PRAISE FOR *RANSOMED DREAMS*

"*Ransomed Dreams* is fast-moving and suspenseful. The author has researched her facts carefully and accurately describes the difficulties that special agents from two different federal agencies face when fate brings them together in an investigation."

JACK BRANSON, retired federal agent

"Amy Wallace weaves an intriguing tale in *Ransomed Dreams*—a most promising debut."

CRESTON MAPES, author of *Dark Star* and *Full Tilt*

"Grab a hanky with one hand and buckle a seat belt with the other when a spirit-wounded FBI agent and a woman recovering from devastating loss pair up to protect children from a vengeful killer. With main characters you'd love to call your friends and villains you'd love to throttle, *Ransomed Dreams* delivers an absorbing read from start to finish."

JILL ELIZABETH NELSON, author of the
To Catch a Thief romantic suspense series

"Amy Wallace is a new talent to watch in romantic suspense."

ELIZABETH WHITE, author of *Fireworks*

"*Ransomed Dreams* is shaped by refreshing storytelling and unique plot twists."

CINDY WOODSMALL, author of *When the H...*

"Steeped in police intrigue and
entertains, educates, and capt
vibrant voice in the Christian n

MARK MYNHEIR, homicide d _ _ _ _ _ of *The Void*

"Amy Wallace is a sparkling new voice in romantic suspense. *Ransomed Dreams* had me hooked from the start and didn't let go until the deeply satisfying ending."

Kristin Billerbeck, author of *What a Girl Wants*

"Amy Wallace handles this difficult story with grace and tenderness—but let's not forget the suspense element that keeps the pages turning. And let's also not forget the heart of the book. Forgiveness is not a tacked-on message but lived out in the lives of these characters."

Tricia Goyer, award-winning author of *Night Song* and *Arms of Deliverance*

DEFENDERS *of* HOPE, BOOK ONE

RANSOMED DREAMS

A NOVEL

AMY WALLACE

Multnomah Books

RANSOMED DREAMS
published by Multnomah Books
A division of Random House, Inc.
© 2007 by Amy Nicole Wallace

International Standard Book Number: 1-59052-747-X

Cover design by James Hall
Cover art by Getty Images, Photos.com, and James Hall
Interior design and typeset by Katherine Lloyd, Sisters, Oregon

Scripture quotations are from:
The Holy Bible, New International Version © 1973, 1984 by International Bible Society, used by permission of Zondervan Publishing House
Also quoted:
Holy Bible, New Living Translation (NLT) © 1996. Used by permission of Tyndale House Publishers, Inc. All rights reserved.
New American Standard Bible® (NASB) © 1960, 1977, 1995 by the Lockman Foundation. Used by permission.

Multnomah is a trademark of Multnomah Publishers, and is registered in the U.S. Patent and Trademark Office. The colophon is a trademark of Multnomah Publishers. Printed in the United States of America

Library of Congress Cataloging-in-Publication Data
Wallace, Amy, 1970-
Ransomed dreams : a novel / Amy Wallace.
    p. cm. -- (Defenders of hope ; bk. 1)
ISBN 1-59052-747-X
1. Forgiveness--Fiction. I. Title.
PS3623.A35974R36 2007
813'.6--dc22

                                                        2007000514
07 08 09 10 11 12—10 9 8 7 6 5 4 3 2 1

To my amazing family.
Without your love, encouragement, cleaning skills,
and prayer support, this book would have remained
simply an entertaining dream.

To Jack and Mary, my favorite federal agent family.
Everything good about Steven, Gracie, Clint, and Sara
is because of you two.

ACKNOWLEDGMENTS

Publishing a book has a lot in common with birthing a baby—from conception onward it's a team effort with God and an amazing cast of characters. Writing the Defenders of Hope series also had a lot in common with my last delivery of a beautiful eleven-pound-eight-ounce baby girl: work, tears, and incredible rejoicing! And lots of people to thank who kept me sane in the process.

A heaping helping of thanks goes to my longsuffering family who have washed, cooked, cleaned, inspired, prayed, encouraged, and loved me anyway. You gave all that so I could do one of the things I know, without a doubt, God created me to do. Thank you, David, for launching my career with your proverbial boot on my backside, which lovingly moved me from typing an action packed dream all the way to a novel I'm proud to hold in my hands.

Thanks to my precious princesses too. Elizabeth, my Sweet Song; Hannah, my Musical Laughter; and Sarah, my Sunshine. You make me want to be a better person. To be like you as you grow to be like Jesus. I love you all—to infinity and beyond.

Other awesome characters who have helped me birth this book include two of the most amazing critique partners known to man. Heartfelt thanks go to my best friend, Jen Keithley, who makes me throw well-aimed rocks at my fictional people to produce a satisfying story rife with conflict and class, sans melodrama. She even allows me to clean her floor when I need a mental break and a good laugh. Then there's Meg Moseley, whose careful eye and flair for detail made my writing look far better than I ever imagined possible. Thanks, you two; I'm forever grateful.

Mom, Dad, Josh, Heidi, Zack, and the Wallace clan—thanks for keeping me grounded and giving me roots.

Julee Schwarzburg, you are an awesome editor and first-class miracle worker. Thanks for taking a chance on the first thing I'd ever written and transforming it into a story that makes me smile and cry at the same time.

A world of thanks goes to the entire team at Multnomah. Being a Multnomah author was my brass ring from the first fiction word I typed, so I thank you all for being a part of making dreams come true.

Many thanks to my Momsloop for your prayers, encouragement, and being a safe place to experience biblical correction and truth spoken in love. What an incredible group of ladies you are! Laurie, Sally, Kirstin, and Heather—you are heart-chocolate to me, my friends.

Shawn and Nathan, thank you for teaching me what whole, full, and healthy looks like. And for showing me how to talk—and listen—to our heavenly Daddy, teddy bear in hand.

Without the over-the-top, wonderful people who make up ACFW, I never would have learned the nuts, bolts, and heart of good writing. I'm so glad I'm part of the family.

There's never been a finer, more beautiful bunch of wordsmiths than The Threshing Floor ladies: Jen, Mary, and Staci. Thank you for teaching me to bleed into my work by sharing my heart, holding up my hands when I am weary, and for showing me how to thank God for the wild ride of writing life. I'm so glad I get to share the roller coaster with you.

My Writers of Remarkable Design group is the best bunch of "non-normals" to hang out with on Tuesday nights. Thanks for being you and for being a vital part of my life. Lindi, Cindy, and Vicki—your friendships are gold. I'm glad we're a team.

Thank you, Les, for believing in The Journey and helping take it all the way to a truly Ransomed Dream.

Beth White, Deb Raney, Jeanne Leach, Tom Chaney, Carolyn Curtis, and Lori Mote—you all were among the first to mentor and encourage me to walk this writing journey one step at a time. What great footsteps you've left for me to follow as we together follow Christ.

Forensics may not be an In Touch CSI (Charles Stanley Institute) thing, but having a passion for God and compassion for people certainly is. Thank you for your prayers and for allowing our family to be part of an incredible ministry.

I'm privileged to be a part of First Baptist Atlanta, especially our awesome student ministry. Thanks to Dr. Stanley and the great people who make up our small part of the Body of Christ. You've taught, equipped, and challenged me well. You've also been and continue to be a place I'm glad to call home.

Finally, to the One who has loved me with an everlasting love before time began and who continues to be my dream come true—thanks, Daddy. It's all because of You.

Do not be afraid, for I have ransomed you.

I have called you by name; you are mine.

When you go through deep waters, I will be with you.

ISAIAH 43:1–2, NLT

PROLOGUE

Gracie's night overflowed with promise.

Uncharacteristic Georgia snow glistened in the front yard, and a cozy fire warmed her living room. She hummed "Silent Night," even though the memory of Christmas grew to the week-old mark. Cider sloshed in her hands as she dodged two-year-old Joshua to find her corner of the couch.

"Mommy, me like da fire truck." Joshua circled the coffee table, making siren noises, as Jake, their golden retriever, beat a quick retreat to his new bed in the corner.

"Come here, little man." Mark flopped down on the floor and tickled the toy away from Joshua.

Gracie smiled at the scene near her feet and caught Mark looking her over. He winked. They'd soon enjoy a private celebration of their seventh anniversary, complete with chocolate, a bubble bath, and massages—after the kiddos were tucked in bed at their grandparents' house a short drive away.

Christmas tree lights twinkled, and candles filled the air with the aromas of vanilla and peppermint. Gracie listened for the oven's beep, indicating her famous chocolate pound cake was finished, but heard nothing except Jake's tail thumping against his pallet.

Elizabeth snuggled up with a book and her pink blanket in the rocking chair across the room. Gracie smiled. "You going to join us, sweetie?"

Her blond curls bounced as she hurried past her daddy's extended hand. Elizabeth preferred books to tickles any day. "I readin' the book you gaved me." She hopped into Gracie's lap. "See the princess? I wanna be like her when I growed up."

11

"You already are a princess." Mark rose to his knees and pretended to bow. Elizabeth rewarded him with little giggles before she disappeared into the book again.

Gracie set her empty mug down and poked at Mark's long, muscular legs with her toes. Tonight couldn't come soon enough.

"Penny for your thoughts, beautiful." He slipped up on the couch and drew her close.

"It'll cost you more than that."

"How 'bout a kiss or two?"

Mark's kisses would buy him anything he wanted. It was a wonder they didn't have more than two children. "I'll tell you, and then we've got to run. Kisses come later." Heat filled her cheeks at the memory of their almost seven years. Guess God knew two little ones were about all she could manage and retain some semblance of sanity. "I don't want to keep my parents waiting, but we can hurry home after."

"No kisses first?" Mark stuck out his bottom lip. His blond, blue-eyed, six-foot frame shrank into the back of the couch with arms folded over his chest. He looked adorable with a pout.

"Don't start, mister. I'll collect my payment later."

His little-boy expression slid into a lazy grin. He planted a kiss on her forehead. "We'd better hustle then."

"You gonna bing da chock-it, Mommy?" Joshua zoomed his fire truck across the table again.

The cake.

She hightailed it into the kitchen. The oven remained cold and dark. No aroma of baking cake. "I don't believe it. I forgot to turn on the oven."

"No chocolate?" Elizabeth hugged her leg. "It'll be okay."

"Elizabeth's right." Mark picked up their pint-sized princess and tickled her tummy. "We'll survive this one New Year's Eve without the cake."

"Hode me too, Daddy." Joshua's lobster claw hands snapping open and shut, begging to be picked up, made Gracie smile.

She checked the creamy brown batter and turned on the oven. "I really don't want to waste all this good chocolate. Besides, it's tradition. So why don't you all head out, and I'll bring the cake in time for dessert." She rubbed Jake's neck as he nudged closer to what he must have hoped would be dinner.

"I'd rather go without the cake than have you miss dinner."

Elizabeth and Joshua nodded.

"I'll just straighten up around here a little and come over as soon as the oven beeps." Gracie tickled Elizabeth's side. "It won't be too long."

Mark hoisted their two kiddos higher on his hips. "Can we survive without Mommy for a few short minutes, my little man and little princess?"

They giggled.

"I'll make sure everything is ready for when we get home." Gracie wiggled her eyebrows.

That made Mark haul the kids out of the kitchen and toward the front door. He wrapped two squirming, laughing children into coats and hats as Jake danced around them, barking.

She adjusted the greenery on the banister. "I'll see you soon."

Mark hustled Elizabeth and Joshua through the kitchen again and out the door to the garage. He turned back toward her. "I'm thinking about a long night in front of the fire."

She walked into his arms and adjusted his scarf. "You are the most wonderful husband in all the world, Mark Lang. I love you—to infinity and beyond."

"Buzz Lightyear you are not, and I'm glad." He wrapped his strong hands around hers and drew her close. When he placed a kiss on each one, she couldn't stop the shiver that trailed up her spine.

Gracie stepped back. "But you'd better go before I decide not to let you out of my sight."

"Come with us then. Turn off the oven and forget the cake."

"Daddy, help peese!" Joshua's voice came through the open door.

Gracie tilted her head to the side and put her hands on her hips.

Mark held up his palms in surrender. "I know. I know. I'm going and I'll be careful. Don't be too long, okay? I love you."

She tipped her chin up and closed her eyes. His lips met hers and deepened the kiss while his arms lifted her off the ground.

With a playful nudge, she pulled back. "Soon."

He set her down, slow and steady. His lingering smile sent a silent promise that warmed her from the inside out.

She couldn't help but giggle when he turned up his jacket collar and winked.

She tossed him the keys and then flipped on the outside light as he buckled two little ones into their old blue minivan and closed the door. "Nice view," she whispered.

Mark backed out of their driveway and into the white-dusted road.

One last wave and he was gone.

Gracie put books and all manner of toys back under the tree. They'd clean up later. Tonight was for fun. And romance.

Then she noticed a little pink teddy bear blanket flopping over the edge of Elizabeth's tiny rocking chair. Elizabeth wouldn't sleep without it.

The grandfather clock in the foyer showed that only three minutes had passed.

"If I know my girl, she's probably asking for it now." Gracie smiled. If she hurried, she'd catch up to Mark's careful un-Atlanta-like driving. Cake or not, she'd rather be with her family.

Then it hit her. She could have her cake and her family too.

She turned off the oven, loaded the still-cold cake into a carrier, and left Jake settled down for a long winter's nap. She hustled into Mark's restored Mustang—pink bear blanket and yummy chocolate in tow.

Within ten minutes, she spotted their van not too far off

Highway 316. A few more turns and she'd have to slow down. The country landscape in the dark with snow falling wasn't a good place to make up time.

Suddenly a fast-moving black truck flashed its brights.

Then everything blurred. Screeching tires. Crunching metal. The truck plowed into the front of their minivan and sent it spinning off the road.

A scream filled the Mustang.

She slammed the brakes and swerved as the black monster barreled toward her. Look! Her mind willed her head to turn away from where the van had disappeared. She caught sight of a young man's wild eyes as the truck sped past.

She pulled over to the shoulder and kicked open the door. As she ran to the edge of the road, her pulse hammered against her temples. The van's engine made the solitary noise at the bottom of a long, steep hill.

"Mark! My babies!"

Police. Ambulance. Phone.

She ran back to the car and fumbled through her purse. Phone shaking in her frozen hands, she called for help.

"Nine-one-one. What's your emergency?"

"Car accident. My family is trapped at the bottom of a hill. Off Highway 316. Past Harbins Road. I need to go help them."

"Ma'am, if you could stay on the line—"

She dropped the phone and ran back to the tire-streaked pavement where the van had disappeared. "Oh, Lord, please let them get here fast."

She fell to the ground and started to slide down into the ravine. Cold seeped into her coat as she pushed heavy branches out of her path, slowing the descent.

Minutes later, sirens split her desperate prayers. The once-quiet scene filled with red and blue lights, voices yelling. Police cars and fire trucks. Men in uniform pulling her back up to the road. Back to Mark's car. Away from her family.

"Ma'am."

Gracie spun around at the slight touch to her elbow.

"Did you see the accident?" An older police officer stood with his notepad and pen motioning toward the hill where firefighters swarmed.

"Yes, they're my…"

"Can you describe in as much detail as possible what you saw?"

Gracie blinked and turned back to the hill. "My husband and two kids are down there. Are they going to be okay? Please tell me they're going to be okay."

"That's your family?" The officer's pen froze. He surveyed the scene and shrugged his black coat closer to his neck. "They're doing all they can, ma'am. We'll hear something soon."

"I was following them. A black truck hit our van and sent it down the hill." Bright white lights and screeching metal filled her mind. Air burned her lungs. Short gulps didn't satisfy, and forcing more words out felt impossible. Within seconds a female officer placed a scratchy blanket around her shoulders.

"Did you see the driver?"

"He was young, had a chubby face. A college student, maybe? I…I'm not sure."

Firefighters started hauling stretchers up the hill. Two of them. The female officer stepped into her view.

Beyond the officer, a heavyset medic clambered up the hill toward a group of uniformed men. "They're gonna be DOA, man. No need to break your neck getting down there."

Her knees buckled. "Oh no. Please. No."

The older officer took her arm and steadied her. "Ma'am, is there anyone we can call to be with you? To bring you to the hospital?"

Tears stung her eyes. She searched the ground for her phone until the female officer placed it in her hand. "My parents…were expecting us." She covered her mouth and tried to get a breath. "Thompson. My daddy." She handed the phone back. "In the contacts."

The last stretcher came up the hill, and Gracie thought she saw a bloody foot move. She fought against the female officer who held her near Mark's Mustang while the firefighters loaded the stretcher into a second ambulance. "It's best that you stay here, ma'am."

"My husband and babies…"

Minutes passed in a haze as other police officers arrived and left. Then her parents pulled into the chaos. Her father took her in his arms and nodded to the remaining officers.

"Daddy, you have to hurry. I saw Elizabeth move. I need to get to them."

All the way to Gwinnett Medical, no one spoke a word.

They're okay. They have to be okay. Over and over the words raced through Gracie's head. Another part of her mind heard *DOA*.

She jumped from the car as soon as her dad pulled up to the ER doors. She rushed straight to the reception desk. "Please, my family. They were brought here. A car accident. I have to see them. My name is Gracie Lang."

The woman forced a smile. "Just a moment."

Police officers milled around just beyond the desk. One of them stepped away from the others. The older officer from the side of the road. "Mrs. Lang?"

"Yes."

Her mother's arms tightened around her waist.

The officer motioned for her to follow him as he walked through the ER doors. "They're in trauma room one."

"Is my family okay? Please tell me they are…"

He stopped just outside the door. His stiff posture softened, and he shifted from one foot to the other. "I'm really sorry, ma'am. The EMTs did everything they could."

"No! This has to be a mistake. I saw my daughter move. They have to be alive." She pushed her mother's arms away. "I need to see them."

The officer stepped away from the door.

"Gracie, I'll go." Her dad's strong hands held her rooted in place. "You stay here with your mother."

"No. I have to see for myself." She forced her legs to walk through the cold metal door. All around, the ER buzzed with voices, clanging metal, and electronic rhythms. An acrid smell assaulted her senses, and she focused on the center of the room.

Three white sheets.

I can't do this.

Every thought of how to survive this moment froze like the December ice outside. Useless muscles refused to move. Warring emotions unraveled the last thread of peace holding her heart together.

Nothing remained.

Gracie fixed her eyes on the lifeless covered bodies.

A mistake. This was all a mistake. A different van. Not her family.

The nurse stood next to a large form covered in sterile white. She waited patiently, eyes filled with compassion.

A traitor to her inner scream to flee, she moved forward. The nurse began folding the sheet down. Gracie closed her eyes.

Maybe it won't be Mark. This is all a mix-up.

She drew in a few shallow breaths and opened her eyes. The blond hair and defined jawline belonged to her husband. No mistake.

An icy hand wrapped around her heart and it exploded.

Oh, Father, why can't this be a mistake?

She reached out quivering fingers and then recoiled at the chill of Mark's cheek. Beneath the bruises and lacerations was the face she had kissed good morning for the past seven years.

The nurse stepped away, but Gracie knew she waited with the police officer, just beyond her view. If she could get through the officer's questions. Beyond her parents' heart-wrenching sobs. Past her front door at home. She would turn the lock and…

Gracie looked at the ceiling. "Please, God. Please let this be a dream."

When she looked back down, nothing had changed.

The nurse had removed the sheet to reveal Mark's face, but Gracie needed to see his hands. She moved the white cotton material away from his side. The sheet felt as cold as his rigid limbs. She'd give anything for one more touch of his gentle hands as they caressed her. Held her together. Lent her courage.

Gracie forced her fingers to move. Her knees quivered as if she'd run a marathon, and she could barely see for the flood of tears that splattered as drops of gray all over the bloodied sheet. She turned away to keep from falling, only to face a sight no mother could bear.

My babies.

Leaden hands muffled the scream that fought its way through her lips. Gracie shut her eyes against the two small covered forms in front of her.

Her burning eyes held no more tears. She didn't want to move. Didn't want to breathe. Didn't want to remember *anything* from this day. The only life she wanted existed before this room.

The joy of Mark's proposal.

The first time she saw Elizabeth and Joshua, red and squalling.

The sweet scent of her newborn babies, or the brush of a kiss on her cheek.

A young nurse pressed two items into Gracie's hands. The pungent odor of blood and hospital antiseptic stung her eyes and nose. The woman whispered something about them being ready to take home.

Home. Gracie stared at the things in her arms. Joshua's fire truck and *Goodnight Moon*, Elizabeth's favorite book, felt like shadows in her arms. They were all she had left.

Gracie turned for one final look before she stepped out to the bustling world whirling without her.

Three white sheets.

1

Today Elizabeth would have been six.

Gracie checked the clock radio on her bedside table. Still dark outside, she had over an hour before the alarm would blare and her feet would have to move. Jake paddled his honey-colored paws, lost in a dream at the foot of her bed. The soft thickness of her rose-patterned comforter bunched around him.

"Wish I could sleep like that."

She slipped out from under the heavy comforter and swung her legs over the side of the bed. Her golden retriever didn't stir. One more week of school and she'd have survived her first year away from home.

Alone.

A photo on the nightstand captured her attention. In an instant she was back in Georgia, sitting on her front porch swing, camera aimed, watching Elizabeth and Joshua play in the yard. The autumn leaves swirled in the wind against a crisp blue sky. From his garage den, a growling daddy "bear" marched into the leaves and stalked the pretend hikers. Two squealing kiddos with carbon copy smiles turned toward him. As he approached, Elizabeth and Joshua reached out to grab hold of the muscled arms of their daddy. Gracie snapped the picture when the trio turned in her direction.

It felt like yesterday.

She climbed back into bed and snuggled under the warm comforter. She smiled as the sweet memory washed over her.

I can hear their laughter.

Then she remembered the three white sheets.

Hot tears spilled down her cheeks. Someone in a raging black truck had ripped her family away from her. And every memory still stung with unfinished business.

That had to change.

A ringing phone made her heart and Jake's body leap. She lunged for the receiver before the deafening noise hammered her brain again. "Hello?"

"Gracie? Did I wake you?"

The voice of her best friend sent her heart back into place. "Under normal circumstances, calling at 4 a.m., it's a good bet I'm still asleep."

Leah ruffled through some papers. "But not today."

"No."

"You going to make it?" Leah McDaniel sounded like a mother hen, but she kept her trial lawyer questioning at bay. For now.

"Elizabeth would have been in my class next year."

Leah sighed.

Gracie knew there was nothing more to say. For two years they'd searched for clues and cried on the anniversary of her family's death and on each of their birthdays. She grew weary of the continuing ache.

"I'm doing something different today, Leah. I'm tired of walking through their birthdays like a zombie with puffy red eyes." Jake scurried back to the bed, dog tags jingling, and she rubbed his warm fur. "This time I'm going to find out what happened. My family deserves justice."

"But you've been there and done that...for the entire first year after the accident."

"It wasn't an accident! That kid must have been drunk, and driving intoxicated isn't an accident. He should be in prison."

"Gracie, we don't know that. The police didn't find much evidence and had no leads. Even with all of us hounding them—you; your parents; me, your brassy lawyer friend way up here in

DC—the officers in charge of the investigation did all they could."

"Well, I'm going to do more."

"When?"

Her old college roommate had gone soft. Gracie's heartbeat surged. She'd run her plan by Leah and succeeded without much of a fight.

"I'll call my parents tonight. Then after I make it through the last week of school, I'll leave for Georgia next Monday or Tuesday." She got out of bed, walked to her closet, and pulled out a soft blue and yellow flowered sundress. Elizabeth's favorite color of sky and Joshua's favorite because it looked like sunshine.

Mark would have loved undoing the bow in the back. She shook that thought away. Over two years as a widow didn't make a body's natural physical responses any easier to manage. Avoiding the thoughts helped a little.

"You'll call with updates? And you know if Kevin and I can do anything to help, we will."

"I know, Leah. And I love you for it." She picked out matching blue slingbacks and moved to the dresser for jewelry.

"I'll be praying too."

"Pray that God will answer sooner than later this time."

"Be careful what you ask for, Gracie."

She knew Leah's heart. But the caution did little to dampen her spirits. Gracie had reignited the fire that had lent her strength during her first year alone. For the first time, a birthday wouldn't send her running to her scrapbooks crying. She'd fight. The powerful zing circulating through her blood did wonders for her energy level.

She ended the call with promises to be careful and not get her hopes up too far. But they already were. This time *would* be different.

Gracie fingered her old-fashioned gold locket. The heavy oval contained pictures of her babies right after they were born.

For them. She'd find answers this time. In the deep places

within her, the truth remained just beyond her reach. But this time she'd take hold of it, and life would make sense again.

Hope Ridge Academy loomed before her.

A year of teaching first grade at the exclusive school hadn't lessened the overwhelming sense that walking through school security was like visiting the president.

Gracie maneuvered her car into her parking place under one of the huge oaks that surrounded the brick federal-style main building. Exiting her still new-smelling red Jeep Wrangler—a birthday gift last month from her parents and sister—she remembered the last phone call from Beth.

"After you finally agreed to let Mom sell the Mustang on eBay, I loaded the Jeep with perfect specs on-line, and Mom and Dad picked it up. It's a great guy-magnet car."

Like Gracie needed that. But she didn't need Mark's car gathering dust in her parents' garage either. Letting go of that piece of her husband pricked at her heart. At the same time, one small shackle to the past fell away.

Now if she could just keep Beth's pestering at bay. Her sister's insistence that she needed to date again dogged her heels. Soon. Because she wasn't getting any younger. Little sisters could be pains, even up to the wise old age of thirty.

Walking past the stately front columns of Hope Ridge reminded her of being in Old Philadelphia, imagining the American Revolution days. Until she stepped inside. There, high-tech surveillance cameras and magnetometers greeted her with beeps and electronic blips.

"Morning, Mrs. Lang. Ready for school's end?"

She returned the older security guard's smile. He'd been like a surrogate grandfather, a true friend she'd eaten lunch with many times over the past year. "Sure am, Mr. Jennings. You and the missus going to travel the country while we teachers catch up on sleep?"

He waved her through the large metal portal. "Believe we will. Not getting any younger, you know. You have big plans besides sleeping?"

In May she'd turned thirty-two and felt every day of it. But Mr. Jennings at sixty-plus acted far younger, with a spring in his step and a twinkle in his eye. Maybe age was all in the mind.

Gracie set down her soft leather briefcase. Teachers and students alike filed past her. Some with Secret Service escorts; others pouting because their cell phones and iPods didn't make it past security. "I'm heading home next week. Going to follow my daddy's old military intelligence ways and become a supersleuth."

His wise old eyes misted. "Going to pester those police about your family?"

She touched his uniformed arm. "I need answers, Mr. Jennings. I need to know that I did all I could."

"Then you'll let it go, honey? You got to let it go sometime."

"I will."

"Mrs. Lang." The gruff voice of a lanky Ichabod Crane look-alike bristled the hair on the back of her neck. "Isn't it past time for K through Third's morning assembly?"

"No, Mr. Perkins, I have ten minutes."

He raised an eyebrow and rubbed his thick brown beard. "Last I checked, I was still the vice principal and school was still in session."

Her experience growing up as a military brat forced her to smile, nod, and keep moving. Not to mention stuffing all the smart-aleck words she'd like to say to her stuffy boss. She hadn't done anything wrong. It didn't stop her from feeling like a kid being called into the principal's office, though.

Or vice principal, as the case was.

Gracie hurried to her room and locked her purse and briefcase in her desk. Little voices filled the hallway just beyond her classroom door. And the lines of tall teachers with fifteen little ducklings following in neat rows made her smile.

They reminded her why she taught: For Elizabeth and

Joshua and all the little minds like theirs who required patient love and gentle direction for their inquisitiveness.

It gave her a small taste of the joy of being a mommy again.

Most days, anyway.

For now, she had a morning assembly to run. Or Mr. Perkins with his curly brown hair tamed perfectly into place would be circling like a vulture ready to peck at her for every second she was late.

There was nothing worse than being called to the vice principal's office the last week of school.

Well, except for the extra paperwork he could dream up to keep her at her desk all summer. He'd tried that last winter break, tasking her with reworking her lessons to better fit his idea of what fancy prep school first graders should learn.

Mr. Perkins had no idea who he'd hired a year ago, though.

She smiled. Leah and her perfect research papers done the night before they were due had nothing on Gracie Lang and her straight A's. A dual Education and Literature major with tons of curriculum paradigms stored on her computer, she matched her college roommate's work grade for grade.

And Mr. Perkins had his new lesson plans before he could blink.

Gathering her silly song list and a bag of musical instruments, Gracie headed for morning assembly. If she could harness the zeal she woke up with this morning, her search for clues next week just might yield some powerful results.

Ones she hoped would help alleviate the fire building in her gut. She didn't want to repeat the ulcers or insomnia of her first year without her family.

Justice. That was her aim. For Mark and Elizabeth and Joshua. Their killer needed to know the impact of three white sheets.

The warm night air whipped his hair as he waited outside Gracie's dark backyard.

"Jake! Jake," she called. "Come on, boy. It's time for bed."

But Gracie's dog liked to take his time sniffing out his domain. After two years, her watcher knew almost everything about the golden retriever and the young widow.

Except how to end her quest for answers.

He crept closer to the wooden fence for a better look. At least she wasn't hard on the eyes.

In the full moon, he could see Gracie's long auburn hair fly free as she wrapped her bathrobe tighter around her athletic body. Her huge dog rushed across the backyard to obey her command.

She and that dog had been in every major newspaper for months after his accident. And following her every night, he'd grown accustomed to her vanilla spice perfume tormenting his senses.

He moved in for a closer look.

Then before she turned to go inside, Jake made an abrupt halt and stood completely still, eyes trained in his direction. The dog's low growl pierced the quiet night.

Every muscle in his body tightened as he clamped his mouth over the curse threatening to spill out.

"Come on, Jake. No one's there. Let's go inside." Her shaky words didn't convince Jake. But he obeyed her command anyway and disappeared inside the small brick house.

He exhaled a slow and controlled breath. If he was caught, his sloppy surveillance skills would cost him everything. His career. His freedom. Juries didn't look in favor on drunk drivers who killed perfect little families.

Or who hid the truth from law-abiding citizens. Especially the mother of two dead children.

But he wouldn't allow himself to be lax again.

Any more than he'd allow Gracie Ann Lang to find long-buried answers.

2

S teven Kessler's Thursday couldn't get much worse.

The J. Edgar Hoover Building buzzed with federal agents hustling to and from desks, myriad tasks on their minds and serious lemon faces straining their features. The steady drone of chatter forced him to curb his observation analysis and finish the trek to his desk.

A weeklong case taunted his patience. Ryan, an eight-year-old boy from Steven's Kentucky hometown, had been tracked to Washington DC. Now it was his job to find the child and bring him home. Alive.

And the sooner he got another lead, the sooner he and Ryan could both sleep a full night—in their own beds. He longed for time off, but only after his job was done. With his first look into his newborn son's face almost six years ago, he'd vowed that nothing would stop him in his new assignment as a Crimes Against Children coordinator. He would bring kidnapped kids home to their families. That one reuniting moment made all the donkeywork and not-so-happy endings worth it.

Steven shook his head to clear the cobwebs. He removed his suit coat and loosened his U of L basketball tie. A million other things held more appeal, but the paperwork stacks required his attention.

"'Bout time you meandered in to work, partner." Clint Rollins slid past the partition that separated them and grinned. Agents passing by straightened their shoulders and sucked in their guts. Nothing like trying to best the Texan's top-cop stature.

"After all these years, I'd think you'd have learned only early birds catch the unit chief's morning lashings. Besides, real agents get coffee first." Steven held up his double espresso and extended his partner's straight black brew.

Clint tipped his imaginary cowboy hat in thanks. "The unit chief was in good form this morning. Even had a compliment for the defense tactics training I did last week."

Steven didn't meet his partner's eye.

Clint stood to his full six foot five inches and rolled his neck from side to side. "Remember? The class you skipped because of your creaking joints?"

"Last I recall, I was escorting a porn ringleader to jail, my creaking joints and all."

Michael Parker, their squad's newest member, pulled his nose out of a book and stopped beside Clint. "Any news on Ryan's case?"

Steven and Clint both shook their heads. Steven wanted to hit the punching bag in the gym or be out with the team surveying the place Ryan was last sighted, but he had paperwork to do.

"You missed a good class, Kessler. I beat your record in tactics and on the track."

Clint slapped the twenty-eight-year-old CACU rookie on the back. The kid's blond hair crowned a smirk the size of Alaska.

"While you and the cowboy here were playing good cop, I was working. Something I suggest the two of you return to."

Clint clucked his tongue. "Don't let his growl scare you, kid. Only his gun's worse than his bark."

Jan Bryant, their favorite administrative assistant, interrupted. "Steven, an Amber Alert just placed Ryan and the perp in Rock Creek Park. You guys bring Ryan home today. And get that son of a—"

"Will do." Steven cut off the string of words he didn't need slamming around his brain. Without thinking, he grabbed his backup Glock, holstered it, and headed for the stairs. Clint and Michael followed close on his heels.

He'd rather avoid killing a man if he could.

But if not...

All that mattered right now was brining Ryan home. As Clint drove, Steven fingered the year-old picture of his son's first day in kindergarten. The one he kept tucked into his vest. James's light brown hair, blue eyes, and full-throttle smile held such promise. Just like Ryan's photo they'd circulated.

Both were like looking into a mirror of the past.

One was safe at Hope Ridge Academy; the other Steven intended to return to his parents' arms. Tonight.

Branches slapped at Steven's face and shoulders as he ran.

Deep into the wooded terrain of Rock Creek's interior, he reached for his radio and called in his position. Up ahead in the small meadow, a heavyset man with wild eyes held tightly to Ryan. His sweaty arms clamped around the boy's neck, and he yelled for them to stay away. Ryan's body hung listlessly.

Steven stopped, close enough to see the severe bruising through Ryan's tattered clothes and his eyes wide with fear.

Hours had stretched into days of looking for Ryan with little hope of finding him. Parker doubted they'd find him still breathing, but they had. Now Steven's job focused on getting the boy away from his captor and home.

Leaves crunched and branches snapped across the clearing.

A gun fired.

The massive perp returned fire. Steven had a clear shot of the man's back and had to act now.

Lining up the target in his sights, he pulled the rifle's trigger. A loud scream sounded. Then silence.

FBI agents rushed into the clearing.

Michael and Clint got there first and pulled the little boy away from the dead man.

Ryan's body fell into Steven's arms, unconscious.

If only I'd found him days ago.

"Ryan's not breathing, Steven."

"Was he shot?" If one of his team members had missed and struck Ryan, there would be hell to pay.

"No." Clint radioed in and requested the medical examiner and an ambulance.

Steven started CPR.

Minutes passed before the medics rushed onto the scene. The clearing was too small for a helicopter. They intubated Ryan and took over for Steven in one swift set of movements. Clint pulled him back.

"We should have gotten here sooner."

"We did all we could, Kessler," Michael said.

Parker's shot had given Steven perfect placement to finish the job. But Ryan wouldn't be going home tonight. Might not make it to the hospital alive.

"Never again. I don't want another child to suffer like that on our watch."

His partner nodded with a slow tilt of his chin. "Let's head to the hospital. And pray."

That attitude kept Clint Walker Rollins doing his job every day and going home to his family sane every night.

Parker scoffed at Clint's comment. Then all three trudged through the thick brush in silence.

It'd been a long time since Steven had held a child in Ryan's condition. Not long enough, though.

Ryan's parents were on their way.

The doctors still didn't have good news to report, but Ryan was on life support and the medical staff was doing everything in their power to keep him breathing. Of that Steven had made sure.

Now he paced. Clint clicked away on Steven's personal laptop in the private patient waiting room, compiling facts and information he'd need to file Ryan's report, no doubt. Having a best friend like Clint to watch his back kept Steven doing this job, year after year. Without drinking to dull the daggers in his conscience.

Not that he hadn't thought about it. He had. But alcohol had ruined enough in his life already. And he had a son to protect.

His phone buzzed, and Steven answered it.

"Agent Kessler, this is Thomas Perkins from Hope Ridge Academy. We've tried to contact your parents to pick up your son, but no one is answering at their residence. He's among the last students left in our after-school care. When can I expect your arrival?"

Steven groaned. He'd forgotten that his dad and stepmom were out of town for the weekend. Too bad his sister, Hanna, didn't live closer. "I'll be right there."

Clint looked up at his muffled curse. "That's not gonna make it better. What's the problem?"

"Dad and Sue are in Baltimore opening a new coffee shop. James is at school waiting for me."

"I can see if Sara will swing back by and pick him up. She should be done with afternoon rounds by now." Clint speed dialed his wife, one of DC's finest oncologists.

Steven closed his partner's phone. "No. I'm not doing any good here. And it's James's last day of kindergarten. I should at least pick up my son once from school."

"Your dad and Sue moved to DC to help, Steven. Cut yourself some slack. Single parenting is hard enough without wallowing in guilt."

Easy for Clint to say. He and Sara made marriage, parenting, and life look rose colored. Together. Steven shook away the green thoughts. "See you in the morning. Call me if anything changes with Ryan's condition."

Beltway traffic didn't help him reach his goal quick enough, and thoughts of Ryan dogged him when Alexandria's red stoplights left him with no cars to pass.

By the time he parked his blue Explorer, showed his credentials, and bypassed the magnetometers, his son sat in the after-school room with a teacher alone. At least James wasn't crying.

Steven leaned against the doorway watching the long-legged teacher invite James to work a puzzle on the floor. The slightly opened door gave him a little cover to observe. Her soft auburn hair, clipped into a ponytail, shook as she laughed with his little all-star.

Steven had never seen a young, attractive woman enjoy spending time with James. It did something to his insides.

Something he hadn't felt in years.

Angela had left when their son was just a baby. Ever since then, James's grandparents or an older nanny cared for him. Better not to have a woman seeking a ready-made family trying to win James's affection. Between James and work, in the last five years dating hadn't made Steven's list of things to do.

Maybe it should have.

"Agent Kessler?"

He turned to face a scrawny flip of a stuffed suit.

"I'm Thomas Perkins, the vice principal." The man reached over and closed the classroom door. "I'd like to discuss your plans future for after-school care. If you intend to keep your son at Hope Ridge, that is."

Steven straightened to a full head over the younger man. "This is the first time James has been picked up late. It won't happen again."

"With your Bureau work, I don't imagine the hours are ever conventional."

"I'll make sure we have other arrangements worked out before school starts in September."

"Good. Please see that the front office is updated as soon as possible." Mr. Perkins strutted down the hall like he owned the world. The thirtysomething official needed an attitude adjustment in a bad way. But not from Steven. Someone else would have to take that guy down a notch.

Steven adjusted his favorite red and black tie. He hoped the five years he had on the vice principal made him far less arrogant, not so quick to try and pick a fight. Like he would have done more than a decade ago.

Before Clint had started feeding him quotes about fools rushing in where angels fear to tread.

He returned his attention to the classroom and its beautiful teacher. Maybe that was Perkins's problem. He'd caught Steven staring at his girlfriend.

Not likely.

The lady still doing puzzles with his son had more class than that. Given her looks and ease with children, she probably had a husband and kids at home too.

Before reaching for the classroom door, he checked his phone one last time to see if Clint had left a message about Ryan.

Nothing.

Maybe no news was good news this time.

"I'm here to pick up James."

Gracie's face flamed. She'd caught a glimpse of the handsome stranger in the hallway earlier, before her boss had closed the door, and she'd been watching for him ever since.

Talk about a candid-camera moment.

After a prolonged pause, she shot to her feet and straightened her white sundress. "I'm sorry; we haven't met. I'll need to see some identification before I can release James."

"Daddy! You're here!" James rushed into the man's arms. No mistake. This was James Kessler's father. Both of them had full heads of light brown hair and the most piercing blue eyes she had ever seen.

"Hey, my little man, it's good to see you." He put James back down onto the linoleum. The boy started talking at the speed of a race car.

Little man.

Mark's pet name for their son sent memories crashing to the surface.

She tried to shake away the snapshots of her smiling little

boy with his adoring daddy. Melting into a tearful mess in front of a parent would draw her boss's ire for sure. Not to mention how it would send James's father running for cover fast. This dad who loved his son like Mark had loved Joshua. What she wouldn't give to be a part of a family again.

Mr. Kessler brought her back to the present with a smile that curled her toes. Then he ruffled James's hair and focused on his son's rapid chatter.

"I'm Steven Kessler, by the way." He managed to get the words in while James took a breath. After that, he reached into his suit coat and handed her what she assumed was photo ID.

His left hand held no trace of a wedding ring. Gracie's face flushed hotter as she realized the direction of her thoughts. Then she dropped his ID.

Steven chuckled.

She wasn't usually this clumsy around men.

His amused grin, as he bent to pick up his ID, didn't help cool her burning cheeks. He returned the ID to her, and she glanced at the picture, now resting firmly in her hand. The man looked even better in person than in his photo.

"I'll get James's things." Gracie stepped around her desk and picked up his red backpack.

"Mrs. Lang is going to be my teacher next year." James pulled out the kindergarten award papers he'd shown her earlier. "Look at this, Daddy!"

As Steven took the extended papers, his phone blared the COPS theme song. He held up one finger to his son. "Kessler."

As his caller's loud jumbled voice filled the room, the FBI agent closed his eyes and ran his free hand through his hair. The muscles in his now-clamped jaw worked up and down.

He slammed his phone shut and cleared his throat. "Could I have my badge, please?"

Gracie took a final look at the badge and placed it in his hand. She smiled at James. "I'm glad to know James's grandparents aren't the only ones I'll get to know next year. I've already heard wonderful things about each of you."

"James's grandparents are the ones you'll see most often."

Steven's blue eyes had aged during the short phone conversation. Whatever had been communicated in that call had turned his warm demeanor to ice.

"Are you okay, Mr. Kessler?"

"I'll be fine, thanks." He looked down at his son. "Come on, little man. I could use some time with my favorite guy. It's been a rough day." Steven hoisted James into his arms.

With a slight wave, the two Kessler men disappeared down the hall.

M etal groaned and scraped against metal as a large blue
minivan tumbled down the hill.

Everything happened in slow motion. Glass shattered.
Screams ripped the air. Gracie smelled gasoline and blood, and the
bottom of the ravine seemed miles away. But she slid down the cold,
slippery mud as fast as her feet would move. By the time she reached
the car, only silence remained.

Blood filled her sight.

Elizabeth and Joshua and Mark sprawled over the cold snowy
ground.

Her stomach clenched and she turned away, the image freezing
her to the core.

A chilling presence drew her attention upward. A man, shrouded
in black, stood motionless. Gracie screamed for help and ran to catch
him as he turned and moved out of sight. She ran closer to him until
he was just within reach.

Then tires squealed and he sped away in a black truck. MVB. She
repeated the license plate letters over and over again.

Her heart felt as if it would slam through her chest, but she had
to get back to save her family. This time they would survive.

But the crash site disappeared, leaving only bright white hospital
lights assaulting her eyes. She stood in the silent emergency room surrounded by three tables covered with sheets. The bodies underneath
terrified her. She couldn't look at them.

"No!" She bolted upright in bed, waking from the nightmare. Her comforter felt like a lead weight. She threw it aside,
heaving for breath.

Jake scrambled from the bed and stood at her bedroom door. Even her dog couldn't handle her emotional outburst.

She clutched a pillow to her chest and fell back, drawing into a ball. The vise grip of grief closed around her heart.

Images of Mark, Elizabeth, and Joshua faded in her mind's eye. Gracie tried to focus, but only watercolor shadows remained. She felt her empty left ring finger.

"Oh, God, why couldn't I have been in the van too?"

Silence answered her.

Moving to the hope chest at the foot of her bed, she uncovered the green velvet case. Its cool softness mocked her. Unlike the first time she'd held that box.

No. Everything had changed since then.

For over two long years she'd been without her family. She'd become one of those lonely women hiding instead of wearing her wedding rings. She'd grown tired of explaining her widowhood and the pitiful, sorrowful looks that accompanied her confession.

Tears dotted the little velvet box. Opening the lid, she fingered the jewelry that had been so much a part of her for seven years. Every time the marquis-cut diamond caught the light, she'd smile with loving memories.

No longer.

She closed the lid and returned the green box to its resting place.

Meeting Steven Kessler must have brought on this dream. A dream she hadn't had in months. She shook her head. More likely it stemmed from her upcoming trip and the anxiety that had been building all weekend.

Still, thinking about Steven Kessler didn't help anything. It only intensified the ache.

The past held her captive. She wasn't free to date again. It didn't matter that her sister and parents said it was time.

Not yet.

Standing up made her head pound. She massaged her temples

and neck while crossing the cold hardwood floor. Moving aside the floor-length rose curtains, she peered into the thick darkness. No moon to soften the blackness. No stars shining. Only clouds and night.

She pressed her forehead onto the cool glass. "Help me find the man who killed my family, Father. Please help me put him in jail." Jake nudged her hand with his nose and she stroked his warm fur.

Nothing would bring them back. But justice had to provide some comfort, some sense of closure to the entire nightmare. If that man were locked behind bars, he could never destroy anyone else's family.

That had to count for something.

She padded over to her dresser. The leather book, placed there last evening, drew her. She flicked on an antique lamp and held the book close to her heart.

The clock flashed 1 a.m. Monday morning. Gracie sat on the bed and pulled the comforter to her waist. Jake settled back down to sleep at her feet. She fingered the worn leather Bible Mark had given her on their fifth wedding anniversary. Flipping through the highlighted passages, her eyes settled on Jeremiah 31:3: "I have loved you with an everlasting love."

She wanted to pray that if God loved her, He'd help her on her quest. But years of Sunday school and listening to her parents share truth about God reminded her that a prayer like that wasn't a guarantee He'd act.

Still, she had a good cause. Justice. And starting tomorrow, she'd force the police to reopen the investigation. After all, she had remembered a partial license plate and the man's features a little more.

Even if it was just a dream, her counselor had alluded to the fact that her subconscious mind might reveal more information when she wasn't trying so hard to remember. And it had happened. Now this information could make all the difference.

❋ ❋ ❋

Gwinnett County's police headquarters didn't impress her Tuesday afternoon.

Neither was the poker-faced officer on duty impressed with her demand to see a detective. Gracie looked around the small waiting room and shifted in the stiff blue plastic chair. Huge portraits of past chiefs dotted the otherwise bare room. People filed up to the large glass windows to lodge complaints, pay fines, and request accident reports.

No one paid her much mind.

"Mrs. Lang?" A man with huge shoulders and biceps worthy of Arnold Schwarzenegger held open a thick gray door. "I'm Detective Calhoun. If you'll come this way, we can discuss your case."

Finally.

Of course she would have waited far longer to be seen.

They sat in a busy office with tiny cubicles. No privacy. Lots of noise. "I'd like to reopen the investigation of my family's death."

Detective Calhoun's blank stare did nothing for her confidence, but she pressed on and explained the details of the accident.

Gracie sucked in a deep breath. She wouldn't cry in front of this stoic officer. She had to hold herself together. But the scene was as vivid as yesterday's nightmare. Unshed tears stung her eyes.

"Mrs. Lang, I'm sure this is difficult for you to recall. But maybe this isn't the best course of action either." The detective lowered his voice. "Have you gone to counseling, ma'am? That might help a great deal."

She didn't know whether to laugh or cry. Or both. She did neither, merely returned his gaze and waited. He wasn't getting rid of her that easy.

"What I mean is, there's really little we can do with the few leads we had two years ago. The officers heading that investigation are no longer in the Accident Investigation Unit, and the paint chips and physical description didn't yield the hoped-for results."

"So my calling ahead nailed the coffin for reopening this case?"

Detective Calhoun chuckled. "No, ma'am. I just like to know what I'm dealing with before I meet with a citizen so I can maximize our time together."

"I have a license plate number."

The detective's eyes narrowed and he leaned forward. "That might get us somewhere."

"It's MVB. And the truck was an older black Ford with a two-door cab."

The officer's pencil stopped midscribble. "That's only a partial plate, Mrs. Lang. Did you stumble across a forgotten note where you'd written it down years ago?"

Her face grew hot. "No. I remembered the license plate from a dream just the other day."

To his credit, the middle-aged detective didn't burst out laughing. His face provided a study for the best card player, though. "We'll do what we can with this information."

"How soon do you expect to call?" Clasping her hands in a tight ball did nothing to still their wobbling. She had to walk out of here with some shred of dignity. Even if all of her summer plans were gone with one five-minute meeting.

"I'll run the plate today and see if we get anything. But it could be up to a week before I can call. Evidence trails take time." He looked down at a thick file on his desk. "Can I reach you at your parents' number, or do you have a cell phone?"

"My parents' phone would be best." She stood and shook the man's hand. A picture of the detective with two little girls caught her eye.

His brown eyes softened as he followed her gaze. "Mrs. Lang, please consider talking to someone about your grief. You had a beautiful family and lost a lot in their accident. But you're still alive. Don't throw that away."

She swallowed hard and forced a smile. "Thank you for your concern, Detective. I look forward to hearing from you soon." Southern pleasantries and a stiff upper lip came in handy at times.

Even if she felt anything but pleasant. Or stiff. She felt like a wrung-out dishrag.

Blinking against the late afternoon sun, she found her red Jeep in the parking lot. Turning right out of the parking lot, she passed the jail and followed the stream of cars onto Highway 316. Thirty years of living in Atlanta made driving on autopilot simple. But when she pulled into the driveway of the home she'd shared with Mark Richard Lang, everything inside of her melted.

Detective Calhoun's words tumbled around her pulsing headache. *Maybe I should see a counselor again.*

No. She'd done that for a year, and progressing past the paralyzing grief had been good. The appointments ended just before her move to DC. A move the counselor felt was a positive step. But it was more than that. Her Christian counselor broached the topic of forgiveness, and she couldn't go there. Didn't want to let go of the fight for justice. Or the fire that burned stronger than tears.

The year in DC had served to gain her some perspective and strength. She wouldn't terrorize the kind detective who was just doing his job. But she wouldn't give up either.

She had a killer to catch.

"Uh, ma'am, you okay?" A tall teenager with dreadlocks stood next to her Jeep. His dark eyes were full of questions and concern.

Grabbing a Kleenex, she dried her face. "Is this your home?"

"For 'bout a year now. My mama bought it for a steal from this nice old couple." He shifted a football from left to right and back again.

"Those were my parents."

The football stopped. "You lived here?" He looked back toward the front door. "You, um, want to come in? My mom keeps the place spotless."

She smiled at the polite teen. "No. But thank you. I'd better go."

With a slight shrug and a nod, he disappeared into the back-yard—past the rosebush she'd received for her first Mother's Day gift. Into the same backyard Elizabeth and Joshua learned to walk in. Where they got their first skinned knees and played for hours in a blow-up pool.

Photographic memories tumbled one after the other as she turned the scrapbook pages of her mommy heart. She put the Jeep in reverse.

A car's engine startled her as she backed out onto the quiet cul-de-sac. She hadn't noticed any cars at home as she drove in. A silver four-door disappeared before she could catch a glimpse of an old neighbor. Maybe it was better that way.

She drove out of the neighborhood, alone again.

It still seemed strange that the only car she heard had appeared and disappeared just as she was leaving. Especially when the neighborhood pool she passed at the subdivision entrance had been overrun with kids, and all the houses on her way in were void of life.

"Overactive imagination," she whispered to her silent Jeep. Mr. Jennings would get a kick out of her current state of para-noia and the conspiracy theories she'd created. Over their lunch breaks, the old security guard often said she needed to apply at the CIA.

Fat chance of that. She couldn't even get local police to take her seriously.

But she kept checking her rearview mirror the entire drive home.

Just in case.

W eeks passed with no phone calls.

Just like they had over two years ago.

Gracie tucked her favorite childhood story, *Anne of Green Gables*, back into the bookcase and then headed downstairs. Even with the air conditioners running full force, the hundred-plus degree temperature outside seeped into her parents' home.

But the oppressive July heat wouldn't deter her parents from celebrating the country's birthday. Growing up military, the sense of patriotism ran deep in her Thompson blood. As it had in the Lang family. So many little things she missed.

Like heated debates with Mark about government reform and domestic policy. He'd tease her parents and her with military reduction suggestions, only to laugh at her daddy's red-faced reply. For seven years, her father had fallen for Mark's riling every time.

Maybe it was a man thing.

Down the long stairwell she followed the scent of coffee and cinnamon rolls to her father's mouthwatering breakfast spread. Fresh fruit, bagels with cream cheese, and gooey pastries filled the table.

To be in the home of Mr. and Mrs. Robert Thompson was to see hospitality in action, right down to the watermelon placemats and summer-themed china. With matching cloth napkins, of course.

Her father hummed the "Star-Spangled Banner" as he bent his strong six-foot frame over the sink of dirty pots and pans, his salt-and-pepper hair in perfect place as he worked.

"You tryin' to make me look like a whale?" She picked at a warm roll and licked thick white icing from her fingers. Leaning against the breakfast bar, she let the gooey treat perk her up.

Her father's dark brown eyes twinkled as he turned toward her, laughing. "No, princess, I'm not. But your mother thinks you still have some room to grow."

"Where is Mom?" She looked around the expansive oak and white kitchen and into the adjoining family room.

"With your big lug of a lapdog."

"Jake's good company. And I take him out for exercise. Three times a week in the morning and to the park on Saturdays."

Daddy stepped away from the sink and wrapped her in a warm hug. "Didn't mean that as criticism, honey."

She relaxed in her father's strong arms. "Sorry, Daddy. I thought Mr. Perkins's amazing job offer and Leah already being in DC would make the move easier. But now my boss's back-handed remarks on everything from my punctuality to my grading routine keep me on edge. Guess I forgot I'm home."

"You could move back. Stay with us till you find a new house. Your mother would love it." He pulled back and looked her square in the face. "Me too. I'd love to have my reading buddy and debate partner back for good."

Her eyes watered. "I can't, Daddy. Everything I see reminds me of Mark and my babies. The pull of the past is too strong here."

Her mom and a worn-out Jake slid into the kitchen. Her daily five-mile trek must have done him in for the day. Jake collapsed on his pallet with a low huff while Mom stood on tiptoes and kissed her husband on the lips. Then she took a seat at the breakfast stool next to Gracie.

"I'm wonderin' if that 'guy magnet' car your sister insisted we give you has anything to do with your staying up North."

Her father grinned. "No diggin' for clues, Marianne."

Mom tidied up her silver hair and straightened her red and

white running clothes. "Oh, all right." She held her head up in mock regality. "Do you, Miss All Grown Up and not dishing to your mother any longer, have a boyfriend you'd like to tell us about?"

Gracie giggled. "No."

"No, you don't have a boyfriend or no, you don't want to tell?"

Her father winked. "She's starting to sound like Beth, don't you think?"

Her mom huffed. "I'm fixin' to call Beth and let her drag it out of you."

Gracie pulled her mom into a hug. "I love you and your nosing around my life. But there's really nothing to tell dating-wise." Gracie stepped back and tugged her robe belt tighter. "But I do need to change before we go shopping and out to the big Patriotic Pops celebration tonight."

Poor Jake stayed sound asleep on his pallet, not even bothering to check her movements as she headed upstairs.

Her stuffed animals tucked into the bookcase sent her thoughts trailing back to Hope Ridge. She actually missed the kids already. Ideas for next year's lesson plans with James Kessler made her smile. If everyone thought she should date again, maybe his handsome father would follow up on that spark of interest she was sure she'd seen in his eyes.

And felt in her full-of-butterflies stomach.

She dressed in a flash and then grabbed the cordless phone. "Hey, little sister. Do you have a minute to chat?" Gracie held her breath; they hadn't talked since her birthday.

Things with Beth had been rocky since the accident. After counseling pushed her past the initial grief, Gracie had chosen to cling to God and her parents' teaching. But Beth had taken the loss of her godchildren and namesake and run from faith of any kind.

She'd run all the way to California, following a man Gracie still despised.

"To what do I owe this out-of-the-blue call?"

Sarcasm or surprise, Gracie couldn't tell. "Because I miss you, Beth. And because I have news about your 'guy magnet' car." That'd get her hopeless romantic of a sister talking.

Beth gasped. "You're dating again? Who-boy, did the cows all come home or what?"

Gracie smiled and flopped onto her just-made bed. California may have claimed her sister as a resident, but nothing could completely remove the Georgia roots, even if none of them had "true Southern" accents. A fact that disappointed her first graders when they learned she was born in the "Deep South," but after too many military moves, she sounded like a Yankee. No *Gone with the Wind* hoopskirts either.

"The cows on the old Ames's farm did come home, believe it or not."

"Whatever. That old man is crazy for pretending he still lives in the country with his cow and his pig and his three-legged hound dog."

They laughed. And a few drips of the iceberg years melted in the warmth.

"So what's his name?" Beth flicked off the background noise of some British sitcom. "The boys are napping and Dennis won't be home 'til way late."

Dennis, her not exactly brother-in-law, whose political aspirations included legalizing marijuana. But only after he made a million as a pharmaceutical rep. At least he and Beth had talked about marriage after Peter and Rob were born. Gracie would ask Mom about the latest tonight. No use going there with Beth yet.

"His name is Steven Kessler, but we're not dating."

"That's no fun. Why not?"

"He hasn't asked yet."

Beth laughed. "So why don't you? This isn't the 1950s, you know."

How could she explain that she wasn't really ready to date but wanted to return to their teen camaraderie of gushing over childhood crushes? "He's tall. Light brown hair and blue eyes. Wears an FBI badge."

"Ohhh, cool." That last bit hooked Beth. "It was the Jeep Wrangler, wasn't it? He saw you cruisin', pulled you over, and couldn't take his eyes off of you. Right? Please tell me it was some romantic meeting like that."

"You watch too many soap operas."

"Nope, I'm composing scenarios in my head as I chase the dynamic duo around."

Gracie hadn't yet seen her nephews, but she'd seen pictures of the toddlers. They had her sister's strawberry blond locks and brown eyes. Her arms ached to hold them. To again hold a baby that shared her blood.

Her flat stomach ached too. She rubbed the empty place under her flag T-shirt. Pregnancy might not be wine and roses, but she loved being a mom. Wanted that title again. Longed to hold a wiggly little baby who clasped a tiny hand around her finger for all it was worth.

Someday.

"Hey. I have an idea. Why don't you ask Mr. FBI Supersleuth to help you find out who killed your family?"

Beth was nothing if not direct. Maybe this was another olive branch like the car, but Gracie didn't know if she should go down that path or not. What could it hurt, though? "I might do that. Especially since the police here are too busy to give much time to my case."

"You gonna keep hounding the cops in Atlanta?"

Gracie sighed. "Probably not. I'm thinking of heading back to DC the end of the month but playing tourist downtown until then."

"Mom will like that."

Gracie looked out her blue and white drapes into the clear July sky. "I miss you, Beth. Sure wish we lived closer."

"Me too. I'm glad you called." The loud noise of a slamming door filled the phone line. "I'd better run. The dynamic duo has awakened and escaped their cribs."

"I'll call again soon."

"Good. And call that handsome FBI guy. I need some vicarious testosterone excitement without diapers and bills to pay."

As Gracie hung up the phone, a new idea took root. She remembered Steven's sad eyes as he and his son left Hope Ridge back in June. Maybe he needed a friend too. And his job as a federal agent could prove helpful to her search.

Even if talking to him came to nothing, at least the possibility had given her an inroad into her sister's heart once more. And that was a place she wanted to be again.

Deep in the heart of her family.

He'd spent a month casing his old college haunts.

Georgia State hadn't changed much in the two years he'd been in DC. Five long years he'd slogged at this institution for higher learning. Mother Dear had been proud of his MBA with honors and his appointment by her snooty school board to the job of vice principal at her highbrow school.

She didn't know about the drinking.

Or the DUIs he and his fraternity buddies had narrowly escaped.

Or the accident.

Tom rubbed his brown beard and looked into the rearview mirror. The past should stay in the past. Right where he intended to keep it.

Even his old girlfriend, who still worked in admissions, hadn't recognized him. Or she'd have slapped him. Hard. Like the last time they talked. The day after her obstetrics appointment when he questioned whether her positive pregnancy test was his concern.

Kimberly still looked good. Slender and young. Not married either.

He took a swig of his Starbuck's iced frappe. No use wasting good coffee while waiting across the street from Gwinnett

County police headquarters. Gracie Lang shouldn't be in there much longer.

Far as he could tell, her quest had turned up dead ends. So today's visit must be to say good-bye. At least Tom hoped that was what her bringing a cake to the station had meant.

He'd snoop through her e-mails later tonight to make sure. A gold mine he'd found from prowling around Georgia State. Meeting with an old frat-budd-turned-computer-instructor and laying on a thick sob story provided the wealth of information he'd needed to tap into Gracie's ISP. With a quick trip to the electronics store, he was in business. And with paying cash, they didn't care to learn his name or anything else.

He loved technology. And all the information money could buy.

Gracie exited the police station without wet cheeks this time. His top-dollar binoculars gave him a sharp picture of her peaches-and-cream face.

His coffee gone, he decided to follow her home once again. Then he'd head back to DC, mission accomplished.

Gracie had found nothing. And once she settled back into DC life, he could keep an eye on her from the comfort of his office desk chair. Far away from her stupid, too-observant dog.

He'd invent extra work for her to do if the sleuthing bug bit her again. He'd dream up ways to scare her if that didn't work.

Or worse.

He had all sorts of ideas and lots of time to perfect them. But that didn't matter. For now, the past was safe.

As long as her search ended here.

5

N auseating described the Baltimore club scene before him.

Pulsating strobe lights distorted the two giggling girls flitting round and irritated Gordon's throbbing temples. As did the smell of sweltering bodies dancing to American "oldies." The late July heat ramped up the displeasure of his chosen assignment.

Olivia Kensington. Daughter of his brother's killer.

While he kept vigilant watch, he drank his bitter with the chill off. Just like home.

Olivia and her seventeen-year-old American friend wouldn't even use the lavatory without hooking arms. Interesting turn of events that fact could bring.

Almost time to play American and dumb down his language. Something he had to do many a day he spent slaving for The Regiment. Something his sister, Charlotte, did with ease, living in this uncultured pastureland.

He rang his sister to reestablish specifics. "Petrol up, my dear?"

"Stop it, Gordon. And yes, everything is as you requested."

A loud wail split his eardrum. "Little one's not happy trapped in his pram?"

"He's like Harry, always moving." Charlotte's words drove his cause. "If you plan to stay out of prison this time, dear brother, I suggest altering your word usage."

He looked like an American; now he needed to sound like one. No need to rouse suspicions. Though he doubted the estimable Sir Walter Kensington even knew his name.

Or his brother's.

Intelligence officers were a dime a dozen to the Crown. That's what Harry had said in their last row on the phone. Too little evidence to send Sir Walter Kensington to jail. Not enough blood to return his brother to him.

Harry's blood had been spent for the corrupt ambassador. Now Sir Kensington's daughter would be returned to him in like manner.

"Remind me again why there's no security for the young beauty queens?" Gordon watched for his moment, when they were too tired to fight and too intoxicated to know the difference. Piece of American cake.

"They've outgrown bodyguards. At seventeen, unless there's a threat, they are on their own."

"Good for us."

"Good for you. I'm not laying a hand on those children. I'll do my part at the embassy." She huffed into his ear. "I never approved of your gray ways, Gordon. And I don't still. But Harry's fresh in his grave, and the ambassador's got to be stopped."

"Always loyal to home, eh?"

"Americans believe loyalty is paramount."

"Be loyal to me, Charlotte. You've little else left and no mum to run home to."

"Be done soon and go home, Gordon."

He shut the phone and considered his approach. Should he offer to buy Olivia a drink? He shook his head and watched the two recent high school graduates dance the Electric Slide. They were sloshed already, and Olivia and her friend, Jordan, were far too young for his nearly forty years. Socializing wouldn't appear proper. All business was right on.

He straightened his black suit and tie. A regular Secret Service bloke—he stopped himself. Even his thoughts had to be American.

A regular Secret Service agent if there was one. Drinking-up time for Sir Walter Kensington's eldest had come.

Weaving through a sea of gyrating bodies, he found his mark at the edge of the mass. "Miss Kensington?" Gordon grabbed her elbow and directed her toward the back door. Jordan followed as predicted. "Your father felt midnight was late enough for your party. It's time to return home."

Both teens, dressed in similar black-and-white minis and halter tops, pouted as they moved through the crowd surrounding the dance floor.

"When's your dad going to figure out all the good stuff happens after midnight?" Jordan drew her overly painted red lips down and huffed her bangs out of her eyes.

Relief that he had no bratty offspring filled him. "Right this way, ladies."

Jordan covered her red cheeks with matching manicured nails as her eyes grew wide. "Livvie! How'd your dad find out about our fake IDs? He's gonna kill you and me too."

"Hush, Jordie."

They slipped out of the blustering dance club without further chatter and didn't arouse a bit of suspicion. He even held the door open for them.

The back alley, devoid of any cars or bodies, felt muggier than the dance club.

Olivia blinked as the sound and smell of the nightclub was silenced with the clank of the heavy metal back door. "You don't…look…like…" The woozy youth cleared her throat and stiffened. "You're not…part of our regular detail. What's your name? I mean, who are you?"

Gordon broke into a grin. Which passport ID to choose? He had to match the dye job and contacts. "Harry Smith. Now if you'll step across the way, our car awaits."

Jordon stumbled over a stray glass bottle. "We don't go out the back way anymore." She waved a hand in front of her nose. "Besides, it stinks out here."

Gordon gave the little snot a push as she fell into the backseat of his rented limo, which was far too easy to land without much of a background check.

Jordan reached out and jerked Olivia's arm to follow her into the car.

A lanky teen tripped out the club's back door. "Hey, mister, where are you taking my date?"

Gordon lowered Olivia's head and thrust her into the car next to Jordon, locking the door with a button's click. Their giggles ended as they watched out the tinted window.

The boy kept walking toward them. As he scanned the license plate, Gordon knew options were limited.

He pulled his silenced Glock 17 and aimed true.

Jordan screamed. He turned back to the car, and Olivia's wide eyes searched his face.

The young fool never knew what hit him.

But these two girls would if they didn't cooperate.

Gordon opened the door, blocking any escape attempt with his body. "Give me your purses. Now."

The two birds turned over their shiny treasures with quivering hands.

Gordon slapped cuffs on both their wrists. All remained quiet as he settled into the driver's side and pointed the black car into traffic. Before they reached the expressway, he threw Jordan's purse out the window. Clue number one would take federal agents weeks to trace, buying him ample time for step two.

But Olivia's purse had a message to deliver.

His calling card of sorts.

Right up to the British embassy front door.

6

There a reason you won't talk about Ryan's funeral?" Clint Rollins leaned on the partition and watched his long-time best friend stiffen like a poker. No matter. Steven needed to talk, or he'd be back like he was when Angela left. Clint had given his partner over a month to process Ryan's death his way. It was time.

"It took all I had to look Ryan's parents in the eyes." Steven kept clicking away at his keyboard. "Besides, what good does it do to rehash it? Doesn't help."

"Neither does stuffing it."

Steven looked up at him. "You're an old mother hen."

"And a darn good lookin' one at that." He pulled his desk chair near Steven's and sat down. "I figure pushing you might backfire, but it's better than watching you close in like you did five years ago."

"Did I tell you about meeting Gracie Lang? She'll be James's teacher next year."

"Is this a clever diversion, or are you going to shoot straight with me?"

Steven held up his hands. "I'll talk about Ryan if it'll stop your bleeding heart."

He shrugged. "Depends on what you say."

"I'm still wrestling with the guilt about being too late to save him. Your praying doesn't work for me, partner. It didn't save my marriage and it doesn't change the fact that kids die. On my watch."

"God's still in control, Steven." Clint lifted his eyebrow. "Not gonna sermonize this, but if you can't pray my way, pray like you did when we first met. With the passion that keeps your backside in that chair when you'd rather be anywhere else."

"Too hard to live like that. It's for younger men." Steven adjusted his favorite photo. One of only two on his desk. "Remember graduation day at Quantico? Ten years ago. Man, we're getting old."

"Speak for yourself. Old is a state of mind and muscle." And his were both in prime shape. So said his beautiful red-haired wife, who still looked as good as that picture his partner liked so much.

"You, me, and Sara bunched together looked like we could take on the world."

"We still do."

Steven sniffed. "A little worse for wear now."

"I remember that my Irish princess tried to get Angela to join us for that photo. Tried for years to get her to open up and let us in."

"This is supposed to help me?"

Clint leaned back in his chair. "Sorry. I just don't get it, even after all these years. She's missed so much of James's life."

"So have I." Steven swiveled his chair to look him in the eyes. "But after I got the call that Ryan died and I had James to take care of without my dad and Sue to help, I realized my little man is too important to keep missing time."

"It's not like you're an absent father, Steven."

"You know as well as I do that I haven't given him everything I can." He straightened his Looney Tunes tie.

Some quirks you never lost. Clint wished Steven played poker because his tie adjusting would be the perfect tell to wipe him clean.

"Don't get stuck here again, Kessler. Think about graduation. How you led our group in prayers. How those young agents looked up to you then." He nodded toward Michael Parker's cubicle. "They still do now."

"I'm pulling seniority, Agent Rollins. I think we need to get back to work."

He pushed his chair back to his desk. "If I had my cowboy hat, I'd tip it to ya."

"Save that for Sara. She's the one who turns to mush when you're in jeans and your Stetson." Steven smirked and waved him on.

"Wonder what your son's teacher would do if she saw you in your workout garb."

"Not gonna know if we don't get work done, will we?"

Clint would leave it there for now. But they'd return to this subject soon. Real soon.

Agent Maxwell's bellow could be heard across the room.

A portent of great things to come. Steven hit the save icon and waited.

"Kessler!" The unit chief stalked toward his desk. "I want you, as the top Crimes Against Children coordinator, heading this investigation and doing lead interviews." Maxwell slapped a file down on his desk and rattled off the highlights. The senior agent reeked of cigar smoke, which only added to Steven's increasing distaste for the assignment.

"This one is a high diplomatic priority. Ambassador's daughter abducted early this morning. Choose your team carefully, Kessler. If all goes well, this will be another one for the books." With a slap on the back, Maxwell disappeared around the corner.

Steven scanned the documents in front of him. So much for an easy Saturday morning at work.

"What'd I tell you? You're a legend in your own time." Clint stood at his side.

Michael Parker joined them. "Who's the vic?"

"Olivia Kensington, seventeen-year-old daughter of the British ambassador to the United States. Kidnapped from a dance club shortly after midnight. The Evidence Response Team has already been dispatched." Steven reached for the phone. "I'm going to set up an organizational meeting with Assistant US Attorney Kenneth Marks, and Special Agent David Adams. He's over the Kensingtons' security details. After that, we'll do a short intro for our team, then head to the embassy." He handed the case folder to Clint. "Ask Jan if she'll prep this for briefing. Then you can push for the ERT's report and round 'em up."

"And head 'em out," Clint said.

Thirty minutes later, Steven drove east across the steel blue Potomac to Massachusetts Avenue. Michael and Clint clicked keyboards, shuffled papers, and talked on cell phones the entire drive. Made of red brick and stone, Sir Walter Kensington's home away from his London home looked like a sprawling English country house.

The place was still crawling with local police and ERT agents. A steaming British ambassador stood right in the center of everything. Clint and Michael jumped out of the car and into the thick of it to organize the scene and take charge of the investigation.

Steven invented a quick parking space amid all the police cars and then rushed up the cobbled sidewalk. Sir Walter made a beeline for him, eyes blazing. The diplomat's slight rugby build and graying hair didn't soften the rage roiling in his features.

"My assistant said you were in charge." Sir Walter began his clipped speech before any typical British formalities. "You'd very well better be the last person I have to deal with today. Your president has given his word, and I expect my daughter returned to safety with haste."

Sticking out his hand, Steven steeled his shoulders and held his chin high. This terrified father needed to see confidence and didn't give a flip about past cases—successes or failures. Ryan's bruised features intruded into Steven's thoughts anyway. He shoved them away.

"I'm Agent Steven Kessler, FBI. Our Rapid Start Team is

already tracking investigative leads." He motioned toward the embassy residence. "Can we find a quieter place to talk?"

Sir Walter shook his hand with a firm grip. But his blood-shot green eyes told a different story. The story of a father whose daughter was God knows where. "In here. Follow me." The ambassador turned with a snap and entered the residence, striding past local officers and FBI personnel with no acknowledgment.

Steven nodded in passing and followed Sir Walter. The high ceilings and ornate decorations as they swept beyond bedrooms and formal halls were cataloged in his memory. Choosing to take the teenager at a dance club rather than her residence was strategic. Small-scope operation. Few people involved.

Leaving Olivia's purse just over the outer fence of the residence hinted at a far more personal motive. One he intended to flesh out today.

On entering the ambassador's library, Sir Walter slammed the outer door. Motioning for Steven to sit, the ambassador stood by a sculpted cherry desk and yelled into the phone. "I will not be disturbed, Charlotte. Is that understood?" He slammed down the receiver.

"Sir Walter, tell me about Olivia and her friend Jordan." Steven hoped the pacing older gentleman would soon take a seat. While he waited for the ambassador to respond, Steven scribbled notes the old-fashioned way—with a pen and yellow legal pad.

"They were impetuous and foolish, but I never dreamed they'd manufacture false identification to go out pubbing." He swore under his breath. "I should have never let them go out celebrating graduation without protection. Seventeen or not, they should have had a Secret Service agent with them."

"You knew about their IDs?"

"Not until a swarm of cops descended and thrust all manner of facts to my attention." Sir Walter slumped into a high-backed leather chair. "This is entirely my fault."

"Sir Walter, I'm sure this is beyond difficult, but let's focus on possible suspects. That will speed up this investigation and help us bring Olivia and Jordan home as fast as possible." Emotional father-speak wasn't his forte, so he switched to his strong suit: facts. "Any threatening calls, recent trouble, or past boyfriends that come to mind?"

"My daughter and her best friend were not, how do you say it? Loose."

"I didn't mean to imply..."

"They were both highly intelligent young ladies who graduated ahead of schedule and wanted to celebrate their achievement. I had no reason to believe they could be in danger. None."

"Yes, sir, I understand that. But you are a man of political importance and anything, no matter how insignificant, could be a great help to our investigation."

Sir Walter steepled his fingers and sat up straight as a rod. "My assistant will give you copies of documented threats and any security concerns. She's been working on that information ever since your police force invaded my home."

"Any significance to you concerning Olivia's purse being returned?"

The ambassador's neck muscles bulged, and his face turned crimson. "I have no idea, Agent Kessler. It's my understanding that falls under your job description."

"Yes, sir."

"How many people are privy to the facts in this case?"

"Besides my team, the Evidence Response Team, the Rapid Start Team from the FBI, and local authorities involved with your 911 call, there's also the Secret Service."

Ambassador Kensington shot to his feet. "I did not want your emergency line contacted, and I do not want any more questions from local authorities." He returned to pacing. "I want only your team involved in any further information sharing. All I need is for your press to find an easy leak and blast my family or impede my work in the United States."

Steven's mind whirled with possibilities. "Who called 911?"

"My assistant, Charlotte Brown. She found the purse and became hysterical. She thought it had Olivia's blood on it."

"Was she close to Olivia?"

"Doubtful."

A knock on the door interrupted the ambassador's pacing. "I do not wish to be disturbed!"

A little sniffling voice called through the library entrance. "But, Papa, I can't find Mum and these men following me won't help."

Steven had a hard time not smiling at the glowing report of the little girl's Secret Service detail. He turned his attention to the files in his lap and waited.

Sir Walter crossed the room and jerked open the door. A little blond-haired girl in a long white sleeveless dress flung herself into his arms. He stroked her bright curls and held her tightly. "I'm sorry, Victoria dear. I'll see if we can raise her on the phone."

The little girl's blue eyes filled with tears as the pair slipped behind the ambassador's desk, and he picked up the receiver. "Eileen, I need you to attend to Victoria." Sir Walter set his daughter on his desk chair and turned his back. "I don't give a... Yes, I do understand. She still needs her mum. Now."

Victoria watched her father's terse conversation with wide eyes. Then she turned toward Steven. "Are you the one who's going to bring my Livvie home?"

He guessed the precocious six-year-old had overheard far more than her little ears needed to know. "I'm going to do all I can."

The little girl cocked her head. "I miss my sister. She was my only friend here in America, even if she was gone too often. Mum is dawdling on where I'm to attend school in September. Livvie was supposed to take me to lessons so we could have time together."

Steven adjusted his tie. This little girl had no real concept of the storm that raged around her. But something in her China doll features made his insides knot in a tighter ball. Too bad she and his son didn't attend the same school. James would have loved being friends with another child his age who spoke as comfortably with adults as he did.

"Are you a papa?"

Steven nodded. "I have a son about your age."

"I should like to meet him." Victoria was well on her way to becoming a charming hostess.

He glanced at his watch and hoped the ambassador wouldn't continue his conversation much longer. Every second counted. At the same time, people in a traumatic circumstance needed careful attention. Even a child, especially one this verbal, could supply helpful information. If he chose his words with care.

"Where did you and Livvie like to spend time together?"

"At the parks. We would walk with those big men following and whisper about being princesses and finding a magic carpet to take us far away. Like Princess Jasmine."

"From *Aladdin*?"

Victoria's face creased with a grin. "You watch Disney movies? I thought all adults watched dull sports or news shows."

Ambassador Kensington ended his conversation. "Are you entertaining or grilling my youngest daughter? Neither will return Olivia, will it?"

Steven stiffened. His time would be better served interviewing the assistants, for all the help Sir Walter had offered between his succinct rants. Nonspecific answers. No possible suspects. Many diplomats had lists of enemies to rattle off at a moment's notice. Finger-pointing and politics seemed to go hand in hand.

"If you have no further questions, I'd like to complete our discussion at this time." Sir Walter passed his chair and moved to the library door.

Steven's cell phone buzzed. Offering up a silent plea, he nodded to the ambassador. "I will be in touch soon, sir."

"Good day."

Steven shook his head as the library door shut on his heels. He flipped open his phone and headed back to his Explorer. "Kessler."

"Got some interesting leads to run by you." Michael Parker's voice boomed through his cell. "And a very irate American father in the command center who's asking for your head. Want to handle it now or later, boss?"

"I'll be right over." Steven returned the phone to his belt clip and checked his watch. Still inside twelve hours. They needed a strong lead—soon. Maybe Jordan's father would supply more information than Sir Walter. Not likely. But he could hope.

Little Victoria's words dogged his footsteps. *When will you bring my Livvie home?* Deep in his gut he felt the teenagers were unharmed. So far. The bits of evidence melding together into a working theory increased his pace through the English estate grounds.

He wouldn't be too late.

Not this time.

T he Assistant US Attorney's office buzzed with activity
early Monday morning.

Steven drummed a pen on the huge mahogany meeting
table. The familiar room hadn't changed since the last time his
team had met with Kenneth Marks. Deep green plants and
expensive framed family pictures separated the floor-to-ceiling
collection of reference books on built-in bookshelves surrounding the room.

His team and two of the Kensingtons' Secret Service detail
flipped through notes and talked shop. He should have called
this first organizational meeting to order ten minutes ago. More
like two days ago. If he had found Olivia Saturday, they wouldn't
have needed this meeting.

But that hadn't happened.

At least Clint knew not to include him in any light conversation today. Working on little sleep and two days of futile leads
in a kidnapping case left Steven a little short on pleasantries.

And even shorter on time.

Kenneth strode into the room and stationed himself at the
head of the ornate table. In a flash, the room grew quiet and male
and female agents took their seats around Steven. "Ladies and
gentlemen, thank you all for coming today. Court ran late, as the
DC system is wont to do. But I assume you've all reviewed Agent
Kessler's extensive case notes so we can skip to the next step in
protection, pursuing Olivia's kidnapper, as well as establishing a
solid case for prosecution. The president is following this case
with interest."

Steven hoped the white-haired attorney wouldn't harp on the lack of quality leads the Rapid Start Team was still researching. Ken had always shown great respect and professionalism in his work with federal agents, even with pressure from the Oval Office. But everyone knew their window for success in this case was closing.

Fast.

Pen in hand, Ken locked eyes with Steven. "Agent Kessler, your team's circulating a physical description. Any updates there?"

The question of the hour. "Brown-haired, dark-eyed men wearing black suits are a dime a dozen in DC. Many at the Baltimore club had noticed our perpetrator leaving with the two girls, but most were too intoxicated or too caught up in their own world to provide useful clues."

But every interview lead and called-in or e-mailed tip had to be followed up, regardless that it was most likely wasted time. Valuable resources detained on rabbit trails. Steven wanted to curse. He had to find Olivia and Jordan soon.

"The Crimes Against Children team has been working all leads throughout the weekend." Steven fought back a yawn. "My interviews with Sir Walter and his staff have given us a few promising suspects. We're bringing two in for questioning later this afternoon when their planes arrive from London."

"Any indication Olivia is still alive? Have ransom demands been received?"

"A few calls to that end, but they've been invalidated." Steven took a deep breath. "Given the clean abduction site, no murder weapon, physical evidence left at the embassy, and no contact with the ambassador, I believe this is a small operation and personal in nature. The two men coming in today could shed some light on those theories."

Ken nodded. "Good. Make sure my office is notified immediately of any case developments and transcripts sent afterward."

"Yes, sir."

Ken turned to the Secret Service Special Agent in Charge at the other end of the conference table. "Agent Adams, I understand the Kensingtons are applying pressure to place their youngest daughter in a protected school next month and to increase her security detail."

Steven braced for the reaction. David Adams despised interference in his protection details. Especially by unpredictable diplomats. Or FBI agents. Steven had gone toe-to-toe with the middle-aged agent on enough cases to steer clear whenever he could.

David clenched his jaw. Brown eyes blazing, he straightened the papers in front of him. "Yes, sir. I've allocated four agents for Victoria Kensington's around-the-clock coverage and met with Lady Kensington."

"Are her requests unreasonable?"

Agent Adams backpedaled at Ken's directness. "Not entirely, sir." He looked at his planner. "She's requested that her detail be removed, which won't happen. And the fixation on this school in Alexandria is a bit extreme."

Steven sat up straighter. This could get interesting.

David continued. "I have an appointment at ten today with the headmistress of Hope Ridge Academy, Janice Hall, and the first-grade teacher who will have Victoria in her class the beginning of September."

Clint raised his eyebrows and nodded at Steven.

"Hope Ridge Academy is perfect placement for Victoria." Steven leaned forward. "She'll be in my son's class, and according to the headmistress, the teacher is one of the best in the school."

Steven met Agent Adams's surprised stare. "Janice Hall is former FBI, and she runs a tight ship at the school regarding security protocol and academics. I met with her a number of times before registering James."

Ken cleared his throat. "Then maybe you should accompany Agent Adams today."

David stiffened and kept his eyes locked on Ken. "Agent Grivens and I can handle things at Hope Ridge."

The seasoned attorney chuckled. "No doubt about that. But given agency stickiness at times, I think having the lead FBI agent brief both the teacher and the headmistress on his investigation would be good PR."

Agent Adams swallowed hard. "If Agent Kessler has the time, he's welcome to join us."

Clint grinned across the table like he'd won a Texas-sized seed-spitting contest. No doubt his partner would torment him over this turn of events. So what? Steven would get to see his son's attractive teacher and get away from his desk for a few short hours today.

No harm in that.

Maria Grivens walked the quiet halls of Hope Ridge Academy, her uncomfortable two-inch heels clicking in step with the vice principal. She noted every escape possibility on the schematics in her hands. A thorough report with all manner of details would be the minimal requirement of her supervisor, David Adams.

Mr. Perkins stepped into her personal space. "Interesting work, guarding a six-year-old?"

Maria bristled. She'd take her licks from coworkers who thought calling her "Teach" was a riot. But she wouldn't accept a slighting comment from some spindly assistant principal. "This is a high-priority diplomatic assignment. I'm honored to be part of Victoria's detail."

The man's warm smile irritated her. She'd been hit on by worse, though. Just not often enough to know how to respond without making everything awkward. "With your black hair and tan skin, I'd guess you're of Hispanic heritage, yes?"

Maria stopped walking and faced Mr. Perkins. "Is that a problem?"

"No. Not at all. You'll fit right in with our multicultural student body." He offered a wide grin. "Except for the weaponry, of course." Perkins started back toward the main office.

Why some men couldn't handle a woman with a gun still riled her. She was a natural-born American, had excelled at every one of her performance ratings during training at Glynco, and had conducted herself with complete professionalism during the meetings with Hope Ridge staff.

One hundred and eighty degrees from the vice principal's behavior.

As she hurried in the opposite direction of the main office, Maria thought back to Perkins's interaction with his mother, the headmistress. Okay, maybe unprofessional was a tad harsh. He'd been perfectly poised at every point except for his tense jawline when Mrs. Hall spoke. Family baggage must run deep.

Knocking on the first-grade classroom door, she watched Gracie jump. Maria smiled. She'd liked Gracie Lang from their first handshake. Even if the sparks between Gracie and Agent Kessler made the green-eyed monster come alive in her thoughts.

"Do you have a minute, Mrs. Lang?"

Gracie held a hand to her heart. "Maria. I mean, Agent Grivens. I'm so glad it's you."

"Maria is fine. But wouldn't you rather it were Agent Kessler at your door?"

Gracie's face turned bright red. "Was I that obvious?" She sat on a plastic chair and motioned for Maria to join her. "I feel like a schoolgirl. Especially considering the gravity of what brings you all to Hope Ridge. I'm so sorry."

"I don't think any of the men noticed." Maria lowered herself into a chair and shielded her paperwork on her lap. "And I can relate. From what I've heard on the Bureau grapevine, Agent Kessler has that effect on most females."

"You too?"

"Yes, but it came to nothing." Maria laughed. "First time I

met Agent Kessler, one of my partners told him I was new to DC and could use a tour guide."

Gracie's eyes grew wide.

"I stammered on about not having time to date, and he just smiled." Maria wondered if getting this personal was a good idea. But Gracie's open communication style drew her. She could use a trustworthy female friend not on Secret Service's payroll. Besides, being comfortable around each other would make her classroom assignment more pleasant.

"So my off-the-wall questions and dropping my notebook at the meeting today didn't make your boss wish he'd chosen a different school? Or at least a different teacher?"

Maria shook her head. "You're fine, Gracie. Agent Adams is very pleased with everything concerning Hope Ridge."

"Will you be here often preparing for the first day of school? Maybe we could grab some lunch one day." Gracie glanced around the room. "I'll be here for a little while most days, getting the room and my lessons ready."

"While I can't discuss protection details beyond what Agent Adams covered, it's safe to say I'll be seeing you here a good bit in August."

A male cough made them both turn toward the door.

"If I'm interrupting a meeting, I can come back later." Agent Kessler's megawatt smile still made Maria pull in her abdominal muscles. At least Gracie hadn't mentioned wanting to sleep with Steven like other agents Maria'd had the misfortune of overhearing.

"No, you're not. Mrs. Lang and I were just getting better acquainted." Maria and Gracie stood at the same time. "But I need to finish my schematics and meet with Agent Adams soon."

She smiled at Gracie. "I look forward to working with you."

"See you soon, Maria. And thanks." Gracie smoothed her straight tan skirt and white blouse, slipping a shy glance at Steven as she spoke.

Maria chuckled to herself and closed the classroom door on

her way out. Someone needed to have a little fun during this assignment.

"Hello, Agent Kessler. How may I help you?"

Steven adjusted his blue silk tie and walked farther into the room. "Steven, please. I wanted to apologize for my abrupt exit last time I was here."

"I'm sure you had important things to do." Gracie moved behind her neat desk.

He noticed the small group of family photos. Including one of Gracie with a man and children. Disappointment derailed his plans. "Is this your family?"

"Yes. Mark, Elizabeth, and Joshua." Gracie fingered her gold locket and stared out the large classroom windows.

"Now it's my turn to ask if you're okay."

Her eyes returned to the silver-framed picture. "Sorry. I'm never sure how to introduce them."

He stepped closer for a better look. "Why is that?"

"They died over two years ago."

Steven froze. "I'm sorry."

Gracie sighed and sat on her simple oak chair. She motioned toward one of two other adult chairs nearby. "If you have a minute, your question actually reminded me of something I've wanted to ask you since our first meeting."

He pulled a chair to the edge of her desk.

"My family was killed in an automobile accident, and I want to find the man responsible. I was wondering if you had any suggestions that could help me."

He studied her face. Time might have given her some perspective and distance, but her hazel eyes held unshed tears. Maybe he'd misread her interest in him. "Did the local police confirm that another car was involved?"

"I watched the accident. And I believe the person in the

truck that hit Mark was drunk. He belongs in jail. But local police couldn't find him."

Gracie's eyes ignited. If a drunk hit-and-run driver had escaped prosecution after killing three people—including two little children—he needed to be found. And if anyone could do that, his friend Justin could.

"I have an old college buddy who's a local PI. I don't have his contact info with me, but I could e-mail it to you if you're interested." Steven pulled a pen and paper from his suit coat. "What's your address?"

"G.Lang@belief.net."

He scribbled a quick note. "Great. I'll send that info this evening." He looked up to see her watching him.

Gracie's face flushed. It had been a long time since he'd made a lady blush. Or cared when a female looked him over. But this time it felt good. Too good. Though the timing stunk.

"Thank you for helping me." She smiled and tapped a pencil on the desk. "Where did you graduate from college?"

The whiplash switch to personal information amused him, but he held back a chuckle. "The University of Louisville. Criminal Justice."

Gracie leaned forward. "And you're wearing a blue tie? I thought Kentuckians' blood ran either Cat blue or Cardinal red and a true fan didn't wear the rival school's colors."

She knew college ball? He couldn't help but grin. Holding out his tie, he cleared his throat and affected a professorial tone. "This is most certainly not a Kentucky blue tie. On the contrary, it was a gift from my stepmom. She said the color matched my eyes and that a Cardinal fan could wear light blue. Just never dark blue."

Gracie laughed.

He enjoyed the sound. "Would you like to watch a game sometime? My partner and his wife catch a few hoops with James and me when we get the chance."

"Mark and I watched college sports all the time. But I'm a little rusty now and never did cheer at the right time."

She glanced out the window again for what felt like an hour. But this time, no tears. Maybe she had enough distance to date, but he'd obviously mistaken her friendliness for something more. Waiting for her polite rejection made his mouth dry. He hadn't asked a woman out in years, and it looked like his one shot was going to be an air ball.

"I might not be good company for basketball, but if you were interested in dinner…"

He leaned back in his chair as a slow smile creased his face. His powers of observation weren't out of tune after all. And she'd practically asked him out. He liked that.

He'd be a fool not to ask now. "Are you free this Friday? I know a great restaurant in Old Town Alexandria."

"I'd like that." Gracie straightened books and lesson plans on her desk that were already in perfect order. "Thanks for saving me from dishonoring my Southern upbringing."

"Never asked a gentleman for a date before?"

"No. And if we don't say our good-byes soon, I might chicken out on accepting your invitation." Gracie stood, her face a study in the color crimson. It went well with her long auburn hair.

"Then I'll be leaving now." Steven headed toward the door. "I'll e-mail you this afternoon. 'Bye, Gracie. It was a pleasure seeing you again."

"Good-bye, Steven. I'll see you Friday."

He smiled, then turned to leave. He could feel her gaze following him down the hall. For the first time in almost five years, he felt excitement about what tomorrow might hold.

Tom had watched unnoticed outside Gracie's classroom door.

Now he paced in his private office with growing frustration.

If she hired a private investigator…

He shook his head and refocused. He'd missed the first part of her conversation with the super-stud FBI agent. The one his mother had praised in their morning meeting for exemplary work as a Crimes Against Children coordinator. A job good old mom had done during her last years in the Florida Bureau office. Too bad she hadn't started a school down there. He would have preferred the Florida sun to the ridiculous winters of his Alexandria hometown.

He took a drink of Coke and wished for something harder.

Mother Dear had offered him a job here though, not in Florida. And it was one he'd mastered with ease. A career his dad would have been proud of. Mother was still too busy recovering from widowhood and a failed second marriage, so he had to work harder to get her attention.

Now Gracie Lang and her FBI date could topple it all.

If only Mother knew about his surveillance work or computer prowess.

Not like that could ever happen.

It was bad enough that his school would be crawling with even more feds in September.

Tom slumped into the leather seat behind his carved cherry-wood desk. Expensive Kandinskys adorned his walls. He was still in charge here. The FBI and Secret Service hotshots would be answering to him come September. Surely he could find a way to stop one little widow from Georgia. Even if she did hire a private investigator.

Tom brushed a hand through his dark curls. Ideas surged through his brain.

Now to pick just the right one.

8

Gordon felt rested after the insufferably long weekend. Couldn't say the same for his pawns locked away in the cellar of the drafty old three-story farmhouse. The girls had screamed 'til they reached exhaustion. With no one around to hear. Poor fools.

He double-checked each window lock in the ramshackle country-bumpkin estate on the outskirts of Alexandria. Curtains drawn against the late Tuesday afternoon sun, he drank his frustration away with an early evening bitter.

Sir Walter Kensington had spent the weekend frantic and fuming at coppers and agents alike. Good. But he hadn't suffered enough. Not nearly enough.

Gordon glanced at his timepiece. The moment to contact Ambassador Kensington had come, but his sister had yet to telephone confirmation of his plan's safety.

When he did e-mail the ambassador, he'd make his demand short and very clear. The FBI would be up all night trying to decipher his note.

To no avail.

He rang his sister first. "Good afternoon, dear Charlotte. Is the estimable Sir Walter Kensington in his office?"

"I knew I shouldn't have answered." She sighed. "I've warned you about calling my cell during the day. The embassy is teeming with agents. I don't want trouble."

"Ah, but trouble has found you, has it not? Thanks to your good employer. Don't forget Harry's blood." Gordon toasted the desolate land outside his temporary residence. The FBI would never follow his paper trail. Ten years in Her Majesty's Special Forces served him well.

"You'd best get this over with soon. Everything is being watched. But you already knew that."

"That I did."

"How will you do it?"

Gordon sneered. "Watching your words, Charlotte? There's no trace on your mobile contraption." He pulled steno notes from his satchel. "No worries about how this will be handled either. Harry and I did our respective work well."

"Harry lived within the law, Gordon."

"Harry was killed because of that." He could see Harry's coffin in his mind. Her Majesty had condescended to allow Gordon a short viewing, thanks to his former clearance.

Harry Landridge died in service to his cherished country.

And now it was as if he never existed.

Harry's killer would soon pay.

The ransom demand would send the coppers and federal agents scurrying for political motive. Experts from London would be retained. No one would ever suspect the Landridge family.

And the results would torture the Queen's representative the entirety of his natural life.

"Be done and go home soon, Gordie." Her line went dead.

His sister's whispered words reminded him of their childhood treasure hunts in the dark. Charlotte had no heart for intrigue or danger, but he needed her now. She would not disappoint him. Or Harry.

Gordon assembled his high-tech office in the front room of the old farmhouse. One thing he would say for America was her fast, efficient black market technology. Once finished, he'd sell the pieces all over the world in channels untraceable. Or even back to Britain through the same pathways Sir Kensington had operated.

God save the Queen.

Thirty minutes later, he connected to Sir Kensington's

personal e-mail account. Gordon sent the encrypted file, then disassembled his equipment. The file contained details of the ransom demand and a few tidbits of incriminating evidence from Harry's investigation. Clues that Sir Kensington would "forget" to share with the FBI.

Then his pure British bloodline would rot in prison.

Steven cursed the Beltway traffic.

He should have known better than to go home today for a shower and dinner with James. His son could have waited one more day.

Olivia might not.

Finally, the Massachusetts Avenue estate drew near. Steven parked his Explorer among a throng of federal vehicles. He was the last to arrive.

Clint met him at the residence entrance, Stetson in hand, wearing blue jeans and leather boots. "Simmer down, partner. You're not too late for the action. Seems Sir Walter delayed contacting us after the ransom demand. The electronic trail could take us a good while to trace, but you have some Intel to work with."

Steven stormed past Clint. "Since the immediate threat is active, why are you here dressed like that?"

Clint caught up to him with quick strides. "Dinner? Family? Ring any bells?"

"Still, we don't need to hand Sir Walter any fodder for dissing us to the unit chief." Steven reached the ambassador's study and stopped, pocketing his credentials. "Why don't you send up some prayers for me? I'm gonna need them to bring those girls home. Especially if the good ambassador isn't being forthright with us."

"Tread carefully. His daughter is still missing."

"I know. All too well."

Steven knocked and entered without waiting for an invitation. "Sir Walter, I've interviewed two possible suspects but had to release them for lack of evidence. Immediate action after that e-mail could have given us the ammunition we needed to find your daughter."

The gray-haired gentleman stood to his full height. "I will not have you barging into my residence like this."

"Do you want your daughter returned?" Steven squared off with the diplomat across his chaotic desk.

The man crumpled into his leather chair. With eyes scanning the thick tan carpet, he rubbed his prominent nose. Even his voice dropped a notch. "Yes. More than anything." He motioned to the guest chairs. "Please, sit. Tell me about your suspects. Given this ransom demand, maybe I can give you something that will constitute reason to detain them again."

Steven squinted. He'd never consulted with the parent of a kidnapped child on a case. He had no intention of starting now. But… "Both British nationals came willingly with the help of your embassy staff. Nothing to hide, it appears."

"You don't believe them?"

"I believe someone kidnapped your daughter and is twisting the knife in your back. I believe Olivia and Jordan are still alive." Steven leaned forward. "But they might not be for long if we don't move quickly."

"I will pay the ransom. I have already wired for my available funds. They should arrive in the morning."

"Ten million dollars? We will not pay possible terrorists, Sir Walter."

The older gentleman's eyes blazed. "If I follow your instruction and my daughter is killed, I will hold you personally responsible."

Great. At least he didn't work in Organized Crime and receive a steady diet of this garbage. "Tell me about the e-mail."

"There was nothing in the e-mail but directions to a location where I will receive my daughter and her friend in exchange for the amount demanded."

Steven met the ambassador's intense gaze. "Nothing else?

Then why did our technicians find British black market references deleted from your e-mail to us? Tampering with a federal investigation is serious business."

The man's face grew pale, and he pointed a bony finger at Steven. "I sent all the information you needed. Must you treat me like a common criminal?"

"Maybe you misunderstand our goals. Our first priority is returning your daughter to safety." Steven leaned back into the cool leather chair. "Your actions place you under intense suspicion."

"I had nothing to do with my daughter's disappearance! You must be mad to think me a suspect."

"Then explain your behavior." Steven could only hope the ambassador would throw him a useful bone. Or Agent Maxwell would have this British citizen deported, without a job or entrance to the United States ever again. Maybe even jail time.

Sir Walter set to pacing behind his desk, passing all manner of classical texts in the bookshelf behind him. "I consider it a threat to implicate me in my daughter's kidnapping."

"Your behavior did more damage than the original e-mail would have done."

Steven considered the diplomat's nervous body language and the obscure references the man had tried to eliminate. None gave them any clue toward Olivia's investigation. In fact, they were dead ends, according to the British Security Service.

Could the ambassador be telling the truth?

"We have a purse with a bloody smear, an abductor who knew about Olivia's whereabouts and lack of security, and no credible eyewitnesses to a murder and double kidnapping. Now a ransom demand via an encrypted e-mail with elements you deleted. I need your full cooperation and disclosure of any relevant information."

Sir Walter slumped into his chair. "There were British consuls under Secret Intelligence Service investigation for black market arms trading. I assisted Her Majesty's forces in apprehending them."

Steven made quick notations on his pad. "I need more information than that."

"Speak with Sir Peter Barnstable. He should verify everything." The ambassador flicked his hand in the air and studied the carpet once again. "The consuls were jailed. I can't imagine their involvement in this. But the references…" He buried his head in his hands. "Could the former consuls have anything to do with my daughter's kidnapping? Please, Agent Kessler. Please find Olivia."

Steven stood and pocketed his notepad and pen. "We're doing everything in our power, Sir Walter."

The man nodded and waved him toward the door.

Clint met him on the other side. "Straight story this time?"

"Nothing simple to validate." Steven loosened his tie. "According to the ambassador, this is home territory trouble. British intelligence, no matter our countries' mutual sharing policy, is not going to break ranks for my investigation."

Clint whistled low and long. "So you believe Sir Walter?"

Steven shrugged. "Not entirely. But now I have something to move ahead with. Our first and only promising lead. Maybe the honorable Peter Barnstable from SIS will be of assistance this time."

They walked out to Steven's SUV, pausing to show credentials a dozen times. "How do you know this Barnstable guy?"

"International training class at Quantico. Not a friendly chap."

Clint leaned against the Explorer. "You need some sleep, partner. Gotta rest up for the big date Friday and all."

"Whatever. With everything that's going on, I may have to cancel."

Clint adjusted the cream-colored Stetson atop his cropped brown hair. "Nothing doing. I can handle things for one night. You're going out two-stepping on the town Friday."

If everything went according to plan in the morning.

If not, time with one Gracie Lang might remain a pipe dream.

9

Wednesday dawned ripe with possibility.

Gracie had an upcoming date for the first time in years, and it didn't feel like betraying Mark. She spun around in her pink flowered sundress. When she stopped, the reflection in her full-length antique mirror caught her off guard.

The skeptical eyes most of all.

"Okay, maybe it feels a little like betrayal." She stroked Jake's honey-colored fur as he watched her every move. "But like Beth said, that's ridiculous. Mark would want me to be happy again. Of course, I think she just wants to meet a real, live FBI agent, but at least Bethy's talking to me like old times."

Jake didn't comment.

She chuckled and gathered her scrapbooks, placed everything on the bed, and sat down. "Today, Jake, I'm going to meet one of Steven's friends who will help us find the awful man in the black truck." Gracie bent down to ruffle the hair on Jake's muzzle. "Once we put that man in prison, that'll be such a weight off my heart. Justice for my family. And maybe Steven will help us celebrate that victory too."

Jake barked.

The phone's loud ring made her scurry to silence the noise-maker. Leah's number. "Aren't you working today, Miss Hotshot District Attorney?"

Her best friend sighed. "I don't think I'll ever get used to caller ID, no matter how long I live. And yes, I am working."

"You're not that old, Leah."

Gracie pictured Leah brushing that comment away like a fly.

Leah was convinced that thirty was old, and she'd passed that number years ago. Gracie didn't agree, but she could only fight that battle every so often. Today was not one of those days.

"I've done some checking on your private investigator, and he sounds like a handful, Gracie. I'd like to join you when you talk with him."

Gracie took the cordless downstairs with her and let Jake out into the backyard. "I'm a big girl. I can handle a churlish grouser."

"I'm sure you can. But Justin Moore's complaining ways aren't my biggest concern. He's respected in DC...for a private eye. I'd just like to make double sure everything he proposes is aboveboard and he's not getting your hopes up."

"My appointment's at ten o'clock. Can you make it to Alexandria in forty-five minutes?"

"See you there."

Gracie tossed the phone on her spotless breakfast bar. Her current home was nothing like life with little ones. She had considered it a good day when her house looked neat. It had hardly ever been spic-and-span clean. One more thing she had yet to get used to about single living.

Time to clean and more time to clean.

But not this weekend. She let Jake into the kitchen and wiped his paws with one of the towels she kept in the bottom drawer of her old-fashioned coatrack near the door. Coming home to muddy tracks didn't make the schedule today.

Thirty minutes later, she parked her Jeep in front of the little brick-house-turned-office suites for Justin Moore, Private Investigator. Leah's silver Lexus pulled in next to hers a few minutes later.

Leah opened her door. "Ready?"

"To take another step forward in putting the past to rest? Yes." Gracie clutched her black leather business folder to her chest. "But I'm terrified too. What if this is just another expensive dead end?"

"Let's go find out." Leah's curve-hugging soft blue suit was tailor-made for her slim form. With straight, natural blond hair, she turned heads wherever she went. As they entered the reception area, Mr. Moore was no exception to the rule. He extended a hand and covertly assessed Leah's figure.

Gracie had tried to get used to that in college. But every once in a while, she wished someone would pay her that kind of attention too.

Like Mark always had. From their first encounter, he had eyes only for her.

"Thank you for altering your schedule to meet with us today." Gracie returned Mr. Moore's firm handshake and followed him into his sparse office.

"Favors for a friend get top priority. Especially when my schedule's relatively open for the morning anyway." He leaned his beer-bellied football physique back in his black swivel chair and chuckled at his own joke.

"I have the copies of police reports you asked to see. And the duplicates of pertinent newspaper articles about the accident." Gracie handed him a manila folder.

Mr. Moore extended his hand across the desk with only a plasma computer screen and a few reference books on it. "Thank you. I've been doing some Internet research in preparation for our meeting, but these will help. Any little bit provides possible leads the police overlooked."

Leah's brow crinkled. "Exactly what do you intend to do that the Gwinnett County police department didn't?"

Mr. Moore steepled his fingers and smiled. "I have great respect for local authorities. Many of my close friends are in law enforcement. But they don't get paid what I do to dig up clues and suggest innovative research techniques."

"Like what?" Gracie had no idea what he might suggest.

"A forensic sketch to circulate on local college campuses. There might be a few folks in the administration from two years ago who would remember." He looked at her. "You did say you saw a college student in the black truck, correct?"

She twisted the hem of her sundress. "I don't know if I remember enough for a detailed picture. I'm sorry."

"We could try hypnotism." He took a drink of black coffee and raised his eyebrows. "Sorry about my lack of manners. Would either of you like a cup?"

She and Leah shook their heads. "No, thank you."

The private investigator continued. "I've read studies done with police investigations where a hypnotized witness remembered facts that turned a case around."

"Let me pray about that."

Mr. Moore almost spit out his second sip of coffee.

"I don't want to implicate an innocent man because my memory wasn't as good as I thought." Gracie bit her lower lip. "I'm not entirely certain it was a college student either."

The muscles working overtime in his jaw could have ripped through steel.

Twenty minutes and a slew of standard questions later, she and Leah exited Mr. Moore's office. "So what do you think? Will he be able to help me?" Gracie fingered her gold locket. She hadn't seen the pictures of her babies in a long time, but knowing they were close brought comfort.

"What is his retainer?"

Gracie unlocked her Jeep. "Enough. But it's coming from the insurance money collecting dust in my savings. If it'll help put that man in jail, it's worth it, right?"

Leah hugged her. "If it'll help you make this last step and move into the future, I'm all for it. Especially if that means you'll be dating again."

Gracie held up her hands. "Uncle. I've heard it all from Beth a thousand times over already. Don't you start too." She smiled. "If things go well Friday, maybe we can double-date sometime. Like we did in college."

"Sounds like a plan." Leah checked her sleek silver-and-gold watch. "I need to get back. I have court in an hour, and

I'd like to review the defense's case one more time."

"Go get 'em." Gracie hugged her best friend one more time. "I'll call you Friday night." She climbed into her Jeep. "If I'm not out too late, that is."

Steven ran his hands through his hair.

Roadblocks all morning had his shoulders in knots. The British Secret Intelligence Service continued to give him the runaround. The men he did speak with knew little of Sir Walter Kensington. That they'd share. Even less about black market arms dealing. Scrolling through pages of investigative leads and searching databases yielded even fewer results.

But nothing that validated or refuted Ambassador Kensington's claims. So Michael Parker volunteered to shadow Sir Walter while following some Internet trails today. The young agent and his laptop were seldom parted.

Steven glanced at his desk clock. Noon. This afternoon's security meeting should be interesting. Convincing Sir Walter to play by FBI and Secret Service rules would be a monumental task. But if it were James's life at stake, Steven would have a hard time following the rules too.

He'd do anything to have his son returned alive.

Steven went back to his computer search. Clint remained at the command center at the embassy in case any phone calls required immediate tracking. They wouldn't lose another opportunity.

His cell phone buzzed. "Kessler."

"Well, Romeo, you didn't tell me Gracie was a knockout." Justin's words slammed against his eardrums. The man talked with the same gusto he'd shown when he played Cardinal football. "Her best friend is quite the looker too. It has been a good day."

Steven walked out of the Crimes Against Children offices. "Tell me you didn't drool. I'm trusting you to help Gracie. She has a worthy case."

"An impossible one, if you ask me."

He took a deep breath. "That's not what I wanted to hear. You can do better than that. It's why I recommended you in the first place."

"Tell me you're at least getting some while I bust my tail and turn over every imaginable rock to unearth something useable."

Steven leaned against a wall in the hallway. "No."

"No, what? You've been batching it too long to play the saint. 'Fess up, Kessler. Make my day a little more interesting."

Telling Justin about Christian values didn't seem appropriate now. Steven had known God, and according to his old college pal, he played the saint part well. But it didn't set right. Still, Justin had asked…

"I have no plans to sleep with Gracie, Justin. Or anyone else. One jumped-the-gun marriage is enough for me, thanks."

"Hey, but Angela was more than any man could handle on his own."

Steven's heart thudded. He'd known this conversation was likely when he contacted Justin. All his college friends had the same opinion of Angela. Surprised he ever got a ring on her finger. Not surprised she ditched him a few short years later.

"Tell me about the case."

"Nice non sequitur there, choirboy, but there's not much to tell."

"Try me."

"Cops in Georgia concur that Gracie's family could have been killed by a drunk college student and that she probably did get a glimpse of his face. But the paint slivers on the van, the yaw marks showing the truck slammed on the brakes too late, and more recently a partial plate that Gracie gave Detective Calhoun, have turned up nada." Justin paused. "This is about as dead a case as I've run into in a long time. Thanks a ton, pal."

"Did you ask Gracie about circulating a sketch?"

"I did. Maybe you could talk her into it. She said something about needing to pray first." Justin blew a puff of air into the phone. "Don't see how that's gonna help things, but whatever."

Steven grimaced. That comment hit too close to his conscience for comfort. "If I can make our date on Friday, I'll ask her. But no promises. I don't mess with people's faith convictions." Steven stepped back into the bustling CAC offices. "Besides, maybe her praying will help you nail this case. From what I understand, you need another good win sometime soon."

"Thanks for the vote of confidence. I'll keep you in the know."

Steven flipped his phone closed. The way his entire life stood now, only God could make his and Gracie's situations resolve well.

Maybe he should try that praying thing again.

Tonight would probably be a good time to start.

10

Tonight he wouldn't be too late.

Steven flashed his credentials and entered the ghostly silent embassy residence. Tonight Olivia and Jordan would come home. The main Hostage Rescue Team was in place at Huntley Meadows Park, and Sir Walter had agreed to stay at the embassy and keep his ten million.

That he had such a healthy private account sent up red flags for Steven—until Sir Peter Barnstable verified all of the ambassador's information. He provided little additional information, though. Except that Sir Walter had descended from money, and he appeared to invest with great wisdom.

Michael Parker emerged from the command center. "Hey, boss. Does Sir Walter really require a babysitter tonight?" The young agent locked eyes with Steven and held his typical military at-ease stance.

"Absolutely." Steven chuckled at the rookie's bored expression. He'd learn in time. Only about 10 percent of an agent's life consisted of heart-pounding excitement.

Unless it was Steven's year.

He'd trade with Parker. Especially tonight.

"Is Sir Walter in his study?" Steven gestured right with his chin.

Michael shrugged. "Snug and boring if you ask me." Then he disappeared into the control room to watch the monitors with the Secret Service.

Steven looked up to the ceiling, thankful he'd miss all the smack talk and female conquest stories. Some things still stung his conscience.

As he walked through the decorated halls, the past invaded his thoughts. When the guys he caught lunch with talked about dates, memories of his ex-wife haunted him. Their passionate arguments and little emotion elsewhere. Even with all of Angela's seductive beauty, it still surprised him that they ever had a child together.

Turning the corner, Steven stopped in front of Sir Walter's study. Most agents ribbed Clint about his perfect life, but they didn't breathe a word of Steven's past or his dateless present. Except to call him a saint behind his back and tell the female agents he was too good for them.

He should face that music soon and put an end to the "saint" and "snob" rumors. Maybe dating Gracie would help. For now, he had to get his head in the case.

Steven checked his watch. Eleven o'clock. The drop would happen in an hour.

A quick knock and he entered the study. Given Sir Walter Kensington's questionable behavior to date, Steven needed the element of surprise his fast entrance offered. Plus, like any good cop, he needed to maintain who was in charge.

He was.

"Must you invade my residence with your American lack of decorum?" Sir Walter motioned to the small mounted camera that moved to catch every inch of the room. "Your obnoxious cameras are intrusion enough."

"You did withhold evidence, Sir Walter." Steven settled into a leather chair. "Even with British Secret Intelligence Service backing, that doesn't set well with me. Our primary objective is to bring Olivia and Jordan home alive."

The man's suit showed a life's worth of worry in every wrinkle. "What I did hasn't hampered that at all. They will be home within the hour."

"What have you done, Ambassador?"

The man jutted his chin upward and tossed a nondescript

note card on the desk. "My daughter should be with a personal friend as we speak."

Steven stood and swore in tandem. Then he invaded Sir Walter's personal space. "Tell me exactly what you have done, or God help me, your diplomatic immunity will mean nothing." Steven opened his cell phone and hit Clint's speed dial while he skimmed the plain white card.

The man's ashen face sent Steven's stomach roiling.

"I...I simply followed the instructions on the note. I couldn't risk Olivia's life. The instructions specified another park, no intelligence officers, or Olivia would be dead upon sighting. That's what I was told happened to an intelligence officer with the arms dealing situation referenced in the e-mail. I had to do as they said."

"Any other bits of information you'd care to share?" Steven held up the note. "Like yet another park switch?"

"N-no. On my life, I swear it's Memorial Hill Park."

"What time?"

His partner answered the phone. "Clint, alert the HRT. Correct hunch."

Sir Walter studied his black shoes.

Steven bent down toward the ambassador. "Exactly when?"

"Twenty past eleven."

"It's going down now, Clint. I'm on my way." Steven stormed out of the study and ran to his vehicle. The Secret Service had seen and heard all they needed to know to stay out of his way.

Steven punched another speed dial as he slammed his foot on the gas. The south side of Alexandria was a formidable distance away. "Michael, call the unit chief and put the ambassador under arrest. Give them the details you recorded."

"Yes, sir."

Michael's unasked question drove Steven hard as he threw his phone onto the passenger seat.

He had to make it in time.

❋ ❋ ❋

Hidden by a moonless night and thick trees, Gordon watched the drop site.

The two girls, in black hoods and bound wrists, remained silent nearby. Duct tape helped squelch their godforsaken moaning. That and the rugged trek with his new Glock 17C prodding them onward. Over streams and logs 'til they had no directional sense left.

If ever they'd had some.

Memorial Hill Park. He chuckled to himself as he leaned against the rough tree. In mere minutes, this day would become immemorial to Sir Walter Kensington. Just like Harry's funeral. And he'd have ten million of the old fool's money. Blood money. What Harry had died trying to find.

Gordon checked his timepiece. Drop-off time had passed.

Sir Kensington had never served in Her Majesty's Special Forces, or he'd have shown and retreated by now.

Olivia fought against the silver bracelets securing her hands behind her. Jordan started her insufferable whines, just out of Olivia's reach.

"It's no use. Be still!" Gordon reacquainted her with his Glock, and she was silenced.

His eyes scoped the darkness, ready to kill two birds in seconds if necessary and leave them for the FBI to find. Then his night-vision goggles showed a single body fast approaching the drop-off mark three meters to his left. Good sport. Seems Sir Kensington had heeded the note he'd sent. Wise bloke. Got himself caught covering his tracks too.

Cheers to 'em. Gordon smiled.

The ransom bag now rested under a ramshackle picnic table near the edge of a slight clearing. He waited for the stupid wally transporting it to disappear into the night.

Within seconds, Gordon shoved the American girl forward, blind and bound, to find her way out of the forest. Take her all night, it would.

He pulled Sir Kensington's eldest along as he reached the bag. This one he wouldn't give up tonight.

An owl hooted overhead. The hair on his neck stood to attention. Looking up, he could see dots of heat nearing from the south. He muffled a curse.

No time to check the bag.

No matter.

He still had leverage.

And a grand escape ahead.

Steven maneuvered back road curves with every defensive driving technique at his disposal.

Pulling into Memorial Hill Park's unchained entrance provided no comfort. Silence greeted him. The park's nine hundred wooded acres yielded no clue to the rescue team's whereabouts. Nor Olivia and Jordan's.

No amount of experience could give him the right search coordinates. His gut said west central, as no west entrance existed beyond the natural boundaries of water, part of a road, and thinning woods. One team had started there, the other from the east.

Clint had known that Steven would approach through the southeast entrance, following the main stream that ran through the park's dense center. He'd phoned to confirm his course seconds after his first call.

Steven killed the motor and quickly slipped into cover, adjusting his night-vision goggles. With as large a range as the present hostage teams had to cover, he hoped none of them felt trigger-happy tonight. Or the ones arriving from the alleged exchange site either. Because vests didn't protect skulls.

Slipping down the hill near the entrance road, he soon waded across the first stream and navigated around fallen trees with silent speed. Within ten minutes, he felt more than saw bodies surrounding him. Then his goggles clued him in on the three men approaching.

Once hand signals were exchanged, Steven continued west while the team worked north. They'd found nothing from the south up.

His breath came in fast gulps as scenarios ricocheted through this mind. Best-case: Two girls wandered this park, searching for a way out. Money could be traced. A specialty of the Secret Service.

Worst-case: Two dead bodies would be found and no money.

Steven crossed the main stream and moved deeper into the forest's interior.

No. Far more formidable was finding no bodies—alive or otherwise—and the money left at the drop-off, mocking them.

No clues. No rescue.

Steven stopped to listen. A slight wind rustled leaves all around him. From the wet ground, moss scents clung to the air currents. "God, a little direction right about now would be good."

The thought of being too late plagued him still. Given the vastness of the dense forest surrounding him, their perp could have slipped through the two smaller teams' search grid.

To a timed pickup.

If their guy escaped, Steven would expand the search for accomplices. Starting with consuls and embassy personnel, even though the staff had already been interviewed ad nauseam.

A twig snap froze his movements.

Then he moved right, circling a wide arc toward the sound.

Infrared sensors showed one body, slight build. No others in radius. Steven watched. A trap set on short notice was unlikely, but rushing in could prove a fatal decision.

The body stumbled toward him and doubled back again.

"Olivia? Jordan?" He called into the greenish darkness.

Muffled wails answered him. She started in his direction and fell.

Steven ran to her side. As he removed the hood and duct tape, the seventeen-year-old screamed like a newborn. "He took Livvie! You have to find her!"

"What direction?"

Jordan looked all around. Tears spilled over her cheeks. "I don't know. I've been walking forever. I…" Sobs replaced words.

"It's okay, Jordan. You're safe." He held the shaking girl in his arms.

The teen's sobs subsided to a slow sniffle. "I want to see my mom."

His cell phone buzzed. Steven pulled it out and prayed Clint's call would mean they had Olivia and her captor in hand.

"Where are you, Steven?" Behind Clint's voice he heard cars.

"About two and a half miles northwest of the entrance. I have Jordan. She's scraped and bruised and asking for her mom. Let them know."

"Ambulance is on the way. Can you manage the trek out?"

"Yes." Steven would have to break Jordan's handcuffs before starting out. He searched for the right-sized rock. If she'd be still, he would manage the middle link and deal with the rest later. "Tell me."

"Nothing."

Steven's chest constricted in a vise.

Too late by half was still too late.

11

Two days and nothing.

Maria sat in the command center at the embassy and watched the surveillance tapes of Victoria's father. Her security detail would begin ten minutes past eight, bright and early Friday morning.

Victoria had requested a park trip today.

Not a chance. Public places with unmanned escape routes were off-limits for the little blond whirlwind's foreseeable future. Thankfully, school started in a month to provide much needed socialization and structure.

Maria returned to viewing the tapes.

Service scuttlebutt said Sir Walter Kensington's deportation loomed over the embassy like a thunderhead. No one on his detail would miss him. Victoria had no inkling. At six, she didn't need to. But it broke Maria's heart that the bright little doll she'd fallen for would have her world turned topsy-turvy in a matter of days.

Agent David Adams entered the command center and slammed the door. "Diplomatic immunity my…"

"Whoa. No sailor-speak. Please." Maria cocked her head to the side and smiled. "Can you start over and explain your outburst?"

Agents around her continued their surveillance. The clicking computer keys didn't even miss a stroke.

David twisted his wedding band and then played like a statue until the red in his face faded. "Between the FBI and the president, Sir Walter will remain in the country in his official capacity indefinitely."

"Why does that steam you?" All other conversation in the room stilled. She hated having an audience.

"Because." David clenched his jaw. "It means the entire diplomatic community will feel empowered to do whatever they..." He took a deep breath. "It sends the message that our government is filled with bleeding hearts who look at a man's circumstances to determine justice."

Maria studied her supervisor's profile. She didn't want to debate, but she believed Steven Kessler had good reason to allow the ambassador to remain in the country. International politics notwithstanding. Therein lay a powder keg she wouldn't broach. "Sir Walter's still under investigation. He won't escape the consequences."

"You sticking up for Kessler? Stand in line behind all the rest of the female population." Other agents snickered as David took a seat behind his makeshift desk—a thin, ornate table from one of the embassy's storage rooms.

Maria ignored the insult and focused on her surroundings as agents returned to work. "Jealous, Agent Adams?" Michael Parker, the token FBI agent left to keep watch over Sir Walter, stood to stretch. He grinned in her direction.

Get real, rookie. Not every woman had the hots for him. Someone should enlighten him about that soon.

Anyone but her.

Michael's reputation preceded him. His loose lips had sunk any hopes of his being worth her time. Maybe Steven Kessler and his tall Texas partner would teach the new CACU agent a thing or two about manners and how to treat women.

"Why are you still here, Agent Parker?" David kept his eyes focused on the computer monitor in front of him. "Now that your boss has left our presence, this is Secret Service territory."

"Cryptographic superiority, maybe?" Michael stood at attention. "FBI ongoing investigation. Because I caught the ambassador's e-mail deletions before you had your first cup of coffee. Take your pick."

David glared.

Michael winked at her.

Her internal alarm said work duties called. With a sigh of relief, she exited the testosterone-filled room.

Victoria and her governess strolled through the embassy's English gardens. High brick walls kept the public out of sight and Victoria safe.

Maria nodded to the other agent, John Reynolds, already posted. They shared this rotation with two other agents. Seniority gave Maria the plum assignment as the little girl's shadow. And in the fall—the classroom with Victoria.

With the threat to Victoria's life still at level red, four agents escorted Victoria outside of embassy grounds when necessary. Until then, two monitored the girl's whereabouts from their office while Maria and John stood guard.

"Maria! You're here!" Victoria yanked away from the stodgy old governess and ran into her arms. Maria laughed. Brit-speak continued to invade her thinking at times.

She returned Victoria's firm hug. The policy of keeping a professional distance from protectees altered with children. In her mind, anyway. "Hello, Miss Victoria. How are you this fine summer day?"

"I'm very well, thank you." Victoria crinkled her nose. "Can we play spies and escape my governess?" She whispered, "She's a bore."

Maria coughed back a chuckle.

"Or let's go to the pool, Maria. You can swim with me." Victoria grabbed her hands and danced in a circle.

"Affirmative." David's voice crackled over her body mic. Great. Now all the testosterone in the command center would focus on her. In a bathing suit.

Agent Reynolds smirked and shrugged. No help there.

"Victoria, I think you and Mrs. Byrd should see if your mum would like to join you in the pool. I'm on duty, remember?" Not a babysitter. Or a lifeguard.

The governess led the trio to Lady Kensington's usual retreat—her drawing room.

Relief coursed through Maria. No tantrums from Victoria and no bathing suit in her near future. Three decades—even with continual physical conditioning—hadn't altered her JLo rearview. The rest of her genetics were gifts from her mama and papa. Black hair she didn't waste good money coloring like the rest of her friends did. Smooth, caramel-colored skin that needed no trips to those awful tanning beds.

Victoria took her hand as they passed Sir Walter's study. "Maria, will you teach me Spanish?"

"Hush, child." Mrs. Byrd's little black eyes drilled into her charge. The little Brit with debutante manners ignored her governess.

Maria knelt to Victoria's level. "I wish I could, honey. But my mother and father felt great pride in their American citizenship, so we only spoke English in my home."

Mrs. Byrd muttered as she continued her amble down the hall. "Americans do not speak proper Queen's English."

Victoria giggled.

Maria smiled. She hoped beyond logic that no harm would come to Victoria Kensington. During Secret Service protection or ever. The little girl's family had already endured so much. One day, Maria wanted a little girl who handled life's trials with similar spunk.

A little girl with Steven Kessler's eyes.

Maria dismissed that crazy thought and walked hand in hand with Victoria. She'd seen the spark between Gracie and Steven. That meant hands off.

"FBI on deck, Maria."

She wished body mic traffic could be squelched. David Adams must have sought revenge for her earlier comments by sharing inflated stories of her pleasant conversations with Steven.

Maria fingered the ivory rosary in her suit pocket while Victoria pleaded her swimming pool case to her mum. Had her grandmother's gift kept her safe during her past six years with the Service? Having listened to Agent Rollins, she doubted that. But like Agent Parker, she questioned the relevance of organized religion.

Victoria continued to employ every sugar-and-spice word she could muster. Maria couldn't help but grin.

"Very well, poppet. I'll join you for a swim." Lady Kensington hadn't looked old before Olivia disappeared. Now she looked more like a grandmother than a fortysomething former debutante. A week of sleepless nights had altered that forever. Her blond hair remained pulled back into a plain brown clip, and her high cheekbones hinted at the woman's staunch refusal to eat.

"I wish Livvie could." Victoria scratched at the wooden floor with her tan sandal.

Lady Kensington straightened her white poet's blouse and blue skirt. Then she collected her daughter in a tear-filled embrace.

Maria felt the familiar stirring in her heart. Surely this ordeal would end soon. For Victoria's sake. And Olivia's. Lady Kensington's as well. Maria wanted to see the perpetrators strung up and Olivia safely in her parents' arms.

Movement outside caught her attention. Michael, Steven, and Clint—the Crimes Against Children superstars—slammed the doors of Steven's Explorer and left in a rush.

That had to mean a viable lead. She hoped beyond hope it meant Olivia's fast return. Alive. Everyone involved with the Kensington task force needed another dose of good news to go along with Jordan's safe return.

Victoria most of all.

Steven had to see the park again. Had to find something. Anything.

No news in two days could mean their kidnapper had

returned to his games. He could demand more money. Inflict more harm.

Or they'd never hear from him or see Olivia again.

"Steven, the ERT has scoured the park already." Clint nodded toward the backseat. "This is not a wise time expenditure."

Michael's key-clicking stilled. "Better than babysitting an irate diplomat." His tapping resumed. "Besides, I'm breezing through my list of donkeywork as we go."

"This perp isn't worried about being caught, but he could have left a tell. Something. Every criminal makes a mistake at some point." Steven drummed his fingers on the steering wheel, willing the stoplight from red to green.

"The fresh air will be good for us." Michael was starting to sound like Aunt Bee from Mayberry. The rookie needed time off as badly as everyone else did.

"You're grasping at straws, bud."

Steven took a deep breath. "I need a lead, Clint. Now." Sleep deprivation and adrenaline forced him into action. James stayed busy with Dad and Sue, so Steven had nothing to do but focus on Olivia's case. Sleep escaped him when he tried to rest. Better to keep moving. Outrun the specters of guilt.

Clint looked out the window. "If we spend an hour there, will you quit and go home?"

"Maybe. Depends on what we find."

Michael slapped his notebook computer shut. "The words are swimming. I need a break."

"Got a date this weekend, Parker?"

Steven shot a glance at his partner. Clint smiled and shrugged.

"Nope. Thought about asking Maria Grivens out, but she's pretty straight-laced from what I hear. I think sleep is in order tonight."

"So Steven's one up on you this weekend. He has a date. With Gracie Lang."

Michael whistled long and low. "I saw the Secret Service

background check. I'd skip sleep for her too."

Steven clenched his jaw. "Want to take my place?"

"Nothing doing, partner. You need this time away. And you'll go if I have to hog-tie you and deliver you to Gracie's porch myself."

Michael snickered. "I'd pay to see that."

"Whatever."

Steven turned right into Memorial Hill Park. Little kids filled the play area and runners took advantage of paved sidewalks and less intense morning temperatures. Parking at the head of a familiar-looking trail, he faced Clint. "I'll go out on this date tonight on one condition."

"I'm all ears." Clint's grin creased his eyes.

"You don't breathe a word about guilt, God, or forgiving myself for being too late." No way could his best friend manage that demand.

"Deal."

Michael and Clint exited the Explorer.

Steven followed. "Just like that?" He joined Michael and Clint in swapping dress shoes for hiking boots, waiting in the charged silence for an answer.

"I accepted your proposition. Wanna spit shake on it?"

Steven shook his head. "You're just going to use other words, aren't you?"

Michael started down the hill, shaking his head.

"You're a man of your word, Steven. So am I." Clint pointed to the woods. "Time's a-wastin'. You've got a hot date to prep for."

A sweat-filled hour later, Steven kicked a dilapidated table near a clearing on the northwest side of the park. The HRT report confirmed that this was the drop site. Always one step behind. That had to change. He moved toward the road forming part of the park's west border and hopped over the stream.

Clint joined him and looked up the steep hill. "Looks like your hunch is on the money. No way he could have managed this himself. Had to have a car drop him off and meet him in a prearranged scheme." Clint pointed into the thick greenery of ancient trees and full bushes. "He hiked in a good ways. Hard to believe that coming from a busy road with two bound teenagers no one noticed."

"Too few people pay attention to what's happening beyond their noses."

Clint grabbed his shoulder. "Let it go, Steven. Even Maxwell said you did everything by the book and did it well. Jordan's home."

"Ryan's not. Neither is Olivia."

His partner exhaled a deep breath. "Compartmentalizing isn't effective for everything. At some point you have to deal with the emotions or you'll explode."

"It didn't used to affect me like this. Maybe I should think about retirement." Steven kicked a rock at his feet.

"Not you. Not now." Clint turned toward their entry route. "Go back to the basics, partner. Talk to your dad. He'll say what I promised I wouldn't. Maybe you'll listen."

"Maybe."

"You know my deal ends tomorrow." Clint slapped him on the shoulder and then ventured back into the dense forest.

Steven would deal with his best friend and his father another day. Another month, if he could hold them off that long.

He followed Clint and stepped over logs as they made their way back to his SUV in silence. He could talk to a trauma counselor again like his unit chief had mentioned yesterday.

Not yet. For now, he only needed to bring Olivia home. Once that happened, life might return to "normal."

And he could go back to pushing papers like a good coordinator.

12

S teven doubted his sanity for agreeing to follow through on this date.

But a hot shower, a quick nap, and a game of checkers with James had helped ease the transition into the normal world. Where normal people went on dates all the time.

Michael did almost every week. His little sister, Hanna, dated some. Even Clint and Sara. And James had wiggled with excitement all afternoon at the thought of Steven going out with his new teacher. The teacher that his son talked about nonstop, day after day.

Steven reknotted his tie while he went over the evening routine with his dad and stepmom, pacing his hardwood foyer as he flipped the yellow silk. "Okay. The fridge is stocked, James's bath things are laid out, and his pajamas are on his bed."

The oriental vase Sue had given him, filled with vibrant pink roses from her garden, shook as he walked past.

Steven startled as Dad draped an arm over his shoulders and held him still. He was a younger clone of his dad, who had always been his hero. Steven envied the joy and peace his father wore like a comfortable baseball cap.

"Everything will be fine, son. You need this break, and we've packed our bags to stay overnight. That way James can stay in his own bed and you can stay out late."

"We'll see, Dad."

"Clint's a good man to push you out of your self-imposed monastic lifestyle."

Dad's intense gaze said he wanted to say more. Most likely that he would be praying.

Steven turned away to retrieve his coat from the coatrack by the stairs.

Sue came over and placed both hands on his chest. A good six inches shorter than he and his father, she held her own in the Kessler family, ruling the roost with her Southern charm. "Hanna said to tease you for her. And I know your mom would have made you laugh with a story of your high school antics. I missed that fun, but I know you're a catch if there ever was one. Relax, honey. Gracie will be blessed just getting to know you; I'm sure of it."

The reminder of his mom felt bittersweet. Over the last eight years, few days had passed when he hadn't wished she'd survived her battle with cancer. But then Sue had stepped into their lives five years ago and honored his mother's memory while pushing them all forward.

Steven reached down and engulfed his stepmom in a bear hug. "Thanks. Mom would have loved you."

His dad's strong hand rested on his shoulder again.

Steven checked his watch. Time to go. He turned to call up the stairs. "Hey, little man, I'm off. Can I get a good-night hug before I head out?"

Thundering through the hallway and skipping stairs, James jumped into his waiting arms, all smiles. Steven felt human again in his son's hug. The weight of the world and his kidnapping investigation faded a little.

But only a little.

James handed him a card made out of yellow construction paper. "This is for Mrs. Lang. It's her favorite color. Will you give it to her?" His son took a quick breath. "Are you going to be out all night, Dad? Are you going to kiss Mrs. Lang? Will she be my real mommy?"

Pain like a glass shard in his heart nailed his tongue down.

No one moved.

"I think you should kiss her." James folded his arms across his chest. "That's what the big kids at the park said everyone does. Maybe then Mrs. Lang will come live with us faster."

Steven forced a smile and put James down. He'd talk to his dad later about a better choice of playmates and ask when the mom talk had started. "Well, regardless of what some people say, I'm not about to kiss Mrs. Lang tonight. Gentlemen don't kiss on the first date." He ruffled his son's sandy brown hair.

Not that I don't miss it.

But distractions like that didn't fit into his life anymore.

"All right, James, let your dad get going. I'm sure he doesn't want to be late." Sue scooped up her grandson and gave him a hug. "You've sure taught him how to be honest, haven't you, Steven?" She laughed while shooing him out the door.

Like it or not, the time for his date was upon him.

Gracie changed clothes for the third time.

She was back to the outfit her sister had suggested in the first place. She studied her dark blue cocktail dress in the full-length mirror and frowned. Then sighed. Giggling with Beth later would be worth a little sucked-in tummy strain.

"I can't believe I'm doing this, Jake. But it'll be good for me. A step into the future."

He continued to stare at her in silence.

Gracie clasped the gold locket around her neck. Then Jake scrambled off the bed and down the stairs, barking at the door.

Steven was here.

Grabbing her matching satin clutch, she steadied herself and moseyed to the door. No use looking like an overeager teen. She took a deep breath and smiled before opening the front door.

According to Steven's appreciative eyes, she had chosen the right dress for the evening.

"Hello, Gracie. You look stunning."

"Thank you." What to do next escaped her.

Jake pushed past her and jumped up on Steven's chest.

"Oh, Jake, get down!" She grabbed his collar, pulling him away. With a stern pointed finger, Gracie directed him to his dog bed in the den where he went, tail tucked. "Sorry about that. He's not used to many visitors."

"Not a problem." Steven brushed off his suit coat. "He's a great-looking golden. Lots of fun too, I imagine."

As she ushered Steven inside, he extended a small bouquet of roses—one yellow and one red nestled in greenery and tied with a lace bow. And a yellow card. "These are for you."

The flowers' sweet smell made her sigh.

Steven followed her down the front hall. "The yellow flower and card are from James. He said they looked like sunshine and you would like that."

"Thank you. He's right." Gracie motioned for Steven to have a seat in the den. "I'll go find a vase and leave myself a note to send James a thank-you card."

Gracie flipped open a few kitchen cabinets looking for a crystal vase and then fiddled with the flowers, watching Steven the entire time. Jake crept over to the couch and nuzzled his offered hand. In turn, Steven rubbed the dog's soft honey coat and glanced around the room.

The den, with its periwinkle walls, lace curtains, and rich oak furniture, was her favorite place to curl up and read. Strange that the approving look from a relative stranger caused the tap dance in her belly to intensify.

Steven stood and scanned the built-in bookshelves by the fireplace packed with a menagerie of eclectic books. She followed his gaze to the adjoining wall where he studied a Ron DiCianni painting of an angel watching over a child in a dark forest. The brass plate below read, "For he will order his angels to protect you wherever you go."

She wondered if Steven knew that verse in Psalms.

He cleared his throat.

Oops, caught staring again. It'd been too long since she'd even noticed another man, let alone had one in her house. And her manners were blaring that fact. Steven would never ask her out again.

Gracie fiddled with her gold locket. "You mentioned our reservations were for eight. Should we be heading out soon?"

Steven's smile crinkled the tanned skin around his stunning blue eyes. He bowed and extended his arm toward her. "As you wish."

Princess Buttercup she was not, but Steven's response reminiscent of Wesley's dialogue in *The Princess Bride* movie broke the ice between them as they laughed.

On the drive to the restaurant, conversation felt more natural. Eighties movie trivia and college basketball facts—Georgia Panthers and Louisville Cardinals—carried them through downtown Alexandria.

Gracie gasped slightly as they pulled up to the beautiful Morrison House. Behind the handsome red brick, a vibrant sunset gilded the finest restaurant in Old Town Alexandria. She hoped this night foreshadowed great things to come.

Maybe even a future date with the handsome FBI agent next to her.

Under the orange and purple watercolor sunset, anything felt possible.

Steven held out Gracie's chair.

Her wide-eyed survey of the restaurant reminded him of James's FAO Schwartz adventure on their only family vacation two years ago. The New York City toy store left children and adults staring in wonder.

Gracie caught him watching her and blushed. She studied her napkin and then met his eyes again. "Do you come here often?"

"No, this is my first time."

She relaxed her shoulders. "Well, I'm very impressed. This restaurant is exceptionally beautiful."

"You fit right in." That sounded so lame. He'd string Clint up for making him come tonight. He had better things to do than sound like a desperate teen on a dead-end date.

But Gracie's blush looked incredible by candlelight.

"Thank you."

Their waiter rattled off specials, prices omitted. Steven ordered two of the mixed salads Gracie had commented on and watched the starched waiter weave through the linen-covered tables. Blue table settings and crystal water goblets dotted tables all over the room, adding to the elegant atmosphere. Everything hinted at a huge bill. Michael hadn't mentioned the expense of his favorite dining recommendation. The rookie would have an earful, come tomorrow afternoon.

Unless they found Olivia tonight.

Then all would be forgiven.

Steven winced at his thoughts. Some phrases stuck like glue.

"You look like you're a million miles away." Gracie dabbed at her mouth. "Is it something I said?"

Steven shook his head. "I'm not doing a good job of leaving work at work. I apologize."

"If it would help to talk things out, I'm a good listener."

And a Christian, if her book selection and shelf of nondusty Bibles were any indication. He didn't want to go deep and hear a lecture. He had Clint for that. Besides, faith and work realities never mixed well. Especially now.

How things had changed. Years ago, he'd sat in Gracie's place with Angela scowling at his God-talk.

Gracie jerked him back to the present with her humming to a James Taylor song in the background.

"You know JT? Aren't you a little young for that?"

She smiled all the way to her eyes. "I cut my musical teeth on my parents' favorite records, James Taylor among many. His lyrics floated through my dreams, and now that I've lived a bit, they make sense. They remind me that life is both good and bad. There's much to be gained in embracing both."

"'Fire and Rain' is my favorite song."

"There's a story in that."

Steven chuckled. An understatement of mammoth proportions, but she didn't push for more information. He respected that. Appreciated her gentle invitations to conversation. Even more, he appreciated the lack of pressure to fill the air with words.

The waiter placed large salads in front of them. "Are you ready to order?"

Steven cleared his throat and remembered Gracie's choice from the specials. "Yes. She'll have the red snapper and I'd like the New York Strip. Medium well."

"Very good. We'll have that out shortly." The young man turned on his heel and speed walked through the dining area.

She bowed her head, presumably to say grace, and Steven shifted in his seat.

Gracie looked up. "I wanted to thank you again for sending me Justin Moore's contact information. I feel hopeful about what he'll add to the investigation. Is he fast with results?"

"It depends on the case." Steven remembered his old friend's assessment of Gracie. In a candlelit room, wearing a curve-defining dress, he concurred. More than beautiful, she possessed something deeper. From the inside out.

Gracie carried the conversation with talk of her parents, her sister, and dreams for the future. Most of it centered on seeing her family's killer locked in jail.

Steven understood that drive for justice. Sometimes it was his singular motivation for getting out of bed. Putting criminals away and watching his son grow. The entirety of his existence.

"I look forward to having James in my class soon. He's a precious little boy."

Steven nodded. "James is looking forward to September too." So was he. To seeing Gracie's smiling face each morning at Hope Ridge.

As their meal drew to a close with the chocolate soufflé and crème brûlée almost gone, Steven wasn't ready to say good night. Putting off tomorrow's inevitable headaches with Gracie's easy company beat staring at his white ceiling any day. "Are you up for a walking tour? I thought you might be interested in seeing some of the historic sites."

"I'd like that very much."

"James and I used to walk the trails throughout downtown. It's a beautiful place." Romantic, even. Not that he'd thought about that when he was carting James around.

Steven remembered his son's flurry of questions before he left the house. Prime among them, *"Are you going to kiss her, Dad?"*

He imagined their after-dinner stroll. He'd stop on the cobblestone path that led down to the Potomac and draw Gracie against his chest. Then he'd cup her blushing cheeks in his hands. Bending down with a slow, restrained movement—

"A penny for your thoughts, Steven?"

"I think they're worth a little more than that." He stood and pulled out Gracie's chair.

She raised her eyebrows. "This should be good."

"James asked if I was going to kiss you tonight. I was thinking about a moonlight walk and wondering if I could keep to what I told him."

"Which was what? Gentlemen don't kiss on first dates?"

Steven let out a hearty laugh. "That's exactly what I said."

It felt nice to spend a Friday night out. On the arm of a handsome man, strolling the sidewalks through Old Town Alexandria, a cool breeze whispering through the trees.

A few starry-eyed couples passed them, each captivated by the other's words. Gracie sighed. Beth and Leah would squeal at her replay of tonight.

"This is wonderful, Steven. Thank you so much for an enchanting evening."

"My pleasure."

They walked along in comfortable silence. But curiosity about Steven's ex-wife spilled from her mouth before she could sensor it. "Would you mind telling me a little about James's mother?"

Pain flashed in his blue eyes. She regretted asking. Once again, inquisitiveness landed her in a tight spot. "Never mind." So much for setting the stage for a follow-up date.

"It's okay. My ex-wife isn't a favorite topic, but since you've been so open with me, I figure your request is a fair one."

Steven turned them back toward the Morrison House, passing the Old Apothecary Shop on their way. "We married right after Angela finished law school. I went to church; she didn't. By the time James came along, we'd grown so far apart we hardly talked. I threw myself into work; Angela invested her time in another man and left when James was a baby."

"I'm so sorry."

Steven shrugged. Then his cell phone played the COPS theme. A fitting ring tone, but a frustrating interruption.

"Kessler."

Gracie watched her first date dissolve into clipped sentences barked through a cell phone and hurried footsteps to Steven's Explorer. She pushed the disappointment aside.

Steven held her door open. "I'm sorry, Gracie. I'll have to drop you off in a hurry. Thankfully, your house is on the way to where I need to be."

"Is this typical for your work?"

"Yes and no." He drove like a NASCAR racer through the dark residential roads of Alexandria, cell phone cradled between his neck and shoulder, more curt sentences blasting into the little silver receptor. When he wasn't talking, his jaw muscles made slicing side to side movements.

Maybe dating needed to return to the back burner of her life. She hadn't invested much beyond time so far. And between ex-wives and work stress, Steven seemed less like a prince and more an example of twenty-first-century reality.

A world she and Mark had never known.

Steven pulled into her subdivision. At the first stop sign, he turned his head toward her. "I'm really sorry, Gracie. Work is erratic and demanding. But if tonight goes like my partner believes it will, life will return to normal. Good, even." He continued to drive and took a right onto her street.

"How about next Friday? I'll make it up to you with an uninterrupted date."

She tried not to get her hopes up again. "Sounds like a plan." She'd give him one more evening.

One date didn't a future make. Not with anyone but Mark.

Steven pulled into her driveway. "I'll call this week." He slipped around to open her door and then hurried back to the driver's side.

"Good night, Steven." No chance of breaking Steven's word to his son about gentlemen and first dates. Better not to awaken long-dormant stirrings with a kiss either.

His SUV disappeared from her street.

Whatever next week held—good or bad—she would walk away with a smile. She'd passed a hurdle. Enjoyed an evening out on the town. Beth would be proud. Leah too.

Even if nothing came of it.

13

G ordon removed Olivia's hood and duct tape.

The seventeen-year-old winced, and her blue eyes watered as she stayed motionless on the floor. But she held her insufferable screams. He supposed a Glock pointed at the heart had that effect.

Gordon unlatched the girl's shackles and took stock. Week-old makeup and stringy blond hair had Olivia looking like a trashed Harrods mannequin.

Charlotte watched every movement with wide eyes and both hands over her mouth.

Sir Walter Kensington would be livid.

He shrugged. What harm could his brother's killer do to him now?

Olivia blinked hard against the bald light that did little more than throw the evening's shadows a step away. But when she fussed over the dirty miniskirt, Gordon had his fill and jerked her to her feet.

"Go easy with her." Charlotte clutched his arm, but he shifted her out of the way.

"Who are you?" Olivia turned her face from his and stared straight into his sister's wide eyes without any clue who she was. Chameleon talents and a vast array of disguises to choose from proved widely helpful. "How could you help this monster? He killed my friend!" The youth dissolved into tears. Gordon pushed her away.

"No, Olivia." Charlotte sank onto the dank floor with the sniveling teen and reached out to stroke her hair.

Olivia slapped at her hand.

"Jordan is home with her family. She's fine, dear. Just fine."

What an idiot his sister could be. Especially driving out here in pearls and ridiculous heels with her long red wig flying everywhere. Only to wallow on the floor so as to give the young Kensington a pat or two.

Motioning Charlotte away, he took hold of Olivia's quivering arm. As they moved over the creaky boards of the farmhouse to his temporary office, Gordon tightened his grip until she stopped all movement. "You will have less than ten seconds to ring the ambassador and demand more ransom." Gordon released her arm and held out the phone. "Surely you are worth more than ten million?"

Olivia studied his face. Then ran for the front door.

He lunged forward, grabbed her long matted hair, and gave a yank. "Not a chance, little bird. You'll not be flying from here."

She tumbled to the floor when he let go.

"Gordon, don't. Go easy." Charlotte held a hand to her face. "She's so thin and filthy. Let me give her a cleanup."

He pulled Olivia to her feet and pointed his new toy's barrel at her head. "If you become more trouble than you're worth, I won't be needing your services much longer."

Charlotte gasped. "You have the ten million. Let it go, Gordon. Go home."

"Shut your yapper. Now." He'd blast her later for her constant interference. But for the moment, there were more important things to attend to.

Olivia watched them with no expression. Interesting. The ambassador's daughter had more pluck than he'd figured.

Too bad.

Gordon turned her to face his written instructions resting on top of the electronic gadgets. Then he handed the receiver over and stood with his gun at the ready. Olivia's trembling hands clutched the cool gray plastic of the phone as Gordon rang Sir Kensington on the ambassador's private line.

"What do you want now? Where's my daughter?"

He pointed his Glock 17 at the writing tablet he'd set in front of her with the exact clipped phrases to repeat.

"Papa." Her voice trembled.

Gordon nudged her. Time was running out.

"He wants more ransom."

She sucked in a breath as he moved to disconnect the call.

"We're at an old farmhouse. Please, Papa…"

Gordon slammed the gun into her face. Stupid little fool! He killed the phone connection and began packing.

"Gordon!" Charlotte ran to Olivia's side and blotted the red stream oozing from the girl's mouth. The teen stayed where she'd fallen on the wooden floor, whimpering, her head cradled in Charlotte's lap.

"This is madness. Harry would not approve. Not at all."

He clenched his jaw and pocketed his gun. "Dear sister, may I remind you that you are party to a wad of felonies from which Her Majesty will not rescue you." He plucked the black hood and a fresh roll of duct tape from the floor. "I could leave the two of you here for the Feds to find."

He shoved Charlotte away and replaced Olivia's bindings and hood. The little rag doll didn't put up a fuss. Too worn out from a week of water and scraps.

No matter.

Weak or not, she still had a part to play in his plans for the ambassador.

"May I remind you, prison is a dank place. Full of rats and all manner of evil vices. Besides, what would become of your Stewart? Can't leave your baby to his American father, now can you?"

Charlotte wagged her finger at him. "Leave my son out of this, Gordon."

He laughed, then turned back to his office, leaving Olivia in the black hood and Charlotte trembling near her. Both of them too afraid to move.

Dismantling his equipment required precious moments, but leaving everything was out of the question. The coppers were too smart. He couldn't leave them more than a scrap.

Not even one of his many latex gloves.

"Take your sniveling self back home, dear. If you hurry, the Feds might not ever know you were here." He narrowed his eyes. "But I'd wager they could track your tire imprints. You might concentrate on distancing yourself from your current convertible and find a sensible mum wagon."

Charlotte clomped through the drafty living quarters and out the door.

Within minutes, he flung Olivia's limp, whining frame into her basement cell. Keeping an eye on her while packing wouldn't do.

Gordon resumed his trek to the black limo with another round of baggage to dispose of en route. Her Majesty's training left him with many options and no need of panic. Worry would only serve the federal idiots well.

Not his plan.

Soon they'd be on their way to Dulles Airport. This bothersome distraction amounted to little more than a nuisance. The game continued. With him at the helm, as always.

The ambassador had yet another little brat at his knee, but Gordon would never have another brother.

Thinking over his next move, he grinned. He would continue to even the odds. All in good time.

Steven's SUV flew outside the Beltway.

Michael's communications expertise had provided a quick triangulation of Olivia's call. She was alive. He still had time.

Steven's white-fingered grip on the steering wheel didn't hold the raging thoughts from tumbling through his head.

Olivia's picture.

Jordan's bruised arms and terror-filled eyes.

So like Ryan's.

When he tried to dismiss those pictures, Gracie's wide-eyed response to their date's ending left a hollow place in his gut. They'd connected. But after tonight?

Steven shook his head. James's hopeful eyes would match his pleading questions in the morning. *Did you kiss her, Daddy? Will she be my new mommy?*

It had to happen sooner or later. James knew that a traditional family required a mother and a father. The boy had never known Angela, had never seen her picture. Maybe that was wrong, but Steven couldn't take the reminder of yet another failure...

Pulling onto the dirt driveway of a rundown farmhouse, he parked behind Clint's truck. The solitary vehicle blended into the evening shadows of tall pines and scrubby brush surrounding them.

"We beat the ERT?" Steven unlatched his holster.

Clint nodded. "The hostage team is on their way too."

Michael joined them.

Steven inched to the edge of the wooded perimeter. The dark and silent three-story presented a quandary.

Do a three-man assault, or wait for the Hostage Rescue Team?

Disrupt a crime scene and possibly save Olivia, or wait on the evidence crew?

Move now and find a hot trail if the farmhouse was deserted, or wait 'til everything went cold?

Steven longed for his hotheaded rookie days when he would have charged into the house and trusted his God and his gun to provide all he needed to survive. But now? Now he had agents under him to protect as well as a teen to rescue.

"Let's do a preliminary, Clint."

Clint worked his jaw muscles while he surveyed the farmhouse structure.

"She could be in there," Steven said. "Almost dead. Just like Ryan."

His partner fixed him with narrowed eyes. "Don't pull that

trash on me. We did all we could. Just like now. Olivia's life isn't in my hands. Or yours."

Steven yanked at his yellow silk tie. "I'm going in."

Clint exhaled. "I'll go low. Watch your back, partner. "

Michael double-checked his sidearm. "I'll start high, up the back stairs."

With a nod, Steven watched his companions circle around to the other side of the house. He crouched down and stayed low as he neared the front porch. Bypassing the holes in the front steps, he tried the door.

Unlocked.

Gun up, he flung the door wide and slipped in.

His breath came in short, shallow bursts. His heart thundering in his ears, the only sound.

He scanned the open room. Nothing. Not a trace of life. Dusty threadbare furniture and a few odds and ends tables. Steven followed the main wall around the front room. At the corner, he paused before entering one of the two closed doors.

The first door creaked open as he touched it. Dust and empty wood floors. Shredded curtains. Faded and peeling paint.

He pushed open the second door and plastered himself to the wall, waiting. Scanning the room, he found more of the same.

Back in the hall, he saw Michael make his way down the rickety stairs. He nodded toward the basement door. No sounds of Clint coming up.

Maybe Clint had found Olivia.

And her captor.

God help us all.

14

T om settled in for a quiet Saturday at work.

He liked the silence of Hope Ridge Academy during summer break, when schoolkids stayed home and teachers didn't laugh and chatter in the halls before or after classes. Days exactly like today.

He rifled through the papers on his desk. Gracie's file lay open on the far left corner. But in front of him, he spread the newspaper clippings from two years ago. Something in all this melodrama played for sympathy had to yield a clue to the woman's weaknesses.

Gracie's visit to a private investigator had precipitated the need for his ideas becoming reality. Finding one place of vulnerability should prove easy. Ten articles later, he realized maybe not.

He grew tired of reading Gracie's long moralisms and the reports full of bleeding hearts longing to help this widow find her family's killer. She wouldn't. Not if he had anything to say about it.

And he did.

So he turned to the Internet. Finding websites on the practices of serial killers provided interesting reading, but nothing he needed for the present.

Medical websites provided a few more fascinating tidbits. Amazing how detailed the World Wide Web had become. A housewife in Iowa could find enough pharmacological information to diagnosis and treat any ailment. Or kill a horse.

Information on how to build a bomb.

Poison a human and not get caught.

Tom shuddered. He wanted none of that last bit of information. Getting that close and personal was not on his agenda. Not yet.

Thoughts of Kimberly gnawed at him. What would life have been like if he married the pretty brunette from Georgia? Loud, emotion-filled fights, no doubt. Punctuated with the wailing of a child that wasn't his.

No thanks.

But watching Gracie at night…

"Tom? What on earth are you doing here so early?" Janice Hall—or Mother Dearest—entered his office.

He swallowed his heart back into his chest and focused on his mother. Perfect black hair fashionably in place. Modest diamond earrings. Designer gray suit and makeup fit for a model. The four-inch stilettos, though, were not a sight he cared to have impressed behind his eyelids.

No sixty-year-old woman should keep up with a twenty-year-old and wear shoes meant to entice. Not even his attractive mother. Especially not when she'd divorced his stepfather. The only man besides his dad who'd given Tom more than expensive toys. All for her job. Everything for her job.

No wonder he'd do anything to keep his.

Janice moved to the desk. "What's all this about Gracie Lang?"

Tom snatched up the newspaper clippings and slid them into a file. "Reviewing her background to make sure she can handle all the upcoming events, that's all. What about you, Mother? Why are you here, dressed to the nines?"

A schoolgirl blush warmed her face. Tom wanted to puke.

"Some personnel business to attend to."

"Dressed like that?" He leaned back in his leather chair, putting his hands behind his head. He enjoyed his mother's discomfort. Living without a father for most of his life, he had no intention of another man muscling into his tidy world.

"Thomas, my private life is mine to manage. Much like you've always demanded that yours stay out of my frame of reference." She moved back to his opened office door. "Unless, of course, you'd like to tell me the truth about that photo of Gracie you were studying when I walked in."

How much had his astute mother seen? Time for damage control that would rock her world so much that she'd forget about newspaper articles and start planning for grandchildren.

"Actually, it's not Gracie I'm interested in. It's the agent who will be working in her classroom. Getting to know Gracie will help me create inroads to spending more time with Maria Grivens."

Janice's smile touched the edges of her steel gray eyes. "Well, Tom. I had no idea." She folded her slender form into his guest chair. "I remember your first real girlfriend like it was yesterday. College, wasn't it?"

A warm fuzzy trip down memory lane held no appeal. But it would serve as an apt distraction. "Yes. College. A lovely season of life."

"Didn't you date that girl for a time?"

"Her name was Kimberly, and we dated for two years when I was in grad school."

And right before he could offer her the tiny diamond he'd scraped to afford, she'd informed him that she was pregnant with someone else's child. A younger college hero with biceps Tom could never rival without steroids.

He stood and walked along the far wall of his office, hands clasped behind his back. His paintings brought no comfort. Neither did the bookshelf full of long-ago memorized leather-bound works of Shakespeare.

"...Maria seems like a very nice woman. Exotic beauty too."

"Yes. A Secret Service agent to boot."

Janice sighed. "I hope you'll let me know more about Maria than you did about that Kimberly." She stood up and crossed the thick cream carpet. "Have a good morning, Tom. I'll check in with you before I leave."

He stood as his mother walked out of his office. Strange emotions rummaged through his mind. His mother blamed him for not talking about Kimberly. Like Mother was ever around to listen.

Funny how time altered perceptions, skewed the facts into unrecognizable bits of information. All according to what one desired to remember. Or forget.

He could only hope that would happen to Gracie as well.

Then when she abandoned her fruitless quest for answers, he could relax. Maybe even pursue a future with Maria Grivens or some other attractive female.

Tom huffed. Thankfully, Agent Steven Kessler's attention was focused on Gracie, not Maria. Like that mattered. FBI hotshots were more her style.

Would Maria ever be interested in him? Yeah, right.

"So how exactly are you gonna top your first date, partner?"

Clint watched for Steven's reaction as he flipped large, juicy burgers on the grill. The savory smell of beef and all the picnic fixin's on the table next to him caused his stomach to growl. Loud.

"Better feed that bottomless pit."

Clint ignored his partner's ribbing. All he had to do was wait and enjoy the beautiful blue Saturday skies overhead. The silence would drag out Steven's dating information.

Jonathan, Susannah, and James squealed in the backyard kiddie pool just beyond the deck he and Steven had built a few years back. And his Irish princess swaggered toward him in a white two-piece under her bathing suit cover-up. The one he'd make disappear after Steven and the kids said good night.

Sara kissed his cheek before going into the house to retrieve one more necessity for their already overflowing table. Maybe she'd break out the homemade ice cream churn.

To any outsider, their life would resemble a summertime spread in *The Saturday Evening Post*.

"I could top the ending of last night's date by not answering the cell phone."

Clint chuckled. "Nice try, Kessler, but I doubt that'll work. If she's going to stick around, she needs to know what to expect. Annoying cell phones are part of the package."

"Who says she's going to stick around?" Steven leaned on the banister to watch the kids splash in the pool.

"My gut instinct."

Steven scowled. "I think you should turn that gut instinct back to our case. I want this thing wrapped up. The sooner, the better."

Clint grunted a reply.

"Think Olivia's still alive?"

One at a time he flipped the dozen hot dogs on the upper rack of the grill. "Don't know. All that duct tape says she was there. Evidence techs found nothing to prove a death occurred on the premises."

"But?"

"But little about this case makes sense—paper trails end with no rhyme or reason, every tip a waste of time, the ambassador's screwy story."

Steven nodded.

"I met with Jordan and her folks Thursday."

"Why didn't I know that?"

"You were busy. I took care of things. It's all in my case notes if you want to do some reading tonight." Clint had no intention of finishing this shoptalk. Or of answering Steven's question. He wanted one Saturday cookout to relax. The problems would still be there come Monday morning.

Was that asking too much?

Sara's soft footsteps behind him didn't fully register until she wrapped her arms around his waist and leaned up to kiss his neck.

Steven groaned. "Can't you two skip the mushy stuff when company's around?"

Sara grinned. "Since when have you been company, Steven Kessler? Besides, according to my handsome husband, you might join couple-land sometime soon." She turned her sparkling green eyes on his partner. "I hear she likes college ball. We might have a double date in our future."

"Your husband talks too much."

Clint transferred the crispy burgers to a serving dish with fish all around the side.

Sara batted her long lashes at him. "Wouldn't our new fish tableware look great with real seashells as decorations? I hear Florida shells are awesome collectibles." She sashayed down the stairs.

Steven spread out knives and forks, a grin lighting his often somber features. "Do I hear a beach vacation in your near future?"

Clint focused on Sara's walking out in the yard with beach towels to wrangle in their little band of waterlogged children. "Like she'd leave her stethoscope for that long."

"Or you a holster."

"Touche." Clint served up hot dogs and potato salad on Jonathan's plate, cutting everything into small bites. No way his two-year-old would choke while he was on duty. "After this case wraps up, I'm fixin' to lay ahold of some vacation time. We all need it."

As everyone gathered around the fancy wrought iron furnishings, Clint nodded for Jonathan to pray.

"God. Food. Amen."

Sara and Susannah shared identical smiles.

James prayed next. "Thanks for the sunshine and hot dogs. Please help us enjoy it. And God, if it's not too much trouble, please let my new teacher be here next time we eat. I'd sure like a mommy like her."

Steven's face contorted into a sour pucker. Nothing like little-kid prayers to surface the big stuff. Clint offered up a short prayer of thanksgiving for food, friends, and safety. A silent addition about Olivia and the Kensington family hung in the air around them.

Just like James's prayer for a mother.

Clint and Sara locked eyes while the rest of the crowd chowed down. Eight years of marriage had perfected their silent language.

He answered her unspoken question with a wink. Clint would do his dead-level best to see Steven do more than talk about dating again.

He needed a woman's influence to soften his rough edges. Especially a praying one. From the first moment Clint had watched the two of them interact, Gracie seemed a perfect fit for the job.

Even now, Clint read in Steven's unspoken words the raw desire for what he and Sara enjoyed almost every day. After five years of praying, it had to be time.

Time for Steven to fall in love.

Time for James to have a mom.

And time for his partner to break open those locked compartments and face the past.

Time to heal.

15

Friday. Another date. A second chance.

Gracie stared into the bathroom mirror and brushed her straight reddish-brown hair with a little more force than necessary. She had a little more quiver to her hands than last weekend. What if Steven never showed?

Or worse, what if the uninterrupted date made clear how incompatible they really were?

How opposite from life with Mark.

She wiped the single tear from her eye. Not the time for makeup messes. She walked out to the dresser, picked up the golden locket, and opened it. Something she had avoided for a year now.

Elizabeth. Red and squalling. With a thick head of light brown hair and a cute little nose. Tiny fists in the air.

Then Mark's little man. Her husband had loved both their children with every cell in his body. Joshua had just awakened something in Mark that Elizabeth and her dolls had done for Gracie. *Someone just like me.*

Tears streaked her makeup. A long-ago song filled her mind. *"Lord, I want to be just like You. 'Cause she wants to be just like me."* Well, the three pastors had sung *he*, but Gracie had always sung the line with *she* because her little Elizabeth had wanted to be a mommy just like her.

Oh, God. Why? Why did You let my family die?

Gracie sank to the floor at the foot of her bed. Jake laid his head on her lap. He'd grown used to the tears and always offered his silent presence. At least she had Jake. He was her only living link to Mark and her babies.

Jake had licked their hands and faces like he slobbered on her at times.

Jake had carted Elizabeth around like a miniature horse more times than Gracie could count. What a dog.

"You miss them too, don't you?"

He released a slow huff of air. She'd take that as a dog form of yes.

Fifteen minutes before she expected Steven at the door, the phone rang. She walked over to the nightstand and stared at her grayish phone. Her hand didn't move. Not answering it felt like the safer course.

The basketballs bouncing in her belly hurt.

She wiped the remaining wetness from her cheeks and forced herself to pick up the phone before the answering machine clicked on. "Hello?"

A muffled word she didn't recognize.

"Who is this?"

Gracie's heartbeat kicked up a notch. All the dreams of Mark's killer calling her on the phone to apologize filtered through her brain. They alternated with other images of the man coming after her with his black truck to finish the job.

"Gracie. Sorry. Thought your answering machine was going to pick up."

Steven's voice. Clipped. Cold.

Her heart didn't return to a normal rhythm. "Is something wrong?"

He sighed into the receiver. "Yes. I'm not going to make our date tonight. Something's come up at work, and I have to deal with it."

"Oh." So much for second chances.

"I'm sorry, Gracie. I have to go."

And with that he disconnected the call. She held the phone in her hands until the dial tone registered with its annoying high-pitched buzz. What had happened to the FBI agent with daz-zling blue eyes who'd wanted to hear about her life? Told her she was beautiful? Made her think about the future?

"He's disappeared without a trace."

Jake lifted his head and turned it to the side. Who says dogs aren't intuitive?

Gracie rubbed his muzzle and let him lick her cheeks. "At least I know you love me, huh, Jake?"

He barked a series of short yips in response and Gracie laughed. Then he ran out the door and down the steps. Her golden retriever hadn't been declaring his undying love. More likely he had to use the bathroom.

Men. Okay, males. Canine or human, they didn't make sense.

She descended the stairs and let her big lug of a dog out into the backyard. She stepped out onto the patio and lowered her-self into a white Adirondack chair, watching the heavy clouds move in to block the fading sunset.

Such was her life. Promising bursts of color clouded by harsh reality.

"God, I don't understand. Where are You? Where's the heal-ing Your Word promises? I've grieved and still sought You. I've tried to move on and find Your purpose, why You left me here."

Gracie rubbed her empty left ring finger. "I thought..." Tears covered her words. "I guess I thought dating Steven was part of Your answer, a promise of something to look forward to again. His help in finding Mark and my babies' killer."

She smoothed the simple white sundress over her stomach. Both her arms and abdomen ached. A soul-searing ache. "I guess I put all my eggs in one basket and hoped...hoped someday I'd be a mom again. A wife again."

Jake trotted over to her chair.

"I was stupid for making so much out of one little date." She rubbed his honey-colored coat. "Well, I won't do that again. Life's better when I avoid letting those longings wake up. I'm a widow.

I had my one dose of happiness. No more kisses or babies or..."

The bitterness in her mouth halted her words. She swallowed it back down.

"Why, God?" Gracie stared into the silent sky. "Why won't You at least help me find the one who ripped it all away from me?"

Or was it God who took everything? His way of teaching her some obscure lesson? He could have saved them. But He didn't. She recalled the well-meaning comments of church folks from years past.

"Honey, maybe God's just gettin' you ready for even more blessing."

"God could be getting your attention to deal with some deep issue."

What, God? What issue had she missed? What sin had she committed to deserve having her life ripped apart by death like that? Did she not believe enough, pray for her family enough, trust God enough?

The comment she'd heard over and over at her family's funeral hit again with the same gut-wrenching force. *"God makes all things good."*

A misquote of Romans 8:28.

A horrible, painful slap in the face. Nothing about watching her family die could ever be made good. Not in a million years. Not even by an all-powerful God.

The God who hadn't rescued her family.

Why would He rescue her now?

Tom watched her from the shadows.

Gracie's stupid dog hadn't detected his scent. Good. And her little tantrum against her God provided a night of free entertainment. No nosy neighbors to report him. Few neighbors even home in the evening; they were too busy. Little ants running here and there with no purpose. Filling the days with useless striving.

Gracie's philosophical musings bled into his thoughts. What if her God did help her find the answers she cried for? He certainly hadn't kept her family from that awful crash.

And Steven Kessler was too wrapped up in saving the children of the world to care about poor Gracie. Too busy rescuing the world to care much about his little boy either. The one who taped pictures to Steven's refrigerator of a cozy threesome. James. Steven. And Gracie.

Oh, yes. He'd expanded his nighttime prowling. Watched Steven some. A fairly boring waste of time.

He watched Gracie's private investigator a little too. Those memories made him chuckle to himself. A PI being stalked by the criminal he'd been hired to catch.

Humorous.

Gracie went inside mumbling to her dog. Something about checking e-mail. This could be good. He'd have to retire early tonight and surf the web, preview Gracie's e-mails.

Delete any from that insufferable do-gooder agent. Add those to the messages that had come from Justin Moore, PI extraordinaire, Deleted. Gone. Too bad people weren't as easily disposable.

Pointing his shiny new SUV toward his townhome in Old Alexandria, he frowned. Back roads and traffic meant that Gracie had probably already read any e-mails he would have normally deleted.

Should have done that first before snooping in her back woods.

He'd remember that for next time

Long minutes later, he flung his keys on the oak entry table. All around him deep blues, greens, and light wood furniture recreated his favorite place of escape. He glanced around the living room toward the picture window overlooking the mighty Potomac, down the slope from his back door. He unbuttoned his white dress shirt. No adoring wife gasped with appreciation. Like that could ever happen.

Turning his focus to the beloved pictures of lighthouses, he studied their majestic peaks surrounded by wild waters. Those hanging over his white fireplace had stormy skies to match the bubbling waters. And others, larger paintings in the dining area, had softer colors. More like the beaches where he'd entertained himself most of his adolescence.

His thoughts trailed off to a distant memory of his family noisily gathering food for a late afternoon picnic on the beach. Waves had crashed just beyond their beachfront home. He'd tasted the salt water as he'd fidgeted with a bag of sand toys, ready to build a huge castle. A whole day with his family; it would have been a great one. But the high-pitched ring of the phone had silenced the activity and turned the day upside down. The Federal Bureau of Investigation had a way of interrupting every family moment.

"Stupid memories." He waved them away and moved to his computer in the spare bedroom-turned-office. Gracie should do the same—wave the past away and get on with life. Just like he'd do when the teacher's quest finally ended.

Something he still scoured the Internet for ways to make happen.

He flipped on a desk light to view e-mails. Gracie had already downloaded all the interesting ones, it seemed. So he switched to work e-mail. Boring.

Growing restless, he closed the files and undressed in his bedroom. After slipping on black shorts, he reclined in the comfort of his favorite chair to ponder his options. Caesar, his black-and-gray striped tabby cat, rubbed against his leg.

"This townhome used to be a retreat for me, but there is no safe place, is there? And we could lose even this unless I find a good way to end Gracie's search. And soon." He reached down to stroke Caesar's fur.

"I could scare her into running home to Mommy and Daddy, vicious letters threatening her safety. Of course the nightly news could do that too." He chuckled. "But that only drives her back to the scene of the crime. Closer to the truth. Away from my keeping."

He shook his head.

"I could rile a few mob interests and point them toward Mr. Moore. They'd have him walking in cement boots before too long."

Nah. That was old news anyway.

Caesar trotted off to his little scratching post.

An idea started to take shape. Medical sites full of information sprang to mind. Yes. His days of research would not prove useless. This was a good plan. A new quest for Gracie Lang.

The shrill ring of his bedroom telephone snapped him to attention. He picked up the cordless phone. Caller ID showed that it was from Out of Area. An international call, perhaps? He pressed the Talk button, but no one answered.

The silence puzzled him. Who would have his unlisted number?

16

T hey found a body."

"I know." For the second time tonight, Olivia's shining blue eyes taunted Steven from her file photo. That was all her parents had now to remember her by. Photos and possessions. No child to watch grow into adulthood.

He wanted to slam his front door into Michael Parker's face. But no use being rude and making him wait outside. Especially with a nasty storm brewing. This failure wasn't the rookie's fault. "Come in, Michael. My father is en route. When he pulls in, we'll head to the scene. Unless you want to go on ahead."

"Clint said to fetch you, so I'll wait. Locals are butting heads with our evidence team. We need your strong-arm diplomacy to get things back on track before the rain washes away evidence."

"Where's Clint? He said he'd handle things when he arrived."

Michael shifted from one foot to the other. "Agent Maxwell called him at the scene and sent him to the embassy to head off any inquisitive local cops and keep Sir Walter from bolting."

Steven clenched his jaw. He shouldn't have listened to Clint's advice to take a break from the case and go out with Gracie tonight. Stupid date. He'd decided to cancel right before the call about Olivia came in, which gave him a valid excuse. And now Maxwell had called Clint to do Steven's job.

Turning his back on Parker, Steven walked into his den and picked up the phone, intending to call Clint and swap assignments. Anything beat seeing another physical reminder of his incompetence.

But he hung up before it rang and leaned into the empty roll-top desk. Clint would only tell him to pray. What use was it? Olivia had been found. Dead.

He was too late again.

"Thought seasoned agents knew how to shake off stuff like this." Michael's quiet words held more concern than challenge. The rookie remained rooted near the front door.

Steven motioned Michael into the den and sat in the brown overstuffed leather recliner. The case was no longer a rescue but a homicide investigation. And his boss had called Clint. Twice. Probably because he had Sara to watch the kids, while Steven had to waste valuable time getting a babysitter on weekends.

He clicked the TV off. With its light gone and the antique lamps around the room dark, he kept his features hidden. No need to bare his soul in the glaring light. "I used to handle it better. Stow it away."

Michael sat on the edge of the matching leather couch. "What changed?"

The front hall light cast shadows all over the room. Steven searched the twenty-eight-year-old's face. "Don't know for sure."

He checked his watch and relaced his black dress shoes. He hadn't bothered to change when Clint's call had come in a few minutes ago.

Steven reknotted his tie and slipped on his FBI jacket. It would keep off the coming rain. And now more than ever he had to look the part. Not let anyone think he was slipping from his game.

Clint knew. So did Parker.

"My father would say I needed to pray again."

Michael groaned. "Not another Clint."

"Yep. But they have peace. They do their jobs and live their lives without spinning their wheels outrunning guilt."

Silence.

"Look, Michael. My problem has been that I let Ryan's case get under my skin. Maybe he looked too much like James. Maybe I've been going too hard for too long without a break. Maybe it's time to…"

"To what? Quit?"

Steven didn't want to admit those were his exact thoughts. "Move to another section. White-collar crimes. Counter-terrorism. Something besides children."

There. He'd given voice to the haunting that dogged his steps. Change. He needed a change.

The sound of his father's Lincoln in the driveway snapped him back into focus. "Let's go. We still have a job to do."

Steven climbed into Michael's black Mustang with a wave to his dad. He'd explain later. For now, he'd analyze the new muscle car's interior. Clean. Leather. Backseat too small for company. Totally fit the rookie's personality.

"You'd really walk away from Crimes Against Children?"

No. He couldn't walk away from making his son's world a safer place. Other cases filtered through his jumbled thoughts. Cases when the child came home. Crying parents with tears of joy. Awards. Respect.

"...all the other agents say you're the best."

Steven grunted, glad he'd missed Michael's review. Listening to your own PR never helped. People either loved or hated you based on something in them. Simple as that. He'd learned from his dad to listen to the criticism with an open mind and dump the glowing praises. Nothing but a big head resulted from them.

Unless it was from his son. He'd accept hero status there. Even if he'd failed James in the worst possible way.

Michael parked his car behind the three cruisers and the FBI evidence team cars lining Memorial Hill Park's west side. The forest below them crawled with little flashlight dots and bigger crime scene lights. Like big, fuzzy fireflies scattering in the humid wind.

An older, rounder version of his first police chief ambled into his sight line. Days like this he'd have rather seen Chief Hopkins scowl and put him on a beat cop's day shift. "You the hotshot head of this crowd?"

Steven and Michael flashed their credentials.

The officer's nameplate said Lieutenant Riddick. "I'm Special Agent Steven Kessler." He pointed his chin toward the glowing forest. "Who found the body?"

"Some unhappy campers called in a disturbance at the Memorial campgrounds. My zone car was the first responder."

"His name?"

Lieutenant Riddick narrowed his eyes. "Officer Taylor did everything by the book."

"I'm sure he did. I'll just need to talk to him. And I'll need a list of every one of your guys who has ventured down this hill."

"Done."

"Did Officer Taylor ever see the source of the disturbance?"

"Nope." Riddick rested his hands on his large gun belt. "Seems to me your boys ought to take it easy barging in here and telling my officers where to go."

Michael stiffened.

There'd be ten sides to this story. Better to get things smoothed out from the top down. And find a credible eyewitness. "The evidence team needs to move in fast to secure a scene." Steven pointed up to the clouds. "Especially with a storm brewing."

The lieutenant nodded.

Owls hooted and a traffic cop behind them shouted for motorists to keep moving. "Where are your officers now?"

"Stationed around the park, directing traffic."

Steven pointed to the other two cruisers. "Those officers?"

Michael cleared his throat. "Probably down in the trees, trying to help."

Lieutenant Riddick jabbed his finger in the rookie's face. "If your people hadn't started barking orders and accusing us of contaminating a crime scene…"

Steven stepped between the two men. "Lieutenant, why don't we go talk to your officers and see how the ERT is progressing?" He'd have words with Parker later.

They sidestepped down the hill and cleared the familiar stream.

A few agents nodded at their arrival. Most he knew on a first-name basis. Good at their work. Quick and quiet. Not stirring things up with the locals. Michael had ruffled the wrong set of feathers this time.

Steven left Lieutenant Riddick observing the agents milling around Olivia's body and calling his men back to their police cars. Another cross-agency skirmish avoided.

Steven moved through the thick trees and stopped near a dilapidated picnic table. They'd been in the right place last time. Just too late to recover Olivia. Steven pushed the rush of regret into his mental lockbox. No time to rehash his dismal failure now.

"What can you tell me, Agent Walters?"

The older man motioned him over to the body. Agent Walters had been the first to tell him Vicks didn't work at crime scenes. The sticky stuff only opened nasal passages further. It didn't mask the scent of death that clung to every fiber and airway.

"Time of death? Best guess right now, a week. I'll let the ME have the final say, though."

Steven stayed upwind of the body. Olivia's blond hair hung limp around the edges of the once-red wooden table. He resisted the urge to vomit.

"Cause of death?"

"Strangulation." Walters frowned. "But this little girl had been worked over long before then."

"Sexual assault?" That didn't play into their scenario. Might make it a whole different ball game too. On so many levels.

"No signs of that, Steven."

He let go of the breath he'd been holding. "Then what?"

"She was pistol-whipped, malnourished, and bound for an extended period. Severe bruising."

Steven shook away the scenes filtering through his mind. "Guess the cloudy weather and cooler temps were on our side for DNA retrieval?"

"Somewhat. Our perp wrapped the body to keep animals out

and covered it well." Agent Walters rubbed his bald head. "Unofficial gut response—this guy's sending someone a message."

Steven massaged the back of his neck and stretched it side to side. "You gonna give me some clues as to who it is and the message he wants to send?"

"I'll do my best, Kessler. My best."

He squeezed the older agent's shoulders. No amount of experience made cases like this easier. Not for him or for top evidence technicians like Philip Walters.

Steven retraced his steps up the hill to where Michael sat in the passenger side of his Mustang, typing away. The Alexandria officers had cleared the forest, and only two remained to deal with this side of the park's traffic.

He checked his cell. No message from Clint.

Steven wondered how the ambassador had taken the news. Yelled for Steven's head, no doubt. *If anything happens to my daughter, I will hold you personally responsible.*

Nothing like a British ambassador's guilt load dumped on his head. Over and over. He already had far more than enough of his own.

Clint watched Sir Walter pace his library like a caged tiger.

"Are you absolutely sure it was my Olivia? You Americans make identification mistakes all the time."

Biting his tongue, Clint nodded from the cold leather chair. They'd covered this territory more than once already, with a room full of expletives and finger-pointing. Clint was glad that he was the one who got stuck relaying the devastating news to the gray-haired diplomat. Steven was better off on scene. His partner was in no place to hear the pain-filled, angry words that spilled from Sir Walter's mouth.

"Would you like some time to speak with your family? Alone?" Clint stood to leave.

The man's shoulders slumped forward as he stared out into

the dark night. "What difference does it make, eh? You will watch my every move and record every word. I should like to leave every one of you and this wretched place far behind."

But he wouldn't. Diplomatic immunity could only carry officials so far. This time the leash would keep the ambassador and his family firmly in the United States. Until they found Olivia's killer. And cleared Sir Walter from suspicion.

Ten million dollars enticed all manner of despicable actions. They had to be sure he hadn't succumbed to the money's draw. Especially given the ambassador's withholding important information.

Clint walked to the library door unnoticed. Turning back to the ambassador, he lifted up a short prayer asking for the truth to be revealed, Steven and their team to be kept safe, and Victoria and her parents to be comforted.

He turned the corner from the library to head toward the original block of offices. Most office lights were off and quiet reigned. Expecting to meet one of the Kensingtons' detail patrolling the grounds, Clint was surprised to see the ambassador's personal assistant walking around the main lobby entrance. She hadn't changed from her office attire, and her long black hair was unkempt. Odd, considering it was almost ten o'clock on a Friday night.

"Mrs. Brown, is there a problem?"

The young woman jumped clear out of her skin. She put a hand to her throat and fingered the strand of pearls. "You startled me, Agent Rollins." Her laugh rang hollow. "I...I decided to stay late to make sure the ambassador and his family were all right. After this evening's news and, you know..."

"They're as good as can be expected." Clint studied the woman's pale skin. "How did you hear of Olivia's death? To my knowledge the ambassador hasn't spoken to anyone since I arrived."

She sucked in a quick breath. "The agents in the control room. I...I was taking them some requested files and I..." She covered her face as her shoulders shook.

Clint didn't bridge the gap between them to offer comfort. A young, attractive woman in relative darkness, alone, didn't need a hug from him. He did shoot a quick prayer heavenward, though. "Were you close to Olivia?"

"Yes. I mean no. I…we talked on a few occasions. She was a lovely girl."

He nodded.

"I would have gone to Lady Kensington, but I can't bear to look her in the eyes. Nor Victoria. I've been pacing in here, trying to work up the courage to offer my condolences and see if there is anything I can manage for them." She searched his face. "Do you know when the body will be released so I can make funeral arrangements? That I could do for them, you know?"

"I'm sure they'd appreciate the help."

Mrs. Brown glanced at the ornate grandfather clock in the lobby. "I should get home. Harry will be worried."

Clint searched his memory. That name didn't sound familiar. And he'd scoured all the employee records every which way more than twice. "I thought your son's name was Stewart."

Her face turned ashen. "Yes. Stew. Isn't that what I said?"

"No, ma'am. You said Harry."

She swallowed hard and set to pacing again.

He waited.

"Harry was my brother. He died only a bit ago, and I suppose facing death again so soon, I…my words slipped."

The words made sense, but something in his brain stood at attention. Every little detail held the possibility of a clue. And every clue mattered. Even now.

"Your brother—remind me of his name again?"

"Landridge. Harry Landridge." She stood like a statue with a quivering hand over her mouth. "Harry died in Her Majesty's service. In May."

"I'm sorry for your loss." He looked around the dimly lit

entryway. "Can I walk you out to your car or call someone to drive you home?"

"No. Thank you. My husband is with Stewart. No worries about me."

Clint shook his head and watched the young woman skitter into her office and retrieve her purse before leaving out the side entrance.

He waited for Mrs. Brown to enter her Mini Cooper 850 and start the engine before he made his way back to the control room. He had to call Steven.

Tonight's impromptu meeting had left Clint's hackles raised. He hoped his partner would be in a frame of mind to help him sort through the nagging impression that something was wrong. Maybe he'd overlooked something in an employee record like he'd missed Mrs. Brown's having a brother who'd died in May.

None of his searching would bring Olivia home, but it could put an end to her killer's freedom. And allow people like Charlotte Brown and the Kensington family to grieve without an investigation hanging over their heads.

17

Sunday morning, a silent house greeted Steven.

No parents dropping by to see if he wanted to go to church. No James bounding around asking for chocolate chip pancakes for breakfast. He missed his son already.

Steven threw back his red and black comforter and dragged himself out of bed. Sun streamed through the curtains. As a child, he'd decorated his room with an ever-changing array of sports team logos. But Angela wouldn't allow him to display any of his collectibles. She hated the Louisville Cardinals. And it seemed everything else Steven had held close to heart.

His faith.

Having a family.

His parents.

Even his alma mater.

After a quick shower, he slipped into some cutoff jeans and an old sleeveless blue T-shirt. His stomach growled. Louder than his partner's ever had. Time for some grub, straight out of a box of sugarcoated cereal.

Who said you had to grow up in everything?

The glow in the dark stars all over James's bedroom ceiling caught his attention as he passed by. Steven admired his son's neatness, the made bed with toys and books all in their proper places. So much like Steven's mom. Neat. Organized. Efficient. His mom had been full of life and fun, though.

Not Steven. Not after Angela left. She'd destroyed more than their wedding vows. She'd taken a big chunk of his heart too.

Leaning on the doorframe, he looked around the quiet room.

His eyes stopped on the well-worn teddy bear he and Angela had picked out when they were shopping for baby clothes, long before he'd had any idea of how his wife had been spending her free time.

The bear now sat atop a comforter decorated with asteroids and planets. Steven was surprised the favorite bear had been left behind. James was probably too excited packing for Space Camp to think about his bedtime buddy. Steven picked up the brown-and-white animal and breathed in his son's fresh-out-of-the-bath scent. He'd be glad when James was home again.

Steven continued on his quest for sugary food. Tempted to slide down the banister, he behaved and took one step at a time down to the kitchen. No use twisting his ankle and getting ribbed hard for it at work Monday.

The "family" pictures of him and James with Gracie caused his neck muscles to tighten. He could call her today. Explain what happened Friday night. At least try to make it up to her. Steven pushed that thought aside and poured a bowl full of milk and pure sugar hearts, moons, stars, and clovers. He ate it standing by the sink.

James would have a blast at Space Camp this week, learning how to become an astronaut while Dad and Sue took a well-deserved vacation and played tourist. Steven ached to join them in Florida. To watch James play in the waves and collect shells.

From the moment James was born, Steven had felt such joy and pride. He and Angela had done at least one thing right. But in the silent moments when work wasn't screaming for his blood, sweat, and tears, he wondered if loving his son was enough. It hadn't been enough just to love Angela. It wasn't enough just to love rescuing children and making the world a safer place.

What was enough?

If James was growing up to be like him, what kind of footprints was Steven leaving him to follow?

A knock on the door put an end to his contemplation. Who

would be out selling things at ten o'clock Sunday morning?

Opening the door, Steven felt a frost come over him.

"Not at church this morning, preacher boy? Interesting." The leggy, raven-haired beauty stepped into his personal space. "How about inviting me in, Steven?"

He stepped back.

With a wicked smile, she floated past him.

"Angela."

"Glad you remembered me." She looked around the foyer and up the carpeted stairs. "Where's my son? Surely you don't let him watch cartoons in his room all morning."

"He doesn't have a TV in his room. And he doesn't watch cartoons."

Angela folded perfectly manicured hands over her toned biceps.

His body responded. Five years, and her short leather skirt, low-cut sleeveless blouse, and suggestive pout still turned him every which way but loose. Too bad she'd shared everything else with someone else. That iced his desire. Quick.

"What are you doing here?" Steven shut the door. "Last I heard, you'd shacked up with that cue ball prof of yours."

"Marcus and I married as soon as my divorce from you was final. The best day of my life." Angela raked her eyes over his entire frame. A spark of interest still smoldered there.

He put both hands behind his neck and clenched his jaw. Nothing like taking up right where you left off. "I'll ask again. Why are you here?"

She walked into the den like she owned it. "Remodeled and redecorated. Do it yourself, stud?" She picked up a picture of James from the built-in bookshelf and folded into the couch without a word. "He's so handsome. Even has my eyes."

"No. He has Kessler eyes. And everything else. But why would you care, Angela? You walked out. On both of us."

His ex-wife smoothed her hand over stomach. "He's my son too, like it or not."

"The one you abandoned."

Angela pinched the bridge of her nose.

Steven must have been imagining things, because he thought he'd seen tears forming in her eyes. But this was Angela Barrett Kessler. No, not Kessler anymore. She was still the hardball attorney, though. No tears. No emotional investment, unless she'd had a few too many drinks.

"I left you and your beloved FBI mistress, Steven. Not my son."

He perched on the arm of his recliner. "You don't even know his name, do you?"

"James. James Andrew Kessler. Named after both of our fathers." She hadn't lifted her eyes from the photo. "A mother doesn't forget the child she gave birth to."

"Unless she's too drunk to give a..."

"Shut up!" Angela stood and stalked over to his side of the den on her four-inch stilettos. "I'm clean now, Stevie. I even have documents from a well-respected facility to prove that. Besides being all grown up, I have a law practice of my own. I want my son. I want a second chance with him."

Now that Steven had raised him to the point she didn't have to get her hands dirty. No diapers to change. Old enough to send to school.

Over his dead body would this woman ever take his son.

His son.

"Let me remind you, I'm married to an attorney too." Angela returned his ice-cold stare. "With friends in the Alexandria court system ready and waiting to help me. I have a stable nine-to-five job. I'm home on the weekends. No being out all night because of surveillance." She held James's kindergarten picture up to him. "And last I heard, you were still playing the saintly monk. All work and no play. No little Kentucky wife, barefoot, pregnant, and in the kitchen baking bread."

Red-hot terror impaled him. Angela's threats were sharpened daggers pointed right at his heart. She wanted his son.

"Your parental rights were severed years ago. You have no leg to stand on, Angela. High-priced sugar daddy or not."

Angela slapped him. Hard.

He caught her arm at the wrist when she tried again and held her close to his chest. "Get out of my house, and stay out of our lives. We've lived well without you, and I intend to keep it that way."

She wrenched her arm away and took a deep breath. After smoothing her skirt, she threw her shoulders back. "We'll see about that."

One hand on the door, she turned back and tossed her black hair over her shoulder. "I've already petitioned the courts to have my rights reinstated. And I'm filing for sole custody. If I win, you'll never see James again."

Steven invaded her personal space and glared down on her. "Why don't you go have your own children with Mr. Cue Ball? Leave me and my son out of it."

She bit her bottom lip.

"Or does the mighty Angela Barrett have a chink in her perfect armor?" Steven hated baiting her like that. Hated the mean little man he'd become in her presence.

"I never forgot my son. I needed time to get clean and..." She looked up at him with tears in her eyes. "I can't have any more children. I want a second chance with my only child."

"Nice act, Angela. You always played the drama queen bit to perfection."

The brief guise of vulnerability quickly morphed into anger. She flung open the door and stepped outside. "You just wait, Stevie. Next time I see you, you'll be waving good-bye to your little Rockwellian fantasy world. James needs a mother, not your always-absent single-parent act."

Watching her strut away, scenario after scenario gnawed at his stomach. A sympathetic female judge might buy Angela's second-chance bit. His ex-wife could tug heartstrings with the best of them.

What if she won even partial custody? Steven closed the door, walked into the den, and sank into his leather chair. She might be clean now, but that could change. His son could be in constant danger. Away from his protection.

His most basic nightmare had become a very present reality.

The day passed in a hazy, stomach-churning blur. Cleaning his guns didn't distract him. Neither did making James's favorite chocolate chip pancakes. But Steven had a freezer full for when his son came home next week. Maybe they would go to church with his parents next Sunday night.

Invite Gracie to come too.

What was he thinking? Playing church and dragging Gracie into his domestic problems wouldn't work. He didn't want to hurt her. Or lie to James and make his son think church could be a large part of their lives as it had once been.

But Steven had to do something.

Fast.

Calling Clint wouldn't help. Steven didn't want to talk about work and hear dead-end theories. Olivia Kensington's case had gone cold a week before they'd found her body in Memorial Hill Park. Besides, his partner was most likely at church serving right alongside his pretty wife.

Steven looked at his kitchen calendar. A little over three weeks until school started, the day after Labor Day. Surely the courts wouldn't uproot James right before school. Not to give him to a mother he'd never seen. The one who'd abandoned him for her whisky bottles and any number of lovers.

But Angela and her new husband were wealthy. Had stable jobs with reasonable hours. Why wouldn't the courts award her sole custody? How could he fight her and win?

He wandered into his son's room and fingered the Bible on the nightstand, the one Dad had given James last year when he got baptized. Why hadn't he taken it to camp?

Steven's old nemesis—guilt—slipped into the room and started pounding away.

What kind of father worked while his son packed for vacation?

What kind of man couldn't keep a wife?

Or find a child before some slimy perpetrator stole his or her last breath?

Steven opened the book to a passage he'd committed to memory as a teenager, one of his mom's favorites. He read out loud. "Come to Me, all who are weary and heavy-laden, and I will give you rest." The words felt like stones in his mouth.

And a knife in his heart.

There was no rest for him. Not when he had a neverending job to do. Faster. Better. Harder. He'd outgrown the Bible stories his parents had raised him on. Moved beyond a belief system that gave total power to someone unseen, whose supposed control of the universe still allowed children to die despicable deaths. This invisible God had allowed Steven's marriage to fall apart, even when he had prayed with every fiber of his faith.

He returned the Bible to its rightful place.

Amid the rocket ships and stars that decorated his son's room, Steven sat at the white desk transfixed, staring at the Bible until the grandfather clock downstairs chimed the hour of midnight.

Right now, he had to get some sleep. He needed energy to plan his attack. He would not allow Angela to rip his world apart ever again. Or destroy his son.

Ever.

Steven dragged himself into his room and collapsed onto his unmade bed. He hoped sleep would come soon, because first thing tomorrow, it was time to find a lawyer.

18

T om read through Gracie's e-mails a second time.

The updates from her private investigator—ones he'd not been able to delete—always ended with, "Let's do a police sketch, soon."

Tomorrow was the day.

And tonight he had to stop her.

As he paced in front of his townhome's large picture window watching Friday's cloudy skies darken, his mind churned with fear. He had the medication he needed, but what if he got caught? Or his timing was off?

His stomach had to be a case study for ulcers. No matter. Soon things would return to normal. Better than normal, maybe.

School started in less than a month. Behind his desk, he felt powerful. He'd also be seeing Agent Grivens every day. That little thought could keep him busy for a while.

Walking into his kitchen, he smelled the remnants of tonight's Chinese takeout. His stomach grumbled for a late snack, so he downed handfuls of trail mix as the clock ticked off the slow minutes until midnight.

After more wasted time with boring e-mails, Tom rechecked the syringes. Each dose of the special anesthetic had been measured for a fatal injection.

He checked his appearance in the bathroom mirror. Too thin. Too ashen. But the tight black outfit highlighted the few muscles he'd managed to build up in the last several months. He looked better than he had in high school.

Far different from his college days too.

The normal drive to Gracie's little brick house might as well have been stop-and-go traffic for all the wear and tear it did on his insides. Pulse thumping out of his chest. Sweaty hands.

All for a stupid cover-up.

Within minutes, Tom gathered his gear and took his usual place watching from the woods behind Gracie's house. Moonlight illuminated all he needed to see while the crickets droned their annoying songs. Most everything else wrapped itself in silent stillness. Not Gracie. She was in the shower upstairs.

Tom packed the binoculars away. No time for distractions tonight. He had a job to do and the quicker, the better.

He searched the backyard for signs of her dog. She usually let him out one last time before retiring for the night. Tom sighted the huge mass of golden fur sniffing through the flower beds at the edge of the woods.

Perfect placement. Lost in the shadows, no one would see a struggle. Or hear the mutt's inevitable barking.

He had to move fast.

He pulled his leather gloves tight against his fingertips. The tiny syringe only required one stick and a few seconds of pushing on the plunger to empty the dose of toxic chemicals.

Then Gracie would have a new quest.

Finding another dog.

Tom watched Jake catch a scent in the still air and pull the guard-dog stance, a low growl rumbling in his throat.

Just a little closer.

Jake snapped the twigs a few feet in front of him and locked his canine eyes on Tom.

Holding his breath, Tom steadied the thick padding on one arm and held the syringe ready in the other.

The dog lunged.

Tom braced for impact and let the dog's huge teeth sink into the padding. He could feel its hot breath in quick bursts.

One stick in Jake's haunches.

A few seconds of wrestling.

Then silence.

Gracie's golden retriever lay on the ground, whimpering, panting.

"Jake!" Gracie's voice split the silent night.

Tom looked up and whispered a curse. How could she have finished so quickly?

No time to make sure his dose had accomplished its purpose. He shoved the arm guard and syringe into his backpack and ran for his rented Lexus with no plates.

He glanced back before he left the woods. No sign of Gracie.

No noise from Jake.

Mission accomplished.

Gracie sped through Alexandria's dark streets, Jake barely panting in her backseat. "Please, God. Keep Jake breathing. I can't lose him."

Tears blurred her vision. She revved the Jeep's motor and fixed her eyes on the small-animal clinic just past the glaring red brake lights holding her captive at the traffic light.

"One. Two. Three..." Counting to ten didn't help.

The red light continued.

Green.

Gracie nearly rammed the truck in front of her, but it took off, leaving her crazy self to pull into the vet's office. Dr. Gregg and two of his staff met her in the parking lot.

She watched them haul Jake out of the car and onto a doggie stretcher. More white sheets.

No. God. Please.

"He's breathing, Gracie." Dr. Gregg and his nurse sped the stretcher into the clinic.

Another employee, a young redhead, held the door. The vet and older nurse disappeared into the back room with their patient.

The young woman touched Gracie's arm. "I hope he'll be okay, Mrs. Lang. He's a strong dog." She motioned into the front room of the clinic. "Would you like some coffee? I can make a fresh pot, fast."

Gracie nodded. "Sure. Thanks."

The redhead flipped on lights as she made her way through the side office. Gracie blinked against the familiar sights all around. Cold linoleum. Bright posters. Hard blue waiting area chairs. Nothing fancy. But this little practice had been willing to open for her tonight. Said they would do everything in their power to help Jake.

Jake.

Gracie's flip-flops thundered as she paced the white floor of the waiting area. The dripping sound and pungent smell of brewing coffee felt strange in the otherwise silent twilight zone she'd tumbled into.

Thirty minutes ago, she'd let Jake out one more time before bed. Like every other night. But this time, he hadn't come running when she opened the door. And when she found him collapsed at the far end of her backyard...

Tears stung her eyes and goose bumps pricked at her arms.

Jake couldn't die.

He was the only other living creature that knew her son's squeals of delight in clutching fistfuls of fur to help him stand. The only one who could drag Elizabeth away from her books for a romp in the sprinklers on a hot August day.

Her only living link to the past.

Jake was also her sanity saver. Without him she wouldn't have made the long trek to an unknown job up north. Not even Leah could have helped make the transition to a new home, a new life as smooth as Jake had done.

He nuzzled her hands when she cried.

Licked her tears away.

Listened without complaint.

When the young woman handed her a cup of steaming

black coffee, Gracie stopped pacing and sat down. "Thank you."

She nodded and left Gracie to her thoughts.

The bitter drink didn't make time speed up or calm her nerves. The caffeine would only increase the jittering in her tired limbs. So after checking the Noah's Ark clock on the opposite wall for the hundredth time, she tossed the full cup in the trash can. No one had returned with an update in the last ten minutes. She needed a distraction.

Leah's son had been up all night last night with an ear infection. No way would Gracie call and wake a tired mother after midnight.

Mom and Dad couldn't help her all the way down in Georgia. No use worrying them.

Steven was out of the question. Why she even considered calling him bothered her, but that was a question for another night.

She had enough trauma to face without adding more angst and questions about relationships.

Beth. Her sister would understand and would still be awake. Gracie punched in the ten digits from memory.

"Hey, sis. You gotta stop calling in the middle of my crime shows." Beth's TV blared in the background.

"I'm at the vet's. Jake might die, Bethy." More tears trailed down her already raw cheeks as she resumed pacing.

Beth gasped and the TV went silent. "What happened? Gracie, are you okay?"

"I don't know. I found Jake in the backyard barely breathing."

"Did he pass out or have a seizure?"

Gracie shook her head and then realized her sister couldn't see her. "I don't think so. Jake's healthy. He's never passed out like that before." She bit her thumbnail.

"Good thing you were still up and found him."

She shuddered at the memory of Jake lying so still in the grass. "Yeah."

"What did the vet say? Will he be okay?"

"I haven't seen the vet since they took Jake back, so I have no idea." Gracie sat on a chair near the door. "This wait is like Chinese water torture."

"Then let's talk about something else. You gonna make it to the PI for your sketch appointment tomorrow?" Beth's normal TV munching sounded like a jackhammer coming through the phone line. "You've been talking about it all week."

Thinking about anything other than her beloved Jake when he might die seemed like a betrayal. "I…I don't know." Gracie sniffled and dried her eyes. "Do you think this is some kind of sign? A warning that I shouldn't go?"

"Would your God be into that kind of cruel stuff? Personally, I think a flat tire would have been a better choice."

Beth's attempt at a joke did nothing to cheer Gracie. She wanted to launch into a Sunday school lesson about God's ways being higher, but that felt like gravel in her mouth. God had let her family die. Why not Jake too?

"I think you should keep the appointment. Even if Jake isn't ready to come home, the doctors will take care of him. And stop thinking about signs. That doesn't sound like you at all."

Dr. Gregg pushed the office door open, scribbling notes on a chart. His face was unreadable.

Gracie jumped out of her chair as her heartbeat kicked up a notch. "Beth, the doctor is here. I gotta go. Call you later."

"Jake will be fine," Dr. Gregg said. "He's sleeping soundly with safe vitals now. I'd like to keep him overnight at a nearby twenty-four-hour hospital. Do some tests. Find out what happened."

She nodded, trying to ignore the calculator ticking off the charges in her head. Jake was worth every penny. "Okay."

"I'll arrange the transport then and have Jake's files delivered." He motioned to the young redhead. "Heather will get you the forms we'll need, and then you're welcome to go get some rest. We'll call when Jake's ready to come home."

Gracie took a shaky breath. "Can I see him first?"

He opened the door and pointed to the left.

Gracie held the tears at bay and let Dr. Gregg lead her. Jake was alive. He'd be fine, the doctor said. Maybe she should go home. Try to sleep. In the morning, she'd go see Justin Moore as planned.

It'd keep her from going crazy waiting to find out what had caused Jake to collapse. He would be home soon. Alive.

That settled the churning acids in her stomach. A little. Maybe God hadn't let this happen to Jake as a sign that she shouldn't keep her appointment with the PI. That she entertained such a thought caused her conscience to stand at attention. But it could have been God's way of getting Jake the help he needed for some seizure disorder or internal problem that had gone unnoticed.

One thing she knew. God had answered her prayers tonight.

Maybe now, the rest of her answers would come as fast.

19

Sweating in his home gym, Steven pressed the weight bar up again, muscles straining with every rep.

"Go easy, partner. Landing yourself in the hospital isn't going to help James." Clint snatched the barbell and let it clang into the rack.

Steven sat up and wiped the sweat from his face and neck. "The lawyer said joint custody is a strong possibility. I can't let that happen."

"Think maybe Angie's changed?"

"No." Steven looked out his basement window. The sunny Saturday morning did nothing for his state of mind. His wife— ex-wife—had haunted his thoughts all week. Meeting with a lawyer had done nothing to assuage the fear knotting itself deeper into his gut.

"You gonna talk, or should I just fill you in on Jonathan's potty training experience?" Clint asked with an exasperated smile.

He groaned. "Been there, done that, don't want details."

Clint laughed and took his turn on the weight bench.

Spotting for Clint had always been an unspoken contest with ribbing galore. Not today. Silence dragged between shoptalk and lame attempts at conversation.

"Heard you had a run-in with Sir Peter Barnstable." Clint slipped more weights onto the bar.

Steven didn't want to cover yet another depressing turn of events on the Kensington case. But it beat reliving the emotions of Angela's visit. "Yes, the honorable Sir Peter dressed me down for snooping into Sir Walter's financial affairs. Said the ambassador had been through enough."

Clint slammed through another set. "Sir Walter hasn't exactly been an angel."

"No. And that hunch of yours about missing pieces in the embassy files still has me up late at night. We're on to something."

"Michael thinks so too," Clint said. "But if Mrs. Brown wasn't married, I'd think she was Michael's new target, not her personnel files."

"Parker's changing."

"After you took him to task about the pretty young ERT tech, I'd think he'd better."

"Not just that. I think he's really listening to you, Clint." Steven rubbed the back of his neck. "In fact, he's pestering me with all sorts of God questions. Why don't you call him off? Or answer him yourself?"

Clint sat up and took a long swig of water. "You answer him."

"Can't."

"Or won't?"

Steven tugged at the towel around his neck. "It's more than that and you know it. How am I supposed to explain all the random violence we see every day? Why God lets kids die and lets ex-wives rip families apart no matter how much I pray?"

Silence.

"Seems better just to tell Parker I don't know than to unload my litany about how cruel and uncaring your God is."

"Tell me about Angie."

What good would that do? Steven had battled picture after picture of his six-year marriage from the honeymoon to the day she'd left. "She still smells like spring and looks like a schoolboy's fantasy." Steven ran a hand through his wet hair. "For a minute, when I held her close…"

"To keep her from slapping you again."

"Yeah, whatever. But…I don't know. I looked into her eyes

and remembered our first kiss. And for a second it felt like I was cruising with the top down—tunes cranked and sun shining. Freedom. I could taste it again." His heart constricted. No matter what happened between them, Angela would always be the first.

"You still love her."

Steven stared at his partner. He wanted no part of this painful trip down memory lane. "No. Not sure I ever did. Maybe I just liked how she made me feel."

Clint shook his head. "You loved her, Steven."

"And she left."

"Have you forgiven her?"

What kind of fool question was that? Steven stalked to the other side of the room. He'd rather hit the punching bag than connect with Clint's chin like he wanted to, so he went after the bag and ignored his best friend.

"You'll be chained to Angie's memory until you let go."

Like it was that easy. Let go and let God.

Steven jabbed hard at the brown target. Praying hadn't worked before, and it wouldn't work now. He'd begged God for his marriage; Angela still left. He didn't need religious psychobabble about forgiveness. He needed a plan of attack. A way to prove she was still a danger to James so she'd leave them alone and never return.

"God didn't cause Angie to leave."

"He didn't stop her either."

Clint stepped on the other side of the bag and held it still. "We make choices. Love or lust. Forgiveness or bitterness. We open the door to the enemy's work when we shove the anger—the hurt—down inside and ignore it. When we let unforgiveness drive us."

"I'm not letting it drive me."

"Then why do you work so hard? Why is every case your personal crusade to fix the world? And why does one threat from Angie send you into a tailspin?" Clint stepped away from the bag.

"Trace it back. Angie's father beat her, you rescued her, but you weren't enough to be her savior. Instead of running to God, she let it all fester, started drinking. Then she skipped out. Now she's back to make you pay again."

Steven shoved the bag and threw down his gloves. His heartbeat thundered in his ears.

"Stop the cycle, Steven. Deal with your heart. Talk to Angie. You can make this work without fighting her tooth and nail in an ugly court battle."

"I'm not letting her take my son."

"Then pray."

"You've got it all figured out, don't you? Kids die and it rolls off your back. Angela leaves and then shows up to take my only son away from me and your answer is to pray." Steven stood toe-to-toe with Clint. "Why? What good will it do? According to you all I have to do is snap my fingers and say a little prayer of forgiveness and it'll all get better. Right?"

Clint stepped back. "None of our job rolls off my back. Neither does your pain. I care, buddy. That's the only reason I'm pushing now. I don't want to see you lose any more years—or your son—to your pride."

Steven wanted to spit. "My pride didn't kill Olivia or Ryan. Didn't make Angela leave."

"No, but dealing with it could break the cycle inside you. Change things for the people your life touches. Help you see beyond your case and your solution and your focus that doesn't extend beyond your nose."

He held back a curse and stomped away.

Clint grabbed his arm. "Pride keeps you from facing the past and dealing with it. It's stealing your edge to do your job well. You think you can handle it all yourself, make up for all the wrongs, but pride will drive you right off the cliff when it comes to James. It'll keep you running from him and from yourself."

"And send him right into Angela's arms? Is that what you're saying?"

His partner's brown eyes were impossible to read. "Don't feed the hate, Steven."

"I love my son. And I loved Angela. But it wasn't enough." *I wasn't enough.* Steven grabbed his towel again. "I'm going to fight. It's what I do."

"What if you don't win?"

Steven narrowed his eyes. "That'd just prove you right, wouldn't it? And you'd say it serves me right for not doing it your way."

"You're believing a lot of lies there."

"So what? Your way doesn't touch the pain. Doesn't fix broken homes or broken bodies."

Clint took a deep breath. "Talk to God about what you're believing. What you think will make it work. Then listen. That'll start the process of healing, and forgiveness will come."

Steven sat on the weight bench and watched Clint for a few long minutes. He was so sure, so confident all his God-talk could fix everything. Steven shouldn't have let the conversation get this close.

"I'm praying." Clint headed upstairs without another word.

No one left to argue with, Steven swallowed hard and rested his forehead in his hands. What if Clint was right? Losing James wasn't an option. Quitting wasn't either.

A knock on the front door drained Steven's last ounce of energy. He was in no shape to face Angela's taunting again. Not today.

He ignored the noise, but the knocking came harder. Deep breath. He walked upstairs and threw open the door.

Justin Moore extended a six-pack. "Came here to share some good news. But you look like you could use a beer first."

Steven stepped back and opened the door wider. Justin's offer was far more tempting than Clint's, but scenes of Angela's drinking binges and the resulting cleanup invaded his thoughts. "No, thanks. But I'm all ears for something good. Come on in."

Justin settled himself in the den and took a swig from his

amber-necked bottle. "Met with your girlfriend this morning, and she gave me a sketch I think might bring this case some action."

Girlfriend? If only.

"She didn't seem too keen on my suggestion to call you about her dog. Guess you blew your chance." Justin's deep laugh filled the room.

"What happened to Jake?"

"She was all shook up about spending last night at the vet's office. The dog passed out or something. He's fine now. Really scared her, though. She went on and on about how Jake and her family did this, and Jake and her family did that. Talk about a private history lesson. But I think for some reason it shook loose a few other memories too. Helpful memories."

"And?"

Justin took another drink. "Like I said, I got a good sketch to start circulating. Think I might slam-dunk this cold case after all."

"Where are you going to circulate it?"

"Gracie thinks the driver might have been a college student. I'll start with the colleges down in Atlanta and use the Internet too." Justin stood and finished his beer.

Steven shook his head. "Let's go shoot some hoops so you can sweat that off."

"Gonna arrest me if I don't?"

"Scared I'll win again?" Steven headed for the back door.

Justin rose to the challenge. But he was better at football than basketball. Three games of one-on-one later, Steven was three for three.

Resting his hands on his knees, Justin bent over double. "I'd better get busy." He scowled when Steven clapped him on the back. "And you could use a shower, pal. Especially if you're planning to see your girlfriend today. If not, I'd be happy to step in for you."

He showed Justin to the door. "Not a chance."

Steven watched his buddy drive away, then walked into the

kitchen and tossed Justin's empty glass bottle into the recycle bin. He grabbed his drink of choice: water. The picture of Gracie on the fridge caught his attention.

He should give her a call. He'd shared a little about Angela with her on their first date. Maybe Gracie would have some tips. She'd be less preachy than Clint. Far nicer to look at too.

Steven headed upstairs for a shower. Maybe he'd e-mail before he called. Typing his reasons for missing their date last week felt like an easier path. Then again, maybe he'd just run by his dad's house to check on things, borrow Sue's sporty little Saturn SC2, and take it for a spin to see if Gracie wanted to grab ice cream or something.

It was sure better than hanging around here waiting for Angela to attack again.

Or for Clint's words to catch up with him.

They would, no matter how far and how fast he ran. But not tonight. James would be home tomorrow, and this week would be relegated to that long queue in the back of his mind. Where every other problem took a number and waited for its turn.

Unfortunately, Ambassador Kensington's case was first in line.

20

A full month with ten million dollars to spend and little to show for it.

Except a new plan. He who dares wins, after all.

Gordon leaned back in his desk chair and stared out into the rainy day outside his flat. Leaving London would do him a good turn. Not Charlotte. She wouldn't be over the moon to see him again. His poor sister still refused his calls and had canceled her cell phone service.

No worries. The little information he'd given to Harry's old mates in the British Secret Intelligence Service would have Ambassador Kensington arrested before too long. Leaving Gordon with only one more detail to attend to.

He'd lost all sense of conscience years ago. With his first kill. Military service required a quick shot and little time to question a superior's orders.

Gordon studied the picture of Harry on his desk. Tall, thin, full topper of red hair all blown about in the wind. Clear skies above his little brother and the deep Pacific below. Harry had loved to surf, to sail. A regular fish, the bloke.

Then came Sir Walter Kensington. Too many black market deals, and the SIS was closing in on him. Or gaining his help to take down shady consuls, depending on who told the tale. But the more Harry had uncovered of their British ambassador, the less he'd thought of him.

Then Harry had been snuffed out. Bullet to the brain. Everything covered. Evidence disappeared. Sir Walter Kensington hailed a regular hero by the Queen.

Gordon knew differently. Served Kensington right to have lost his eldest child.

"This is madness. Harry would not approve. Not at all." Charlotte's words filtered through the angry haze, but Harry wasn't here to stop Gordon's plans. Not this time. So he dialed the DC number and listened for an answer.

He wouldn't leave a message. Too traceable. He'd keep calling or catch the next hop back to the States. Either way, his target would become the perfect depository for the ambassador's money. How fitting. Blackmail and blood money breeding more blood.

It wouldn't resurrect Harry, but it would come closer to evening the score. And that was all that mattered.

Tom eyed the ringing phone's caller ID. Another Out of Area call. Strange. But he had nothing better to do than torment a telemarketer on the last Monday in August.

Better than studying more poisons on the Internet. Especially after his first failed foray into forensic anesthesiology. Stupid dog. His time would come.

"Hello."

"Is this the residence of one Thomas Perkins?"

The male voice sounded too highbrow to be a pimpled teen trying to earn a living. "Yes. How may I help you?" Tom settled down into his leather couch, resting his highball on his leg while he clicked through channels on his flat-screened plasma TV.

"I have a business proposition for you."

Tom clicked the Off button on his television. "Who are you and what type of business?" Nerve endings on the back of his neck felt like icy heat.

"Let's start with a few facts you might find interesting." No background noise. Nothing to place this caller beyond a modulated voice. "Gracie Lang's family is dead and her very busy private investigator is circulating a picture of their killer."

Tom spit the bitter whisky onto the wood floor. "Who *are* you?"

"A man with a need that you can fill."

Sweat beaded on his forehead. How had anyone deciphered his connection to Gracie Lang? Better to play it calm and see what the man wanted. He'd find out the rest soon enough. "How so?"

"Supply information on Hope Ridge Academy's security for 8 September. Not much to ask, is it?"

"Why?" Tom wished for the millionth time he had his mother's high-tech gadgets that she'd used to track Internet predators and bring down pornography rings. They'd come in handy right about now.

"The less you know about my plans, the better. Fewer bodies to dispose of that way."

Tom's mouth felt like the Sahara. He needed some foothold in this spiraling phone conversation. "How do I know you won't take what you want and kill me anyway?"

"You don't. But the alternative to not helping me is the loss of everything you hold dear."

"How do you figure that?"

"It's my understanding of your law that drunk drivers who kill people go to jail. Especially those who perpetrate a hit-and-run killing of two innocent children."

Tom's stomach filled with lava rocks scorching every cell. "What does that have to do with me?"

"Nice try, but your picture on the Hope Ridge website bears an uncanny resemblance to a police sketch I happened to notice in researching the backgrounds of your academy staff. Fancy none of your colleagues made the connection."

"Why me?"

"The rest of your staff tracks squeaky clean. Which leaves you. The only one with a past worth purchasing."

Tom stood and paced in front of his picture window. A way out. He needed a way out. Removing this mystery man would prove too difficult. Gracie would be an easier target. But he couldn't even kill her stupid dog. How would he manage disposing of her? And what good would that do if this caller could ID him as the DUI killer? Maybe he should just up and disappear for a time.

But that would require more money than he had at present. An idea crawled through Tom's desperate mind. An idea to free himself from both his past mistakes and the future trouble he was sliding into. Along with money to help him forget.

"Since you have a need to fill, what are you offering in return for my help?"

"Besides forgetting your past and not sending you to prison?"

Tom swallowed the bile climbing his throat. "I could deny everything. Besides, I'm your only way into Hope Ridge Academy. I get you in, and then you help me disappear afterward."

Silence.

Tom held his breath.

"I'm offering two million dollars. Everything goes as planned and you will never hear from me again."

"Three million, one up front, and no further questions," Tom said. "Once I receive the money, I'll send you security schematics and code that will get you on and off of our school grounds for one day." He didn't want to know what the man would do with them.

"Good. I'll send you a series of routing numbers to access your new bank account tomorrow. Then another set when my task is accomplished."

Tom couldn't squelch the curiosity clawing at him. "Why September?"

"Three million and no more questions. That was our deal."

"Yes. But September, especially the first week of school, security is extra tight and schedules vary with students settling into new routines. October might be a better choice."

Silence.

The extra month might give him some clues to this man's

identity. And more time to set in motion a complete way out of this mess.

Tom had killed three people, but that was an accident. This…this business transaction could be even worse.

He sat back down on his couch and took a long drink of his highball. Appearing too anxious might become a fatal mistake with this caller.

"Very well," the caller said. "October it is. I'll be in contact again soon."

The phone went dead.

Much like his hope for a quick and easy resolution to what used to be a very simple problem. It was simple no longer. But the core issue remained the same.

Gracie Lang's infernal quest for answers.

21

A Saturday morning jog in Chinquapin Park had been just what the doctor ordered.

Or the vet, in Jake's case. Breathing hard from the brisk run, Gracie inhaled fresh air with a hint of fall whispering through the massive oak trees. Two weeks since Jake's emergency and she was ready to put the awful experience behind her and return to a normal exercise routine.

She retied her tennis shoes and then gave her beautiful dog a good head-scratching before they resumed their cooldown walk through the park.

Last week, Mom and Dad had suggested returning to Atlanta so they could care for Jake when she went to work. Beth had said to forget that night in the animal hospital and to suck it up and call Steven.

Gracie couldn't manage to do either. Not that she hadn't tried. Or at least thought about it. But she couldn't completely forget how close she'd come to losing Jake, and she wouldn't call Steven. She had hoped he'd try to contact her, though.

But nothing. No phone messages or e-mails explaining the canceled date.

She stopped and took a long drink from her water bottle. She didn't want to return to Georgia. Not yet. The upcoming school year gave her something to look forward to. One day, maybe she'd see Steven and they could talk.

Her vet had given no answers as to what happened. Inconclusive blood work didn't concern Dr. Gregg because the rest of Jake's testing came out fine. So he pronounced him healthy as a horse. And Justin seemed to think her fears about someone's wanting to hurt her dog were ridiculous. But he hadn't come out and said that. He'd suggested she call Steven and get a security system if it would help her sleep better at night.

Gracie stopped to watch the fluffy white cumulus clouds that dotted the blue skies above her. Then a familiar twosome of Kessler men caught her attention. Playing Frisbee and laughing together, they made a great picture.

Jake tugged on the leash until he was near the picnic area and then sat down. Far enough away not to be noticed. But close enough to watch.

Sadness washed over her. The hope of one day being part of a scene like this with Steven and James gnawed at her heart.

Steven's back was toward her, but she couldn't help noticing how well his red T-shirt and jeans fit. It was obvious from glancing around that a few other females enjoyed the same view.

James's loud call drew Gracie out of her daydream. "Mrs. Lang, Mrs. Lang, come play Frisbee with us!" All giggles, he sprinted past Steven and flopped down in front of Jake. "What's his name?"

"Hello there, James." She bent down to the boy's level and rubbed her dog's head. "His name is Jake."

Her golden retriever licked the boy's face and reveled in his hugs and pats.

Steven brushed off his jeans, then meandered toward them, flashing his toe-curling smile. "Gracie."

She stood up so fast she felt light-headed.

He steadied her. "I've tried e-mailing you, but I suppose you've been busy."

She blinked a few times before the words registered. He'd tried to e-mail? "I haven't received anything from you. Must have been a server glitch or something. Why didn't you call?" Her face warmed as she finally got a handle on her overflowing mouth.

He tossed James the Frisbee. "Hey, little man. Why don't you see if Jake will play catch for a few minutes." Steven looked her in the eyes. "If that's okay with you?"

"Sure."

She released the leash and watched boy and dog run in the open area. She hadn't expected her heart and stomach to flutter with such force. From the corner of her eye, she watched Steven's smile widen.

"I need to get James a dog. He loves animals."

She fingered her gold locket.

"I'm really sorry I didn't call, Gracie. I wanted to, but things have gotten complicated with work, and I…well, I thought you'd e-mail back. When you didn't, I let the time get away from me."

"It's okay." She studied the grass under her feet.

Steven bent down to get her attention. "No, it's not. I should have called. It's not because I didn't want to see you again. I hope you know that."

Gracie wanted to pretend the last three weeks hadn't happened and that she and Steven were still at the Morrison House enjoying a wonderful meal with easy conversation. Things had felt less complicated for those few short hours.

Before ringing cell phones and the ugly side of life had interrupted.

The warmth of Steven's hand encircling hers and gently stroking her fingers startled her. "I hope you're a believer in second chances."

"You'd be working on the third at this point."

Steven laughed but didn't release her hand.

"Hey, Dad. Come play." James ran up and Steven let go of her hand. "Will you come too, Mrs. Lang? It'd be a lot of fun if you joined us."

James's blue eyes twinkled like his father's. How could she resist?

Steven watched Gracie and James chase the dog all over the picnic area, then circle back around. Her ponytail flipped with every movement. A better place to focus than her athletic legs and running shorts.

"Can I have my water, Dad?" James collapsed on the concrete bench where their picnic basket rested. The one Sue had packed for them before shooing him out of the house.

Gracie and Jake caught their breath, standing by the table too.

"Three waters, coming up." Steven handed out the ice-cold bottles.

James guzzled his and went back to playing. Jake followed, close at his son's heels.

"I'm glad Jake's okay. Justin said you'd had a scare with him."

Gracie fingered her gold locket, a habit he'd noticed before. One day soon he'd ask about it. But for now it seemed a little too personal.

"Yes. The vet says he had some sort of seizure. But no explanation why it happened or if it'll happen again."

"Could he have gotten dehydrated?"

"Maybe." Gracie met his eyes. "I'd rather not talk about it, if that's okay."

"Sure." He spread out three plates and piled sandwiches and chips onto them. "Will you join us for lunch?"

"You packed for three?"

Steven chuckled. "Sort of. Sue packs extras, hoping we'll either eat them all or make a new friend to share them with."

"She sounds like a great lady. Takes care of you both, from what I remember of James's family history." Gracie nibbled on a chip and sipped her water.

"Did I ever really apologize for being so late that day?" Steven hoped he'd used better manners than he could recall. After the phone call about Ryan, little else that day stuck with him. Except Gracie's smile.

She shrugged. "I don't remember."

He caught her slight blush before she turned away and fixed her eyes on James and Jake, still playing catch with the Frisbee. For whatever reason, her blush made Steven feel important. Like what he did mattered to her. He liked the feeling.

"What a cozy little picture." A female voice purred behind him.

Steven held back a response. He turned to see his ex-wife standing beside him, wearing a running bra and tight shorts. She crossed her arms and smirked.

Gracie's wide eyes met his.

How in the world would he manage this minefield?

Angela took care of that. "Are you one of Steven's friends?" She looked Gracie up and down.

Gracie retied her ponytail and stood. "Yes. Gracie Lang. And you are?"

Angela smiled her crafty lawyer grin. "Angela Barrett Carter. Pleased to meet you." She turned to face him. "Don't let me break up your little party. Your dad mentioned I might find you here. So I thought I'd get some exercise in before seeing if we could talk."

Gracie smoothed her white T-shirt. "I'd better head back home. Thanks for lunch, Steven." Turning to Angela, Gracie managed a quick smile. "It was nice to meet you."

"I'll call you soon, Gracie," Steven said

But she was walking away already, without responding. Gracie widened the distance between them with a few long strides. Then she bent down and talked to James while she reclipped Jake's leash.

"She's attractive. In a down home, girl next door sort of way."

Steven clenched his fists. "Stop it, Angela. My life is none of your business."

"My son is."

The ice forming between them kept them both frozen to the spot, eyes fixed on James walking Gracie to her car.

"Save it for the courts." Steven stepped between his ex and her focus on their son. "James doesn't know who you are, and I want it kept that way. But if you insist on barging into our lives like this, I'll let him know just what type of person you are."

Her glare connected. "You wouldn't dare."

His teeth ground side to side. Would he?

"Well, it looks like your lady friend is gone for the time being." She cocked her head.

"Jealous, Angela?"

"Want me to introduce myself to James?"

His son waved good-bye as Gracie drove away. Then turning back to the picnic area, he headed straight for them.

Steven's jaw tightened. "I want you to leave. Now."

James stepped close to his leg and took his hand. "Hello. I'm James. Do you know my daddy?"

Steven held his breath and narrowed his eyes.

For once, Angela took the warning. "Hello, James. Nice to meet you." Her eyes blinked rapidly. "I knew your father a long time ago, but he can tell you more about that."

She stayed rooted in place, taking in every detail of James's face. Steven could see Angela in the angle of his son's chin, his high cheekbones.

His stomach lurched.

James kicked at a pebble by his shoe.

"Weren't you just leaving?" Steven swallowed the other words he wanted to let loose.

Angela smiled at their son. "'Bye, James. I hope we'll meet again. Soon." She turned on her heel and started a slow, controlled jog across the picnic area and back to the trail.

Steven watched until she disappeared between the huge oak trees lining the walking path.

"Who was she, Daddy?"

"An old acquaintance." He ruffled James's hair and pointed to the picnic table. Now was not the time to explain the ticking bomb his ex-wife had just set in motion.

They dug into their sandwiches and chips in silence. How long did he have before everything blew up in his face?

22

Maria Grivens walked behind Victoria and Lady Kensington as they entered Hope Ridge Academy for the first time together. Maria bypassed the magnetometer while the other two waited their turns amid squealing kindergarten students and sullen teens. Victoria stepped through the huge metal portal with no bounce, her curls flat all around her head.

Lady Kensington's once-dancing eyes looked dead as well.

Maria's heart constricted. Olivia had not come home, and the gray cloud of grief hung over every person in the British embassy. Not even the first day of school—a day Victoria had been asking about hourly before Olivia's funeral—enticed the little girl to smile.

Maybe new friends and Gracie Lang could do the trick.

Wide-eyed children and hurried parents swarmed around them as they walked down the long hall to Gracie's classroom in silence.

Gracie waved to another parent and then smiled at Maria. "Good morning, Lady Kensington. Victoria." She bent down to the little girl's eye level. "I'm so glad you're here today."

Victoria gave a small curtsy. "Thank you, Mrs. Lang."

Lady Kensington hugged Victoria for a long moment. Then she gave a quick nod and straightened her black skirt and simple white blouse before turning to leave. A month since her daughter's murder, and black still clung to every pore.

Maria swallowed hard. She'd become too emotionally involved. Any more distraction allowance and she'd have to resign from this case. Victoria's safety mattered more than Maria's care for this wounded family.

She followed Victoria into the classroom.

Gracie smiled and touched her arm. "Good morning to you too, Maria. It's good to see you."

Because of recent case developments, the Secret Service's plans to have Maria work in the classroom as a teacher's assistant had changed. Now both she and Agent John Reynolds would stand guard in the room. Each would become a statue. A non-person for the duration of each school day.

Victoria clutched at Maria's hand, tears spilling over her little white cheeks. "I want to go home. Please may I go home, Maria?"

She blinked and looked at John, who didn't move.

Her supervisor's voice crackled through her earpiece. "Negative. We're set to roost for the day."

Maria hated the microphone chatter. No emotion. Just the cold reality that there was a job to do and it would be done, no matter how broken Victoria's heart.

Maria knelt and was instantly wrapped up in the arms of the little China doll. "We're here for a time, Tori. Let's make the best of it, okay?"

Victoria sniffled. "Yes, ma'am."

A little boy with sandy brown hair and striking blue eyes stood by Victoria. "Hi. I'm James. Would you like to do a puzzle with me?"

Victoria glanced up, tearful eyes asking the question, and Maria nodded.

The two scampered off.

Maria took inventory of Gracie's decorations for the first week of school. Hey Diddle Diddle posters and cutout cows and moons surrounded the excited children filling the room and finding their cubbies to store their backpacks. When the children were directed to look up, each found their name in calligraphy on a shining star that dangled from the ceiling.

"That's me!" Pointing to their stars, little girls and boys giggled and spelled out their names for their new teacher. Gracie smiled and looked each first grader in the eyes as she spoke.

Reach for your dreams. Catch your star. The bulletin board banner made Maria wish she'd had such a teacher to begin her school career. From the special book nook with stuffed animals to the myriad puzzles and math games all coordinated to the nursery rhyme's theme, these children would be in good hands. They would learn with their new friends and remember their first-grade teacher with much fondness in the years to come.

A concept Gracie called "circle time" transformed a zoo of wiggly children to a quiet, orderly collection of students, each seated on a brightly colored carpet square, entranced by her reading of *Good Night Moon*.

Maria watched from her grown-up sized plastic chair by the door. Every once in a while, she would nod and even smile at children who looked her way. But John stayed rigid like a British sentry at Buckingham Palace, eyes studying every move both inside and outside the classroom.

Between the two of them, they shared concerns about many places in this room. Gracie's class was the last on the hall with a door that opened to the outside. Great for necessary escape routes, bad for allowing another point of entry to keep secured. Then there was the minimal long-distance visibility with the large oaks and thick underbrush encircling the small open area just beyond the door. But the huge, ceiling-to-waist windows allowed plenty of visual coverage for recess time.

Maria almost yawned as Gracie covered her mouth at the end of her story to pretend to sleep. Fifteen little pairs of hands followed her lead. What a great way to calm everyone down without yelling at them to sit and be quiet.

Introductions around the morning circle included a favorite Mother Goose story along with names and ages.

"I'm James Kessler and my favorite nursery rhyme is Baa Baa Black Sheep because the little boy gives out wool to help his neighbors."

Gracie handed James a white wooly blanket. "That's wonderful, James. Would you like to recite your rhyme in costume?"

Wrapped in white wool, Steven's son hammed up the short poem and baa'd the best sheep impression Maria had heard in years. Of course it wasn't a matter of routine to hear Secret Service agents making animal noises. Unless they were playing basketball in the gym.

When Victoria's turn came, Maria held her breath. The girl had done little besides a puzzle with James. And she'd sat with perfect posture, silent while the rest of her class wiggled like normal six-year-olds.

"My name is Victoria Kensington. My favorite Mother Goose is Humpty Dumpty. But I don't like that they couldn't put him back together again."

Gracie's eyes watered.

Maria made a mental note to talk to Lady Kensington again about art therapy for Victoria. The little girl needed a child-friendly way to process the pain that she now wore like a cloak.

"Victoria, why don't you recite your nursery rhyme and then, together as a class, we can put our special Humpty Dumpty puzzle all back together again."

Even Agent Reynolds's face softened at Gracie's gracious gift to the little girl.

Maria mouthed a silent *Thank you* when Gracie caught her gaze.

Gracie beamed.

The morning flew by, much to Maria's surprise. The rest of her detail could tease all they wanted, but this assignment would be one of the few she would enjoy each and every day.

Hope Ridge was everything Steven Kessler had said it would be. Perfect.

While the children worked with what Gracie called math manipulatives, Maria joined Gracie at her desk.

"Never underestimate the power of a great teacher," Maria whispered to her friend. "You were so gentle with Victoria.

Thank you. Under your care, she may well recover."

"I'm praying she will, Maria. She's a precious child." Gracie scribbled a few notes on her lesson plans about adding more art activities, all the while keeping an eye on every one of the four tables in the middle of her classroom.

Gracie would make a good federal agent.

John and the others in Victoria's detail were committed to keeping that same vigilant watch. But looking out the large classroom windows into the swaying green trees, she couldn't help wonder how long this idyllic scene would last.

Victoria had already started to come out of her shell and Maria was glad.

Still, the feeling that the other shoe was about to drop never strayed far from her thoughts.

Gracie waved a drowsy good-bye as Maria and John left with the Kensingtons' nanny.

"See you tomorrow, Mrs. Lang!" Victoria waved back and bounced down the hall.

If only Victoria's mother could see the girl now. What a change from the reserved little diplomat who had entered her classroom that morning. In large part due to James Kessler.

Gracie watched him gather all the puzzles and return them to the wooden rack near her desk. The precious boy was everything she'd imagined her own Joshua growing up to be.

Careful. She hated how easily she let her heart daydream sometimes. And the certain themes that kept intruding. Twinkling blue eyes and toe-curling grins at the top of the list.

Beth would be thrilled. But she still didn't know about the park outing and the black-haired siren that had disrupted a wonderful Saturday picnic.

Or the resulting decision Gracie had made about Steven Kessler. The parent she was most thankful not to have seen this morning.

Parents and nannies arrived one by one to pick up their children. That kept her mind busy, but her face started to hurt with all the smiling.

"Mrs. Lang. For you. A picture." Akemi, a senator's adopted daughter, bowed her head and waited for a response.

Gracie knelt in front of her and took one of her hands. "This is a gorgeous rose, Akemi. May I put it on our bulletin board?"

The little girl's short black bob shook as she nodded. "Oh yes. Thank you." She returned to the center art table and giggled through a tic-tac-toe game with her new friend, Susannah Rollins.

Gracie watched Susannah's fiery red locks escape her white bows while she played. The daughter of Steven's partner was the spitting image of her mother, Sara, and as free with a smile as Agent Rollins had been the first time Gracie met him.

She would have liked to get to know the Rollins family better outside of Hope Ridge Academy. Not a possibility anymore, though. But among Akemi, Susannah, and Victoria, Gracie's days would be filled with beautifully drawn flower gifts and gentle manners.

A knock sounded at the door. *Please, don't let this be Steven.*

She opened the door. Breath catching in her lungs, she forced a smile. "Good afternoon, Steven."

"Hello, Gracie." His eyes searched her face. "I'd like to speak with you a minute if I could."

Part of her job consisted of short, impromptu parent-teacher conferences at the door with concerned parents. She'd already endured the usual round of "Did she cry long after I left?" to the academic grilling, "My son made straight A's today, yes?" Gracie tried to comfort and reassure each parent and affirm their love for their offspring.

But talking with Steven felt unsettling, which had nothing to do with his son and everything to do with her resolve crumbling as she looked into his pained blue eyes.

"I feel like I've said 'I'm sorry' far too much already." He ran a hand through his thick brown hair. "Last Saturday at the park, I—"

She held up a hand. "You don't owe me an explanation. I think maybe we'd better keep things focused on James." She glanced over her shoulder into the classroom. "He's a wonderful little boy, and I'm so thankful he's in my class."

Steven clenched his jaw. A carbon copy of the last look she'd seen from him on Saturday.

"James made fast friends with every one of his classmates and was especially kind to Victoria. I believe this will be a good year for both of them."

"With you as their teacher, I'm sure it will."

The compliment heated her cheeks. One more brick fell from her wall of resolve. "Thank you. I'll go get his things."

Steven touched her hand. "That woman was Angela. My ex-wife. I didn't want her there, Gracie."

She swallowed the lump rising in her throat and placed ten more bricks on her wall. No way did she want to stand in between Steven and the ex-wife whose glance could slice steel. The same woman who still elicited powerful emotions in her ex-husband.

Love and hate weren't opposites. Love and indifference were. And Steven was as far from unaffected as a sloth was fast.

"I'm sorry, Steven." She gripped the door with white knuckles.

"I'd like to explain. May I call you tonight?"

Thomas Perkins walked down the hall, eyes fixed on her. The vice principal stiffened as he stepped to Steven's side. "Is there a problem here, Mrs. Lang?"

"No, sir. I was just getting James."

Gracie turned away from the door and Steven's once again clenched jaw. She heard the vice principal's clipped tones, something about dating and maintaining decorum, and cringed. Maybe she should give Steven another chance. At least listen to him, let him talk out whatever had morphed his entrancing eyes into heated lasers of pain.

She and James walked to the door, gathering art projects as they went.

"Daddy!" James rushed into his father's open arms.

"Hey, little man. I heard you had an awesome first day." Steven's eyes, focused on his son, resumed some of their former twinkle.

Mr. Perkins turned on his heel and left without a word.

"I'm sorry about that."

He shifted James to his hip, a smile nowhere to be found. "Not a problem and not your fault. We'll see you another afternoon, Mrs. Lang."

"'Bye, Mrs. Lang." James waved. "See you tomorrow!"

Gracie waved like a robot and held her breath until the pair disappeared down the hall. Tears fought for release. Steven's pleasant but clear dismissal replayed in her mind as she shut her classroom door.

So much for second chances.

23

Thursday morning's early teleconference with Britain's Security Service and Secret Intelligence Service had Steven's boss fuming.

Steven leaned back in one of the conference room's leather chairs and smirked at the backpedaling the Brits were doing because of the unit chief's bellowing.

"You mean to tell me you believe you were justified in withholding information from my agents conducting a federal investigation?" Agent Maxwell barked at the large video screen. Clint and Michael stayed focused straight ahead and said nothing.

The honorable Sir Peter Barnstable closed his eyes and took a deep breath before answering. "Agent Maxwell, you are aware we have similar protocols to your American agencies in regards to protected information."

"My agents requested information on Harry Landridge the eleventh of August and were told he died of natural causes after working for years as a glorified file clerk for your agency. Now you're telling me he was actually killed in the line of duty as an SIS officer investigating arms deals that you now believe involved Ambassador Walter Kensington? The same ambassador we've been investigating concerning his daughter's kidnapping and subsequent death?"

"Yes."

"Agent Kessler, what were we told about the ambassador?" Maxwell's face grew redder with every tick of the clock.

Steven flipped open his case file. "That the investigation concerning Sir Walter's consuls had been closed satisfactorily, that the ambassador was independently wealthy, and any further investigation into his character was unnecessary."

"That was *after* we'd been told none of the ransom note's black market references were relevant to our investigation." Michael spoke to Agent Maxwell, then crossed his arms and glared at the video screen.

"Our new information has only recently been authenticated…"

"It's high time you came clean with us." Maxwell stood and jabbed a finger toward the stuffy British officer. "Exactly what information do you now have?"

Sir Peter's stony disposition set Steven's jaw on edge.

"Because our intelligence officers are reopening this case, we cannot acquiesce to your further demands for information. This is a British security concern. As a courtesy toward your government, we will keep you apprised of our investigation."

Maxwell paced around the conference table. "You'll do better than that."

Sir Peter opened his mouth to reply, but Steven held up a hand. "Sir Barnstable, we understand that you have an open investigation, but we have a homicide that occurred on American soil we are tasked with solving. We need to know the information pertinent to our apprehending the killer."

It was a good thing the Brits were safely across the pond because their stretching silence had Maxwell ready for blood.

Clint's bowed head went wholly unnoticed by everyone else in the room. Steven didn't know what to make of his partner's way of handling the standoff. But he hoped the prayer worked.

The Brits shuffled papers and a few Security Service officers clicked away on their keyboards. Nothing moved in the FBI conference room.

Sir Peter cleared his throat. "Our information on Ambassador Kensington was received from Harry's brother, Gordon Landridge, former SAS officer."

"Special forces soldier and SIS officer. That explains why neither brother appears in Charlotte Brown's file." Clint shook his head. "I'd say we have motive and strong evidence Gordon is capable of everything we've seen thus far."

Maxwell returned to his chair. "Where is Landridge now?"

"Unknown."

"Rollins, I want warrants for Charlotte Brown's phone records. Parker, get surveillance on Brown's house. Kessler…"

"I'm on my way." Steven hotfooted it out of the Hoover building. He would have liked to stay and hear the full dressing-down Chief Maxwell was sure to unload, but he had a killer to catch and the gut assurance that they'd finally gotten the break they needed.

The embassy was fast becoming Steven's least favorite place.

Right up there with anywhere Angela Carter could be found. Funny how Pavlovian instincts hooked Angela's name to the stress of an adrenaline rush.

He maneuvered in and out of DC traffic, letting his mind spiral through what he would say to Charlotte. He'd spoken with her supervisor and verified that she was at her desk. Now all he had to do was get there and not arouse suspicion before he secured concrete evidence of Gordon's whereabouts. Surely she'd make a slip like she'd done with Clint a few weeks ago. Then they'd find Landridge. Make an arrest. And put this case far behind them.

Rush-hour gridlock forced the other mental balls he was juggling to the forefront, stealing his focus. Gracie's obvious disinterest still stung. And he could do without her bothersome boss. Something about the vice principal nagged at his conscience.

Just like Gracie's smile refused to disappear from his dreams.

Then there were his father's words about the whole fiasco with Angela at the park. His dad had only meant to help by directing her to Chinquapin. Like Clint, he had wanted Steven to work things out with Angela, for James's sake. Dad sure had to be disappointed with Saturday's fallout and the problems that had started over a decade ago with the proposal.

All his father's logic hadn't swayed Steven. Angela wasn't a Christian. Right after college wasn't the ideal time for marriage. Not even his dad's insistence that things weren't what they appeared had altered Steven's course.

It hit him now with perfect clarity. Dad had been right. About all of it. And Steven had paid the price ever since for ignoring him.

He carried the glass shard of Angela's rejection in his heart. Every memory twisted it deeper. Seeing her again at the park had ripped the still-bleeding scab clear off.

No Band-Aid could cover it either. Nor could Clint's theories linking bitterness and revenge and his solution of forgiveness. Things were far too complex for a simple cure.

Just like the Kensington case.

But the ambassador was now Attorney Kenneth Marks's nightmare. Not Steven's headache any longer.

Finding Olivia's killer was.

As he entered the embassy from the rear, Steven adjusted his suit coat at the waist to reveal his credentials. He walked the residence halls listening for signs of life. Little beyond electronic buzzing caught his attention, so he proceeded over the bridge and into the original offices.

"I'm here to see Mrs. Charlotte Brown."

"You're a bit late, Agent Kessler. She's just left on holiday and won't be back for an entire month." The gold-streaked brunette sitting behind Charlotte's desk leaned forward. "But I'm Dottie Evans. And I'd be delighted to help you."

Steven stepped away from the desk, flipped open his phone, and pressed the number three speed dial. "Clint. Charlotte Brown's not here. We need to check her residence and see if she's taken her son. Alert transportation routes too. Let's see if we can find her before she leaves the US."

"I'm on it."

Returning to the assistant's desk, he narrowed his eyes. "I spoke with Mrs. Brown's supervisor this morning. She didn't mention a planned vacation."

Ms. Evans laughed nervously.

"Something funny in that?"

She stood and straightened her tight gray suit. "Follow me, Agent Kessler. I'll explain in the records room."

He heard the electronic whir of a surveillance camera turning. Most likely to watch the attractive assistant saunter across the room. Childishness existed everywhere. But there could be a lead to unearth, and he needed the patience to find it.

Ms. Evans unlocked the secluded file room and held the door for him. The room was still tapped, so he was covered should her story about their talk differ from his. Didn't give him much breathing room, though.

The scent of lavender and lemon quickly overpowered the little room. Less was always more with perfume. "You were going to explain."

"Charlotte would come back here and put on her little black fan," Ms. Evans pointed to a back corner of the room. "So as not to be caught on tape when she called her boyfriend, Gordon."

"What?"

The woman nodded with a wide grin. "No worries, mate. I'm sure you can track 'em down with your supersleuthing. I'd bet the moon that's where she's run off to so fast. Find Charlotte's bloke and you'll find your answers."

How right she was. And if he could verify Ms. Evans's claim, that would link Charlotte as a coconspirator and possibly lead them to Gordon's hideout. "How do you know this? And why did you wait until now to reveal it?"

Her face lost some color under her caked makeup. "I'm not in trouble, am I?"

"That depends."

She wrung her hands. "You see, well, Charlotte was a friend, and her private affairs weren't my business. But when she begged me to file her holiday paperwork request just a short while ago, I knew something was wrong."

Just a short time ago?

Maybe he wasn't too late. "Is there anything else you'd like to tell me? Any other memory that seems worth mentioning now?"

"No, Agent Kessler. I only heard the one conversation, and Charlotte would never answer any inquiry into her beau. Very closed to discussion, she was. But she did talk about her little Stewart. Nonstop. Maybe that will help you find her."

Clint was already all over that angle. Steven would be too as soon as he could get away from here. "Thank you. We'll need to get a sworn statement." He opened the door and held it. "If you'll follow me, we can take care of that."

"Am I in trouble?"

"Not unless you're lying." Steven almost chuckled at her wide-eyed response.

He led Ms. Evans toward the Secret Service office space in the residence area. After a few paperwork details, he'd join in the footwork that got his blood circulating. Nabbing a suspect beat desk donkeywork any day.

Even more when it ended in arrests and airtight court cases.

Bureau assessments still loomed, case overload or not.

Clint laced his tennis shoes and stretched. The headquarters' gym smelled of sweat and Old Spice, even on a Friday morning. He watched through the front glass doors for any sign of his partner.

Fifteen minutes to seven, Steven slammed through the door and tossed his gym bag on the first bench. Clint joined him.

"Nice of you to show up, given that our HIP assessments are scheduled for next week and I need the practice. Especially on the range."

Steven grunted. "After yesterday's disappointments, I need the physical challenge. Health Improvement Program garbage or not."

"Wasn't your fault, Steven. We followed the lead and got the warrants as fast as humanly possible."

"Too late to do much good. Charlotte and Gordon have disappeared. No trace."

Michael entered the floor from the locker room. "I think she's still on US soil. Besides, her son is here. She couldn't have gone too far. Or for long."

Clint had seen just that thing happen more often than he cared to remember. Give the rookie ten years, and he'd learn.

"You're a conspiracy theorist, and I don't have the brain power to hear it today." Steven crossed the gym and headed up the stairs to the upper level track.

"What's his problem?"

Clint shook his head. "He's the coordinator. It's his behind that'll be chewed if every lead turns up a day or even a minute late."

"Steven's done everything by the book. We'll find Olivia's murderer sooner or later." Michael jutted his chin toward the stairs. "He should loosen up, or a heart attack will be crouching at his door."

Michael had no idea how close his words came to Clint's own thoughts. In fact, his partner's heart had been the focus of his and Sara's prayers for a long time last night. God had to be at work, or Steven wouldn't be fighting the truth so hard and on every possible front. Work. James. His dad. Angela. Even Gracie. A name Clint hadn't heard in far too long. He'd see what he could do about changing that.

Steven wouldn't run from his questions forever.

Clint took the stairs two at a time and then positioned himself next to Steven on the track. They waited for Michael's starting call.

The rookie dropped his hands and shouted. "Go!"

Clint felt every muscle in his body burn with the exertion. Keeping up with Steven's unrealistic pace wouldn't benefit him in the end. He watched his partner's back for the first mile, then increased his stride and pushed harder.

Sara would be proud. And he'd enjoy a good rubdown after their date tonight. Since he couldn't do anything about the image of his wife's curves right now, he put the mental charge to good use and drove his muscles harder. By the third lap, sweat soaked both his and Steven's muscle shirts.

He pulled even with his younger partner by the home-stretch. But then Steven kicked it up even further and passed the finish line two strides ahead of him.

They walked off the muscle cramps and heaving lungs in silence.

Michael joined them. "If office scuttlebutt is on, you both just bombed your last assessment times by 20 blips."

"Say again in old folks' English?" Steven stretched his neck.

Clint shook his head. At thirty-five, Steven didn't know old yet. Wait till the big four-o started breathing down his neck. Clint knew that experience all too well. "Michael said we beat our Quantico records."

"Good." Steven grabbed a white towel. "Now if we can manage that on the range too, we'll snap the assessments."

Snap? "Old folk talk, huh?"

Steven quirked a lopsided grin. "That was for you, pops."

Showers and promising range scores served to improve Friday's outlook. But there was still paperwork to do before clocking out tonight. Clint bent his aching six feet five inches into the silver and gray thing the FBI called an ergonomic chair. Torture device fit better.

He wanted his cowboy boots, Stetson, and some of Sara's true Southern sweet tea.

His partner's typing on the other side of the partition halted. "Clint? Remember graduation? Those were the days, weren't they? No heating pads necessary after assessments."

"If I didn't know better, I'd think you were coming up on a birthday or something. Thinking about your creaking joints, old man?" Clint stood and leaned against the partition. "Hey, wait. You are coming up on a birthday, aren't you?"

"Leave it to you to remember things like birthdays. I'm trying to forget." Steven returned to typing.

"Come on now, you know Sara and I wouldn't forget. James is looking forward to the party too. Don't get all grumpy on us and ruin it."

"All right. All right." Steven held up his hands. "I wish you had planned a surprise party though, so I could be spared this constant bother from your whole family. By the way, the over-the-hill e-card from your kids was a real highlight of my day."

Clint laughed.

Steven shook his head as he pulled up the dancing Kentucky blue teddy bears in tutus. "I should have hit Delete and not even acknowledged it."

"Yeah, well, you always were a softie, weren't you?"

"Whatever." Steven pulled another file from his top drawer and added it to his completed case notes stack. "Don't forget, I beat your stellar record today. On the range and on the track."

"Old men live in their pasts, partner."

Steven turned to face him. "Want to try again tomorrow?"

Clint chuckled. "No way am I going to rain on your parade. Sara and the kids are joining me to do some hunting for all things black tomorrow. Just the ticket to throw your mammoth birthday shindig on the twenty-third."

"You've got some nerve. I'd have expected a respectful lull in the smack talk. You just wait 'til I tell Sara about our times today."

Steven and Sara would make Clint's old bones creak all the louder with their joshing. He could take it, though, given that Sara's eyes still lit on fire when he stepped out of the shower.

"Hey, before I forget: When are you going to call Gracie and invite her to the party?"

Steven grimaced. "I'm not. The thing with Angela at the park last Saturday cooled Gracie's interest."

Clint's smile disappeared. "What do you mean?"

"She didn't want to hear my explanation and suggested we keep our focus on James." Steven leaned back in his chair.

"Decoded, that means 'Get lost, buster.' I'm not begging for another chance."

The faraway look in Steven's eyes told a different story. "You just can't get her out of your mind, can you? Been there, done that, got the ring to prove it."

Steven shrugged. "Doesn't matter, does it? Not if she's crossed me off her list."

Nodding his head toward the picture of Sara, Steven, and himself taken a decade ago at their graduation ceremony, Clint exhaled long and slow. Sara had beamed between him and Steven, but Angela hadn't been interested in joining the celebration. Clint had tried to get her to warm up to them. She never did. That still stung Steven even now.

More so, since Angela had arrived on the scene again. If Clint didn't step in and do something fast, Gracie would disappear under the weight of Angela's memory.

"Don't give up, partner. You know Sara's first reaction to me." Dr. Sara O'Toole's daunting green eyes and fiery red hair had made even the pain of a broken wrist disappear.

"Wait. Let me see if I recall that story." Steven cleared his throat.

Michael Parker joined them. Clint wished he'd kept his mouth shut.

"Here's how it went—you immediately impressed Doctor Sara with your brave handling of that old sports injury, and she fell madly and totally in love at first sight. Right?" Steven laughed at his own parody.

They both knew full well that was not how it happened. Clint had pursued Sara for months after their first meeting in the Anderson ER. Phone calls, cards, and flowers. She finally gave in and went out on a date.

The rest and two kids was a sweet success story. One Steven needed too.

"My point, wise guy, is that you should ask Gracie out again. For your birthday party. Don't let that spark I see in your eyes go out so easily." Clint leaned against Steven's desk. "Gracie's a keeper. Just like Sara."

Michael folded his arms over his chest. "So you're saying, if at first you don't succeed, try, try again?"

Clint affected his worst Irish brogue. "You might just find yer big ol' pot o' gold."

Steven and Michael both rolled their eyes. *"Right."*

Michael went back to his desk.

"You gonna call?"

"Yes, Clint. If it'll get you off my back."

"I'm just covering your six and your thick skull. My job, you know."

"I thought that was God's."

Clint grinned. The God-talk about Angela three weeks ago must be working, at least a little bit. "Hey, make the call soon, or I'll invite Gracie myself."

He settled back at his desk and checked for updates on the Browns' phone record warrant he'd filed for yesterday. Something good had to give in this case and in his partner's personal life. Soon.

Clint put his money on God and Gracie. Between the two of them, at least Steven's hardness toward God was toast.

24

Steven's phone buzzed.

"Kessler." He maneuvered off I-395 toward Pentagon City for the short trek to Russell Road.

"Got a line into SIS," Michael said. "A chatty Cathy by the name of Thomason remembers both Harry and Gordon Landridge. He also elaborated on what Sir Peter was reluctant to share."

"You mean they're being cooperative now?"

"That and staying away from any further videoconferences." Michael chuckled. "Thomason said the tip that reopened the arms case consisted of cell phone transcripts from Harry's last conversation with Gordon."

"Tell me you're already working that cell number."

"As we speak, boss."

"Still nothing from the surveillance at the Brown home?"

"No. It's been a week. Charlotte will check on her son soon. You wait and see."

Steven hoped so. Charlotte or Gordon had to slip soon, or this case could drag for eons. All he needed was one bite, one physical lead, and he could reel in this investigation and hand it off to the Assistant US Attorney for prosecution. "You talked to Sir Walter yet about the Landridge family?"

"No. Thought you'd want to take that one."

Steven pulled into Hope Ridge Academy's parking lot. "More like no one else wants to two-step with the angry ambassador."

"You got that right."

Michael was a straight shooter. Steven liked that. He didn't like that he'd get stuck going one more round with Sir Walter. But now they had a blueprint. Unpack and prove the motive. Bring in the bad guys.

Not a slam dunk, but possible. Finally, a ray of hope in this case. "Thanks, Michael. I'll tangle with Sir Walter soon."

The sunny afternoon skies made him smile as he scribbled a few notes before heading in to pick up James and see Gracie. She'd agreed, with some reservation, to attend his birthday party next week.

Maybe turning thirty-six wouldn't be so bad after all.

"Hello, Stevie." Angela appeared suddenly at his door. "I have an early birthday present for you." She stood by his Explorer in her two thousand-dollar power suit.

On second thought, with birthday presents from Angela, turning thirty-six with his sanity or heart intact might not happen. Steven clenched his jaw. "What?"

"Court-ordered temporary visitation rights." She extended an official-looking document through his open window with her perfect French-manicured nails. "Read it and weep."

He took the papers and read through them. He should have known Gracie's "yes" and his upcoming birthday party wouldn't hold a candle to the facts of his life. Things like dead children and custody battles. Those made up his reality.

His nightmare.

"So now you'll have to introduce me properly to my son." Angela motioned to the front office doors of Hope Ridge. "We'll start with placing me in his file and working out a schedule for me to pick him up from school."

"Why don't you and Mr. Cue Ball lawyer go have a few drinks to celebrate instead? I'm not letting you be alone with my son. Not until a court says I have to."

"They have."

Steven stepped out of his SUV and shoved the papers back into Angela's hands. "No. This says you have the right to see James, not unchaperoned visitation. Big difference."

She stiffened. Her stupid heels made her taller, so she almost met him eye to eye. "Marcus will be with us. He'd like to get to know his stepson too. And he'll make a great father. Unlike you."

Steven closed his eyes and tried to remember that Angela had a heart buried somewhere inside. His neglect of his wife and not sharing the hell of chasing drug lords and doing hostage rescues with the Hostage Rescue Team at Quantico had hurt Angela so badly she wanted revenge. Revenge intended to draw blood.

His.

And his son's.

At least that was Clint's take on the situation. And his partner thought facing lies and extending forgiveness would solve everything and wrap it up with a neat little bow. No way.

Black suits and uniformed children passed in a blur beyond Steven's SUV. The occasional mother in a tennis outfit flitted near them. Many of the suits were his colleagues. Not the place for a scene.

"I'm sorry I did so much wrong in our marriage. I wish I could change that. But I can't." He stepped closer and felt her retreat even though her feet stayed still. "Don't punish James to get back at me."

"This is not about you, Steven. The world does not revolve around you and your playing Superman." Her voice softened. "I just want to know my son."

He searched her dark brown eyes. The eyes he'd fallen for and had never recovered from. He knew then how right Clint had been, and a new emotion vied for first place against the guilt raging in his gut.

Sorrow.

Gracie's second week of school drew to a close with a tired smile.

It'd been a good Friday. Her students were settling into a

routine, and they'd even managed to remain calm on the craziest day of the week.

"Mrs. Lang?" Akemi tugged on her coral sundress. "Will you play pick-up sticks with James and me, please?"

Gracie knelt down and hugged Akemi. In just under two weeks, the shy little girl had started to invite people into her play. It was a joy to watch. Even more of a joy to be included. No matter how many candles on her birthday cake, being welcomed into a group made Gracie feel wanted. Special.

She settled into a child-sized chair with the last two students waiting for their parents. James dumped the multicolored sticks onto the center table. Akemi went first and managed to untangle three sticks before making one move.

James tried for the hardest stick first. Some things had to be genetic. Gracie smiled as the little boy dislodged two difficult red sticks from the pile.

She just touched a yellow stick when a knock on the door made her jump and spoil her turn. "Oh, well." Ruffling James's hair, she stood. "Your turn, Akemi. I'll try again in a minute."

Gracie opened the door and fought the urge to slam it closed. Instead, she plastered on a welcoming smile. "Hello, Steven. Angela."

"Hey, Gracie." Steven's smile looked plastic. Like a large part of the raven-haired model standing next to him. "I know the two of you have met already. But I needed to let you know, Angela is being added to James's file, and she may be picking him up from school in the near future."

Steven's ex stepped closer to him. "So. You're my son's teacher. How quaint."

"*Angela.*" Steven's voice came out as a low growl.

Gracie felt dizzy with all the electricity exploding around her. "I'll gather your son's things and let him know you're here." She shut the door and took a few deep breaths. "James, it's time to go."

"Can I finish our game?" His pleading blue eyes held no hint of the way his world was about to be turned inside out.

She felt like a traitor, but no amount of protective instincts could shield James now. "Maybe on Monday. For today, it's time to go home."

Akemi waited with her hands in her lap and smiled at James.

Gracie extended her hand and walked with him to the door. As they stepped into the hall, he moved back against her leg. "Hey, dad." He looked into Angela's face. "Why are you here?"

Tension and Angela's thinly veiled temper sucked all the oxygen from Gracie's personal space. She returned James's tightened grip on her hand.

Steven knelt down and opened his arms, keeping his eyes fastened on Gracie.

James stepped into his father's embrace. "I want to finish my game with Mrs. Lang."

"This probably isn't the best time or place, but this..." Steven motioned to Angela. "This is your mother, James."

The little boy's eyes widened, but he said nothing.

Angela knelt also, snuggled into Steven's side, and opened her arms. "I've been waiting so long to meet you. Can I give you a hug?"

At least she'd asked, unlike other plastic people who demanded their due attention from teacher and child alike. Gracie wanted to escape the scene unfolding before her— Angela's strong musk perfume, her perfect proportions, especially the intimate space she occupied with Steven, talking to their son.

Who would never be Gracie's son.

"...we're going to take, Angela, I mean, your mom, out to dinner tonight." Steven stood and settled James in his arms, his ex-wife right in time with every movement.

"Can Mrs. Lang come?" James's sad eyes locked on to hers. "I really want her to come too."

Gracie's mouth felt like cotton, and her face burned with the fiery darts shooting from Angela Carter's eyes. *God, a little help here would be good.* No words came.

Steven cleared his throat. "I'm sure Gracie will join us another time."

She nodded. "I'll see you on Monday, James." She turned to Angela. "Nice to see you again." Turning toward the door, she entered her classroom and quickly shut out the perfect little family scene in the hall.

She wanted nothing more than to run home and collapse into Mark's arms. But that wouldn't happen. Ever again.

How in the world would she survive the mammoth ache growing in her heart?

25

A week hadn't touched the knot of fear in her stomach. Gracie and her doggie shadow had managed an early morning run, a few loads of laundry, and cleaning the bathrooms that weren't in need of cleaning. Usual Saturday chores. But everything else was so far from normal.

In a few hours she'd have to face Steven again. Alone.

She checked the clock above the spotless white sink and sighed. Spotless had never described her kitchen when two sets of pint-sized hands and feet kept things looking lived-in. When tiny handprints and mud tracked in from a full day of summer play. She'd take that look any day.

Leaning back onto her white Corian countertops, she debated calling Beth or Leah. Beth would put on her cheerleader voice and try to psyche Gracie up for an evening of romance with Steven. A place she wanted to avoid.

She called Leah instead.

"I think I'm going to be sick." Gracie opened one honey oak cabinet after another, gathering ingredients.

"Hello to you too." Leah laughed into the phone. "All butter-flies and smiles about your big birthday party date tonight?"

"More like I want to avoid the whole thing."

To keep her mind occupied and her hands busy, Gracie bustled around the kitchen with the phone tucked between her shoulder and cheek, working on a peach cobbler. A gift for the Rollins family. Southern hospitality still reigned, even if she lived near Washington DC.

"Don't you dare. I think you need to decode what's going on

with Angela and Steven and go from there." Leah said. "Then give him the thoughtful gift you agonized over and let his gorgeous smile warm your toes."

Gracie groaned. Thinking about Steven's smile and searching blue eyes didn't help her rumbling insides. "What if he's still in love with his ex-wife? She's like a dark-headed Barbie doll with a law degree. I can't compete with that."

"You don't have to."

"I feel like I do." Gracie chopped soft, fuzzy peaches. Their smell settled her nerves a little, reminding her of Mom and home and all things sweet and safe. "I mean, it seems like I'm being swept into a relationship that's more like a tornado than the enjoyable companionship I'd hoped for."

"No man, not even a handsome FBI agent, will ever come close to what you had with Mark. You two were college sweethearts. You filled a room with honey just looking at each other."

Gracie's chest constricted and her eyes watered. "Leah, don't."

"You know I love you, but you need to hear this. God doesn't have you there anymore. And you can't compare now with then. Or yourself with another woman." Her best friend's words were soft and painful.

"Care to explain God again? Why He took my family and left me with this confusing mess? James is a joy and reminds me of my son. Steven has a pull that's…that's…" She struggled to find the right words. "Irresistible. Deep melancholy and electric at the same time. But I can't…I don't know what to do."

Leah's background noises changed from Saturday morning cartoons to her backyard full of bird sounds. "I don't have an answer for the whys. It'd be pat and bad theology to say God allowed your family to die so you could step into Steven's family and help them. God is far too complex for human reasoning like that." Leah's voice dropped lower. "It's what you're thinking though, isn't it? You're trying to figure it all out and line it up logically."

"Sometimes I hate that you know me so well." Gracie mixed the sugar and flour with shaking hands. This train of thought never failed to derail her composure. But no amount of Bible verses made sense of it. Maybe that was the point—trusting God when nothing added up and pain and joy were so clearly two sides of the same coin.

I just feel so helpless...

"I'm praying, Gracie. God is good and has a good plan, whether we understand it or not. That's where you anchor. Right now that plan includes a classroom full of kids who adore you like my William will next year and an FBI agent who's searching for something."

"What if I can't help him?"

"After all our years of friendship, I've earned the right to tell you this..."

Gracie gulped a swig of water to help swallow the lump in her throat and then folded the liquid and dry ingredients together in the bowl.

"Be who and where you are, Gracie. Free, when you rest in God. Alive. Loving. If He's doing something with you and Steven, relax and let it come. In God's time. Enjoy the journey."

"Enjoy." Gracie folded the peaches into the mixture and then slipped the glass pan into the oven. "That was my word for this year, my goal. Learning to enjoy God again, to enjoy life."

"You're doing it as well. Every time I listen to you talk about school. When you paint your watercolors, like the sunset you saw on your first date with Steven. And when you take your Bible out on the back porch and listen." Leah's voice drifted through the phone line and straight into Gracie's heart. "You're coming alive again, and it's a beautiful sight."

"You're good for my ego, you know."

"I'd like to think for your heart too."

"Yeah, well, maybe."

Jake nuzzled her thigh. Time for a snack before a quick shower and another round of closet gymnastics to find the right outfit for tonight.

"Gotta scoot, give Jake some treats, and get ready." Gracie

rubbed his soft warm fur. "Any parting words of wisdom to settle my stormy stomach?"

"How about my favorite paraphrase of C. S. Lewis?"

Leah was such a mom. Reading Narnia to her son and dispensing good theology in child-sized bites with every exciting scene. Just the size Gracie needed.

"Is Aslan safe? No, he's not safe...but he is good."

"Dad, are you coming with us?" James's excited voice called out from the foyer.

Steven finished wiping off the kitchen counter, dumping the last of the mess from their cake-baking extravaganza into the disposal. "No. Your grandma and grandpa are taking you early to help decorate. I'll be there later with Mrs. Lang."

Lack of sleep all week and the emotional turmoil from last Friday's dinner with Angela still weighed heavy. But spending time with James and his way of lighting up the room had made it a good day. After all, it was Steven's birthday. He deserved one day to forget the world's cares.

"Happy birthday, Daddy!" James hollered for about the tenth time that day. "I love you!" He ran in and opened his arms wide for a hug.

Steven picked up his son and held him a moment longer than usual. The sweet scent of childhood and the softness of James's hair, being wrapped in his strong little arms, brought a rush of memories. His little boy was fast becoming a miniature man, his heart still soft, undamaged by life...so far.

Angela's face on their wedding day flashed across Steven's mind. Followed close by the day she left him mingled with the images of her recent appearance back into his life. Her demand for time with James. Full custody. The threat couldn't be escaped, birthday or no birthday.

James pulled back and looked him in the eyes. "Daddy, are you okay?"

"Yes." Steven received another bear hug. "Thanks for making this the best birthday ever."

"I'm glad you're not working today." James had no idea how that comment cut to the core. "Do you really think Mrs. Lang will come over tomorrow and eat some of our cake?" No mention of Angela, as if meeting his mother had never happened.

Steven's thoughts swirled with training quotes about children's resiliency to stress. Maybe meeting Angela hadn't been as problematic as he feared it would be. Then again, James was so much like him it hurt. Bury it deep and smile.

Steven looked up at the sound of masculine throat-clearing. Dad and Sue grinned from the kitchen doorway just as they had earlier when James insisted they invite Gracie to join them after church. His son's motives were obvious. So were Dad and Sue's.

"I'll ask her, James. I know she enjoys spending time with you." Steven glanced at their lopsided chocolate cake and smiled. "And I think she'll also like the cake."

"We'd better get a move on if we're going to be any help setting up." Sue held out her hand to James.

"I love you, James." Steven mouthed a heartfelt *thank you* to his dad and stepmom.

"I love you too!"

Steven watched them leave, then took a long look in the foyer mirror, staring at his reflection. Clint and Sara must have been praying hard this week, because Steven's thoughts kept flying back to God and how to rid himself of the haunted look in his eyes. How to keep his son from falling under his ex-wife's spell, especially if Angela kept showing up at school and hounding him about time alone with James. Time Steven wasn't ready to give.

The grandfather clock in the living room chimed five times. If he was going to smooth things out with Gracie before the party, like he'd tried and failed to do all week at school, he'd better hustle.

He headed upstairs to get ready and took his usual five-minute shower and then slipped into jeans and a white button-up. He grabbed his key ring by the back door, then started the thirty-minute drive to Gracie's little brick house. The one with paintings that quoted Scripture. He shook his thoughts loose and turned on the radio for something to lighten his mood.

Some soft rock, even if it was on an oldies variety station, would do the trick. Windows down, tunes up, crooning to Dobie Gray's seventies hit *Drift Away* made the fall air feel like an endless summer night.

By the time he stood on Gracie's front porch with a bouquet of daisies and red and yellow carnations, he felt human again. Taking a beautiful date to his birthday party for the first time in years reminded him of Friday night football games in high school—teenaged hormones on alert and heart aching with dreams about forever.

He'd been married long enough to know what his teenaged hormones hadn't known, but he wasn't old enough yet to have forgotten. Not by a long shot.

Gracie opened the door wearing a fitted white blouse over a red-and-black plaid skirt. His mouth curled into a huge grin. She'd remembered his college colors. Or she and Sara Rollins had been talking. Maybe he read more into it than intended, but right now he didn't care.

"You look incredible. I'm glad you accepted my invitation." He stuck the flowers into her hands before he said something high schoolish and inane. Or drooled.

Gracie blushed.

He chuckled and watched her golden retriever nose his way out the front door. "Hey, Jake. Not gonna knock me down this time?" Steven rubbed the dog's fur.

"Thank you for the flowers. They're wonderful." Gracie stepped back and held the door open wide.

He followed her graceful walk down the hall with his eyes and then willed his feet to move forward. "I know I'm a little early." He closed the front door and sucked in a deep breath. "But

I'd hoped we'd have a few minutes to talk about what happened with Angela last week and clear the air between us."

Arranging the flowers into a crystal vase, Gracie nodded and pointed to a tall white breakfast bar chair. "You really don't have to explain anything, Steven."

He pulled the chair out and sat down. "But I want to. My partner will have my hide if I keep messing up dates with you. He and Sara think you're the best thing since sliced bread." He grimaced inwardly at the cliché. "I mean, they think you're an awesome teacher and…so do I. I'd like to continue building on the good time we had on our first date."

"Then why don't we save the heavier discussion for after the party?" Gracie put a hand over her stomach. "I'm nervous enough as it is, wondering who I'll be meeting and what you'll think of the gift I have for you."

A gift? He hadn't considered telling her not to buy anything, but there hadn't been many conversations between them. "I'm sure I'll love the gift, and you already know the Rollinses and my parents from school. No reason to be nervous there. They like you."

His smile didn't seem to assuage her fears.

"All righty then." She scurried to the den, stopping by the couch, and held out a large blue-and-white striped gift bag. "Would you like to open it now?"

He joined her in the den and sat on her overstuffed beige couch. Then he remembered a gentleman should remain standing in the presence of a lady. Too late.

She sat on the far side of the couch and extended the slightly quivering bag in his direction. He milked the moment for all it was worth, slowly taking the bag and carefully lifting out each piece of blue tissue paper surrounding a large, thin square.

"You're not being kind. Just open it already." She rolled her eyes.

It was hard not to laugh. This little interaction was far more fun than he'd expected. He bowed toward her. "As you wish."

She giggled.

Ripping through tissue paper taped on the large square, Steven held the old-fashioned vinyl record of greatest hits in his hands. The simple pearlized cover with a list of song titles like "Sweet Baby James" and "Something in the Way She Moves" grabbed his heart and didn't let go. "You remembered?"

"Even if you are too young to be a James Taylor fan, I thought you'd like the album."

Her smile stirred up more than gratitude in his chest. "You can tell a lot about a person from the gifts she gives." He held up the record but looked over the top of it, taking in every line of her beautiful oval face. "This says you're observant, thoughtful, and someone I want to know better."

She lowered her head and started picking up the pieces of tissue paper between them.

He stood, tucked the prized album under his arm, and extended his other hand. "We'd better head over to Clint's house. Don't want to miss the party."

Or let himself get carried away by haunting nostalgia driven by a longing more potent than fire. Any more time alone with Gracie and he'd be singing with his new JT album about not wanting to be lonely tonight.

Clint checked his watch for the fourth time in fifteen minutes. His living room had filled with balloons and little-kid laughter.

But no Steven.

Steven's parents, Michael and his perfect-ten date, and a few other squad members and their wives milled about eating Sara's amazing hors d'oeuvres. It wasn't like Steven to be late. Or Gracie.

Steven had called half an hour ago saying he and Gracie were going to take a short drive and listen to his birthday gift. Not the vinyl record, but Steven's CD of the same James Taylor hits. Gracie had scored big with that gift.

Clint smiled. Then he pulled back the front drapes and watched the driveway.

Sara slipped her arms around his waist. "They're all grown up, cowboy. And it's not like it's midnight and they're parked somewhere making out."

"That gives me an idea for tonight."

Sara poked him in the ribs and huffed at the ceiling.

A few minutes later, Steven pulled up in his spit-and-polished SUV and walked to the passenger side to retrieve Gracie. They shared a long look before he tucked her hand around his arm.

"Now if that doesn't make the fall air sizzle." Sara wiggled her eyebrows.

Praying must have done more than he and Sara had asked or expected.

Steven gave a knock, then entered.

Clint followed his almost skipping wife into the foyer to meet them. "Hey, you two. Glad you could make it."

Sara nudged him with her elbow. "So, how's the birthday boy?" She gave Steven a hug then turned to Gracie. "Welcome. I'm so glad you're here. Come on in and join the chaos."

Gracie extended a pie carrier. "Hope you don't mind that I made a peach cobbler for your family to enjoy later."

Sara took the dessert with an amused smile. "Thank you. Why don't you all follow Clint into the living room, and I'll store this away so no one devours it before dinner."

Clint's stomach rumbled. Gracie had scored points in his book too.

Steven stage-whispered into Gracie's ear. "See? They like you."

Her face blazed as she leaned into Steven's arm. Her eyes scanned the room, settling on Sara's favorite painting of a beach at sunset over the fireplace. Not his thing, but Gracie seemed to like it.

"Your home is beautiful, Clint." Her blush had faded, and her shoulders relaxed a little. Good sign.

"Thanks." Before Clint could ask about their little drive, Steven scooped James into his arms and made his way around the room with introductions and polite conversation, spending the most time with Andrew and Sue. The wink from father to son was not lost on Clint. Or Gracie either.

Only Michael's fidgeting as they talked shop about the Kensington case hinted at any less-than-calm emotions around the small group. The rookie was probably anxious to get on with the rest of his plans for the night.

Clint winced inside. He needed to stop reading into Michael's actions. Steven had been right. Michael was changing. Not singing in the choir yet, but he'd done almost a 180 from the playboy image he'd been touting when he first started working for the Bureau.

Soon the smells of steak and homemade rolls filled the house. As everyone took a seat in front of the place cards that James and Susannah had decorated with leaves and brown raffia, Clint stood at the head of the table to offer the blessing.

"Lord, we thank You for this night to celebrate with friends. We lift the Kensingtons to You and ask Your guidance in all the work of our hands that's never far from our minds." He peeked at his kids to be sure they were behaving. Susannah caught his gaze and smiled, then closed her eyes and bowed her head. He continued.

"But tonight, we pause to give thanks for great food, for Steven making it to thirty-six, and for all the good You still have in store for him and each one of us. Amen."

Sara's spicy blend of Caesar dressing and tons of salad veggies disappeared as fast as the shoptalk had when the kids all took their seats.

"So when are the roasting stories about my son going to start? You promised a good show tonight, Clint." Andrew Kessler's blue eyes held as much mischief as Steven's sometimes did.

Steven groaned. "Thanks a lot, Dad. Just wait till your birthday. Paybacks and all, you know."

"We could always start with Steven's storming into that factory basement to rescue the eight-year-old twins a few years back." Michael loved retelling the story he'd heard through office gossip.

Whoever said women were the only ones who told tons of tales hadn't been in the headquarters' break room during a decompression session.

Clint took over before Michael had the chance to give more details than young ears needed to hear. "That was a Superman moment if there ever was one, huh, Steven?"

His partner shook his head. "For the uninitiated, that little story has been inflated over the years. All I did was break up a blackjack game and miss a few punches before finding two adorable little girls with cornrows hiding in a back room."

"Breaking up an organized crime game room is more like it."

Clint shot Michael a look and nodded toward the children at the other end of the large dining room. "Like I said, it was one of Steven's more heroic moments."

"Not at all like his Quantico days, though." Michael was asking for a beating at the gym when they practiced takedowns next week.

Gracie's puzzled look at the other agents' laughter made Clint remember his manners. "Suffice it to say, Steven tried to sleep through some classes when our benevolent teachers thought he needed to pay more attention." Clint watched Steven study his almost empty plate. "One time, we all had to do laps because Steven's snoring was loud enough to make our profiling instructor hit the roof. A member of our class hated running so much that he targeted Steven for a little righteous indignation."

"To the tune of trying to make my face meet the mud every time we passed Agent Lechter." Steven smirked. "He got me once. Then I used some of Clint's fancy Texas sidesteps, and the poor guy met more mud than the Amazon River in the rainy season."

Gracie put her napkin up to her mouth to catch the sweet tea that almost escaped. "You didn't?"

"Sure enough did." Steven nudged her with his shoulder and then draped a protective arm around her chair.

Interesting.

Soon after, Clint escaped the tall tales going around about their rookie years. He reappeared from the kitchen, followed by three little ones carrying a cake glowing bright with mostly black candles. Sara had made him add a few red ones for Steven's University of Louisville.

The room exploded with a rendition of "Happy Birthday" that could have been rivaled only by a circus parade.

Clint and Sara dispensed cake and ice cream as Andrew peppered the discourse with tales of Steven and his sister's childhood mischief and antics. Too bad Hanna's work kept her in Kentucky. She'd have had some roof-raising anecdotes. But James added his own funny stories about his dad, and the children's laughter blended with the adults'.

No one mentioned Angela. FBI compartmentalizing at its finest. It was like that period of his partner's life had never existed. But it had. And it was still affecting life today. More than Steven wanted to admit.

It wasn't the time or place, but Clint wanted to know more about Steven's budding romance and how he planned to balance it with the upcoming custody battle that Angela had promised.

Steven and Gracie's close contact throughout the rest of the evening made Clint glad on one hand. On the other, a new romance might distract Steven from his work when the Kensington case was so close to breaking.

It might even keep him running from God.

Clint's stomach tightened. His wife may have had the intuition of an old-time biblical prophet, but he had his share of gut-level hunches. And one kept buzzing to the surface.

No doubt about it. Dangerous waters lay ahead.

26

I want to see my son, Gordon."
In the last two and a half weeks, Charlotte had become more insufferable than Sir Kensington's brat. Gordon closed the tiny kitchen curtain, blocking out the gray Monday skies. The rented flat, eighty kilometers outside of Alexandria, served to keep them hidden and sheltered. Little more than that.

"I will not go to prison because you can't stand a holiday from Stewart."

She stepped closer. "How long, Gordon? We have new passports, tickets, and…" Charlotte ran her hand through her now cropped reddish hair. "I look like nothing Stew would recognize. I can't bear this much longer, and why should I? Just so you can torment the ambassador? You've done enough. Let's go home for good. Today."

"No." He glared at his sister with steel resolve. "I will finish what that fool started. He has other children. I won't ever have another brother."

The mention of Harry sent Charlotte into another crying jag.

Gordon let her run into the postage stamp-sized bedroom and have her fill of tears. He threw back the last swallow of another bitter. What he wouldn't give to be home in his pub, dossing about with people who spoke the Queen's English.

Not the American tourist trash he'd succumbed to once again.

He was as ready as his sister to return to Piccadilly Circus, but the time of departure had yet to arrive.

Soon. Three weeks from tomorrow. October seventeenth.

A slamming door set his senses on alert. Charlotte knew better than to leave in the daylight, but starting another bitter took precedence over chasing his stupid sister out of the nearby park. He'd fetch her in a few minutes.

Why she couldn't wait two more days blustered him. Wednesday night they'd grab Stew at his nanny's, and Gordon would put the two of them onto a transport bound for Heathrow. Her American bloke of a husband could rot.

That blighter and his computer girlfriends weren't Gordon's concern. Except that Jimmy could help the coppers if he'd kept his fool ears open. But he hadn't yet. Never even knew they'd been near the house. As observant as the FBI rookies had been during the wee hours of the morning.

Gordon grabbed his rental keys in a huff and drove on the wrong side of the road to the little park Charlotte had found as an escape in the past few days. He'd likely find her perched on a swing, singing some incessant nursery song.

The park came into view. But no Charlotte.

"Where are you, dear sister?"

He remembered her tear-drenched words about leaving today. Surely not. He pointed his tan family wagon toward Alexandria.

Once he throttled her for risking everything just to leave the US early, he'd have to give her a cheers for stuffing her money and trying to make a go of it on her own. As long as she didn't get caught.

Midday was no time for evading the FBI.

She couldn't have much more than a quarter hour on him, and only if she'd found a taxi as soon as she left the flat. She may have rung one before slamming the door. His baby sister had proved not to be so daft. A true Landridge, after all.

Harry would have been proud.

Gordon drove around the two federal cars outside of Charlotte's tiny flat, cursing all the way to their little subdivision park, the one Stewart used to prattle on about. Her wally of a husband must have called the coppers in as soon as Charlotte set foot in the door.

He parked on the outskirts of the little park and disappeared into a tangle of trees where he had a good sight line to her house. Things had been ghostly when he'd driven past earlier, but he couldn't risk making that trek again. He needed his rental a few more days. Then again, he might trade it in today in case some FBI bloke noted his tag.

Charlotte's new red bob came into view, walking out of her front door. Flanked by two suits. Gordon guessed the well-over-six-foot bloke was the Texan who Charlotte spoke of fondly. The one who had shown her kindness after the Kensingtons found out about Olivia's demise.

Wonder what his sister thought now.

Gordon killed every urge to start shooting and race his sister and nephew to safety. He was too far in to stop now. The plan had to be completed. Then he would deal with Charlotte and Stew, dead FBI agents or not.

He packed up his gear and left the little park, heading west. He would ditch this rental near Dulles Airport at a place he'd spotted on his last visit.

"Be loyal to me, Charlotte." If she fouled his October plans, he'd have to disappear with unfinished business. How that thought lit a fire through him.

No loose ends. Not this time.

He swapped the tan wagon for another nondescript rental. The promise of a better flat and a pint or two to relax tonight doused his flames.

If his sister kept her gob shut, she would use her brain and play dumb. No doubt she'd lost track of his few secrets she might have remembered. She knew nothing specific of his intentions for Sir Kensington's other child. And probably less than the FBI had already uncovered about him. Which, thanks to a few loyal blokes in SIS, amounted to precious little. All his sister thought of was Stew, anyway.

On his drive back to Alexandria, Gordon tried to conjure a way to follow her progress through the American court system. No doubt she'd be out on bail in less than a bit. Just to be safe, he'd scour their flat clean, and then pay a visit to an American bloke who might be of some use for the million he'd already paid him.

One Yank that would ensure his last bit of business in the US went on as planned.

The late evening storm captured Tom's attention.

Better than "Monday Night Football." He clicked off the television. With his brandy, he toasted Caesar. The tabby had taken to hiding under the bed during storms. Maybe he should do the same. Because with every flash of lightning, childhood fears mixed with overanxious thoughts of prison bars and million-dollar routing numbers.

Disappearing was his only option, thanks to Gracie.

A knock on the door kicked his heart up to his Adam's apple. So not a good feeling.

Who was there? Visions of his mother came to mind. "Sorry, Mother. I'll get the door."

"Not your mum, I think."

Tom startled at the well-built, deep-voiced Brit who stood on his porch. "No, but I recognize the voice."

"A million dollars does wonders for the senses, eh?" The man strode into the townhome like he owned it.

Shutting the door, Tom motioned to the living room couch. "Care to join me for a brandy? Or do you prefer, what do you call it? A bitter?"

"With the chill off, if you have it." The man sat at the small dining room table and leaned back in the expensive Chippendale chair.

The man's dark tan and muscled arms gave Tom pause. This was a guy who could snap his neck if the mood struck. Tom swallowed back the caustic comments on the tip of his tongue. "Sorry. We Americans keep our beer cold."

"It'll do."

Tom poured himself a shot of dark amber liquid and guzzled it in the kitchen before bringing out a tall glass and the beer to his guest. "Care to share a name with me, or is this all CIA secretive?"

"You can call me Joe. That's a name I've never used on any documents." Joe drank his bitter from the bottle. "Due to unforeseen circumstances, we need to move our target date ahead. Send me the new codes and security schedule on October tenth. I'll pay a visit on the eleventh, and if all goes well, your remaining wad will hit the Swiss bank by the fourteenth."

Two and a half weeks. Tom nodded. Plenty of time to finalize his new living arrangements and book tickets across the big blue ocean. He'd always dreamed of a European vacation. Maybe even some plastic surgery. Men were gaining on their female counterparts in the realm of surgery for vanity—or, in his case, for safety. He couldn't hide quite as well as this mystery man at his dining room table. But taking care of one loose end might wrap it all up nicely.

"One question. How good of a shot are you?"

Joe studied him a full minute before responding. "Marksman. Why? Want to pay me a million for a quick hit on a first-grade teacher's pet?"

"No. Just a first-grade teacher."

Joe whistled. "You Americans and your thwarted love lives. So soap opera. Can't you simply walk away from the lass and find another? Or has the alimony got you in a dither?"

"Nothing like that." Tom drained his last shot and stood, grabbing the back of his chair to steady himself. The wooziness had caught up to him quicker than usual.

"Ah, now it comes to me. Your Gracie problem. Pretty bird, she is. Too bad for her FBI bloke if I agree to this new twist."

"How do you do that? I mean, your piecing together my past

was bad enough. But how do you know what's going on with Gracie and Kessler?"

"To say my life is now entwined with theirs is a gross understatement."

Tom didn't want to decipher the pensive Brit's comments. The less he knew, the less likely this man would remember him past October. Better to forge ahead and be done with the entire mess. Freedom. Greek beaches. Paris romances. Dreams finally becoming reality. Without the threat of Gracie uncovering some speck of truth and destroying it all. Dead men, or women, tell no tales.

If all went according to plan, live Brits wouldn't either. Especially ones who had no proof but Gracie's stupid sketch. The one that would rate the trash can when her great PI lost his retainer due to a client's untimely death.

Tom gripped the back of his chair and looked into the Brit's green eyes. "I'd be more than happy to call us even financially if you'd use two bullets and help me out of my situation."

"Freedom's worth two million to you, is it now?" Joe's face erupted into a Cheshire grin.

Tom swallowed hard. "Yes."

Hopefully Joe's business at Hope Ridge would drive him so deep no one would ever find him. After all, killing a federal agent ranked higher on America's Most Wanted than a drunk driving accident years ago.

Joe nodded and drained his beer. "Cheers to you. We'll call it even after all is complete October eleventh." The man stood and left without another word, closing the door behind him.

Good riddance. Tom threw his empty bottle in the trash and set the glasses in the dishwasher. Time to pack and make a list of things to do before he bid the United States a fond farewell. Forever.

Less than three weeks. Freedom had never tasted so good.

27

S teven flipped thin strips of beef in the skillet while Gracie sat munching carrot sticks with dip at his breakfast bar, talking about school.

His mind kept slipping back to the case. Almost two weeks, and their amazing break in the Kensington investigation had stopped cold. Charlotte Brown's dual citizenship added more frustrating threads to untangle, and her house arrest as a precautionary measure left more work for Steven's team, which had fewer agents working all the angles of information she'd supplied.

He doubted her truth-telling ability. She was a staunch and proper Brit to the core, and he'd never seen more loyal blood. Not even he and Clint could drag additional information from her. She had her son, and for her, that was all that mattered.

Not Olivia's death. Not Sir Walter's future, especially since the older man didn't even recall the name Landridge. Certainly not Steven's investigation and attempts to put her only other living relative behind bars for life.

Steven added green and yellow peppers to the strips of sizzling steak, trying to push work aside and enjoy a Friday night off at home. James was spending the night at his grandparents'.

Gracie's amused look made him laugh out loud. "What did you think I was fixing for dinner, peanut butter sandwiches?" He set out sour cream, cheese, and salsa, then put the tortillas in a terra-cotta serving dish to keep them warm.

"Can't I help just a little?"

"No. You sit there looking beautiful. Dinner will be served

momentarily." He slipped the steak into another warming dish and set the table.

Minutes later, he held out a high-backed and seldom-used formal dining room chair and waited for Gracie to settle. He flipped the cloth napkin and rested it in her lap with a dignified bow.

She covered her grin with her hand. "This is too much, even for you."

Steven looked over what she had called her cream-colored tunic sweater and long moleskin skirt. "From where I stand, you deserve every bit of it."

She blushed.

They'd covered a lot of ground in the two weeks since his birthday. Getting-to-know-each-other e-mails, more pleasant conversations at school, and no ex-wife trouble had helped. He'd even begun to rib her a little.

After making sure the soft jazz music was good to go, Steven served the Caesar salads. It felt great to relax. To forget the world for one night and enjoy the company of a beautiful woman, whom his son and parents adored.

"This is wonderful." She dabbed the corners of her mouth. "Is this Sara's recipe, or did she and Clint sneak all this ready made into your fridge?"

"I think I've been insulted."

"Not exactly."

He was thankful she'd only bowed her head for a quick moment before starting her salad. He still wondered if he should have tried to pray for her sake. But he nudged the serving dish closer to her and decided to take the plunge into deeper conversation.

"How do you let go of what happened to your family?" He hadn't expected the grief that flashed across her face. He wished for a way to retract the abrupt question. "I'm sorry. I didn't mean to hurt you. I shouldn't have asked."

"No. You didn't hurt me. It's just that I've been wondering

about it too. Wondering if I'll ever know who killed my family. Justin had high hopes for the sketch I did back in August. But he's been delayed and hasn't gotten much feedback from the colleges he's contacted in Atlanta."

Steven piled sizzling steak, veggies, salsa, and sour cream onto his tortilla. "Isn't he making a trip down there in a few weeks?"

"Yes. I'm going home for Thanksgiving, but Justin thinks he'll have some information for me well before then. Says the personal touch draws lots of leads."

Steven doubted it but kept that thought to himself. His PI buddy was doing all he knew to do. Maybe Steven would ask his dad and Clint to be praying more specifically for Gracie's investigation. What could it hurt?

She placed smaller servings onto her plate and added a little bit of shredded cheese. "Since the last time I talked to Justin, I've been rereading my journals. Praying about whether to keep searching or to let it go. But I can't stop now." She fingered the locket that hung around her neck.

"Pictures of your children?"

She glanced down at the locket. Her lips smiled, and her eyes misted. Maybe he should stick with surface talk about their jobs and leave the heavy stuff for wiser people. People like Clint.

"Yes, these are Elizabeth and Joshua's birth pictures." She opened the delicate locket and held it out to him.

He leaned in for a closer look. The tiny pictures reminded him of James's birth. All red and screaming. Then Angela had disappeared a few weeks later, leaving a note about her professor and wishing Steven a nice life.

"I'm struggling to accept that there's so much I may never understand this side of heaven," she said. "I ask the questions anyway, and I let God have it every once in a while. He can handle it. I want to believe I don't need the answers, that God is enough. That He has good in store, like my best friend tells me."

"Does it work?" Snapshots of missing children and those

who would never return home slammed against his skull. This conversation had landed too close to his struggles, his questions about life's mysteries.

Come Monday, he'd talk this out with his partner. Clint and Sara must be at home praying something fierce.

For now, Steven could only attack his steak fajita.

Gracie took a deep breath. "I believe despite what I feel sometimes. Jesus came so that we might have life. He never promised a long or easy life, but He promised us Himself and eternity in a perfect place with no tears or sadness."

Her chin quivered, but her eyes blazed. "I don't understand why Mark and our children died. I don't understand why God didn't take me too. But I choose to believe God has a purpose. I know my family is in His arms. I find great comfort in that."

Steven clenched his jaw. Gracie was talking about the family she loved and lost and, as natural as breathing, telling him about Jesus. How could he ever measure up to that? Guilt gnawed at the steak in his gut.

At least she hadn't offered simple Sunday school answers. She lived what she said. Compassion showed in her eyes and in her touch as she placed her hand on his arm.

"Peace comes from knowing God, not from having answers to every question. The answer is faith. Trusting Him."

"My partner thinks forgiveness is what turns life all rosy."

Gracie cut her fajita and chewed a small bite. "Well, I can't speak to that one. In fact, I'd say that's my Achilles' heel. I can't imagine forgiving the man who stole my family from me. Not until after he rots in jail. If then."

"Think you'll be able to move past it if you don't find the guy?" He appreciated that she'd admitted to an imperfect walk with God. Maybe there was hope for him yet.

"I'm not willing to cross that bridge yet. Not until I've exhausted all possibilities." She studied his face. "For right now, I'm working on trusting God to get me through today. The rest will have to wait."

She leaned forward and met him with a piercing look. "What about you? From what Clint tells me, it sounds like you and God parted ways about six years ago. Right after Angela left."

Steven took a long drink of tea. Sweet stuff that Sue had made special for him. And for Gracie. "Touché. I kinda figured you wanted to know more about Angela than you let on."

He thought of Angela and all their fights about religion. Nothing like this time with Gracie. Not even close. Most of his God-talk had met with belligerence, Angela being loose lipped under the influence of alcohol.

"Angela and I argued about everything. But about God, more than anything else."

Gracie's expression didn't waver as she finished her fajita and waited for him to continue. Did she already know he'd walked in her Christian shoes before? He'd done the talk but had gotten burned too much to stick with the walk.

"Are you still in love with her?"

Ouch. Gracie, like Clint, didn't mince words. Or skirt around the tough stuff.

"I did love Angela. I still struggle with being attracted to her. Guess you picked up on that."

"We react with powerful emotions toward those people we feel most strongly about."

Good answer. True. Not the end of the story, though. "I don't want a future with Angela. Once I'm given full custody, she's out of my life."

Gracie cocked her head to the side. "Maybe Clint is right about forgiveness. Seems to me you won't be completely free of your ex-wife until you forgive her. Your body language screams that truth."

Steven looked down at his clenched fists and folded arms. It wasn't forgiveness or the lack of it that had him riled. It was the thought of the upcoming custody battle and what would happen if it didn't get Angela out of his life for good.

What if she had never really stopped drinking? Sharing joint custody and leaving his son in a potentially dangerous environment wouldn't ever happen. But what if she was clean? She had a right to know her son. According to her, James was the only child she would ever have.

Steven's heart felt gripped in a vise. He didn't understand the strange feelings stirring around inside.

Snippets of Clint's booming voice thundered in his ears. Daggered words about pride and how Steven wouldn't be able to make up for the past or be free of it without forgiveness.

"Steven?" Gracie waved a hand in front of his face. "I think you have a visitor at your front door."

He shook his head. "Sorry. I got lost for a minute."

She smiled. "I'll start clearing dishes, and you can go check to see if you need the latest magazine subscription some poor high school kid is trying to sell."

Steven walked to the front door. A salesman on a Friday night? He opened the heavy wooden door. Worse than a salesman. "Angela. What brings you here this evening?"

She extended a dish and smiled. "A peace offering. Derby pie. I hope it's still your favorite." She stepped forward and raised her eyebrow when he blocked the doorway.

"Where's your husband?"

She took a deep breath. "After our dinner a few weeks ago, I went home and had a long talk with Marcus. He agrees that you and I should try to work out our differences. In fact, he'd like to come with me next time work slows down and I'm here for a visit. He'd like to meet you and James."

So that was why she disappeared in between her bomb-dropping missions. She was as busy with her career as he was with his. That information would serve him well in court. Steven swallowed the next set of words that leaped to his mind. Did he really want to meet the man Angela had slept with before and after bearing his son?

Only a paternity test and a newborn had kept Steven from ripping good ole Marcus's head from his body six years ago when he'd first found out about his wife's affair. That feeling hadn't lessened much since then. Seeing the jerk wouldn't help matters.

Gracie laid a hand on his shoulder and then quickly retracted it when she saw Angela in the doorway.

Angela stiffened her back and pasted on an if-looks-could-kill smile. "Well, well. My son's favorite teacher looks like she's fast becoming my husband's favorite date too."

"It's none of your business. We're not married anymore, Angela."

"But we were." Her long fingers tightened on the pie plate she held as she focused on Gracie. "Watch yourself, Mrs. Lang. He looks like a perfect Romeo now and talks a good game until he gets you between the sheets. But his mistress will always be the FBI." She raked her eyes over Gracie. "And if I couldn't keep him interested, I doubt that you can."

Gracie bowed her head and tightened her lips.

Steven wanted to throttle Angela. He may have messed her over and broken her heart, but Gracie didn't deserve those caustic comments.

"Angela, it's past time for you to go. Keep your peace offering." He touched Gracie's arm but kept his eyes on Angela's face. "You didn't stick around long enough to work things out years ago. I doubt you will this time. But if you do see Gracie again, I expect you to behave like an adult. One with a little common decency and courtesy."

"Oh, you'll both see me again." Angela flipped her black hair over her shoulder. "November eighth. In court, if not before. I'm serious about gaining custody of my son. Before I lose him to some *elementary teacher*." She turned and stalked down the front walk toward her Mercedes.

Steven closed the door and drew Gracie into his arms. This was not the way he'd imagined holding her for the first time. "I'm so sorry."

She put a hand to his chest and pulled back. "That wasn't your fault. She's obviously afraid James would rather spend time with me than her, and she's handling it the only way she knows how." Gracie's shaking hands belied her calm words.

"She was wrong to attack you. You're beautiful inside and out and an excellent teacher who makes a difference in children's lives. That matters." He led her into the den to sit on the leather couch. "I hope this doesn't scare you away."

"No. But maybe we should go a little slower. Wait until after the custody hearing to have another date at your house."

He'd waited years for a woman he felt as comfortable around as Gracie, and he wasn't about to lose the ground they'd gained tonight. "Why don't we double with Clint and Sara? Or your friend Leah and her husband?"

"What if I pray about it and let you know?" She smiled, but a hint of fear showed in her pretty hazel eyes.

Steven nodded. If he could keep the frustrating Kensington case from dividing his mind and get the stupid custody hearing over with, surely Gracie would see he was worth her time.

Far more than Angela ever had.

Then again, maybe he was better off alone. But that was what he'd done for the last five years, and it hadn't worked

Maybe Clint and Gracie were right. It was past time for a real change. He just didn't know where to start. Or how.

28

October's morning crispness forced Gracie's tired eyes open as she ran her standard three miles.

But not even Jake's steady panting beside her or Wednesday's school lessons kept her mind from wandering back to her last conversation with Steven. It had been another tense phone call about his being busy with work and not picking James up this week. Either Steven's case was gathering steam toward a conviction, or they'd gotten too honest last Friday and backpedaling had become the order of the day.

Her pocketed cell phone buzzed. *Who in the world?*

"Gracie, are you okay?" Beth's panicked voice flew through the phone lines.

She slowed to a cooldown pace and looked around her sleepy neighborhood, still dark with tons of eerie shadows. The question made goose bumps crawl over her skin.

She laughed it off. "I'm almost home from jogging. No broken body parts or stalkers lurking, so I think I'm okay." She looked at her sports watch. "But you're up way before the workaholics leave for the office. California time it's two in the morning. What's up with that?"

Silence.

"Beth?"

Then sniffles. "I just couldn't get back to sleep. I kept seeing you in my dreams."

"And that's such an awful thing?" Gracie unlocked her front door and released Jake's leash. She needed a quick shower, or she'd never make it to work on time. That'd give her vice principal ample ammunition for caustic remarks. Something he'd been doing more often lately.

"I'm serious. I'm worried about you. Seeing you tumble down a hill in the Jeep I bought for you doesn't make for a good night."

"Sorry, Beth."

"Will you stay home from work today?"

She moved to the kitchen and took a long drink of water, considering her sister's tearful request. They'd grown close again, but Beth and tears still ranked up there as one of life's paradoxes. "I can't. It's too late to call in a substitute, and I have Secret Service company to entertain."

"Will you call Steven and ask him to pick you up on his way with James?"

"No."

Beth blew her nose. Not a great sound amplified over phone lines. "Don't tell me you're ditching him because he's not a perfect Christian like Mark."

"Mark wasn't perfect and neither am I, Beth. We've covered this. Can't we let it alone?" Turning thirty hadn't made Beth any less like a playground bully when she didn't get her way.

"Why won't you call him then?"

Gracie thought of Steven in his tailored suits, with the little-boy grin that made butterflies multiply in her belly. His love for James. All the FBI stories she'd heard on his birthday and since then made him seem like a living superhero. Why wouldn't she call?

She put a hand to her mouth. "Fear."

"Of what? That he's too good to be true?"

Good question. "I'm not sure. Fear of the future? Not wanting to get my heart broken because some cute guy acts as if he likes me sometimes and then other times not?" Gracie headed upstairs. "I'm too old to play the dating game. Besides, I have other issues that require my attention. School, for one."

"And your investigation."

"Yes."

"I'll fly out today if you'll call in sick and come pick me up at the airport."

"Beth, go back to sleep. I'll be fine. And you can save your plane ticket for Thanksgiving. I'd love to see you and your family then."

Her baby sister sighed long and loud. Their mom would have laughed at Beth's drama queen act.

Within an hour, Gracie was leaning against her classroom windows admiring the reds and yellows of autumn leaves that swirled in the cool mid-October breeze. In the fall, Hope Ridge's elegant brick buildings and white columns dressed to impress in the bright sunlight.

She couldn't have ordered a more perfect day. Except for Beth's phone call worries. And the whole situation with Steven. Gracie rubbed her arms, chilled despite her coral sweater and long woolen skirt.

Thomas Perkins opened her classroom door and startled when he saw her. "At work early this morning, Mrs. Lang?"

He wasn't in his traditional black suit. His blue jeans and green button-up looked as out of place as the carefree look he'd worn before he noticed her.

"I had a few things to do before school begins." She slipped her journal notebook into her leather satchel. "And you? You're looking touristy today."

His jaw muscles clenched. "I had some menial work to attend to." He checked his watch, a new Rolex if Gracie guessed right. "Best get ready for school now. Like you. Good day."

He closed the door, disrupting wall posters with hurried ripples of air.

"How weird." Gracie shut down her overactive imagination and turned her attention to the room setup for the day.

An hour later children began their clockwork arrivals, and the over-the-workweek hump passed in a blur of glue and paint, giggles and requests for help.

They'd begun a unit study on the classic children's book *The*

Story About Ping. Duck-themed math equations, vocabulary words written on construction paper eggs, and beautiful pictures of bird drawings filled their cubbies.

"Will you read the story again, please?" Akemi took Gracie's hand and tugged her toward the middle of the classroom where book center beanbags lay scattered. The other children were busy in various other activity centers or the art table.

James flopped a beanbag chair between him and Victoria. "That's for you, Mrs. Lang." His smile mirrored his handsome father's.

Akemi sat in Gracie's lap and handed her the storybook.

"Where does this Ping live?" Tori asked.

"In China." Akemi held her head up proudly. "Where I was born."

"Very good, Akemi. Who'd like to get the globe so we can find China?"

Tori hopped up and walked across the room to retrieve the requested item.

Maria kept her watchful eyes trained on Victoria's every movement. It had become second nature to have the two agents always in the room. But every once in a while, Gracie had noticed their listening to her as she read and smiling at her interactions with the children.

It warmed her insides to know she'd earned their respect.

"I can walk like the little duck in the story." James tucked his hands under his arms and waddled around, waiting for Tori and Akemi to find China on the globe. Gracie laughed. Once the girls had found the country, everyone settled back down to finish the story.

"Would you three like to make a duck puppet? We can make the first ones, then you can help me show the others." The three children rushed to the art table and began to remove scissors, pens, and the basket of yarn, feathers, and other assorted supplies.

Gracie stood and stretched before joining the children.

A deafening noise thundered through the room. Glass

shards exploded from the windows. Akemi screamed.

James tried to tackle Victoria. Agent Reynolds ran in front of Gracie, blocking her view. When she tried to locate all of her students and direct them toward the door, Victoria was gone.

Gracie ran toward Akemi and James, who were standing like statues in the middle of the room.

Another explosion.

Everything in Gracie's sight went white.

Then black.

"Two shots fired. Teacher. Two students down." Maria screamed into her body mic as she ran through the empty halls.

Agent Reynolds barked clipped syllables into his mic behind her. "No visual, moving to southwest escape route."

Maria's heart felt as if it would explode through her chest.

Victoria's nails dug into her neck.

Curious teachers down the hall stuck their heads out of classroom doors.

"Lock it down!" Maria yelled. Black suits flew past her as classroom locks echoed over the linoleum.

Over the din of Secret Service orders and frightened children, Maria fixated on her target. She pushed her body harder and sprinted faster toward the rehearsed escape route.

Flinging open the heavy metal door, she blinked against the blinding sunlight.

She charged past the gymnasium into the side parking lot and stopped at the waiting car.

Agent Reynolds started the Grand Marquis as she secured a whimpering Tori in the backseat beside her. Radio static filled the car as they sped off Hope Ridge grounds.

"My friends." Tori gulped in air. "Akemi had blood."

Maria pulled the little girl's shaking shoulders into her chest. Their heartbeats and breathing hammered over the busy radio and her partner's broken sentences.

"What about Mrs. Lang?" Tori's lungs heaved. The little girl's eyes were wide with fear, and her hands trembled as she clutched the silver bracelet on her wrist. "Olivia gave this to me. I want my Livvie!"

"Shhh, honey. I've got you." She wiped Tori's tears and held back her own.

This had to be over soon.

29

"Where is my son?"

Steven ignored his conscience. He didn't care that the young woman at Alexandria Community's ER counter looked terrified. Fear drove him. "My son, James Kessler, is here. I want to see him. *Now*." He spoke in sharp bursts as he gripped the tall white countertop that partially shielded the receptionist. "Hope Ridge. A shooting in the classroom. They told me he's here."

The woman fluttered through files and phone calls to answer his demand. Phone still in hand, she pointed to the door behind her. "He's in exam room three, but…"

They could call security for all he cared. He slammed the door open and stormed down the hall. No one stopped him. No one would dare.

"James." Steven's breath stopped in his throat. His son's blood covered the bedsheet.

A short man in a white coat and scrubs turned to face him. "Who are you?"

Steven flipped open his credentials before thinking, his eyes fixed on the small form on the bed. The blood smear on James's cheek about did him in. "That's my son. What are you doing to him?"

A soft moan lit a fire under his legs, and he moved to James's side.

"Daddy?"

"I'm here, James." He stroked a tiny, limp arm.

"Your son sustained a few minor injuries—a number of bumps and bruises, seven hairline stitches."

"The glass, Daddy. Glass was everywhere." James tried to sit up, but Steven eased him back down. "Akemi kept screaming, and there was blood all over her face…" Tears cut off his words.

Steven touched James's straight brown hair, avoiding the Frankenstein threads. "I'll make sure Akemi is okay after we get you taken care of. It'll be all right."

"Tori disappeared."

The words sucker punched him. Charlotte's brother had tried to kill Victoria and wounded James instead? Rage like he'd never felt ripped through Steven's veins.

"Is Mrs. Lang okay?"

Steven blinked. What had happened to Gracie?

The doctor scribbled notes on his clipboard and rechecked James's chest and arms. "Your son will need to rest. Keep the stitches clean and bandaged." He wiped the remaining blood away and taped gauze in place. Then he pointed behind Steven. "The nurse will make sure you have full instructions in the discharge papers. She'll be in shortly." He scurried out of the door and closed it behind him.

Steven felt torn between comforting James and finding out what had happened to Gracie. And Susannah. He felt sure Maria had done her job and moved Victoria to safety, but he needed to know whether or not Hope Ridge security had taken down the shooter. Better for Gordon Landridge, or his hired gun, if they took him out instead of into custody.

"Daddy. I heard her praying, after the noise. There were two big cracks. Like thunder." His body started to shake as his eyes watered. .

Stroking his son's hair, Steven exhaled as adrenaline rushed through his body. "You're safe now, James. Rest. I'll find out how everyone's doing." He pulled out his cell phone and dialed Hope Ridge. "I'm going to find out about Gracie and Susannah." And Gordon.

The main line rang with a busy signal. He hung up and tried again. Three times. Finally, he got through to the headmistress.

"Mrs. Hall, I understand that you can't give out medical information to nonfamily members; I just want to know if Gracie is alive." Steven paced at James's bedside. "Yes. Okay. Her parents. Thank you."

Steven's phone beeped before he'd disconnected from the headmistress. Being FBI hadn't gained him any extra access there. "Kessler."

"James okay?" His partner's voice needed no introduction.

"Stitches. Bruises. We'll talk to the trauma counselor soon too." Steven ran a hand through his sweaty hair. "Susannah?"

"Lots of tears, but nothing else. She and most of the class were checked out by the school doctor and released. Sara's staying home with her now." Honking horns blared through the phone. "I'm on my way back to the office. You stay with James. The ERT is crawling over the school. Got a gun. Casings. No shooter."

Steven kicked the wall.

"Daddy?"

"Sorry, James." He turned away from his son's bed. "What about Gracie? No one will release info except to next of kin. I'm guessing she's alive or someone would have given that away at first question."

"Yep. From what I heard at the school, she's giving the hospital docs a run for their money. She fought the paramedics too. Wanted to make sure all her kids were safe."

Gracie was alive but hurt. He had to find out more soon.

"Nothing like being on-site for updates." Steven turned back to his son. "What about Akemi? James said she was hurt."

"I'll check with her parents and get back to you when I come up for air."

"I'll be in as soon as Dad gets here."

"Go see Gracie. She's at Alexandria Community. I'll cover here 'til you get back."

That would wait till James was on his way home. Steven punched his dad's number.

"You're both okay, then?" His dad let out a long breath and

mumbled to Sue. "We're almost to the hospital now, five minutes tops. We'll get James home and settled in bed in a jiffy so you can go catch this guy."

"Thanks."

"You'll get him, Steven. I know you."

Steven didn't know anymore. Too many times in the last few months he'd been too late to do much good. Killed one perp. Wanted to kill another. Especially if he'd hurt Gracie as bad as Steven feared. But he hadn't stopped the man from taking a child's life. Or hurting James.

"Are you going to call Angela?" his dad asked.

The question sucked the air out of the room. "I hadn't thought about it." Steven didn't want to face the tongue-lashing she'd unload, blaming him for James getting hurt. Never mind the guy who pulled the trigger.

"How about I call her when we get home? She can come see James at the house."

"That works. Thanks, Dad." Steven flipped the phone shut and checked his watch. He needed to find out about Gracie and get back to his desk. Follow up with forensics and then see about taking down this Brit before he fled the country.

Unless he wasn't going anywhere. He'd call Agent David Adams on his way back to headquarters. "You doing okay, James?"

"My head hurts. The doctor said I'd be sore for a good while."

Steven sat next to the bed. "I'm sorry I wasn't here faster."

"One of the school nurses stayed with me some, and I was brave."

"I'm proud of you. Really proud."

"Mr. Kessler, I have your son's discharge paperwork right here." The middle-aged nurse entered the room and shut the door without making eye contact. Then she looked up. "Oh. My. You're the one…" She clamped her mouth shut.

"One what?" Steven towered over her as he took the clipboard and started signing his name everywhere. He returned the papers.

"The one they were talking about out there." She jerked her thumb toward the door.

"Where can I find out about my son's teacher? She was brought in with James." He gave James a soft squeeze on his shoulder. "She's a family friend."

"A girlfriend?" The nurse hugged the clipboard to her chest. Juicy gossip trumped disappointment fast.

"Yes."

James smiled.

"Last I heard, she was in surgery. Her parents are flying in today."

Finally, some answers. Nothing like in-person influence to get the information he needed.

The nurse handed Steven a stack of papers. "Here are your discharge instructions. Pain meds script. Someone from insurance will be in, and then you'll be discharged right after that. Do you have any questions?"

"No. Thank you."

The nurse checked James's bandages and left without another word.

A few minutes later, the door opened again. "James. Steven. Thank God you're both okay." Sue hugged Steven and gripped James's arm. Then she bent down to kiss him on the cheek.

Dad shook his head. "Never a dull day with my boys, is there?"

Dad and Sue hovered over James, who scooted up in bed and told the story of his stitches and how brave he'd been.

"Hey, little man." Steven smoothed James's hair away from his stitches again. "I'm gonna go find out about Gracie before I have to head back to work." He hated to leave, but his parents could watch James sleep as well as he could. Steven had a shooter to catch. "Save a story for me tonight, okay?"

"I love you, Daddy."

Steven kissed his son's forehead. "I love you too, James. I'm so glad you're okay." Tears threatened. He needed to go.

Time to turn off the emotion and get back to work. There was a stupid, albeit determined, shooter at large. One who'd just made things personal.

Gracie blinked against the harsh lights.

"Where am I?" Her voice sounded like sandpaper and felt about the same.

Beth's tiny frame came into focus, standing at her bedside. "In the hospital, big sis. When you do it, you sure do it living large."

"Honey." Mom's whitened face leaned over an IV pole.

IV pole? Hospital? "What happened to me?"

Mom and Dad looked at each other and then down at her. "There was a shooting at Hope Ridge Academy yesterday."

Gracie bit the inside of her lip and tried to focus on her dad's words and mesh them with the aches and pains starting to wake up with her brain. "I was shot."

"Yes, ma'am. And that FBI boyfriend must be wearing on you because the nurses said you fought the paramedics to even get you here." Beth giggled.

Dad cleared his throat.

"Are my kids okay? Please tell me. I saw Akemi with blood on her face and James next to her. Please, Daddy, what happened to them?"

He nudged her shoulder back into the bed. "Calm down, princess. Your headmistress was here last night and assured us everyone was okay."

"James?"

"Steven said his son had seven stitches but was resting at home." Mom smiled and patted her arm.

"You talked to Steven?"

Beth sighed. "He's even better than you described. Totally into you too. All the nurses said he asked about you and kept calling to check until he talked to Mom last night."

"*Beth.*" Dad's stern voice held a hint of amusement.

Gracie tried to process all the jumbled thoughts. Steven was here. She'd been shot. James was okay.

A tall, skinny doctor in a white coat tapped the door and walked in. "Well, good morning, Superwoman." He extended a hand and shook with Mom, Dad, and Beth. "I have a note in your file that says to put all your nurses out of their misery and let you know all your students are fine."

Beth covered her mouth to stifle a laugh. Mom and Dad smiled.

The doctor continued. "Even Akemi. She had stitches, a broken arm, but she's home now. Her parents said to give you their thanks."

"Why are they thanking me? Their daughter got hurt in my classroom." Gracie's side started to sear when she tried to sit up.

The brown-headed doctor looked around the room. "I need to do a quick exam, gang. Would you all mind stepping into the hall for a few minutes?"

When the door closed, the man loosened bandages in places Gracie didn't know had so many screaming nerve endings. She focused on his face, guessing him to be in his early thirties. Around her age. "Could you tell me what happened exactly? And include why I hurt so much."

"I'll order some more pain meds." He jotted a note on her patient file and grinned. "Doctor McGregor, not MacGyver, at your service, by the way." He laughed at his own joke.

Gracie groaned.

"Sorry. Anyway, back to your question." He retaped bandages on her side and leg. "You're a hero because when you were found, after being shot in your side, you were holding on to Akemi and trying to comfort her. Apparently you shielded her and made sure your other students were okay. Brave woman, I'd say."

"I don't remember any of that."

Dr. McGregor narrowed his eyes and flipped through her file. "Neuro assessments and scans checked out fine. Slight concussion, but no bleeding on the brain. Can you tell me what you do remember?"

"I remember the glass shattering and blood on Akemi's face. Maria and Victoria raced from the room. Then a few mumbled conversations last night. But I couldn't tell you who they were with or what was discussed." Gracie blinked away the images of blood and terror-filled faces. She'd see those in her dreams for a long while.

He exhaled. "That's expected. You were still pretty groggy for a long time after the surgery. Your chart says you requested pain meds a few times last night."

"Surgery? Did I lose my spleen?"

Dr. McGregor chuckled. "Nope. Not only brave, you're lucky. Clean shot. Point of entry and point of exit missed all your vital organs. It knicked a few things we needed to sew up and fractured a few ribs." He motioned to her leg. "You also have a few slices on your right leg, but other than that, you're all in one piece."

As if on cue, every bone in her rib cage throbbed. She winced. A testimony to the power of suggestion. "So I can go home when?"

"In a few days." He tucked the file under his arm. "Let's get you up and walking around. Make sure your digestive system is in good order. Then we'll talk about after-care."

"How long will I be away from work?" She figured Mom knew all the specifics on her injuries, but better to find out what only the doctor could say for sure.

"Let's plan on six weeks. You have one of the cleanest cases I've ever handled, but risk of infection is still high. A gunshot wound is a severe trauma to the body. Rest is what you can do best to help your body heal."

She'd talk to Mrs. Hall to make sure her class would be well covered through the holidays. Better plan for the worst and pray for the best. "Thank you."

"Any more questions?"

"Not right now, but I'm sure there'll be more."

Dr. McGregor smiled. "I'm sure there will. I'll be back to see you in the morning. Until then, try to get some sleep and don't yell at the nurses too much when they make you stand up."

Gracie stared at the doctor's disappearing back. Stand? She wanted to sleep away six weeks of bed rest and boredom. Her C-section with Joshua had taught her a few tricks. Keep a pillow handy if you have to laugh. Walking helped. They only get you out of bed to prevent blood clots, not for pure torture. This too will pass.

But this was nothing like a C-section. Her heart, ribs, legs, head, and every other inch of skin throbbed a bothersome cadence. She needed more pain meds. Not only that, when she went home, she'd go empty handed. No baby to hold to make the pain worth it.

A slight tap at the door distracted her.

Steven leaned against the little sink outside her bathroom, muscles visible through his suit shirt, his basketball tie slightly askew. "Need any help there?" Gorgeous blue eyes searched her face.

"Steven." She waved him in. "It's so good to see you. James is okay?"

He walked over to her bedside with a smile, avoiding the bandages and IV lines to give her a gentle half hug. "He insisted I give you this." Steven held up a huge yellow card with a beautiful bouquet of flowers and smiley faces.

"I miss him and my other kids already." A stray tear slid down her cheek. "I'll have to stay home and rest for a few weeks."

"I know. You'll make it. I'll help." Steven rubbed the back of her hand, the one without the bruises, tape, and IV lines.

"I'm going home to Georgia when I'm ready to travel."

Steven's forehead creased, and his eyes asked the question. One she didn't have an answer for yet.

"Suppose you don't think I can change bandages or wait on

you hand and foot?" His smile faded when she didn't respond.

Gracie shifted in her hospital bed. The smell of blood and antiseptic made her stomach roil. "I'm sure you can. And I appreciate that you want to. But I need time, Steven. Time without the…the…turmoil that follows you. Late-night calls for you to work. Canceled dates. Angela. I just can't deal with it right now."

He studied the white floor tiles. "I understand. Don't like it, though."

Everything in her wanted to be held. Wanted Steven to promise the cares and pain away. She wished for more and yet…it wasn't time. Maybe it never would be.

Another knock sounded.

Gracie's eyes felt heavy. She didn't know how much more emotional drain she could tolerate. Where were Mom and Dad? Probably giving her and Steven room to kiss and make sure all was well, given their excited looks whenever Beth talked about her FBI boyfriend.

Boyfriend? Not quite.

James hurried to her bedside and snuggled into his dad's arms. "You're okay! I was praying for you. I bugged Angela so much she said she'd bring me. I'm sorry you're hurting. Did you see my card?"

Steven smiled, hugged James, and rested his head, eyes closed, on his son's brownish mop.

Gracie held out her hand and squeezed the little boy's soft fingers. "Thank you for praying, James. I know God hears and He'll help us both get better." She looked at the bandages on his forehead and the bruises on his face. He must have fallen at some point. Hard.

"I'm sorry you were hurt, Mrs. Lang." Angela's voice startled her. She looked pale without makeup and uncomfortable, rubbing both hands over her smooth leather duster. "Thank you for making sure James was okay. He's talked about it nonstop."

Gracie nodded.

Steven worked his jaw back and forth.

Not again. She couldn't handle the verbal barbs. The emotional tension. Georgia looked more and more appealing every second.

"I just brought James because he was so concerned about you." Angela looked at Steven. "Andrew said you'd be here. I hope it was okay that I asked your dad if I could spend some time with James and bring him over to see you."

Steven's exhalation was long and loud. Like the cares of the world had driven the fight from him. Gracie hoped it wasn't on account of her requesting space and time.

Angela turned her attention to Gracie and stared at her and James holding hands. "I'm sorry about the other night too. I was rude."

Gracie's eyes grew wide as she sat up straighter, which sent a searing pain down her neck. "Thank you, Angela."

The two Kessler men watched as if it were a live soap opera playing out in front of them. She and Angela would never be friends. But maybe, in time, they could move a little past civil to friendly.

If Gracie agreed to see Steven again.

A big if.

"I really need to get some sleep." Gracie squeezed James's hand. "Thanks again for the card, sweetie. Keep praying for me, okay?"

He nodded with sad eyes. "Are you going to be back to school next week?"

Gracie fought tears. "No. Not until after Thanksgiving." James looked like he was about to cry. "But maybe you and your dad can call me at my parents' house in Georgia. Would you do that?"

Steven's half smile said he read more into that request than she'd meant. Then again, maybe she'd meant more than she thought.

"Yes," James said. "And maybe we can come visit too. If Dad can take some time off work."

Angela bristled but said nothing. *Thank You, Lord.*

"We'll see." Steven straightened to his tall and disarming height. "Gracie needs to rest." He touched his lips to her forehead and then moved to the door with James.

Beth was right. Steven was gorgeous. *"Totally into you,"* her sister had said. Maybe. The care and compassion in his eyes made Gracie's sore insides soften a little.

She hoped striking blue eyes and the heat of a kiss left on her temple didn't keep her awake long.

Or make her run where she wasn't ready to go.

30

Friday the thirteenth. How fitting.

Tom stormed through his house, gathering the last of his things and throwing clothes into his carry-on. He'd buy new toiletries on the way out of town. Who cared if his fast flight tipped the FBI that he was the inside man? They'd figure it out soon enough, what with super agent Kessler on the job.

A child. Joe had tried to shoot a child.

One more reason not to look in the mirror.

He stopped in front of his favorite lighthouse picture. Second guesses about his flight overseas made his breathing quicken. He'd never see his one-of-a-kind art pieces again. And he couldn't afford to replace them after needing surgery and phony paperwork to start another life.

Even with the changes, he'd always be a hunted man. Someone like Joe, who could stay hidden right under the FBI's noses, would track him to the ends of the earth and back.

Joe had made it clear his job wasn't finished unless body bags left Hope Ridge. They hadn't on Wednesday.

And if Tom had anything to do with it, they never would. He'd never meant it to go this far. Not to the point of killing a child.

His ringing doorbell shot his blood pressure higher than his vaulted ceiling. He looked at the suitcase at his feet. Better hide that.

"Who is it?" He leaned into the door, hoping the visitor would disappear. Maybe he could slip out the patio door and slide past whoever kept banging on his front door. But he knew better. He opened the door.

Joe strutted in like he hadn't a care in the world. "Going someplace, mate?" Piercing green eyes bored a hole through Tom's skull.

"Yes. Early retirement. I did what you paid me to do, and I'm leaving before the FBI puts the remaining pieces together."

"Not so fast. Job's not complete."

Tom's fear loosened his tongue. "That's not my fault. You missed the shot. It's your problem now."

Joe's crushing fingers around his throat cut off his airflow. Maybe death would come soon and his mother would never discover the gory details of his road to perdition. Pain became his only thought, black oblivion his only focus.

"You have no idea who I am." Joe released his grip.

Tom slumped to the floor, gasping. He'd learned enough in the last few seconds. "What do you want from me? Security will be too tight for me to help again."

"I need to make sure your lips are sealed. Or you'll be belly-up in the Potomac."

Tom walked to the kitchen and poured a shot of whisky. One or two wouldn't hurt. He'd stay alert enough to listen for a way out of this nightmare. "I have nothing to tell."

"Ah, but your flying away like a frightened bird says you don't have enough invested to stay quiet when the FBI begins interrogations." Joe reclined in a dining room chair.

Tom stood in the kitchen doorway. "So leave me to disappear."

"Botching things up is not my way. Loose threads, even less. And besides, you're worth more here alive than dead. For now."

"What do you want?" Tom had so little bargaining room.

"I need you to gen up facts on the FBI's search. Inform me of Victoria Kensington's whereabouts." Joe pointed to the kitchen. "Got any bitters for an old mate?"

Friend? Right. Tom escaped farther into the kitchen and poured another shot. Then he grabbed his last beer. If Joe had done it right the first time, Tom would have been flying to the Greek islands tomorrow as planned. If only. Armed with a little liquid courage, he felt a new plan slipping into his hazy brain.

"By the way, mate." Joe's volume hit his ears with force. "You've no idea how to disappear. One call from me and you will be at Her Majesty's pleasure."

Tom gripped the gray countertop. Prison. For the rest of his life, if Joe was still breathing, prison was one phone call away. Gracie's breathing meant the very same thing. Her going back to Georgia with all day to think about her family and time to do her investigator's errands in person almost guaranteed his approaching arrest.

No. He'd come too far, tasted the aphrodisiac of freedom. If he played his cards right, his European relocation was still in his grasp.

One tiny, simple plan away.

Steven fought the traffic into Alexandria Friday afternoon, his thoughts trailing down one path more often than any other. Gracie. Her mother had kept him informed.

And even if Gracie would have rather he remained in the dark, the scraps of knowledge Marianne Thompson threw his way kept him sane. Knowledge was power. He needed every ounce of it.

Staying in good with Gracie's mom wouldn't hurt either. Neither would another trip to the hospital with James.

He drummed his fingers to one of Sara's Irish instrumental CDs. Too many pieces of his life mismatched his hopes and dreams. Keeping his son, always at the forefront of his mind, proved the most troublesome. Angela had become friendly. Too friendly. No more peace offerings.

Now she was just killing him with kindness. Trying to earn points with the custody judge by way of his son and her former in-laws. Steven needed to go another round with his punching bag. If his ex kept up the charade until November eighth, he'd be seeing more of Angela than he had when they were married.

With none of the payoff.

Not that he wanted it. Not from Angela, anyway. Holding Gracie had proven two things that he'd not soon forget. One: He couldn't return to bachelorhood as easily as he had when Angela left and hate trumped desire. Two: When Gracie folded into his arms and fit like the last puzzle piece finishing the picture, it destroyed the illusion that God had forgotten him.

Clint drove home that point regularly. Little comments about James's survival when bullets ripped through his classroom. Reminders of past successes. Cases solved with one spark of an idea. Everything pointed to God's active pursuit of a man on the run.

James and his bedtime prayers for Gracie accomplished the same thing.

And Gracie's words about faith and forgiveness haunted Steven's waking hours like her smiling face sweetened his dreams.

As he parked his Explorer in front of Charlotte Brown's house, Steven shook his head to rattle things back into their assigned compartments. For now he had to be a master interrogator. One man—even former British Special Forces—couldn't hide forever.

Steven had technology, manpower, and his team's passion for tracking down and bringing to justice people who hurt kids. Most of his colleagues agreed with John Walsh from *America's Most Wanted*. There was a special place in hell for child murderers.

He didn't know the Bible's answer to that, but he knew full well there were special places in jail that handled men who hurt kids. Justice came in all shapes and sizes.

Steven knocked on the front door. Charlotte opened it a crack. Her wide eyes met his and then studied the floor. "I suppose I have to speak with you?"

"Yes." In almost three weeks, her sophisticated disguise with a stylish red bob had dissolved into a harried TV housewife. Minus the husband. He'd packed up the day she came home.

"Nice anklet. It goes so well with your bathrobe."

Charlotte sneered. "To ensure I won't jump the drawbridge of this wonderland castle."

Steven walked into the living area and sat on her stained couch. "I'll make this short and sweet. I want your brother's alias that he most likely used this last trip through Alexandria."

"I'll return your sentiment and keep it clipped. You jolly well know where to go." Charlotte stood in front of the living room window with her back to him.

Maybe his crack about the electronic monitor on her ankle wasn't the best way to start this conversation. "I already have your brother's motive, timeline, and enough bits of evidence to put Gordon away for life. You too, when the courts grind into action." He forced himself to stay seated. "You help us, and we'll work a deal for you to watch Stewart grow up."

Charlotte's shoulders slumped. "I'm not handing my brother over to you."

"Gordon missed his hit. Did you know that?"

She whirled around to face him. "You're lying."

"They say all criminals make fatal mistakes when they're running scared."

"Mum!" Stewart wailed from the back room.

Charlotte didn't move. "Gordon is not running scared. You are. Why else would you be here bothering with me?" She pointed a finger toward his chest. "You have nothing. And soon enough, we'll all walk away."

Steven narrowed his eyes. "Clothing fibers on Olivia's body put you with her at the time of death. No judge will let you off scot-free." He leaned forward. "We have far more than circumstantial evidence, Mrs. Brown."

"I'm a Landridge, married or not."

"Either way. Your son will grow up without a mother if you have nothing else to say." Steven stood. "You risked your freedom to see Stewart. Why throw him away now?"

She buried her face in her hands and collapsed into a brown

recliner. "Gordon told me nothing. You already know all I know."

Stewart called again.

"One name, Charlotte. That's all I need. Then you can comfort yourself with the fact that you only participated in murdering one child."

She shook her tangled mass of reddish hair.

"You could help save a little six-year-old's life. She's just a little girl." He waited. She was so close to breaking.

Charlotte disappeared into Stewart's room and stayed for a few minutes. When she returned, her red eyes and tear-streaked face screamed her fear.

"I saw one of his passports the day I came home." Her hands shook as she fiddled with her robe.

He sat still. Waiting. So close…

"Danny. Danny Johnson." The fire in Charlotte's eyes extinguished. "Now if you'll excuse me, I intend to make the best of my last few days with my son."

She'd just handed him Gordon on a silver platter.

Steven let himself out and spoke to the agents on-site. "Put her under suicide watch."

He slipped into his Explorer and speed dialed Michael. With some of the rookie's computer-genius elbow grease, they'd find Gordon Landridge before the weekend was out.

Olivia's autopsy report slammed against Steven's memory. There were days he could walk away from this job and never look back.

But not until he'd slapped the cuffs on one more killer.

Unless something else went wrong first.

31

Gracie's whole body hurt.

Two weeks and the endless bandage changes had grown old. Unlike the memory of metal ripping through her flesh or the smell of blood pervading her entire classroom. She glanced out the airplane window. The little toy houses and antlike cars grew larger as they made their final descent to Hartsfield International Airport.

Home.

In a few minutes she'd be back on Georgia soil. The flood of emotions, many she couldn't even identify, shook her body.

"You okay, sis?" Beth's chocolate-colored eyes held a lifetime of concern. Her gentle caretaking the last few weeks bridged what was left of the gap between them. At least something good had come of the bullets that had shattered Gracie's quiet life.

"I'll make it." She took a deep breath, pressing her hand on the healing wounds in her side. God had protected her just like James had said. But why it all had to happen in the first place still confused her. Add that *why* to all the others that would haunt her on this trip home.

She returned to the book on her lap and read a quote by Muriel Rukeyser: "However confused the scene of our life appears, however torn we may be who now do face that scene, it can be faced, and we can go on to be whole."

Whole? How? Father, I need You. I feel so helpless and so like Victoria's Humpty Dumpty. How will the pieces all get put back together again?

She closed her eyes and thought about recent conversations

with Maria and Victoria, James and Steven. Even Mrs. Hall had called often. Everyone kept assuring Gracie that her students were being well cared for, talking to counselors, and back at school in a cleaned-up and cheery classroom with a loving substitute teacher.

Maria's comments hit Gracie the strongest. *"Tori misses you but is glad to be back at school. She's facing her fears. The shooting got her talking about Olivia. It's good."*

Good. She only hoped she'd echo Tori's attitude someday.

"Hey, daydreamer. Mom and Dad said they'd bring Peter and Rob with them to the airport because Dennis had to get back to work." Beth sighed. "It'll be so good to hold them again."

Gracie bit her lip. Seeing her sister as a mom for the first time, watching their joyful reunion, would be hard to survive. But maybe holding her nephews would prove more healing than hurtful.

She missed Jake, especially when the tears threatened, which seemed often. But she couldn't cry on his furry shoulder this trip, because he was staying with Steven and James.

Beth grimaced. "I'm so sorry. I didn't think about how you might feel seeing...well. watching me with my boys."

She put a hand on Beth's arm. "It'll be good to see you in action with Peter and Rob, to finally meet them. You've been a huge help staying at my house when Mom and Dad had to get home. I appreciate everything you did for me—the time away from your family, spending your vacation waiting on me. Thank you."

Beth grinned and nodded, tears in her eyes.

Time for a distraction. No weeping messes to meet Mom and Dad. Gracie handed Beth her book to put away. Two weeks had taught Gracie to let her sister do the bending and stretching work, along with just about every other chore.

After the plane landed, they waited till the other passengers disembarked. Less chance of getting jostled, and she could take her sweet time walking off the plane to the wheelchair Beth had insisted on. Hartsfield was a huge airport in which to maneuver, even in the best of health.

Within minutes, Beth wheeled her through the crowd and down the elevator toward the awful train that barked orders like a military drill sergeant. They couldn't talk much in the noise or with the press of the people surrounding them, so Gracie rested her eyes and let her mind travel back to last night's dream. Lost in a dark cave, all she felt were cobwebs and a chilling wind. She hadn't been able to undo the blindfold around her eyes, no matter how hard she tried. Fear paralyzed her.

Even now, in the middle of sweaty and heavily perfumed travelers, fear gripped her heart and squeezed tight.

But the dream hadn't ended there. After she struggled with the blindfold for a long time, a hand reached down and led her through a maze of stone, along narrow paths, and up steep hills. She struggled against the hand too, but she soon came to realize it led her out of the cave and toward the warm sun. But she had woken up before she felt the fullness of the light that remained just beyond her reach.

Rather than forget the dream, the longing had grown, the desire to step out of the cave and fully into the light. Maybe Mom and Dad would help her figure out what it all meant. Not that understanding a dream would help her face the part of her trip she dreaded most.

A visit to the cemetery.

Gracie stood on her parents' staircase looking at the photos lining the walls. She'd passed by them for days now, but today she had to stop. She needed to look, to store up all the good snapshots she could to help her face the afternoon's trip.

Her parents' wedding photos. Beth and herself as kids. Their thick silver braces and big hair brought a smile. The pictures of Mark, Elizabeth, and Joshua still caught Gracie's breath and held it captive. She fingered her gold locket.

"What do you think of my family picture up there?" Beth stood on the carpeted stair below her. "I'm still shocked they put it up, with us not being married and all."

Gracie took her sister's hand. "I love you, Beth. So do Mom and Dad. No requirements for that."

Beth studied the carpet. "I'm glad you're my sister."

"Me too." Gracie wrapped her arms around Beth and gave a gentle squeeze.

Steady footfalls in the hallway above them prevented a further journey into mushiness. Dressed in a tailored business suit, Robert Thompson looked as handsome as he did in the wedding photos on the wall.

"Hey, princesses. How are you two this beautiful morning?"

"Ready for a nap," Beth said. "The boys were up all night. I should have slept in with them."

Gracie followed Beth down the steps, holding on to the rail and moving slow and steady. The less jarring the movement, the better.

Dad put one hand on each of their shoulders as they walked into the kitchen. "I've heard that little boys will do that to you." His smile eased the stinging reminder of over two years without the happy exhaustion that a day with little children provided.

Gracie fought tears once again. Being home was turning her into a puddle. She couldn't stay much longer, but she wasn't ready to return to Alexandria either.

Mom looked up from her devotion reading at the kitchen table and smoothed her black-and-pink jogging suit. "If I remember correctly, little girls do their share of wearing parents out too." Everyone chuckled.

Then Gracie's mind flashed back to one difficult day when Elizabeth's traumatic twos were in full swing. She'd wrestled with Elizabeth and potty training as well as disciplined her over and over for drawing on the walls with her sparkly crayons. Long before naptime, Gracie had collapsed onto the couch, wanting to cry. Elizabeth had mimicked her manner of sitting but put a soft, tiny hand on her leg and said, "I tink we need to talk a Jesus."

What she wouldn't give for crayon marks and tiny hands now.

Before she dissolved into another mess of tears, she breathed in and out a few times through her nose. A rich, chocolaty aroma that smelled like home curbed the waterworks and brought her back to the present.

Beth flopped down at the large oak table decorated with bright pumpkins and Indian corn. Autumn leaf placemats surrounded the centerpiece that even included a few of the handprint turkeys the sisters had made in grade school. Mom kept everything.

"Have some fruit, girls." Mom scooted a wooden dish loaded with grapes, bananas, and freshly picked figs across the table. "There are chocolate chip waffles warming in the oven too."

Gracie leaned against the breakfast bar and breathed in the peace wrapped in warm chocolate that characterized her parents' home. Heart-chocolate. That was what her parents provided without even trying. A safe place. Kind words. Gentle hugs. Happy memories. Hope. The kind of chocolate nourishment that didn't line her hips and thighs.

Dad grabbed a fresh bagel from the fridge and wrapped it in a paper towel. "I need to head out if I'm going to be on time for our afternoon trip." He kissed Mom's cheek and turned to Gracie. "We can stop by the florist's on the way."

"Thank you, Daddy."

His strong arms encircling her felt so safe. "I'll see you soon, princess. I love you."

Beth joined their little circle with a contented sigh.

He smiled. "It's good to be a daddy to two princesses. Love you both." He kissed their heads and then exited by way of the garage door.

"I think I'm going to catch some Z's before the boys start tearing through the house." Beth stretched her neck. "I'll see you before you leave."

Gracie nodded but couldn't speak. She didn't want to think about this afternoon.

Beth scooted out of the kitchen before Gracie's stomach rumbled like a volcano. "I think I'll get some waffles before my belly wakes Peter and Rob." Gracie started to move toward the oven, but Mom nudged her back to the table.

"You sit." Mom gathered the leaf-bordered plates from the counter and loaded one with crisp golden squares. "Even if you're as strong as your dad, you're still here to be waited on, and I intend to do just that."

Gracie slipped into a padded oak chair. "Mom, I know you and Dad said that God would show me the meaning of my dream about the cave, but I still don't understand. It feels like I'm so close to something, but I'm afraid it's only another cliff."

Mom gave her a glass of milk and a warm plate of gooey chocolate waffles dripping with organic maple syrup. "You eat. I'll talk. I've been praying for an opportunity like this since you mentioned your dream."

Gracie felt like a teenager sneaking home after curfew. Not at all prepared for a "talk." She bowed her head and prayed for a quick and painless lecture.

"Don't give me that look, Gracie Ann. I know you're a grown lady." Mom quirked a grin with raised eyebrows. "I just want to share something that the Lord's been showing me. I think with all you've been through lately, it'll help."

"Okay." The warm chocolate slid over her tongue and she relaxed. A little.

"You said what you felt from that dream was fear, right?"

Gracie nodded and kept eating.

"Fear of what?"

Good question. "Fear of never getting out of the cave and into the sunlight?"

"What about how you felt with the blindfold and the hand directing you?"

"Helpless." She didn't like where her mom was heading.

She'd talked to the counselor a year ago about her anger. Someone had killed her family. She'd watched it happen but couldn't prevent it. Now she couldn't find the man who'd taken them from her.

Helpless. The word also described what she felt with Steven and his custody battle and Angela's constant involvement in their life.

"That makes perfect sense." Mom leaned forward. "But it's a lie. You're not helpless. That lie is the thing that's binding you like the blindfold in your dream."

"And I thought you'd say unforgiveness was holding me back." Gracie hated the anger rising inside. A lie wasn't what drove her life. Feeling helpless was only an emotion. Nothing more.

"That's an issue too, but first you need to face that you're living a lie. Your quest to find the man in the black truck is one way you're trying to prove you're not helpless. So is keeping everything in your life in perfect order. Your house. Your lesson plans."

Gracie stiffened. The sounds of gunfire and shattering glass ricocheted through her memory. Perfect lesson plans hadn't helped that day.

She pushed those thoughts down. Way down. "No, keeping things in order is called being responsible. No one else thinks I'm being anal."

Mom cocked her head and frowned. Referring to body parts, especially posterior ones, didn't go over well.

"Sorry." Gracie took a long drink of cold milk.

"It sure looks good on the outside, but not on the inside. Not when that raw hunger to fix and understand it all gets thwarted. That only leads to anger at God, which leads you farther away from the only One who can help your heart heal."

Something deep inside resonated with the truth Mom spoke. But Gracie couldn't face it. She was terrified to think that the healing, the moving out of captivity to her past, rested in her power.

"The One who heals you doesn't need your ability to fix it." Mom's brown eyes glistened with the love only a mom could give while spooning up bitter medicine.

"It's not like I haven't been praying or reading my Bible. I haven't walked away from God."

A sad smile curved Mom's lips. "But are you really experiencing Him? Hearing His voice? There's a world of difference between the fear I see in your eyes and the peace I see when I spend time looking into God's eyes, into His truth."

Gracie pushed her plate away, no longer hungry. "I'm not God, so there isn't perfect peace. But I do feel God when I read the Bible. I have joy when I teach. I've learned to move past the anger."

Mom reached across the table to put a hand on hers. "Mothers see things, honey. I see shadows in your eyes maybe no one else notices. I hear the fear and excitement in your voice when you talk to James and Steven on the phone. But this lie about who you think you are—a victim—is blinding you, holding you back from stepping fully out of the dark cave and into the sun."

"So I just run to God and tell Him I feel helpless? And He does what, whisper some Bible verse that's supposed to make it all better?" Gracie pulled away and stood. "I've tried, Mom. I have. I can't keep dredging up those emotions over and over. It hurts too much."

Her mom nodded. "Burying or running from them hurts worse." She stood and wrapped an arm around Gracie. "Test me on this. Step into God's arms and spill out what you've believed about yourself—that you're helpless, maybe not good enough, abandoned. Then admit you've lived trying to prove those lies aren't real instead of receiving what God says about you.

"Let yourself feel His forgiveness and then listen to His truth. I believe He has something incredible to share with you." Mom wiped Gracie's tears with her soft thumbs.

"But I can't just tell my private investigator to forget it."

"I didn't say you had to. I only said to go to God where you are and see what He says."

Gracie sniffled. She wouldn't give up her quest. And she wouldn't go to her family's grave site today either. Too much emotion. Too many thoughts swirling around her brain.

Maybe she should try Mom's way. Bitter acid burned her throat at all the memories.

The black truck speeding away.

Her children's blood on the ambulance stretchers.

Three white sheets.

Even if Mom was right and forgiveness flowed naturally from facing God with the lies in her heart, one thing kept her from it: She'd have to let the killer go. And then she'd have nothing to hold on to.

Her quest to see him pay, the anger that still simmered below the surface, gave her more strength than crumpling in her sadness. Seeing him in jail might not give her peace or rid her of the lies her mother said she'd been living, but it would get that man off the streets and out of her head.

She wasn't ready to give that up.

Not now. Maybe not ever.

Forgiveness required much too high a price.

32

J oe knew how to evade the FBI.

That fact had kept Tom out of prison. Armed with that realization and the courage that accompanied the dawning of his freedom plans, he walked around his office, letting the rush of adrenaline escape.

He'd survived his questioning by the FBI about Gracie's shooting weeks ago. He could answer honestly that he knew nothing about a Gordon Landridge. Or a Danny Johnson—obviously one of Joe's aliases. That was easy. He'd handled this morning's repeat of questions with equal finesse. A great way to kick off his last month in Alexandria.

After Thanksgiving he'd bask on an Australian beach. Far better than Greece. Travel research had kept him focused. Unwavering in his duties at Hope Ridge. Unbroken by the FBI's constant bother. Committed to carrying out his plan.

November down under and the promise of summer's freedom made him strong.

The FBI had given him bits of information on Joe or Gordon or whatever the man's real name was. Not that Tom would do anything with it. Yet. But information could prove a treasure with which to ransom freedom. If his carefully laid plan didn't work.

His telephone buzzed. "Yes."

"There's a Justin Moore to see you, Mr. Perkins."

His earlier adrenaline rush slammed through his veins once more. "Please show him in, Alice." He sat behind his impressive cherrywood desk and waited.

Alice entered and showed Gracie's private investigator into

the room, then left without a word, closing the door behind her.

"Welcome to Hope Ridge, Mr. Moore. Please, have a seat." Tom motioned to the leather chairs in front of his desk.

"Thank you." Both men sat down.

Mr. Moore's broad shoulders stuffed into a tan sports coat weren't nearly as threatening as Joe's muscular build. But his reason for this unscheduled visit could prove even more destructive.

Tom waited.

Mr. Moore handed him a sketch. "This picture is from Gracie Lang's description of the man who ran her family off the road over two years ago, killing her husband and two children."

"I'm familiar with the story. Terribly tragic." Tom handed the picture back without so much as a tremor to his hands. "But I'm not sure what that has to do with your business here today."

"Everything."

The knots in his shoulders and neck tightened, but he couldn't let it show. He had to play this meeting cool like his interactions with Gracie and the FBI agents crawling through his school. "I'm sorry, but I don't follow you."

Justin narrowed his eyes. "I've talked to some people at Georgia State who remember the man in this drawing."

Tom sat forward. "I imagine Mrs. Lang is thrilled with your detective work. Will you be turning over your findings to the local police soon?"

"After I speak with her."

Leaning back in his chair, Tom smiled. "This is wonderful news. I'm still not sure why I need to know this information, though."

Justin studied his hands, and then his gaze roved over Tom's desk. "The people at Georgia State named you, Mr. Perkins."

Tom's stomach plummeted to the floor as his mind sorted through names from school. None would have connected Gracie's sketch to him. They'd all swept through grad school too busy or too drunk to remember him.

Except one.

But if this PI thought he could bluff his way through to get a nervous confession, he had another thing coming. Not a snowball's chance there.

Tom rested his arms on the side of his leather chair. Time for more information gathering.

"Is that your only lead, Mr. Moore? I'd hate to think you'd accuse an innocent man with nothing more than a young lady's attempt at revenge."

Justin's gaze didn't waver. "I never said who I spoke with."

"But the fact that I know who it was has to give some credibility to my innocence. Do you have any other leads on the real killer on which to base your case to Mrs. Lang and the police?"

Mr. Moore stiffened. "I have more work to do, but I'm confident the information I received in Georgia is reliable." The man set the sketch on Tom's desk. "Mind telling me where you were on New Year's Eve two years ago?"

"That's easy. I was at home in my apartment." Tom forced his breathing to remain calm, steady. "Planning to propose until I found out my girlfriend was pregnant. If you'd like to speak with her, I'm sure she could validate my whereabouts. I doubt she's forgotten that very long night." Except for the time she was passed out cold and he'd slipped away to find the nearest bar.

The gumshoe had nowhere to go with this line of questioning. If Moore's flimsy case even made it past the police officers' laughing, Tom had a watertight alibi. One Kimberly couldn't help but substantiate. How ironic that her attempt at revenge would only serve to strengthen his claims.

This news did mean he'd have to move fast now. No time left to unfurl his plan as neat and untraceable as he'd hoped.

Surely Joe knew by now that Ambassador Kensington was being deported sometime this week. His British "mate" would call for exact information, and Tom had easy access to it as Victoria's vice principal. Joe's insane focus on unfinished business would be Tom's lucky break.

Soon.

He ended the meeting with a frustrated Mr. Moore receiving no information to dredge up any new leads. The poor man wouldn't be Tom's problem much longer.

As he closed his office door and relished the silence, Tom could feel the balmy air of the southern hemisphere. Taste the tang of a well-concocted martini he'd use to toast the FBI and British Intelligence that would never find him.

Not even Joe.

Tom had practiced and prepared well for the biggest day of his life. He was ready. Everything would fall into place. And Justin Moore, private investigator extraordinaire, was none the wiser for all his attempts to rattle his prey.

It hadn't worked.

Nothing would alter the plans now.

Steven sat on his back deck, the phone warm in his hand despite the cool evening breeze.

Gracie was sharing about her visit to her favorite Whole Foods store and all the samples she'd tasted earlier that day. He rubbed Jake's soft fur while the dog dozed beside the deck chair. Between calls with Gracie and the loveable golden retriever his son adored, home had become a fun escape. Jake's slobbered affection on James had helped his son on so many levels. Steven too.

"So you're cooking me filet mignon for dinner when I get back?" Gracie's playful voice kicked his hope up a notch. They'd been flirting on the phone about every other day for the past few weeks, and she seemed more than ready to come back to Alexandria.

He hoped her reasoning included him and not just escaping memories.

"As you wish, my lady."

Gracie giggled.

He could imagine her crimson cheeks and dancing hazel eyes. The ache to hold her, to kiss her, had only grown during her recovery time in Georgia. Every night, the memory of her smile kept him from going crazy over one more frustrating development in the Kensington case. Or going insane with fearful scenarios of what the judge would say on Wednesday at the final custody hearing.

Steven stuffed those depressing thoughts. "I hope I can always make you blush like that and be with you to see it."

Gracie's soft breathing made him wonder if he'd pushed too much with those comments. He waited to see if she'd change the subject.

"You probably always will, Steven."

He felt like he'd scored a game-winning slam dunk. Why his thoughts flew back to high school whenever he and Gracie spoke, he couldn't imagine. Unless it was because the possibility of enjoying a relationship again reminded him of the only other time he'd allowed unbridled hope and hormones to make him believe in future dreams.

Except this time he'd keep his hormones in check. Gracie was worth waiting for.

His call-waiting beeped, and he glanced at the screen. Angela's number. "Hey, Gracie. Can I call you back? James is on the other line."

"Sure. I'll be awake a little while longer."

He pushed away the images that comment conjured and clicked over. "Hey, little man. What's up?"

Steven had figured his son's first overnight with Angela might not last too long, and it might be time for a ride home. This little trial run had been his attempt to reciprocate Angela's desire for peace. Maybe joint custody, a likely option, wouldn't be so bad after all.

"Daddy, I need you to come get me." His son's sniffles magnified through the phone line.

Steven stood and walked inside, heading for his car keys.

Jake scrambled inside with him. "What's wrong, son? Are you hurt?" Surely Angela could manage to make sure James's still tender stitch site was okay.

"Angela, I mean, Mom, is being real loud and I can't sleep."

Steven remembered Angela's loud yelling. Most times a drink in hand had accompanied the ear-splitting shrieks. *Not again.*

"I tried to sneak out, but her husband yelled at me to go to bed." James's trembling voice was barely above a whisper.

Keys cutting into his palm, he loaded Jake into his Explorer and waited for the garage door to open. "I'm on my way. You stay tucked in bed, and I'll be there in a few minutes."

He clenched the steering wheel, listening to Jake's panting in the backseat.

Thankful for the cell phone he'd tucked in James's bag, Steven sped toward Angela's condo. The one she and the professor had rented just outside Old Town Alexandria so they could stay close by and keep James on the weekends she was in town.

Which wouldn't happen again if Angela was drunk tonight.

Images of shot glasses shattering against the wall, curses full of venom, and what Angela could be screaming at James made his pulse accelerate faster than his SUV as he pressed hard on the gas pedal. James had been through enough in the past month, and Steven had just led his son into a lion's den with no protection.

"Mom," James had called her. Only because Angela begged him to. That alone rankled Steven, but he had played along.

Stupid.

He'd fallen under his ex-wife's spell again. Hoped for the best. Gotten snowed like always where she was concerned. This time would be the last. He'd do everything to convince the judge that his son belonged with him and was in danger if Angela had any involvement in his life.

Once Angela was out of the picture—again—things would settle down. Gracie would be home soon, and she could provide the female role model the courts were sure to insist James needed.

If only life worked like his best-laid plans.

Steven pulled into the condo parking lot and turned off the ignition. He took a few deep breaths to steady himself. No need to give Angela any ammunition for court.

He rubbed Jake's fur and then walked to the condo door. If Clint were here, he'd remind Steven to pray. No time for that. But he'd talk to Clint at work tomorrow. Remind them to pray hard on Wednesday.

He rang the doorbell. A short, bald man answered. "Steven. What are you doing here?"

Marcus, the one she'd left Steven for. He sized up the middle-aged man and wondered for the thousandth time why. Why had Angela left him for a little mouse of a man? The same man who'd had the gall to yell at James.

Steven relaxed his balled fists. "Don't ever raise your voice to my son."

Marcus's face turned a pasty shade of white. "Angie, baby, you have a visitor."

The mouse wasn't a gentleman either. Hadn't even tried to protect Angela. If James's future wasn't at stake, Steven would have liked to take the professor out back and throttle him till he squeaked.

Angela staggered to the doorway, her wide eyes registering his presence. "What do you want, Stevie?" Her breath smelled of stale Maker's Mark. Bourbon. Her liquor of choice.

Steven fought the memories of that smell. The empty promises to quit. The lies about rehab. Nothing had changed. Not even his own stupid naiveté.

"I want my son." Steven stepped between his drunken ex-wife and the mousy professor.

Angela sunk her claws into his bicep. "You can't barge into my home like this."

"I can when you've put my son at risk." He shook her hands away. "He called me to say he was scared. Terrified of your loud squawking and whatever else you were doing."

Steven shot a glance at Marcus. The man said nothing.

Angela's brave face crumpled. "He wouldn't stop talking about Gracie. Gracie prayed this and Gracie did that. I had to beg him to call me Mom. I shouldn't have to beg my son to call me Mom."

"Being a mother goes far beyond just giving birth; something you didn't stick around to find out."

She cocked a hand to slap him, but Steven caught her wrist. "Never again, Angela. You may not have changed, but I have. You lose this time."

Steven stormed unhindered to the back bedroom. James was lying in his bed, shaking under the covers. Steven collected his son and his backpack. "I'm here, James. We're going home."

He buried his face in Steven's chest and clung to him.

Steven paused at the front door while Marcus and Angela stood rooted to their previous spots. "I'll see you in court. If you're sober enough to stand, that is." He exited the condo, and the door slammed behind him.

Come Wednesday, this nightmare would be over. One less problem to solve. One less heartache to face.

And he'd lock the memory of Angela Barrett from his mind forever.

33

S itting in Hartsfield's concourse B at the farthest gate, Gracie's side ached.

Normal breathing hadn't happened since Justin Moore's frazzled phone call yesterday. He claimed to have e-mailed her details that required her attention, but she hadn't responded. So he'd called.

"I believe Thomas Perkins is the man you saw the night your family was killed."

But Justin had no proof. And she was sure her private investigator was wrong. Dead wrong. She couldn't let an innocent man be harassed by the police because of a drawing she'd probably imagined. There had to be a reasonable explanation for her vice principal's being named from the sketch she never should have given.

Maybe his constant hovering at school and his distinctive Ichabod Crane nose had colored her memories. She'd done Justin's sketch from a nightmare more than from a real memory.

Her cell phone rang. Now she could be like the million other Atlanta travelers with a silver attachment in their ears.

"Beth? What are you doing calling me so early in the morning?" Her sister had flown home with her adorable twins last week. Gracie missed them something fierce.

"Mom said you were flying back to Virginia already. I thought the doc said you'd be off work until after Thanksgiving." Beth yawned.

"You gotta stop having dreams about me, you know." Gracie's tone didn't match her attempt at humor. "Steven's custody hearing is tomorrow. I told him I'd be back for that."

Not the entire reason, but one Beth would be happy to hear.

"So you've decided to embrace the boyfriend thing?" Beth's coffee machine gurgled to life in the background. "That's worth waking up for, even at six west coast time. Details, please. I'd like some juicy tidbits before I have to slave away at my desk pushing grant papers all day while the boys make Play-Doh statues at day care. What a life."

"Nothing new. Like I told you before you left, I'm proceeding cautiously. A lot depends on how Steven handles the results of the custody hearing."

"But you'll be at his side, fighting the evil ex-wife, and then ride off into the east coast sunset." Beth giggled at her own parody.

"Not quite."

"Is Steven picking you up at the airport?"

Gracie heard her row number being called. "Leah's dropping me off at school. I may call Steven to pick me up from there."

"School? Please don't tell me you're going to visit your classroom. You barely survived Peter and Rob's hugs. Those first graders are likely to tackle you if you show up there."

That would be a welcome diversion. "I'll be careful. Talk to you soon, Beth. I love you."

The plane ride home passed with little fanfare. Her seatmates all kept their noses in fiction books while Gracie tried to doze. She'd need all her strength to face what awaited her back in Alexandria.

At Dulles Airport, Leah pulled her into a light hug and insisted she wait on the sidewalk for the car. Gracie had tried to grab her suitcase from the silver luggage carousel earlier, but Leah had bulldozed her away from that too.

This was worse than being hovered over by her mother at home. Thankfully, on the ride to Hope Ridge, they focused on Leah's upcoming trip to visit her parents in Colorado for Thanksgiving.

"You're going home for the holidays, right?"

Leah's Lexus smelled like Yankee Candle's sage and citrus

scent. A mix of beach and citrus and summer breezes. Gracie wouldn't mind a walk on the Destin beaches she and Mark had often visited for family vacations.

She wondered if Steven liked beaches.

"Earth to Gracie. You dreaming about your FBI beau?"

Caught red-handed. Or in her case, red-faced again. She needed to get past Beth's romantic fantasies and back to the real world. Past everyone's notion of her and Steven getting married and living happily ever after.

"Please don't echo Beth. I need you to be Leah, the strong and wise district attorney."

Leah laughed. "I'll unpack my Superwoman cape for you when I get home."

They pulled into Hope Ridge Academy grounds. "Why am I dropping you off here again?"

Leah's upcoming trip must have made her a little at loose ends. That worked for Gracie. Less explanation required. The fewer people who knew about Justin Moore's ridiculous claims, the better. Especially if she still wanted a job to return to after the holidays.

"I need to meet with Mr. Perkins, and then I'll see if Steven can take me home. That way you and William don't have to wait for me."

Leah shot her a knowing look. "Very magnanimous of you."

Gracie rolled her eyes. She'd play along. For now. It was better than imagining her world without Steven after his custody hearing. If it went badly, she'd have to find a way to untangle from Steven and Angela's emotional mess and wait until he was ready to move past his past.

A challenge that neither of them was ready to tackle.

Gracie fidgeted with her blue-and-white checked jumper as she waited in the main office. Skirts and dresses were still more comfortable on her incision sites than pants. Better to focus on her wardrobe than on her "worked in" meeting with Mr. Perkins.

Everyone had been so happy to see her. They spoke of how well her students were doing, but also about how much they missed her. Like she missed them. Getting back into her classroom might be hard, but she'd face her fears just like Victoria had done.

That little girl was an inspiration. After all she'd been through in the last few months, the little blonde had regained her smile. And Maria said it hadn't disappeared when she returned to school after the shooting.

"Mrs. Lang? Mr. Perkins will see you now." Alice led her back to the private office.

Her boss stood as she entered. "Hello, Mrs. Lang."

"Thank you for meeting me on such short notice. I appreciate it."

He motioned for her to sit. "Glad to help. Now, what can I do for you today?"

She brushed the traveling wrinkles from her jumper. "I know my private investigator was here to see you. I…I just wanted to clear up any misunderstandings and make sure everything was still in place for my return after Thanksgiving."

"There's no problem on our end."

His dark eyes held her attention. "I was wondering if you could explain why someone from Georgia State would name you as the person in my police sketch. That makes no sense, and it'll bother me until I have an explanation."

He leaned back in his chair and steepled his fingers. "I have a theory. It's a simple case of revenge, Mrs. Lang. The woman your PI must have spoken with, Kimberly Beam, is a jilted girlfriend. She must have seen the sketch and thought it resembled me, just enough so she could use it to cause some trouble in my life."

"But why would an old girlfriend do something like that?" She was having a hard time wrapping her mind around all the recent updates Justin had given her.

"Like I explained to Mr. Moore, I'd planned to propose to

Kimberly on New Year's Eve two years ago. But she let it slip that she was pregnant. With someone else's child." He took a deep breath. "I'm sure you can understand why I didn't follow through with the proposal and why she would want to tarnish my name at any opportunity. I was her ticket out of single mother-hood, but I didn't play along."

His story made sense. Gracie's gut said there was more to it than that, but she was too jet-lagged to continue the conversation. The rest was none of her business anyway. She wanted to get home, fall into her bed, and sleep for days.

"Well then, I'm glad it's so easily explained. Thank you for your time, Mr. Perkins. I'm sorry I bothered you."

"No problem." He stood to show her out. "Would you like Alice to call you a cab, or do you have another way home? You look too tired to drive right now."

She was. Too exhausted to talk to Steven too. "That would be wonderful, since a friend dropped me off. Thank you."

On the taxi ride home, thoughts of her bed and her sweet, lonesome dog kept Gracie's eyes open. She'd call Steven tonight and see if he could bring Jake home.

She needed the peaceful surroundings of her home and Jake's warm presence to set her wobbling world spinning back on its axis. She'd deal with her nerves when she saw Steven later.

After a good nap.

Everything looked better after a good rest.

Gracie answered the door with sleep-mussed hair.

Steven smiled when she yawned and said hello at the same time. But Jake beat him through the door, jumping on his owner, making circles around her legs. She kept him away from her side and bent down to nuzzle his neck.

Lucky dog.

"How did you know I was home? I'd planned to call this evening."

He stepped inside and closed the front door. "Your mom called and said Leah was picking you up at the airport but that you'd be thrilled if I brought Jake home around dinnertime."

She groaned. "Dinner?"

"Don't worry. Your mom suggested I stop by a deli and grab something for both of us." He held up a white sack and then walked to the kitchen.

"She's got it covered. *Fiddler on the Roof*'s matchmaker has nothing on my mother." She flopped onto a breakfast chair.

Steven considered breaking into one of his favorite musical's numbers, but one look at Gracie's tired eyes and he decided against it. He rummaged through her cabinets for plates instead.

"Steven, have you ever been shot?" The question startled him.

"Years ago." He piled two pink plates with chips, pickles, and turkey club sandwiches. "Clint risked his life to pull me to safety."

"Were you in a lot of pain?"

He considered giving her the trauma counselor's number he'd been taking James to visit. He'd find the card tonight and suggest it soon.

"Yes, I still remember the searing pain. The fear too. I had no idea at first if I would return to work, and I struggled with that." He took their plates to her kitchen table and waited while she bowed her head to pray.

"What about you? How are you handling it?"

"I'm dealing with it. I talked to my counselor in Georgia a little." She munched on her pickle first. Jake sat statuelike waiting for a bite. "Your work is very important to you, isn't it?"

"Yes." He needed to tread carefully with this new subject. Angela's words about work being his mistress could color what Gracie heard, and he wanted to ease her fears, not add to them.

"When an assignment is complete and a child is returned to his or her parents, or when a case goes to trial so airtight that there's no way for justice not to be served, the emotions are incredible. It's an awesome privilege to put that kind of joy in someone's eyes. And when I see the perps sentenced so they never have a chance to do it again, that makes my job worth all the risks."

"I can't pretend to comprehend the magnitude of your job. But it's obvious you give your all to whatever you do. That I understand." She nibbled at her sandwich. "What about your family, Steven? How do you balance time with James and a demanding work schedule?"

Was she asking about how he'd make time for her too? He could only hope. "You ask hard questions, you know that?"

"I've just had a lot of time to think. Tomorrow will be a turning point of sorts for your life, and I'd like to know where that leaves me." She played with her napkin. "I mean, Beth and my mom and dad already have us walking the aisle, but I'm not sure where things are headed."

Neither was he. But spending more time with Gracie made the top of his wish list. Marriage? Maybe. That would have to wait till Angela disappeared.

Gracie chewed on her lip and focused on the table.

"You look like you're dying to say something. What is it?"

"Okay. You asked for it, remember."

He smiled.

She took a deep breath. "The way I see it, Angela was responsible for her own choices. Just like you're responsible for the choices you make now. Clint is right. Until you forgive her, you're not totally free. You choose."

Finishing off his sandwich, he looked straight into her eyes. "You going to take your own advice?"

"Touché." She stared out the dining room windows for a long time while the dog's eyes stayed trained on her, and his tail thumped the floor.

"I loved Angela. I've been honest with you about that. She rocked my foundation when she ran off and left me with a newborn and the accusations about my work." Thoughts of Angela's actions Monday night hit him again. "I blamed her for everything. Hated her. That served me well for a long time. Kept me from feeling the hurt and dwelling on the past. But lately, I've realized that I failed her too." Steven leaned over on his knees and raked his hand through his hair. "I'm still working all that out."

"I can live with that. I still have things to deal with too. A lot, if you listen to my mother."

Marianne might have invited him into their lives from their first meeting at the hospital, but asking her about Gracie's issues wasn't his style. He'd wait till she was ready to share.

He held her hand and rubbed his thumb across her knuckles. "I need you to know tomorrow could get ugly. Angela was drunk on Monday night when James called. Very drunk."

Gracie gasped. "I'm so sorry."

"Me too."

"You know Angela's drinking is not your fault, right?" She squeezed his hand as he scooted his kitchen chair closer. "Each of us makes our own choices."

Her words were accomplishing in minutes what Clint had tried to hammer home for the past five years. Or maybe one had set the stage for the other. Either way, the guilt Steven had allowed free reign shriveled a little. But only a little. And he'd still have to follow the logic through and face a ton of mistakes by looking in the mirror.

After he survived the custody hearing.

"I'm praying for you, Steven."

He pulled her to her feet and drew her close. Then he tilted her chin up and lowered his lips to hers. Gracie's kiss was everything all at once. Gentle. Passionate. Innocent. Electrifying. With only a narrow hold on the passion stirring within him, he pulled back slightly and rested his forehead on hers.

Gracie's eyes were still closed. She inhaled a deep, ragged breath and slowly released it.

"Thank you for coming back. Your presence and your prayers matter." He traced her jawline with his thumb.

Whatever tomorrow held, with Gracie at his side, he felt strong. Hopeful.

More than he'd felt in years.

34

"Hello, mate. I hear you have some news."

Tom gripped his new cell phone with sweaty hands, hoping he'd given Joe this number. If not, Joe was right. Tom had no idea how to disappear or utilize an alias.

Wednesday had not begun on a good note.

He walked around his office desk and studied the Kandinsky he'd purchased at the height of his financial prowess. Then his stocks tanked, and he had to live like the rest of the middle class. Except now he had a cool million in an offshore account.

"This has to be last, Joe. The feds will be clocking in by six." The placid darkness outside rested in stark contrast to his chaotic life. At least the FBI hadn't bugged his office. Had they tapped the phones? Probably. But he doubted that they had any reason to suspect him.

"Shoot."

Joe's word choice sent icy barbs down Tom's spine. "She's leaving in two days, bound for Heathrow. From what I've gathered in snatches of conversation and paperwork, she'll be at Hope Ridge until eleven in the morning. Then the Kensingtons will leave together from their residence for an afternoon flight."

"So my best chance is high noon at the embassy? So American."

"That's up to you. I'm done." Tom ran through his mental checklist while Joe went on with details about Friday. The Brit must have blown a keg last night. Bored or scared, Tom didn't know. Nor did he care. But the information Joe rattled off would serve Tom well. What a gift a drunk "bloke" could be.

"…and Bob's your uncle, mate."

Tom stopped wearing a path in his thick cream carpet. "What?"

Joe's long exhalation shouted through the phone. "It means that's that. We're done, eh?"

"Yes. Finished. Have a great life, Joe."

"Supposing that's your American way of telling me to disappear, let me remind you of a few things. I still control that million-dollar account, and I've evaded the FBI for months. You've not walked a centimeter in my boots. Watch yerself."

Tom had reached his boiling point. Nicing things up with a drunken Brit didn't fit into the schedule today. "I'm hanging up, now. Good-bye, Joe."

"Cheerio, mate."

He straightened his deep blue power tie and the one expensive suit he planned to pack. Who needed suits to lounge on the beach down under?

In some small way, he hoped his mother would see all his genius in untangling the messes he'd made. Then she'd respect him. Even though he'd never see her again after Friday.

The federal-style brick of the 18th Judicial District Court's calm and dignified exterior belied the shattered lives represented within.

One of which could be Steven's. And his son's.

He tried to focus on the ornate white interior and ignore Angela's feral pacing of the waiting area outside the courtroom. She'd dressed to impress in her expensive slate-colored suit, as had her husband in his Valentino. Neither spoke to each other or to him.

Steven's lawyer sat stone-still beside him, sizing up the competition. Suit for suit, they were evenly matched. That fact brought Steven no comfort.

Angela wasn't evil or trying to destroy him. Maybe that had

never been her intent. Even when she left. His conscience shouted that his marriage hadn't been void of good times. But the scene Monday night and countless others like it screamed that the fight for full custody of his son wasn't personal. James's safety was at stake.

Gracie's hand on his arm provided a small amount of comfort. Her presence, and no doubt her prayers, gave him a reason to hope. Clint and Sara and his family would be praying as well. James too. His son's light brown hair and blue eyes dominated Steven's thoughts.

First steps.

Soccer games and playing Frisbee at the park.

Good-night hugs and stories read over and over again.

"I love you, Daddy! You're the best." Tears threatened at the memory of James's words. Words Angela would never hear.

Why he kept coming back to pity and sorrow for her didn't make sense. It was as if two warring forces vied for his attention, both flinging memories and whispers, none of which he understood.

He hoped God wouldn't abandon him now. For James's sake. Surely He wouldn't punish James because of Steven's choices. Still, Clint's confusing lectures attacked his brain. Clint said he had to face the lies that drove him, controlled him. *"Lies like you're not good enough, Steven. That's one of your biggest."*

His partner's deep and compassionate eyes had challenged him with those words. His purpose undoubtedly had been to nudge Steven toward God. All it did was spin him into more confusion.

"You want to walk outside and talk?" Gracie's soft invitation came with a gorgeous smile.

Steven checked his watch. One-thirty. Their case was first on Wednesday's docket in thirty minutes. The chilly November air would do him good. Might chase away the hounding thoughts, for a while, at least.

"Sure."

Angela stiffened as he stood. "If you leave before our case is called, it's a criminal offense." She crossed her arms and drummed her peach fingernails on her suit coat. The open foyer echoed her words, despite the large number of people milling around.

He straightened the cross-and-handprint tie James had picked out last night. The same one his son had made with puffy red and yellow finger paints for Father's Day this year. "I'm not here to pay you back, Angela. You started this process. I'll see it through to the end. For James."

She muttered something under her breath. The last few months she'd been on a mission, using perfect manners. Not anymore. Par for the course when it suited her.

Steven shook his head and took Gracie's hand. He double-checked his watch. Still time for a short escape outside.

The bright sun and cloudless sky did nothing for his mood. "Sorry about that. I know it bothers you to see that interplay."

"It hurts me for your sake, Steven, and for James." She turned to face him and rubbed his biceps in slow up-and-down motions. "Remember James. Remember that you did love Angela and you can forgive her."

He looked down into Gracie's eyes. She was as much a Christian bulldog as Clint. But for once, it didn't irritate him. This time it felt endearing. Truthful.

As they walked around the court building, her words about his job flashed to mind. *"God didn't put you here to save the world. He already did that."*

Good thing, because Steven didn't play the savior role too well.

"You know you're responsible for the choices you make now. In there." Gracie pointed her thumb toward the brick building. "Understanding comes *after* you choose to trust Him. It's your move."

Christian bulldog for sure. He stopped walking. "I know I need to forgive Angela. I'm working on that."

She searched his face with hopeful eyes. "God will hear you, no matter how long it's been since you prayed."

He cupped her chin in his hands. "I know you care. And for that I'm thankful." Softening his voice, he continued. "But I think I'm getting it."

She blushed.

"And if you keep going, I'm gonna pull out a tape recorder and play the words back to you. Over and over and over."

She held up her hands, a playful glint in her eyes. "I'm working on it too. Besides, isn't it illegal to record an American citizen without consent?"

Steven grinned. Then he noticed Angela glaring at them from the courthouse steps.

His stomach acids churned faster. Skipping breakfast and lunch had not been a wise decision. He checked his watch again. "We'd better head back inside."

Gracie took his hand and matched his quick pace without a word.

She was definitely a reminder that God hadn't forgotten him.

When their case was called, Steven, Gracie, and his lawyer followed Angela and Marcus into the courtroom. No one spoke. But the voices of those still waiting for their turn in court blended around them, filling the void.

Two o'clock sharp. At least a few agencies besides the FBI and Secret Service worked on time, if only for today.

Steven tried to block out all the testimony given by Angela and her slick lawyer-husband. They called no witnesses, though, and submitted no documents to the court. Not even her high-brow treatment facility information.

She was running scared. At some point in the last few days she must have considered all the factors upon which the judge would base his decision. If Steven knew how to decode body language, and he did, the judge wasn't the close personal friend Angela had hoped would adjudicate this hearing either.

Steven gave his testimony, keeping it clear and focused on the facts. No emotional outbursts. No pointing fingers. His lawyer submitted the information about Angela's drinking, and

Steven only affirmed what he'd seen in their six short years of marriage. Worse, what he'd seen Monday night.

Gracie sat behind him. He could feel her presence as he fixed his eyes on the black-robed judge. Steven focused on the gavel, willing it to pound out a decision soon.

Angela shot him a sideways glance and smiled. Her substance abuse weighed against the testimony given concerning her financial prowess, his current lack of a marital commitment, disturbing details of his work requirements, and her impassioned desire for a second chance with her only child. She looked so put together while he felt the tremors in his heart increase.

Mercifully, the judge was ready to declare his verdict before dinnertime.

The lawyers and he and Angela stood.

Judge Larry Benson's voice boomed through the chamber. "In consideration of the appearance and manner of the witnesses on the stand and their credibility, my decision in particular course after considering all the factors…"

Steven held his breath. *God, please.* If God really was listening, He'd have to read minds, because Steven couldn't form any other intelligible communication.

"…is to award sole physical and legal custody to the father."

Angela gripped the table in front of her. Marcus moved to her side and kept her standing.

The rush of relief was tangible, but what Steven had thought would bring him great joy only served to sear his conscience. His ex-wife's trembling hands and streaming tears made victory bittersweet.

Judge Benson adjusted his black robe. "Based on two predominant factors, one being the out-of-state residence of the non-custodial mother and the other being the clear admission of substance abuse on the part of the mother, visitation rights awarded by this court will be at the discretion of the father. It is my opinion that overnight visitation be restrained until further successful rehabilitation is demonstrated."

Angela flinched with each pound of the gavel.

Justice had been served. James was safe. But as Steven watched his ex-wife leave the courtroom with slumped shoulders and soft sniffles, something in him broke.

Do justly, love mercy.

His father's continual Old Testament teachings had stuck deep. But in this case, what did mercy mean?

35

Tom tossed his suitcases into the back of his rented silver Impala. The early afternoon sun failed to warm the air, and shivers trailed his spine.

Today was the big day.

He'd leave his mother to sort through what memorabilia she wanted to keep or pitch, including his beloved Vette. He'd find another one in Australia. A convertible, since the weather there was more reasonable than DC's frosty winters.

Thankfully, all the yuppies and DINKs had vacated the upscale townhome community at the crack of dawn. All the little ants and their high-powered jobs. Not him. Not any longer.

So no one had seen anything. Even if some snoopy neighbor paid attention, he'd be long gone before the local cops got a clue. But he had a lot of work to do before he could start living the good life. Free. With no shadows of the past.

He made his way through traffic on the Beltway and exited onto the Anacostia Freeway. First stop—3100 Massachusetts Avenue.

Tom had learned a few things from Joe, even more from the Internet, and he'd drained his savings and bank accounts slowly and steadily with one purchase here and another there. No suspicious activity. Only a few thousand cash.

Parking a good ways from the ambassador's estate, he found a nice full spot of foliage across the main street at an angle from the British residence. Nearby houses were for the most part uninhabited at this time of day.

He'd scoped out this area at three different times and learned that the afternoon was optimal for his plan to unfold with the least amount of interference.

And now he waited.

Sweat beads trailed down to the small of his back despite the afternoon's brisk temperatures. Little wind. Low clouds. High visibility. According to his calculations and view through the binoculars, he had a perfect vantage point to the little Kensington family's last-minute packing.

No doubt Joe did too. But there was so much Joe didn't know.

And with one move from the British killer-slash-former British Special Forces "mate," Tom would have one chance to finish his business and move on to stage two. Ending in a late evening flight out of his adopted hometown of Atlanta.

Not that he liked the faux Southern city that moved at the speed of light. But it would be fitting to have started and to finally end his criminal descent in the same location.

If only Kimberly had been faithful, he might have proposed like he'd planned. But he hadn't. Instead, he'd had far too many shots for those wretched backwoods curves. He shouldn't have taken that last drink. Without it, he might've missed that stupid blue van.

A slight glint of metal flashed, and Tom locked onto the coordinates. How fitting that Joe's money had gained Tom plenty of new toys and weeks of private instruction on how to use them well. Tom adjusted his scope and repositioned the top-of-the-line sniper rifle against his shoulder.

Steven listened to the brittle tree branches snap just yards in front of him.

The steep upward gradient of the British residence gave him the advantage. Clint off to his right and another two-man team approaching from the left provided a constant reminder of the need for a perfect shot.

One chance.

Michael's team would honor Steven's order to have first shot. He got into position and waited.

Months of searching. Endless paperwork. Dead end after dead end. Every member of the CACU had a vested interest in ending this case. Today.

Gordon Landridge aimed at the Kensington entourage.

Steven took a deep breath and focused his rifle on Gordon's chest.

A shot rang out.

Gordon shielded his face from the bark flying.

Someone's total miss. Before his target disappeared, Steven took a hurried shot and watched more tree bark fly.

Gordon ducked from the second round. They'd missed. Twice.

He left his Barrett sniper rifle and dove for tree cover. Pulling out his Glock 17, he kept going down the hill toward the embassy. One chance left. He'd make his mark this time and then leave the United States far behind.

More shots exploded around him. He kept moving closer to the target and opened fire. Sir Walter Kensington disappeared under a shield of black suits.

Gordon fired at the embassy door, stopping the suits by their cars. He was still in control of this scene.

Slamming into a large tree, he fought for balance and aimed again. A flip of blond hair caught his attention. He swung his handgun left and fired. Victoria's protection shoved the little bird into a black car. He aimed at the windshield. He was far from finished.

But before he could fire another round, heat exploded through his leg and chest.

"Move in. Slow." Steven barked into his body mic. He and Clint stayed low as they stepped down the steep, leaf-covered slope.

The snapping of branches echoed as his FBI team descended.

Secret Service cars rushed the ambassador and his family away before he reached the body. Michael approached the black-clothed figure sprawled facedown on the ground and scooted Gordon's Glock out of reach. Blood oozed from the massive leg and chest wounds.

Clint turned him over and felt for a pulse, but Steven, Michael, and Lee kept their pieces aimed at Gordon's head.

The smell of death clung to the musty woods.

"He has a pulse, but not for long." Clint cut into Landridge's clothes and tried to stem the bleeding with makeshift pressure bandages. Lee knelt to assist.

Steven secured his rifle and called in an ambulance.

Michael kept his eyes on Gordon. "One to the chest or one to the head. We'll take 'em breathing but prefer them dead."

"So you're the hotshot who took the first bead." Steven glared. "I lost my aim when your round sliced the trees instead of Landridge."

Michael stared at him with a confused look. "I didn't shoot."

"You didn't—" Steven looked around at the other two men. "Clint?"

"Nope."

"Lee?"

The thirty-three-year-old agent shook his dark head. "Not me, boss."

Steven's pulse kicked up with a fury. "If none of you took the first shot, where'd the other tree splitter come from?"

There had been no other human noise in the woods behind the embassy. He dialed Agent Adams. Within a minute his status report came back negative. No Secret Service agents had fired before the ambush.

Steven's mind whirled with possibilities. Slipping on gloves, he retrieved Gordon's knapsack and poked through it, disrupting as little as possible so the evidence team wouldn't pitch a fit. "Got a key card. No chain logo."

Michael let down his weapon and bent to recheck Gordon's

vitals. "No pulse. Our perp has expired."

Clint ignored him and started CPR while Lee kept pressure on both wounds.

"Okay, Michael." Steven handed him the hotel card. "Follow this trail and see if it leads to whoever took that first shot. You can do that here at the embassy." He squinted and surveyed the relatively quiet residence below. "I'm gonna see if I can find something else in his pack."

Clint and Lee kept busy, ignoring the reality that Landridge's vengeance had cost the man his life.

Steven's gut twisted into knots. Two shots and a mystery shooter on the loose. Even with Gordon dead, this case wasn't over.

Far from it.

36

Part two of Tom's plan would require stretching the bounds of his creativity.

And his newfound depravity. Too bad he hadn't finished off the Brit, but surely the FBI had. Even so, he had precious little time to pull this off before he disappeared.

Tom pulled his rental car into Gracie's driveway and cut the ignition. Straightening his usual black suit and blue power tie, he intended to look the part of his "official business" call.

He stepped out of the car and shivered. More from what the next twelve hours would hold than from the frigid air. But he had to finish what he'd started. Freedom was too close now to quit. Before knocking at the door, he slipped around to the back fence. He knew this ground well, and he wanted nothing to do with Gracie's dog.

The dog was lounging on the back porch, oblivious to Tom and his plans. Good. Without protection, that mutt could defend Gracie and destroy an unprotected man's arms.

Two things Tom wouldn't allow.

He sauntered up to the front porch. Gracie answered the door in white sweatpants and a blue-and-red Braves sweatshirt. "Mr. Perkins? What are you doing here?"

"Good afternoon, Mrs. Lang." He paused, his forehead creased in concern. "There's a situation at school...with Akemi...that I believe you could help us diffuse."

"Why didn't you call?"

He cleared his throat. "I wasn't sure you were up to driving. And you live so close, I thought it would be easier if I simply picked you up." Tom checked his watch. "But we don't have much time. School will be out shortly, and I'd like to see your students calm when their parents arrive."

She tightened her hands on the front door, then wrapped one arm around her waist.

Was she in pain? That could prove useful.

If she didn't come willingly, he'd be forced to resort to the handcuffs and Sig Sauer he'd purchased a few months ago. But he'd rather go slow and remain calm. They had a long trip ahead.

"What's wrong with Akemi?"

He checked his watch again. "It would be better to explain while we're on our way and save time. She was hysterical when I left, and I imagine it's only getting worse."

"Let me grab my things." She left the door open and retrieved her backpack-looking brown purse and a long wool coat.

As Tom helped her into the coat, Gracie flinched when she put her left arm in. Good sign. Still weak from the bullet wounds. She'd put up less of a fight when his plans became clear.

He escorted her to his silver Impala and held the door open so she could slide inside. Closing the door, he breathed a little easier. Step one down without a problem.

"Would you please tell me about the situation with Akemi?" She studied the bare trees and bright skies out the window.

Settling into the driver's seat, he willed his breathing to remain steady. As they pulled away from the curb, he scanned the houses on either side of Gracie's. No nosy neighbors peeking out from behind their curtains. Good.

"Mr. Perkins?"

"Sorry." He turned right out of her subdivision and loosened his death grip on the steering wheel. "Akemi, like most of your class, has been unsettled since the unfortunate situation last month." Pointing the Impala toward the interstate, he hoped casual conversation would distract her. For a while, anyway. "She's been asking for you and became hysterical today when the substitute said you wouldn't be back."

She sat up stiff and straight. "I will be returning. After Thanksgiving." Gracie studied his face and then looked back out the window. "I hope my visit today won't make things worse for Akemi."

He turned right onto I-395, away from Hope Ridge Academy.

She turned from the window, her brow a study in deepening wrinkles. "This isn't the way to school. Where are we going?"

"On a field trip of sorts." Tom caught a glimpse of her whitening face and smiled. He moved his suit coat back to reveal his loaded holster. "Don't want you leaving the party before the final performance now, do we?"

She gasped. "What's going on? I...I don't understand." Fear colored her hazel eyes.

"Give it some time. I'm sure you'll figure it out."

Silence stretched over the ten minutes it took to clear the Beltway. Once on I-95, Tom hit cruise control at seventy-five and eased his foot away from the pedal. At one-thirty in the afternoon, he couldn't attract attention by doing ninety like he'd prefer.

The sooner he handled this mess, the better. He didn't like the feel of blood on his hands. Or Gracie's piercing look. Especially without a drink to numb what sliver of conscience remained.

The young widow didn't respond for a long time. She only studied his face and then her tennis shoes. So he filled in some details to chase away the uncomfortable quiet. "Your private investigator was so close, Gracie. Too close. With the look you got that New Year's Eve long ago and your recent police sketch, you've become a major problem."

She stared at him with wide eyes. "You? You were the one who killed my family?" Her hands started to shake.

Too bad she was getting the last piece of the puzzle too late to do anything about it.

The miles flew by in silence. It felt good to be on Joe's end of the game this time. In control. Of everything.

"Why did you run my family off the road?"

"It was an accident." He gripped the steering wheel. "But you had to make such a fuss in the media! As if I'd planned to run your family off the road all along. I didn't."

"But you didn't even stop to help." She buried her face in her hands. Soon her shoulders shook as the sniffles increased.

"And end up in jail? No. I had enough brainpower left to realize nothing I could do would change the facts. The van came out of nowhere and disappeared just as fast. For all I knew, I had daydreamed the entire thing."

"You killed my husband and my two children." She uncovered her face. Her tears had stopped. In their place was a cold fire. "You'll pay for this."

He took a deep breath. "I figured as much, which is why we're going to part ways in the mountains of South Carolina, where no one will find you for years, possibly. And I'll be long gone from the good old US of A."

Gracie dove for her purse and grabbed a cell phone.

Tom unlatched his holster and pointed his new handgun at her temple.

She froze before even opening the phone. So like a woman.

With few other drivers around them, he pulled into the far right lane and slowed a little. "Throw it out the window, Gracie. Your purse too." He nudged her with the barrel.

She obeyed with stiff, robotic motions. The purse and cell crashed on the pavement behind them. One less clue to dispose of later.

He returned the gun to its holster. "Good girl. Keep that up and the rest of our trip will go well."

"Except that in the end I die anyway."

Tom could feel her frosty glare without turning his head from the road. No matter. He'd grown accustomed to that look from women.

"Sad to say, but yes. If only you had given up your little crusade and settled down with your FBI boyfriend. Life could have had a happily ever after ending."

She bowed her head and refused any further conversation.

Let her pray to her God.

It wouldn't do any good.

Gracie's hands felt like ice.

Just like her heart.

Why, God? Why now?

She thought back over the last few days. Steven's kisses. James's joy at hearing he'd be staying with his dad for good. The hope of returning to school. The lessening pain from her gun-shot wound

Alexandria had finally started to feel like home. A safe place with a future.

But now? Now she was helpless once again. And would be dead soon, at the hands of the man who'd killed her family. If this was the way God answered her prayers, what was the point of praying again?

Gracie's last conversation with her mom haunted her.

"Deal with your lies, honey. And listen to God's truth. Then let His truth and the resulting forgiveness set you free. Really free."

She'd never be free now.

As she watched I-95 turn into I-85 outside of Richmond, the hours of silence stretched her to the point of screaming. Small talk wouldn't help. And she couldn't release the tension fraying her nerves—it wouldn't help either. She'd probably end up pistol-whipped if she screamed. So she stared at the gray-black road outside her window. The one that wouldn't take her all the way home to Atlanta. No, she'd be dead long before then.

Focusing on the growing number of pine trees and foothills, she tried to pray. But the words wouldn't come. How could God let her quest for answers end this way? Facing the man she knew she had to forgive, only to have him kill her anyway.

Maybe she could escape. Prove once and for all that she wasn't helpless.

She sat up straighter and flexed her legs. "I really need to use the restroom. Can we stop at a rest area soon?"

"No chance of that in the daylight." Tom kept his cold eyes trained on the road.

As if on cue, her stomach started to rumble. "A drive-thru then?" She'd been in too huge a hurry to leave with Tom that she'd forgotten her watch. But she guessed the time around four o'clock. Maybe five.

He looked around and studied road signs in silence for miles.

Praying for one small break, she counted the rest area signs flying past and held her breath as Tom slowed to exit. Her one chance.

With sweaty palms and her heart slamming against her ribs, she exited the car. Tom's nails dug into her right arm.

"Do not make me regret this," he growled into her ear.

Gracie walked close by his side and tried to make eye contact with the few people leaving the mostly deserted facility. No one looked. Not a good sign. Little opportunity for screams to do more than scare people back into their cars. Someone might call the cops, though. But that wouldn't help if Tom killed her before they arrived.

Better to play it smart.

At the women's restroom, Tom released her arm. "Make it fast. Take more than two minutes and I come in." He raked his eyes down her torso. "Any bright ideas will cost you."

Gracie's mind refused to process what the cost of her escape plan would be if she failed. So she wouldn't fail.

Opening the cold door handle to the restroom, she shot up a quick prayer. She'd use the facilities and look for another door out. The trees around the rest area wouldn't hide her for long, but maybe she could make it up to the interstate before Tom realized she was gone.

Gracie hadn't resumed her daily running yet, but she'd been walking with Jake. How she wished he were here. If he'd been in the house, Jake would have taken that man down and she could have called the cops. Or Steven.

The thought of Steven made her eyes sting with tears. She'd never see him again. He'd be at her house tonight, ready for another date and she'd be…where? Dead someplace in South Carolina.

No!

She'd show Thomas Perkins. Walking around the corner to the far end of the restroom, she noticed a door. *Thank You, God.* But coming closer, it looked like bank vault. Locked down tight. No alarm visible, though.

A cleaning lady plopped down her yellow Wet Floor sign and began to mop, taking no notice of Gracie by the door. The woman's bent back and leathery wrinkles seemed like a beacon of hope. Maybe she'd unlock the bathroom fortress.

Gracie's two minutes were disappearing fast.

"Please, could you unlock the outside door?" Gracie tried to sound sane. "Or a phone. Do you have a phone I could use, please?"

"*No entiendo.*" The woman's black eyes lifted briefly, then returned to the floor.

Gracie's insides felt like they would explode. She had less than a minute.

A large key ring on the cleaning supply cart caught her attention. She lunged for it and ran past the older woman to the locked door.

The cleaning lady screeched.

Gracie's hands shook as she tried the keys one at a time. *Please, God.*

The woman shuffled toward her.

Then a key clicked and the door gave way.

Gracie almost tripped on the concrete but steadied herself with the door. Every instinct on full alert, she shot out of the bathroom. Her thigh muscles protested before she'd made it two strides past the door.

A tree root caught her running shoe and she stumbled. Not

able to right herself in time, she hit the dry dirt with splitting pain searing up her left side. She could hear the cleaning lady yelling behind her in Spanish.

The loose rocks bit into her sweaty palms. She ignored them and pushed herself to her feet. Gulping for air, she fixed her eyes on the gray road in front of her and stepped ahead.

But a vise clamped around her arm. "I don't think so, Gracie." Tom pulled her close. His narrowed eyes bore into her and burned their image on her soul. "We had a deal, did we not?"

Catching her breath was near impossible as Tom yanked her toward the front of the rest area. The clanging bathroom door echoed in her ears.

"Help! Somebody…"

Tom jerked her in front of him and shook her. Hard. "No use of that." He pointed to the solitary car halfway down the on-ramp. "There's no one left to rescue you now."

Pain messages slammed into her brain from all directions as they neared Tom's car. She should have screamed when she'd had the chance. Stupid. So stupid. No way she'd have another opportunity like this one.

And she'd failed.

What that would cost her, she wouldn't let herself imagine as Tom shoved her into the Impala and headed back toward the interstate. Watching trees and cars blur past her window, there were no tears left to cry.

She'd be dead soon.

Worse yet, she'd just about stopped caring.

37

With Gordon's computer and luggage that were stashed in his rental now in their possession, Steven's entire team worked hard putting the finishing touches on this case. It would wrap up neat and clean.

Steven floored his Explorer and headed toward Alexandria.

From Gordon's e-mails to Thomas Perkins, they'd retrieved a series of routing numbers to an offshore account, which connected the two men with the attempt on Victoria. And they had clothing fibers that Steven felt sure would match Landridge's.

Now all he had to do was bag Hope Ridge Academy's vice principal and turn him over to the lockup. A few days behind bars would have the man spilling every last detail.

"You really think the mild-mannered VP of Hope Ridge made that attempt on Gordon?" Clint shook his head.

"That stuffed shirt's been boiling under the surface for a long time."

He punched the speed dial to Gracie's number for what felt like the hundredth time this afternoon. No ring. No answer. He couldn't wait until their date tonight to make sure she was okay. He dialed again.

Nothing. His gut clenched.

"Justin sent you all the info he'd uncovered on Tom?"

"That's why we're moving now."

Between Gordon and Tom's computers and Justin's research, Thomas Perkins was looking at serious jail time. And that was only if he hadn't touched Gracie.

If he had...the man would be looking down the barrel of Steven's backup piece.

Clint tapped away on his laptop. "Gordon never figured he'd get caught."

"No. But Tom will."

Clint faced him. "Michael's running down Tom's recent purchases and the aliases he might be using. We'll get an APB out as soon as we dig up a few more details from Tom's computer."

"That could be too late to do any good." Steven focused on the road ahead. The one he'd driven just days ago to drop Gracie off after Wednesday's court date.

"She could be asleep."

"At three o'clock in the afternoon? With Thomas Perkins missing from Hope Ridge since before he took that shot on Gordon?"

"You can't head the team going after her if she's missing. You know that, right?"

Steven parked the Explorer in Gracie's driveway and faced off with his partner. "Clint, I'm going after her. Tom is still the main suspect on my case." He checked his watch. "I didn't lose my son Wednesday, and I'm sure not going to lose Gracie today."

He stormed up the sidewalk. On instinct, he drew his gun and tried Gracie's front door. Unlocked.

Not good.

He proceeded inside. Clint followed. With every step Steven's heart raced faster. He was walking into his worst nightmare.

They moved through each of the open rooms of the main floor, then to the staircase.

Nothing moved.

Steven knew he'd find the upstairs empty too, but training and hope spurred him on.

"It's clean, Steven." Clint holstered his gun and pulled out a cell phone. "An ERT is on the way."

A high-pitched whimper drove him to the back door. Jake.

Steven stepped onto the back patio and nearly fell over as the trembling dog leaped on his chest. "Down, boy. Come on, Jake, come in here." The dog was cold and very hungry. Not good at all.

The dog raced into the kitchen and made short work of devouring his food and water and begged for more. "Come on, boy. We need to go." He grabbed Jake's collar and headed to Gracie's next-door neighbor.

Clint could deal with the evidence team and whichever agent would head up the search for Gracie. For all he knew, they were too late anyway.

His lungs fought to expand as a lead weight of hopelessness slammed into him. But that wouldn't stop him from trying. As soon as he could, he'd tear away from FBI red tape and get on the road. Regardless of what Clint had to say about interfering with an open missing person's investigation, this had been his case first.

Long before he'd known Gracie would be at risk.

He couldn't lose her. Not now.

Steven knocked on the door of her favorite older neighbor. The eyes and ears of the block, Gracie had called her. "Mrs. Davidson, did you talk to Gracie this morning?"

"No, Steven, I didn't get to hear her talk about you today." The woman smiled. "I don't get out anymore like I used to. In fact, I decided to stay in bed till late this morning. But I did notice a spindly young man taking her for a drive a few hours ago."

His pulse kicked up a notch. "What did he look like and when was that exactly?"

A large van pulled into Gracie's drive and evidence techs scrambled out.

She stepped out on the porch. "What in the world is going on? Is Gracie going back to the hospital? Oh my heavens, is she okay?"

"It's all right, Mrs. Davidson. Gracie is fine." *Please, let that not be a lie.* "The crowd will be leaving shortly."

The elderly woman eyed the people next door with suspicion. Jake growled.

Steven led her back inside with Jake. "The man that Gracie

left with…can you give me any details?"

"He was in a black suit. Thick curly hair." She stared at her ceiling. "I believe that was about one o'clock. Not too long after I downed my laxative—"

"Thanks, Mrs. Davidson." His stomach churned as he checked his watch. "I really appreciate your watching Jake." Steven stepped off the porch and hurried across the yard to meet Clint.

"Agent Kessler." The agent in charge of the evidence team approached. "I need to ask you a few questions."

"I really need to get going. Can we wrap this up fast?" Steven forced his jaw to relax. Appearing too anxious might raise some red flags.

Clint raised his eyebrow.

"Do you know if Mrs. Lang had any enemies, anyone who might be responsible for her disappearance?"

"Yes. Thomas Perkins. You can get the details from Agent Parker with the Crimes Against Children Unit."

The young agent took far more notes than the words Steven had just given. "Know where they might be headed?"

"Georgia."

The agent stopped writing. "How can you be sure?"

"A hunch." Steven pulled keys from his pants pocket. "I need to head out. Call if you find something." He handed the agent his business card.

He checked his watch again. Every minute he stayed rooted in Alexandria…

Steven shoved those thoughts aside.

He had to keep one focus—finding Gracie.

Today.

Alive.

"Hand me your keys, Steven. I'm driving." Clint stood his ground next to the driver's side door. "You're in no shape to drive. Off duty or not."

Steven handed him the keys and strapped into the passenger's side. "Tom has a two hour or more lead on us."

"I called Agent Maxwell. Told him we're following our suspect." Clint headed the Explorer toward I-95. "We're clear, and I'm flooring it, partner. We'll catch him."

"We'd better. Before he hurts Gracie."

Clint would likely have a few hours to reason with Steven, but he couldn't think of a good segue into all that needed to be said. So he prayed.

And waited.

Steven kept his focus on the asphalt in front of them, mouth set and jaw clenched. "How are you going to cut a two-hour lead?"

"I'll cut it to less than one right here." He pegged the speedometer well past ninety. "And maybe Gracie used her ingenuity and stalled for time someplace too."

Silence.

"Tell me about Wednesday, Steven. That should pass the time." Clint needed a distraction. Something to get the image of Gracie's dead body out of his mind.

Steven slumped in his seat. "I told you. I won custody. Angela disappeared. It's over."

"Not by a long shot."

His partner looked out the window. "She was so defeated. It hurt, Clint. I didn't intend to destroy her. I only wanted to keep James safe."

"What are you going to do now?"

Steven didn't change his focus on the window. "Find Gracie. Raise my son."

Clint held the wheel with both hands and white knuckles, adrenaline pumping. Not a good feeling. He was getting too old for this high-speed chase scene. And even more tired of waiting on Steven to deal with the past.

Clint started coughing and fought to maintain speed. He set the cruise control.

"You getting sick?" Steven turned concerned eyes his way.

"No. Don't change the subject." Clint pushed down all the questions Sara would have if she knew about his recent cough and night sweats. Taking a fast drink of water, he pushed his mind to stay present. "I've heard what Gracie's had to say to you. She's echoed what I've been saying for years. Tell me you're not ignoring her too."

"That's a low blow."

"Tell me I'm wrong. She cares about you, Steven. But you're not free of the past or free to start something good with Gracie until you forgive Angela. Forgive yourself too. And you can't do that until you deal with the lie you blame on your ex-wife."

Pulling a Bible from his coat pocket, Steven held it up. "See this? I'm carrying it now because Gracie said James was talking about how my dad carries a Bible everywhere. But since I don't, James decided he didn't need to bring his to school anymore either."

Clint winced. Nothing like a child's footsteps to jerk a man into the right path.

If the man listened.

"So I'm working on the rest, okay?" Steven pocketed his Gideon's Bible and turned back to the window. "Let's stick to finding Gracie right now. My heathen soul can wait."

"We have a few hours to kill. I think we should stick with the current conversation until we're finished."

Steven huffed. "I know you do. You and Gracie are like pit bulls, but I don't want to deal with it right now. Especially not when she could be dead already. Like Olivia."

Clint gripped the wheel harder and whipped in and out of the fast lane a few times. "God's in control, Steven. I don't understand the harsh realities of our job, but I choose to hold on to what I know. I know God is good."

Clint's cell phone buzzed.

Steven picked it up. "It's the unit chief."

Listening to his partner's side of the conversation, Clint tried to mesh bits and pieces of it together as the car headed into slower and slower traffic.

"Basically, locals have kept the Bureau informed on the recent APB." Steven tossed the phone on the console between them. "There was a sighting near South Hill about thirty minutes ago. We're close on his tracks."

"See? God's at work."

More silence.

Clint wanted to push on Steven's belief that he'd never be good enough. To share that no matter what Angela said or did or thought, that was not what God said. But Steven had thrown up a wall.

And nothing but God could crash that one down.

Thirty long, silent minutes later, Clint's cell buzzed again.

Steven grabbed it, listened, and took a map from the glove compartment. "Got it. ETA twenty minutes."

"What's the latest?"

His partner snapped the phone shut. "Local cops just got a call about a disturbance this side of Greensboro, at a little mom-and-pop gas station. Fits our APB." Steven sat stiffer and checked his watch.

"Now would be a good time to pray, partner." Clint floored the accelerator. He'd drive fast and pray faster.

No telling what Thomas Perkins would do if this turned into a hostage situation. The local cops could be unpredictable too. Clint wondered how Gracie was holding up.

So many wild thoughts bounced around his head, but he kept his mouth closed because none of them offered much hope. He'd seen too many standoffs end with multiple casualties. Crazy men backed into a corner often chose death by cop over jail.

Which meant Gracie...

Clint slapped that thought down.

They would *not* be too late this time.

38

Gracie huddled against the passenger side door. Tom had stopped at a little mom-and-pop gas station somewhere in Podunk, South Carolina.

"If you so much as squeak, I'll take you and the two old people in the little mart down. You hear?"

She nodded and stayed still. But when the owner and his wife stepped out to wave while Tom pumped gasoline, she reacted on instinct.

She waved back. "Oh, Tom, honey," she practically yelled with a mock Southern drawl as she got out of the car. "I do need to use the facilities. I'll just be a sec."

Tom had little choice. Shoot everyone in sight, or let her go to the bathroom alone.

He grabbed her arm and traced the bruise on her face. "Don't make me hurt them because you opened your mouth."

The little gray-haired woman walked her to the tiny restroom in silence. Gracie stayed quiet under Tom's watchful eye but deliberately turned her reddened cheek toward the woman, hoping a long look would motivate her to call the police.

Escaping into the little bathroom, Gracie locked the door and leaned against it. There wasn't anywhere to run. A few trees. One road. Nowhere safe for her to go in the growing darkness. She wouldn't make it far anyway with an aching side and a burning left cheek.

She spied a supply closet door and rushed to open it. Instead of cleaning items, there was a small storage area full of boxes with another door that looked like it opened into the mart.

Moving as fast as she could without making noise, she barricaded both of the doors with a few heavy boxes.

Outside, a car screeched its tires.

She jumped and the stack of empty boxes beside her hit the floor. Her blood pressure climbed with the slight noise she made. Gracie held her breath and waited, praying the police would come before Tom could find her.

The gas station bell clanged and the outside door slammed. "Where is my wife?"

Tom sounded close enough to reach through the wall and pull her out of hiding. He sure put on a good act with the concern in his voice. Of course, he'd been doing a master act for the last year. So much made sense now. All the extra assignments he'd slapped her with every break during the school year. His snooping around her classroom. Especially the day she was shot.

Poor Victoria.

One by one, her students came to mind. She held on to the thought of James the longest. She ached to see her students again. And one parent in particular.

Tom's voice forced her back to the present. "My wife is sick and off her medications. She could be passed out in the bathroom. Let me in so I can check on her."

Gracie shuddered at his tearjerker story. She prayed for the kind store owners, hoping they wouldn't believe him. And that if they continued to stall for her, Tom wouldn't wave his menacing gun in their faces. Or worse.

She wouldn't die by this coward's hand. She'd fight. And pray no one else got hurt.

A noise outside made Gracie hold her breath.

Someone slipped into the bathroom and the door lock clicked. Gracie willed herself not to make the slightest sound.

"Honey," the woman whispered into the supply closet. "You okay in there?"

Gracie wanted to answer but didn't know if Tom was there too. So she held her tongue.

"I called the police. Should be hearing them any minute now, I suspect."

A deep sigh escaped. This would be over soon. Gracie whispered, "Thank you."

The bathroom door opened and closed again.

Minutes dragged on, and Gracie's eyes adjusted to the dark. Tall cardboard boxes lined the four walls. Not much else but cobwebs and the musty smell that permeated the little room like a long-abandoned basement.

Abandoned. That fit.

The men's voices had gone silent, but no one opened the storage room door. Then she heard sirens. Lots of them.

"Get back here, Pops." Tom's voice drew nearer to her hiding place. "You're my only ticket out of this miserable place."

"Please, don't hurt him." A quivery voice stabbed at Gracie's conscience. "He has a weak heart. You could kill him, choking him like that."

Wiping her sweaty hands on her sweatpants, she prayed for direction. She considered going out the bathroom door. Maybe she could sneak around the side of the mart and explain everything to the police, show them the back way into the store. But the locked storage room door would be a problem. As would leaving the kind couple at the mercy of Tom Perkins. The man who wouldn't stop killing until he was free.

Or dead.

She prayed Steven was on his way. Surely by now he'd figured out all the details Tom had bragged on almost the entire trip.

How could she have ever thought Tom was innocent? Why hadn't she listened to Justin and stayed far away from her vice principal like he'd warned? She should have told Steven everything the private investigator had said the night she got back to Alexandria.

But Steven's kiss had silenced every logical thought then. And the custody hearing Wednesday didn't allow for much talk other than James's safety.

Gracie shook her head. Now was not the time to recount her stupidity. She'd have plenty of time for that later.

If she survived.

But she couldn't stay hidden and let two more innocent people die. She pounded on the storage room door. "Tom! I'm in here. Let them go."

On shaky feet she stood by the door and moved the boxes out of the way. Then she waited, praying.

"Open that door. Now."

Keys jangled. Someone sniffled. The sweet older woman?

When the door flung open, Gracie stepped through it and blinked against the store's light. Outside, the sun was setting. Darkness would move the balance of favor into Tom's court.

"I'm so sorry, hon," the gray-haired woman said. "Our local boys will get you out."

"Get out. Both of you." Tom shoved the woman's husband with a gun between the shoulder blades. "Walk slowly."

As they stepped out the front door, Tom wrapped his arm around Gracie's neck and yanked her toward the back exit. "What a hero you are, giving up your freedom to purchase another few years for those two old fogies. Lot of good that did you."

He walked backward, one slow step at a time. "You're still going to die tonight. And I'm going to make my flight." Tom kept his spine pressed against the wall as they neared the back door.

Flashing blue lights swirled outside the glass front of the store. Three cop cars. A few rifles pointed at Tom's head. But they wouldn't shoot. Wouldn't risk hitting her.

And so Tom would drag her back to the car, and they'd die in some high-speed car chase.

Gracie's heart stuck in her throat. She'd die like her family had died, after all.

At the hands of the same man.

Tom opened the back door and the cool night air made her shiver.

No police in the back parking lot. No flashing lights. No knights in shining armor, either.

God, where are You?

Like she'd figured, Tom had moved his car to the backside of the little mart. The gray building would keep them sheltered until they were in the silver Impala and on their way.

Tom shoved her into the front seat, keeping his eyes fixed forward. She ducked down into the seat when he entered and reached for the ignition.

A soft click changed him to stone.

Her mind fought to process what was happening.

"Don't move, Perkins," Steven commanded from the backseat. "Gracie, take the keys and his gun and slide out your side. Clint and the other officers are right around the corner."

She nodded in the dark but sat frozen to the seat.

"Gracie. I need you to move. Now."

With shaking hands she closed her fingers around the silver metal of Tom's disgusting gun.

Tom kept a tight hold.

"Steven?" She glanced back and tried to keep her shaking hands around the gun.

Steven kept his eyes fixed straight ahead and pushed the gun barrel into Tom's neck.

Tom released his gun.

She clamped one hand around it. With her other hand she took the keys from the steering column. Sliding out of the car, she hoped Steven would look up, but he stared at the back of Tom's head, unmoving.

Numb, she walked to the edge of the building and then glanced back one more time. Steven still hadn't moved.

"I'm coming around the side." She held her hands high in the air and walked forward. "Don't shoot."

A few of the officers chuckled.

She couldn't imagine laughing at a time like this, but she'd heard that cops either laughed at tense situations or went crazy.

Clint stepped into her path. "Gracie, thank God you're okay."

She collapsed into his arms and cried the storehouse of tears she'd pushed aside for the last five hours. Tears for the family she'd lost. Tears for the people she loved and thought she'd never see again. Beth. Mom and Dad. Leah. James. Steven.

An eerie silence met her when she sniffled back the last of the tears. She looked up into Clint's face. Judging from the hard lines of his set jaw, something was wrong. Very wrong.

"Gracie. I need you to wait here with the sheriff." Clint pointed toward the swirling blue lights. "I'll be back in a sec."

Clint unsnapped his gun belt and disappeared around the side of the building.

Had Tom gotten away?

"Holster your gun, Steven. Let it go. We got him." Clint's voice boomed from behind the mart.

Silence.

Handcuffs clicked and all the cops let out a collective breath.

Clint marched Tom toward the nearest patrol car. The man's once impressive suit now looked like it'd been trampled.

Tom stopped near her and his harsh glare froze her heart. "It's not over."

Clint shoved Tom forward and into the patrol car, slamming the door.

Steven followed, head down, shoulders drooping. He ran his hands through his thick brown hair and stopped in front of the gas station.

She ran to him and wrapped her arms around his waist, shaking. "Steven, I can't believe you got him. He's going to jail where he can't escape, right?"

Steven didn't look up. Didn't move.

So she pulled back and cupped his face in her hands, making him turn his eyes to meet hers.

"I wanted to kill him, Gracie. In cold blood. I almost did."

Rubbing his arms, she prayed for the right words. "But you didn't, Steven. And you saved me." She tried to smile.

He rested his hands on her shoulders. "You're okay?" He touched the bruise on her left cheek.

She flinched.

"We need to get you checked out at the hospital before we head home." Steven put an arm around her shoulders and walked toward one of the police cars.

"Where's the nearest hospital?"

A short, stocky officer motioned them over to his cruiser. "I'll give you an escort there." He looked Gracie over. "We'll make sure they take the very best care of you too, ma'am."

"The owners? Are they okay?" Gracie scanned the parking lot.

"Deputy took them to be checked out too. They'll be okay, no doubt. But I reckon they'll be home before we make it to the ER."

"We'll follow you over." Steven's voice was hollow, lifeless.

No one spoke the entire drive. And by the time they arrived at the little community hospital, Gracie had decided two things.

One, she had a piece of her mind to let loose on God the minute she had some time alone.

And two, she was going home to Atlanta again. Maybe for good.

Far away from haunted looks.

Far away from the smell of blood.

And as far away as she could run from anything related to guns.

39

Thanksgiving yesterday had come and gone in a total blur. Steven had wrapped up the Kensington case and handed it over for prosecution. He'd have to testify, but that wouldn't be for a while. As for today, he was on vacation.

With nothing to do but fix chocolate chip pancakes for his son and wonder why Gracie wouldn't take his calls.

Still, something was thawing inside.

Whisking the pancake batter, he checked the clock. James would be up soon.

Over Thanksgiving dinner, his dad's prayers had included Steven, James, and Gracie. Angela too. Then his sister, Hanna, had hugged him and told him she'd missed him.

Steven had started to realize how much he missed himself too. The young man who had talked—and listened—to God. The man who had held his crying newborn boy and realized all life ultimately rested in God's all-sufficient hands.

Not in Steven's.

When had he forgotten? And when had he become a man who'd actually consider killing in cold blood?

"That's not who you are, Steven." Clint had spoken those words over and over the last few weeks. He'd also said that feelings weren't truth. Maybe it was starting to sink in.

Steven poured batter onto the hot griddle and then pushed Play on his sister's portable CD player. She'd insisted he borrow her favorite CD, *Casting Crowns*. He understood why as the third song hit him with utter clarity. The words lined up with all Clint and Gracie had been trying to tell him. The passionate and smooth lyrics spoke of all the voices crying out, saying he'd never win.

Steven could relate. Even felt like the warriors quaking in their armor wishing for the strength to stand. But the words that registered the loudest brought to mind a mountain peak and watching an eagle fly right into the storm clouds and soar.

"Listen to the truth, Steven." God's voice came to him with the distinct Texas drawl of his best friend. Listen. To the voice of truth.

Then, as if to pen an exclamation point on the story being rewritten inside of him, the next song was titled, "Who Am I." The answer was straight from his dad's Old Testament teaching on Jeremiah and Isaiah. "I have loved you with an everlasting love. I have called you by name; you are Mine."

No matter how long it took Steven to listen.

Little-boy steps hit the stairs running and interrupted his thoughts. Steven poured milk and set out the maple syrup.

"Hey, Dad!" James stopped at the table with wide eyes. "Wow, pancakes. Just like Grandpa fixes."

Steven smiled. It felt good to be compared to his dad again. They sat at the table and Steven held out his hand. "Let's pray."

James blinked a few times before bowing his head.

"Lord, You are good and You are in control. Guide our hands and words today. Amen."

His son inhaled the first plate of gooey chocolate pancakes and asked for more.

Steven flipped two more onto James's plate and sat down. "Chew, James." He ruffled his little boy's still sleep-rumpled hair. "What say we go cut down a Christmas tree today?"

"Woo-hoo!" James shoved a sticky fist in the air.

"And take it over to your mom's condo."

"But she left weeks ago." James sucked in his bottom lip. "And never called."

"She's at the condo packing it up to sell." Steven knelt by his son's chair. "I think we should take her a tree and let her know we'd like her to stay in our lives. She's your mom, after all."

James hugged his neck hard. "I love you, Daddy." Big blue eyes searched his. "Does this mean it's okay if I like her? I mean, if she stops drinking, then she can be my mommy?"

"I'm praying she'll get the help she needs, son." He picked up James. "And I think she will. She loves you. And she's talking to some good counselors who help people deal with tough things."

Wiggling out of his arms, James ran to the door and stopped. "I'll get dressed fast. Then we can take the ornaments I made when I was little. Mom will like those, right?"

"Yes."

Steven cleaned the kitchen and thought back over all the Christmases James had spent without a mom to bake cookies with or sing him carols at bedtime. Steven had tried, but there were things that moms did best. That huggy, mushy, soft stuff, wrapped in warm vanilla.

He wasn't ready to give Angela overnights or school vacation weeks yet; she still had a lot of treatment ahead. But the time had come to let the past go, to move ahead. To try for peace in a challenging situation.

Angela had left him for another man, and he'd spent the better part of their marriage and the five years since trying to prove he was good enough. A man. But today, he'd experienced the words he'd heard growing up at his dad's knee.

God was the only One to whom he stood or fell. And He'd already paid for the fall so His children could stand. With Him. No matter what.

"Daddy! Let's go get a tree!"

Bundled in warm jackets and wool hats, they left to find what Steven hoped would be the perfect bridge. A tree had served that purpose two thousand years ago.

Maybe it would again today.

"Hi, Mom! We brought you an early Christmas present." James jumped around, totally missing his mother's open-mouthed stare as they stood outside her expensive ground-floor condo.

Steven held his breath and kept the big, prickly tree standing upright.

"We want you to keep your house here so I can visit." James looked back at him. "Daddy says we'll work it out as we go."

Angela knelt down and touched James's coat sleeve.

"Please, will you stay?" James pointed to the tree Steven held. "I even brought my ornaments to decorate it."

Angela smoothed her expensive black running suit and looked over their son's head, meeting Steven's eyes. Questions filled the silence between them.

"You're his mom, Angela. We both want you to be part of his life." He didn't try to figure out the undefined parameters of this new journey. That could wait.

Today was for forging a new path.

She stood and opened the door wide. "Come on in. I think I have the perfect place for that beautiful tree."

James ran next to the large stack of packing boxes and tore off his winter bundling. Gloves and scarves flew across the floor. At least there were no pictures or fragile things sitting out to break.

Angela touched his arm. "Thank you. This…this means more than you know."

He nodded with a half smile. "So where would you like your tree?"

She pointed to an empty space beside the sliding glass doors and held the tree while he took off his coat. James helped him secure the tree in its base.

"Where's Gracie?" Angela asked.

He searched for the right words. They were especially important in front of his son. "She's had a rough couple of months, and she's back in Atlanta taking it easy for a little while."

Better to avoid the details of her kidnapping and that Steven didn't know when or if she'd ever come back to Alexandria. He wanted to hold her in his arms again. Longed for it so much it hurt.

But this time, he'd pray.

Something he hadn't done when he fell in love with Angela. He hadn't waited much with his career either. Pushing, solving cases, depending on his own abilities—he'd forged ahead without much thought for God.

That was changing.

And so, he'd wait.

Because the best was always worth waiting for.

40

I t wouldn't snow in Georgia. Not in December.

It hadn't for any of Gracie's childhood. Except for three years ago. Looking forward to celebrating her seventh wedding anniversary, she'd thought the snow was a sign of good things to come. Everything white and beautiful.

Now white reminded her of hospital sheets. Not beauty. Or hope.

She walked across the cemetery lawn under foreboding gray skies. Weather reports hinted at a possible snow flurry, but she doubted it.

Her dad took her hand and stopped next to a bare maple tree swaying in the wind. "Honey, you know we love you and we've enjoyed having you home for Thanksgiving. Beth too, and the twins."

Gracie tried to smile. It had been good to be around little ones over the holidays. Then again, it also increased the ache inside to have what her baby sister had—children. A strong sense of family. Laughter. Hope and a future.

Beth's live-in boyfriend had even hinted at a ring for Christmas.

Something Gracie would never have again.

If she was really honest, what hurt the most wasn't the past. Though memories of the man who killed her family still haunted her. What hurt to the core was a fear of the future. Fear that she couldn't handle the life Steven represented. Guns and danger. That he could die on any one of his assignments. And yet she missed him with a longing that took her breath away.

"Remember your mom's wise words: 'Face the past and you'll find your dreams for the future.'" With a kiss on her head, her dad left her to her thoughts and made his way to the other side of the grounds to visit his mother's grave site.

Gracie sat between the headstones marking her husband and children's resting places. The wind whipped the loose hair around her face, and she pulled her leather coat tighter.

She fingered the velvet petals of the white and red roses she'd chosen for today. Similar flowers had graced her family's markers every month she'd lived in Atlanta. Mark had always brought home red and white roses on special occasions. Red for the fierce love he felt for them and white for the purity he saw when he looked at Elizabeth and Joshua.

"I miss you so much." Tears stung her eyes as she fingered the lettering of their names.

Elizabeth Anne Lang. Dearly loved daughter of Mark and Gracie Lang. Resting in the arms of Jesus. Little roses decorated the words carefully chosen during the darkest days of her life.

Joshua Allen Lang. Dearly loved son of Mark and Gracie Lang. Resting in the arms of Jesus. Simple strands of metal ribbon flowed around the words.

It was almost more than her heart could handle. But she put the two small bouquets of roses on each of their headstones.

"Mommy loves you." She fingered the gold locket, tiny and cold in her coat pocket. Then she moved to the next headstone.

Mark Richard Lang. Dearly loved husband of Gracie Lang. Resting in the arms of Jesus. A simple cross and Bible flanked the words.

Gracie placed the last and largest bouquet of flowers in the heavy vase at the base of Mark's headstone. Turning over the heavy container and dusting the cobwebs from it had provided a measure of distraction to regain her composure.

She stood and wiped her hands together. The roses were vibrant against the bleak sky. She took a deep breath and returned to her children's grave markers. "So much has happened since last year. In spite of…everything, my job is wonderful. The children remind me of the joy I had being your mommy. I miss you. I miss hearing your sweet voices."

Gracie strained hard to hear the faint sound of her memories. Two little voices singing in church choirs and on long car rides became clearer. *'Jesus lob me, dis I no.'* A slight smile turned her cheeks upward. She'd loved to sing along with her precious little ones. Her throat stung with unsung choruses, and her arms ached with shadow memories of holding her two little babies.

"I still have the locket you gave me for Christmas." She rubbed the delicate gold oval now resting in her hand. Placing a kiss on her fingertips, she touched Elizabeth and Joshua's names again.

It was time to say good-bye, but she would always hold them in her heart.

She moved to her husband's headstone. "Mark, I miss you more than I can put into words."

Gracie pictured his gentle eyes caressing her. She could almost feel his thick blond hair beneath her fingertips. In her mind's eye, she traced his smooth face and muscled arms. She had never loved or been so deeply loved in her life.

She wiped her eyes for what felt like the hundredth time and then wrapped her arms around her knees. So much had happened in the last five months. Meeting Steven. Getting shot. Then getting kidnapped. Learning the identity of the man who had killed her family, the one who'd tried to kill her too.

Looking up into the sky, she recalled her mom's words about facing the past and finding her dreams. Words she'd run from. Until now. Today they'd caught up to her. And she was too tired to keep up the grueling pace of fear.

"Step into God's arms and spill out what you've believed about yourself—that you're helpless, abandoned—and admit you've lived trying to prove those lies aren't real instead of receiving what God says about you. Let yourself feel His forgiveness. And then listen to His truth."

Was it really that easy?

She'd known God's comforting arms many times. But this time, telling Him what He already knew and she didn't want to admit, felt awkward. Like a teenager's first date.

"Mom's right. I know You know that, Daddy." Wouldn't Mom love to hear this? "I felt abandoned by You for a long time. By my family, too, even though it wasn't their fault. And I still feel totally helpless."

She rested her forehead on her knee. "I couldn't get justice for my family by finding the man who killed them. But he found me and tried to kill me. He almost succeeded too. Because even after two chances, I couldn't figure out how to escape."

Anger heated her face and coursed through her limbs.

"I hate feeling helpless. Useless. I don't know why You still want me to talk to You. I can't do anything right. I can't even hear the truth Mom said You'd speak to me."

Hot tears forced themselves over her eyelids, and she flicked them away.

A picture of Elizabeth as a newborn, wailing in her crib, filled Gracie's mind. As helpless as a newborn. The old saying felt like it'd been spoken over her shoulder.

She knelt and looked around, but no one else braved the cemetery on December's first cold Saturday morning. Pulling her coat tighter, she studied Elizabeth's gravestone.

She'd never thought of her children as helpless. Not in a bad way, anyway. They simply needed her and she took care of them. Loved them. Took joy in holding them.

That's how I love you.

Little shivers ran down her arms.

As a mother comforts her child, as she gently cares for her little ones, so I will care for you.

Truth. This was what her mother had meant by listening to God's truth. Too full for words, she looked up into the sky again. Only this time, joy slipped inside and took root deep in her heart.

A chilly breeze rustled the trees. And the sky blew out a few little drops of rain. She stood and let the blood return to her numb legs.

Her mom's words about facing the past and finding her dreams finally made sense.

The gentle love of a mother to her newborn baby—God's love for her—chased away the fear and left in its place a tentative excitement about the future.

There was one thing she had to do first, though, before stepping into that future. A part of her heart was still bolted shut. She wasn't totally sure how to turn the lock and open it wide.

But now she had the key. And God's loving arms surrounding her, comforting, caring, and spurring her to step ahead and leave the consequences in His able hands.

She pulled her leather coat around her and headed toward her dad's warm car. The rain had stopped, but as she brushed the newest wet drops off of her sleeve, she noticed something that made her smile.

The rain had a few tiny snowflakes mixed in.

Gracie parked her parents' Navigator and stared at the huge flag fluttering in front of a large, dreary gray building. The thick barbed wire of the familiar police headquarters next door did nothing to encourage her feet forward.

She rubbed the arms of her down jacket and put one tennis-shoed foot ahead of the other. Crossing the full parking lot, she walked through the double doors and into a large space with a few fake potted trees here and there and rows of plastic chairs dotting its perimeter. Tall windows streamed sunlight into the open waiting room.

Stomach rumbles and taut shoulder muscles made her reconsider this visit. But she stepped in line behind a somber group anyway. The men in light brown uniforms took her coat, purse, and every bit of metal she'd carried into the correctional facility off High Hope Road.

She'd always thought that was a weird name for a street winding past a high-security prison. A place she never thought she'd find herself in the middle of December.

Or any other time.

"Please step through." A bored guard ushered her forward. "You can pick up a visitor's badge once you pass those doors." He pointed to a heavy, dark door at the far end of the waiting room.

Gracie swallowed the butterflies fluttering from her stomach to her throat. "Will I go in alone?"

"No, you'll get an escort." The bulky sheriff looked at her and jabbed a thumb over his shoulder. "They got a group of religious folks waiting to go back. Reckon you'll go in with them."

Minutes later, a suffocating feeling pressed into her as huge glass sliding doors closed behind her before the one in front of her had opened.

Trapped. The word kept bouncing around her brain.

The small group of local church people in front of her walked in silence, their soft-soled shoes making little noise over the white linoleum floor. Every time they passed a few glass windows at shoulder level, she wanted to duck so as not to be seen by the inmates playing different sports in the little gyms.

When they arrived at the small visitation room, she considered telling the guard that she'd changed her mind. But she'd have to wait for this group of two ministers and their wives to finish speaking with those they came to encourage.

So she pulled a plastic chair up to the glass that would separate her from the man she needed to face.

And there she waited.

Small gray partitions between the visitors gave little privacy, but she tried not to listen to the conversations around her.

Maybe he'd refused to see her.

That would make her life easier. She'd been obedient to that still, small prompting at the cemetery a few weeks ago. She'd shown up. The rest was up to God.

Before she could slide her chair backward to go wait by the door, Thomas Perkins entered the room on the other side of the glass. His cold black eyes hadn't changed since the last time she'd seen him, when he'd glared at her from the other end of his gun barrel.

He sat in an identical plastic chair, silent and staring right through her.

She bit her lip. All the practiced words escaped her.

"Let's get this over with, shall we, Gracie?"

Jumping at his words, she tried to breathe slowly and steadily.

"I know why you're here. Your good little Christian self came to say you've forgiven me." His face stretched into a cold, hard grin. "Or to tell me to burn in hell because you finally got justice for your family."

Anger churned in her stomach at his taunts.

She felt like Corrie ten Boom extending her weathered old hand toward the SS trooper who'd tortured and killed her sister. But Gracie knew what she'd come to this prison to do. Unlike Corrie's soldier, the man opposite her had not sought forgiveness. Tom had only glared and taunted.

And yet her situation was similar. Nothing existed inside of Gracie's shaking skeleton that could grant the needed strength to do what she'd come to do.

The picture of a newborn baby cradled in great—yet gentle— hands came to mind.

She wasn't helpless. She was held in the hands of a God who simply bid her to love with His love. It was His love that would unlock this door in her heart. And believing in His truth would set her free.

Regardless of how the man facing her responded.

"Yes, Tom. I did come to tell you that I've forgiven you." Gracie's voice quivered. "Even before I knew that you killed my family, I'd had my hand around your throat, wanting justice at the cost of your last breath."

"Well, now you have your justice." He spit the words out. "Happy?"

"No. Not because you're in prison." She held her chin up. "I'm relieved that you can't hurt anyone else. But what makes me feel the freedom you gave up by drinking and killing three innocent people is that I've made a choice to release you. I'm no longer bound to you through unforgiveness."

Tom leaned forward. "Thanks. That makes me feel so much better."

"That part wasn't for you. It was for me." She pointed to the guard still standing by the door. "I've left a Bible for you, but only if you're interested. If not, they'll give it to someone else. What I came to tell you was that the freedom I've found, you can find too. It's available even behind metal prison bars."

"Not interested in your God-talk. It's bored me since I was a kid. And I have no need of it in here." He stood. "Thanks for nothing."

Tom walked to the guard by the door and exited without looking back.

Maybe she could have said that better or quoted some of the many Bible verses she'd studied before coming today. But maybe it just wasn't time for Tom to understand the truth. She'd continue to pray for him, though.

When she'd finally let go of trying to make Tom pay her back for stealing her family and trying to kill her, she'd been surprised at the prayer rising in her mind. A short prayer. A simple request that God would capture Tom with His truth. And hold him like a newborn baby.

Minutes later, Gracie passed through all the sliding glass doors, retrieved her belongings, and stepped into the bright winter day. Into a place where the air was cold and the wind tasted of freedom.

In a few minutes, she'd swing by her parents' house and let

them drive her downtown. Then she'd walk through Hartsfield's doors and away from her childhood home.

But right now, right here, she'd taken the most important step. She'd faced the past and found her dreams. Her golden locket would soon rest in the hope chest next to her precious wedding rings. Because even though Mark, Elizabeth, and Joshua would always hold a special place in her heart, it was time to move out of the past. Time to step into the future.

A place that overflowed with promise.

Her dream of the future hadn't taken clear shape yet. But there were three things she could see with perfect clarity: a pair of gorgeous blue eyes, a toe-curling smile.

And the picture of a newborn baby resting in vast—yet gentle—hands.

EPILOGUE

Not even waiting by Gracie's front porch swing on a frigid Christmas afternoon could dampen the nervous energy building inside Steven.

He slipped off a leather glove and fingered the small package burning a hole in his pocket. Gracie couldn't be gone much longer. They'd agreed to exchange gifts this afternoon, well before the big celebration at Dad's later tonight.

As she came up the street, he could tell the exact moment when she registered his presence on her porch. Jake strained at his leash and helped pull her toward the steps, a little faster than she'd intended to go.

The smile on her face made his heart rate double.

"Hey, there. Aren't you early? I still have the cooldown part of our walk left." She gulped in a few quick breaths and bent down to rest her hands on her perfect-fitting jeans.

He stepped closer and ruffled Jake's head as she straightened. "Want me to walk the last lap with you?"

"That would defeat the cooldown part."

Steven grinned.

Gracie's hands covered her mouth as her face glowed crimson. "I said that out loud?"

"Sure did."

"Then I might as well tell you that I was having a *Top Gun* 'Take My Breath Away' moment watching you lounge on my front porch." She stepped into his arms.

He pictured the exact scene, complete with flowing white curtains and Berlin's female vocals crooning in the background.

But he'd fought similar images in his dreams too often since Gracie's return.

Today he needed to dismiss them even faster. He was already hovering too close to the danger zone.

Kissing her forehead, he stepped back. "Ready for presents?" He rubbed his hands together.

"How about 'Merry Christmas' and a cup of hot cocoa first?" She laughed and unlocked her front door. Then she let Jake off his leash after they'd stepped inside.

He took their coats and hung them in the hall closet while Gracie and Jake disappeared into the kitchen to make hot chocolate.

"Here, let me do that." He stirred the mixture on the stove as she got out two huge mugs and took a seat at the breakfast bar.

"Is James with your parents?"

"Yep." He yawned. "We've all been up since before the crack of dawn. I think even Hanna is out cold in the guest room now."

"What about Angela and Marcus? Will they be at your parents' tonight?"

Dumping a little more milk and another spoonful of sugar into the pan, he shook his head. "Nope. Just family tonight."

"She is James's family."

They'd talked long and detailed about his marriage, his divorce, and forgiving Angela. A recent development Gracie had been very excited to hear.

"My son and I want to spend Christmas with you."

She cocked her head and smiled.

"Angela will be part of the equation we'll have to navigate for holidays and vacations. But only after she's done with rehab, and even then only after we've taken some overnights nice and slow." He filled their mugs with the warm cocoa and plopped in a few marshmallows. "James loves his mom. Their relationship is growing. But we'd still like to spend this special day with you, Gracie."

"Sounds like a nice dose of heart-chocolate for the holidays." He held out his arm to escort her into the den.

She giggled and slipped her hand around his arm just like she'd done on their first date. Good ole Jake was already snoozing on his pallet, completely unaware of anything around him. Gracie turned on her favorite Christmas CD—Steven Curtis Chapman's *The Music of Christmas*.

She sat on the couch and pulled a Noah's Ark Christmas afghan up around her shoulders. Only the top of her burgundy cable knit sweater showed. Good thing too. He didn't need to keep noticing how well everything she wore fit.

"Would you like me to start the fire?"

She nodded. "That would be nice."

He set about the task of turning Gracie's white fireplace into the storybook roaring fire right out of *Beauty and the Beast*. Gracie's favorite movie, he'd recently learned.

The white Christmas lights blinked off and on in a slow, soothing rhythm. He took a seat on the couch and slipped her legs onto his lap. They watched the lights in comfortable silence for a few minutes.

"I'm curious, Steven…"

"That's nothing new."

She sat up and nudged his shoulder. "I'm trying to be serious."

He smiled and thought about giving her a foot massage, then quickly decided against that. It wasn't time to get that intimate. Not yet. "Serious is highly overrated."

"Even so." She gave him a firm teacher-slash-mom look and leaned back into the couch. "I've been thinking about New Year's Eve." Her eyes studied the afghan over her legs. "You haven't mentioned doing anything yet."

"I wasn't quite ready to ask." He drew his leg up onto the couch and turned to face her. "I know it'll be a hard day for you, and I didn't think it'd be a good idea to suggest a big party."

"Probably not. I never liked big parties anyway." She poked him with her foot. "Go on."

"I also thought about doing something small and quiet,

maybe a late dinner with a few close friends. Say, at Clint and Sara's house?"

"Why do I get the feeling you've already made plans?"

"Because I have." He took a sip of lukewarm cocoa. Even cold, chocolate tasted good. "Leah and Kevin will be there. Clint and Sara set Michael up with their babysitter, Erica."

"He agreed? Mr. Hotshot FBI Agent didn't already have a date?"

Steven shook his head. "Nope. Michael's been talking to Clint more about stuff and I can see a real difference. The rookie hasn't had a date since my birthday in September."

She pursed her lips together. "Long time."

He shrugged. "He's never been married. Not having a date for three months is a little different for a reformed single guy."

"I suppose." Sitting up, she finished off her chocolate. "Have you been talking to Clint about…stuff?"

"I'm going to start calling you *bulldog* if you keep that up." He tucked a strand of auburn hair behind her ear.

She grabbed his hand and held it. "I just know last time we talked about your forgiving Angela, you still had the biggest thing ahead to look at."

"Forgiving myself."

She waited.

Knowing this topic would come up, he should have opted for a velvet pillow for Gracie's gift. The little box of jewelry continued to dig into his leg, but this wasn't the time to present it.

"I've thought a lot about your choosing to forgive Tom." He rubbed Gracie's knuckles with his thumb. "And I decided to let go of my own neck. After Angela and Marcus, it seemed almost natural."

"But not quite."

"No. I've spent a long time flopping from the end of a perfection hook. A self-inflicted capture." Laying his head back on the couch, he looked for a long time at the painting over Gracie's piano. The one of a young boy in a dark wood being guarded by an angel. "I finally understood that forgiving myself was a choice too. A decision to make, not because I deserved a break, but because God had already paid the price. My guilt payment couldn't compete with that."

"It takes time and practice for that choice to impact our knee-jerk feelings."

Wise words. From a woman he wanted to kiss more than he wanted to breathe.

Gracie must have read his mind. Or his eyes. She said they told far more than his words ever did. She snuggled into his chest and released a long sigh.

"I know you'll remind me of those wise words," he whispered into her strawberry-smelling hair. "Often."

She elbowed him. "Hey, what about my Christmas present? Didn't we agree to exchange gifts before we went to your parents' house?"

"We did." He fingered the jewelry box. "But I think it should be ladies giving first."

Standing up from the couch, she crossed the den and slid a very large rectangular package wrapped in blue and silver paper from under the tree.

"You bought me six more James Taylor albums and taped them together? That's awesome."

She laid the heavy package on his lap.

"So, can I open it now?"

She pushed his knee with her foot.

Ripping and tossing the paper just like James had done with every gift this morning, he stopped and stared at a large, ornately framed painting very similar to the one above Gracie's piano. Except his picture had a grown man hugging his son. A hallway mirror reflected a younger man holding a baby. The Scripture plate read, "I have loved you with an everlasting love... Jeremiah 31:3."

The little boy looked just like James. And him.

Blinking his watery eyes, he turned toward Gracie. "It's beautiful. And perfect."

"That's how you're loved, Steven." She laid a hand on his arm. "Fiercely and gently at the same time. Wrapped in God's strong arms."

"Thank you." What an awesome daily reminder this painting would be. "Now it's your turn." He set the painting on the coffee table. "But you have to close your eyes." Turning to face her, he put a hand into his pocket.

"Why?"

"Do you trust me?"

She closed her eyes and harrumphed.

He'd take that as a "yes." But just in case, he waved his hands in front of her face.

"I'm not peeking. Hurry up, though."

He placed the gold-wrapped box with a bright red ribbon into her hands, straightening the top bow a little. "You can open your eyes now."

Sitting with wide eyes, her hands shook a little.

"I hope it's the right size."

Her face turned a deep shade of red.

"Think I'll always be able to make you blush?"

Swallowing hard, she lifted her eyes to search his face. "Probably."

A wide smile stretched his cheek muscles. "Don't look so scared. Just open it."

"I'm not scared." Slowly, she untied the bow. "Surprised, maybe."

Moving closer to her side, he tugged on the last of the soft red bow. "But you don't know what's inside."

"That's why I'm opening it. Hush." With careful hands, she set aside the gold paper and lifted the small velvet lid. A laugh escaped her lips.

"Do you like it?"

She nodded, two tears slipping down her still rosy cheeks. "It's beautiful." She fingered the gold-filigree heart locket. "For new memories?"

"Yes." He slipped an arm around her shoulder. "I got you, didn't I?"

She elbowed him. Then turning her back to him, she held up her hair. "Will you fasten it?"

He fastened the clasp and kissed the crook of her neck.

She shivered and turned to face him, drawing in a ragged breath.

He'd waited for this moment for almost a month. And he'd prayed just as long for the control to keep things pure. She was one of the very best things in his life. And worth waiting for, no matter how hard that proved to be.

Wiping the little wet streaks on her face with his thumb, he eased her closer and then rested her head on his chest. The warm fire and soft lights, the scent of Christmas all around, and the feel of her silky hair spilling over his fingers, nearly broke his resolve.

She ran her soft hands over his forearm.

His turn for a ragged breath.

Gracie leaned back and reached her hands around his neck, running her fingers through his hair. Her eyes drew him in and held him still at the same time.

Their lips met softly at first, then deepened into a kiss full of passion and promise. He closed his eyes and pulled back, keeping her pressed against him. Then with only a thin hold on his self-control, he stood them both up beside the couch.

"I think we'd better head over to my parents' house."

"You're a smart man, Steven Kessler. But I hope you won't wait forever to try your little surprise jewelry gift again. For real, next time."

Jake barked his agreement.

Steven laughed and smoothed the dog's fur. When he looked up, a stunning smile filled Gracie's beautiful face. He would see that smile again. Over and over in his dreams.

"So you want another locket for Christmas next year?"

She threw crumpled wrapping paper at him.

"Okay. Maybe not. How about I try for a bracelet on Saint Patrick's Day?"

"Oh, you."

He pulled her against his chest and kissed the top of her head. He would wait for the right moment. But it wouldn't be next Christmas. Valentine's Day might work. After all, didn't diamonds and chocolate go together well?

They put out the fire in the fireplace and then headed to the front door. It'd be a fun night recounting this afternoon to his parents and James.

Watching Gracie blush all over again.

Teasing her about what the future held.

As he helped her into her long coat, he noticed the pocket watch James had given him earlier this morning poking up from his jeans. A soaring eagle decorated the pewter cover. What a perfect picture for Christmas day. A day for dreaming dreams, enjoying family, and soaring high above the clouds.

The infant in the cradle, resting in the shadow of the cross, reminded him to dream big. Soar high. Believe the truth.

Listen.

Steven walked out into the late afternoon's winter chill with Gracie on his arm. Listen he would. Just like Clint and Gracie had been encouraging him to do all along. Listen and trust the one voice that brought every good dream to life. The Voice of truth.

Dear Reader:

Thank you for taking this journey with me through Gracie and Steven's eyes. As I typed the beginning of this story—that of Gracie losing the family she loved so much—I worked through seeing my worst nightmare appear on the page. I saw in my mind's eye what Gracie saw. Only it felt like it was my blue mini-van tumbling off the road, my children on stretchers. Some nights it was hard to remember I was writing fiction. Especially when I'd look at the photos on my desk of my precious children and strain to hear the sound of them returning from errands. On the many evenings they returned late, the sound of the garage door and their giggles were some of the most precious sounds I've known.

Another way I experienced Gracie and Steven's story is that they struggled with believing some of the same lies I've believed. Those awful words in my head that say I'm not good enough. I'm helpless. I'm unlovable. But one thing I've learned about God after many years of living from a heart filled with lies is that His truth truly does trump those lies. It took some tears and time with God to get to that place where His Word didn't just bounce off my hurting heart. That hard work was time well spent.

Like I've shared with my daughters and my high school seniors at church, getting with God and letting out the pain we too often try to ignore is the first step to healing. Real healing. Not the religious Band-Aids we like to think will work eventually, but healing that allows God to remove the rocky lies in our hearts and replace them with His truth—His Word, whispered into our inmost being. It's when we hear those words and believe those words that we are changed. Made more and more like our loving heavenly Daddy. More like Christ.

As I've allowed God to heal my heart, I've become more open to a very painful and often misunderstood part of the Christian walk—forgiveness. In allowing the Lord to speak His truth to me, my eyes and heart have been opened to the things

I've buried, to the people who continued to hurt me. But that pain only compounded when I held on to them with a death grip, trying to get them to make up for the heartache. Together with the Lord I've learned how to let that grip loosen. I've learned to forgive. From the heart. Like Jesus calls us to do.

My prayer for you is that the Lord will continue to speak His words of truth into your heart and that you will join Him on the path of heart healing, continue into forgiveness, and then rest in the abundant life that He is. He is amazing at taking shattered dreams and making all things new.

Because of His grace,
Amy Wallace

If you'd like to know more about heart healing, please come hang out with me at my website—Heart Chocolate (www.amywallace.com)—and check out the Bible studies on the topic of heart healing. Another place to find me on the web is the Defenders of Hope website (www.defendersofhope.com), where you can go behind the scenes and learn the stories behind the novels. Don't forget to drop me an e-mail; I'd love to hear from you!

PLEASE LOOK FOR THE NEXT INSTALLMENT
IN THE DEFENDERS OF HOPE SERIES—
CLINT AND SARA'S STORY.
COMING APRIL 2008!

DISCUSSION QUESTIONS

1. Gracie struggled with feeling helpless and allowed that to drive her life in many areas, trying to prove she *wasn't* powerless. What lies do you struggle with? How do they keep you from living? Or drive you so hard you don't enjoy the life you have?

2. Another common lie we believe is "I'm not good enough." How did Steven handle this lie and find freedom? What helped him decide others' opinions don't define him? If what other people think about us doesn't define us, then what does?

3. When you read Jeremiah 31:3 about God's everlasting love, what does that stir up in you? If we lived like we believed this verse, how would our actions show it?

4. What do Isaiah 43:1; Zephaniah 3:17; John 13:34; and Ephesians 5:1 say about how God thinks about you? Is it difficult to believe God really feels this way? Why?

5. It can be so hard to trust God and believe that He loves us when life screams differently. Read Psalm 91 and John 16:33. How do those Scriptures go together?

6. How does Philippians 4:6–7 help us to believe that even when life is hard, God is still good?

7. One huge thing Steven struggled with was the question *why?* He fumed at Clint about why children die and why

marriages fail—even when people pray. He turned away from God because of his hurt and unanswered questions. Can you relate to Steven or do you know someone who does? How?

8. Is it okay to fume at God and ask why? I love the book of Job because Job gets real with God and demands an answer from the Almighty concerning his heartache. What does he receive? Job 38:1 says God answered. What was Job's response? Read Job 40:3–5.

9. While there are no easy answers, here are a few verses to ponder and discuss with regard to the deep-seated "why" questions in our lives: Jeremiah 31:18; Romans 5:1–5; 2 Corinthians 1:3–6; 7:10; 1 Peter 2:19–24; 4:12–19. How do these verses impact your "why" questions?

10. Sometimes we won't find or understand the answers to our "why" questions. It seems life would be better if we had no trouble (or at least less trouble) and that the Christian life should guarantee fewer problems. Consider Joseph, King David, Job, Daniel, and Paul. More often than not, they didn't have complete answers to the trials they endured. How did they respond? Read Genesis 50:19–20; 2 Samuel 12; Job 13:15; Daniel 6; and 2 Corinthians 12:9. How did they benefit from their responses? How have we benefited from their examples?

11. What did you think about Gracie's picture of forgiveness? How did emotionally keeping her hand around the neck of the one who'd hurt her cause her more pain?

12. Forgiving those who have hurt us is a painful and difficult choice. But to live in unforgiveness is far worse. Matthew 18:23–33 shows some very painful consequences of

unforgiveness and not receiving God's forgiveness for ourselves. How did Gracie and Steven suffer for choosing not to forgive?

13. What does it mean to forgive from your heart? Gracie found she could truly forgive only after she'd taken her lies about herself to God and heard His truth. First Peter 1:22 talks about being cleansed by obeying the truth, then loving deeply from the heart. How do you think it would help you to forgive if you took your hurt and lies to God first and allowed Him to cleanse you and speak truth?

14. Who is harder to forgive—yourself or others? Why?

15. As Gracie became aware of the need to deal with her lies and forgive, she described what her parents provided as heart-chocolate. My definition of that phrase is: "words that wrap around the heart and bring excitement, comfort, and an expanded perspective of how awesome God is." Can you think of some heart-chocolate in your own life, a moment when you experienced God and it encouraged you? How can you share that same type of encouragement with others?